Author photo by Lisa Cooper, New York

About the Author

An independent art historian and writer with a bachelor's degree in Art History and English Literature from Hamilton College in Clinton, New York, Lucy Paquette studied with the British and European Studies Group, London (B.E.S.G.L.), 9 York Terrace East. After beginning her career in marketing and copywriting in Washington, D.C., she became a freelance writer for publications including *Signature*, a publication of the Women's National Book Association, and *Maquette*, the journal of the International Sculpture Center. Her research on James Tissot has been published in *The Burlington Magazine* and online by the Victorian Web, and she presented a paper by invitation at the Closing Symposium of *James Tissot: Fashion and Faith* at the Legion of Honor in San Francisco, California on February 8, 2020.

Using dozens of contemporary sources, she has rebuilt Tissot's life to shed light on a fascinating but little-known figure embroiled in the birth of Impressionism and modern art.

ಎಎಎ

The Hammock

A novel based on the true story of
French painter James Tissot

Lucy Paquette

ಎಎಎ

Also available as an ebook, illustrated with
seventeen stunning, high-resolution fine art
images in full color courtesy of
The Bridgeman Art Library:
ISBN 978-0-615-68267-9 (ePub)

THE HAMMOCK Cover and Title page design:
Emilie Misset, New York

Front cover image: *The Hammock* (*Le hamac*), 1880,
etching and drypoint, by James Jacques Joseph Tissot
(1836-1902), Courtesy National Gallery of Art,
Washington, D.C., Ailsa Mellon Bruce Fund, 1972.26.2.

Back cover image: *Portrait of James Tissot* (Jacques
Joseph Tissot, 1836-1902), albumen print by Carjat & Cie,
Carnavalet Museum, History of Paris, PH57071 (CC0 1.0)

THE HAMMOCK: A novel based on the true story
of French painter James Tissot, by Lucy Paquette
Paperback edition published in 2020 by Lucille Paquette
Zuercher. ISBN (pbk.): 978-0-578-73522-1.

This work was originally published as an ebook:
(295 pages; ISBN (ePub): 978-0-615-68267-9).
THE HAMMOCK: A novel based on the true story
of French painter James Tissot, by Lucy Paquette
© Copyright 2012 by Lucille Paquette Zuercher.
U.S. Library of Congress registration available upon request.

To

Alex, my inspiration and guiding spirit

and

To

Julia, who makes everything possible

ббб

≈≈≈

Author's Note

When my son suggested that I write a novel set in the Victorian Age, I began looking for inspiration in paintings of the time. James Tissot's paintings of beautiful women beckoned with the promise of romance, and I soon found myself intrigued by his life. The more I researched the few biographical details that are known, the more I was curious about the unknown, and the unknowable. The novel grew from my desire to make sense of the events and decisions that shaped Tissot's career and personal relationships.

James Tissot was close to a great many of the most prominent people of his day. It would have overwhelmed the reader to portray him among his wider acquaintance of artists, authors, poets, playwrights and composers. In the novel, Tissot is shown amid just a few recurring characters, with references to the fact that he enjoyed a vast circle of intellectual and artistic friends.

When Tissot went to Paris in 1859, he befriended James McNeill Whistler, Edgar Degas, Édouard Manet, and Lawrence Alma-Tadema, and he knew others including Berthe Morisot and her husband-to-be, Eugène Manet. During the Franco-Prussian War, the artists Étienne-Prosper Berne-Bellecour, Joseph Cuvelier and Henri Regnault were among those fighting alongside Tissot to defend France.

In England, Tissot befriended journalist Tommy Bowles, John and Effie Millais, Louise Jopling and others including the actor Henry Irving, the novelist Ouida and the composer, Sir Jules Benedict.

I have attempted to present each character accurately on each date they are depicted, showing where they were and interweaving their career progression and personal life with Tissot's. I spent months researching the individuals I portrayed, including their faces and dress, personalities and motivations, attitudes and wit.

As much as possible, dialogue and situations are drawn from the individual's own words, in their letters or autobiographies, or from those of a contemporary. My aim was to let the characters speak for themselves and to blend imagined dialogue for a seamless recreation of these fascinating individuals playing off each other as they might have in life.

A few characters had to be relocated to appear in a scene. The essence of the characters and the timeline was preserved, to bring these people to life in the most accurate context of an extraordinary decade.

My deepest appreciation goes to Suzanne Freeman, Lee Viverette and Michelle Hevron at the Virginia Museum of Fine Arts Library, and the reference librarians at the Twin Hickory Area Public Library for securing all my many interlibrary loan requests. I'm also grateful to all my family and friends for their encouragement, and especially to Jake Reilly for his practical assistance. And, of course, I could not have written this book without Rick's belief in me from the very beginning.

THE HAMMOCK

᳚᳚᳚

Prologue

The Hammock

A NOVEL BASED ON THE TRUE STORY
OF FRENCH PAINTER JAMES TISSOT

LUCY PAQUETTE

James Tissot, c. 1865 albumen print by Carjat & Cie.
CC0 1.0 Paris Musées/Musée Carnavalet, Histoire de Paris.

Prologue

On September 22, 1999, a private collector lent a painting to the Yale Center for British Art in New Haven, Connecticut, for an exhibition called "James Tissot: Victorian Life/Modern Love."

The painting, which had recently turned up for auction at Sotheby's, was about four feet tall and three feet wide, in an elaborate gilt frame of the period. The surface of the canvas was so polished that the artist's brushstrokes could hardly be detected, yet the textures – the cast iron colonnade behind the glassy pond, the billowing foliage, and the lush grass – were so richly depicted that they looked real.

The artist had framed the scene in his suburban garden as if it were a photograph, cropped along the vertical lines of the trees that flanked its subject: a young woman lounging in a hammock reading the newspaper, her elegant black gown draping over the straw matting below, revealing a white flash of petticoat where her ankles crossed in their shining leather boots. The lady, painted throughout the 1870s by the same artist, had been known only as *"La Mystérieuse"* until her identity was discovered by a London journalist in 1946.

The painting itself was known only from a photograph album kept by the multimillionaire French artist during the height of his success, when the British public bought his pictures for vast sums.

The first and only time the painting had been shown was in London in 1879. Critics condemned it as immoral. The picture of Paradise in his back yard ultimately shattered James Tissot's career.

The Hammock had not been seen in public in one hundred and twenty years.

Chapter I

Château de Malmaison, Rueil, France
October 21, 1870

Tissot stood in the arched opening of the highest point in the château's crumbling stone ring wall. He balanced his long *chassepot* rifle, lined up the enemy soldier in his ladder sight, and pressed the trigger.

"James, you are fearless!" marveled Berne-Bellecour. He stepped out from behind the wall and craned his neck to get a better view of the dead Prussian soldier at the edge of the woods. "He didn't even see you before he fell."

Tissot picked his way down the treacherous foot holds that led to the worn-away rampart. "The trick is," he chuckled, "to stay alive so as to kill as many as one can." He pulled back the cold steel bolt of his *chassepot* to reload a cartridge into the breech. "*La bataille de la vie.*" *The battle of life.*

Berne-Bellecour grinned through his fine dark beard and mustache. In his blue Guard tunic, with its double rows of silver buttons, he had as fine a military bearing as if he were commander of the French troops. He held his hands behind his back, and in them was his sketchbook and pencil. "Listen to them, shooting off their cannons across the fields. D'Hurcourt says he saw their horses all saddled for a hasty retreat." He sat down again on the grass near the ruins of the rose border and continued to sketch everything he saw around him. It was his way of coping with the anxiety during the lull in combat.

"We might take Versailles back, before they know what's happened," said Tissot, in a tone of bravado. The French sharpshooters, and the cannons on the hill, had beaten the Prussians back across the fields and into the deep pine woods. It was their first serious sortie outside the fortified walls of the city, and now they were encircled by the grey stone wall of the Emperor's run-down château. The Prussians and the French continued to hurl bombs at each other's batteries.

On the brittle stone steps to the lookout, Tissot's friend Joseph Cuvelier stood guard above them. The sharpshooters suspected the Prussian troops were forming their lines for a counterattack. Cuvelier was watching, waiting.

On the green banks of the River Seine seven miles west of Tissot's elegant new house in Paris, the pointed towers and sloping roofs of the Château de Malmaison rose behind them against the bright afternoon sky. The hundred and fifty acres of meadows and woods beyond the château's grounds had become the front line of the defense of the capital. The vineyards and autumn grass were crushed, and in their place were makeshift fortifications, thrown together from straw, earth and pieces of lumber from the little farmhouses.

A Prussian shell exploded on one of the houses dotting

the farm fields, and a man and his wife and baby emerged. The farmer and his wife seemed unconcerned that their house had been hit, though the baby screamed. They strolled over to Tissot and Berne-Bellecour and handed them a large basket of salamis and oval country bread to feed the Guardsmen defending them.

Tissot pointed behind them. "Your house is on fire."

The farmer waved goodbye and said, "It's nothing. We have another up the road."

Tissot exchanged a glance with Cuvelier up on the lookout and saw that he was laughing. Tissot had met him through Degas. Cuvelier was generally reserved in groups, growing animated only when alone in his sculpting studio with his intimate friends. Now he called down, "D'Hurcourt, come enjoy the view!"

D'Hurcourt clambered up the precarious foot-holds to the stone rampart to join Cuvelier. He was only seventeen, slight as a girl. Tissot and the others referred to him as "*Le petit*" – the kid – with full respect for his courage. After the Emperor had been deposed in August and the French had suffered unthinkable losses, *le petit* had run away from home and volunteered for the National Guard against his parents' will.

Berne-Bellecour sat in the grass and sketched the broken walls surrounding them and the fields beyond, dotted with farmhouses. He penciled in his companions, showing the minute details of their buttoned uniform tunics, their trousers with the stripe down the side, their spat-covered leather boots and their brimmed kepi hats. Without raising his eyes, he remarked to Tissot, "As soon as this war is over, souvenirs of the battles will be all the rage."

"You may be right," Tissot replied slyly, "but I can't wait to get right back to painting beautiful women."

Tissot did not want to draw the scenes that seemed so

fascinating to Berne-Bellecour. He felt a little stir-crazy, listening to the ongoing roar of the Prussian artillery in the distance across the fields of Malmaison. Pulling off his red kepi hat, he ran a hand through his thick hair. *It must be nearly three o'clock*, he thought. Were the Prussians going to make them wait all day, and attack after dark? He used the kepi to wave a fly off his nose and watched the men who waited behind the château wall with him.

"Regnault, what are you writing?" Tissot teased the younger man. "A love-letter to your fiancée? Your engagement broke the hearts of every woman in Paris under thirty."

Regnault's muscular shoulders were bent over a small white stationery card. His blush made his face glow like a hero from a romance novel, but he assumed an arrogant tone and shot back, "Tissot, I hope you will console as many of them as possible."

"I don't need your permission!" They did not know about the *affaire d'*Angelique. "I'm just grateful that Berne-Bellecour is married – happily. I wouldn't stand a chance, next to him."

Berne-Bellecour glanced up absently from his sketch pad and resumed his work.

From his post on the high stone wall, Cuvelier suddenly fired, then shouted, "Tissot!"

The laughter dissipated from Tissot's eyes, and he raised his sleek *chassepot* rifle. It was four feet long, taller than Tissot when the bayonet was fixed. *Capitaine* Dumas told them that the *Tirailleurs de la Seine* – the Sharpshooters of the River Seine – would be considered elite among the irregular units, when the company was established last month. He was satisfied that the artists' brigade was well-armed at least; the *chassepot* was the most coveted weapon manufactured in Europe.

Tissot squinted through the sight and took aim just below the tall steel-spiked leather helmet of one of the dozen Prussians coming at them through the thicket. He saw that the man had watery blue eyes and pockmarks on his cheeks. Tissot pressed the trigger. The soldier cried out, and blood spurted from his face when he dropped like lead to the ground. Tissot crouched and reloaded. He hadn't seen the blood of the other one he'd shot.

Dirt and debris flew into his hair from an enemy shell that exploded on the other side of the wall. The sharpshooters grabbed their rifles and burst out from behind the wall, firing one after the other, and reloading or covering their comrades in their turn. Tissot coughed as a cloud of smoke and dust enveloped them. There were more French sharpshooters than Prussians, this time. The *tirailleurs* had littered the field with dead bodies. D'Hurcourt, from outside the wall, gave a low whistle: the all clear. That was the thing about *le petit*: he could slip from place to place so quickly.

When Tissot passed back through the wall under the château for more ammunition, Cuvelier lay dead, with a single bullet to the throat. He had toppled down the rocky, steeply winding path to the lookout and lay face down in a pool of his own blood in the dirt.

"Joseph! Ah, Holy Mother of God, *non...*" Tissot, feeling his heart in his mouth, crossed himself and knelt at his friend's side.

Cuvelier, so clear-headed, resolute as he watched over every detail of the fabrication of his sculptures, anticipating the time when his long years of work would pay off in the renown he deserved. Only when he was satisfied that he could do no more, did he sign his works. Tissot lay his hand on Joseph's cheek and felt tears rising, but he could not afford to shed them. He was fighting for his own life. He swallowed hard and loaded another lead *cartouche* into the breech of his *chassepot*.

When Tissot raised his eyes to the rampart where Cuvelier had been, he saw d'Hurcourt, the kid, calmly standing guard in Joseph's place.

Once the battle began, Tissot never saw the face of another Prussian soldier. He found himself lying in a field with his comrades, straining to see into a cloud of bluish smoke without any idea of his distance from the enemy, and side by side with the others, firing into the sulfurous haze and clamor on the command of *Capitaine* Dumas.

Ten paces ahead, Tissot heard a comrade receive a ball in the chest and collapse to the ground. He plunged ahead, coughing in the smoke that filled his lungs and stung his dry, itchy eyes. Prussian shells tore through the air and rained down on the field. One burst to his left and threw shrapnel into his legs, above his leather boots. He crouched and ran his hand down his thigh. A sharp stick had pierced his skin about six inches below his hip, and he pulled it out. *Bruised, not wounded*, he thought.

The guttural accents of three, four, and more Prussian soldiers emerged from the smoke. Tissot fixed his bayonet and thrust it forward. He knocked away the needle gun of one soldier and stabbed him between the rows of buttons along his chest. He squinted in the encompassing smoke, pressed the trigger, heard another soldier thud backward onto the hard, packed dirt of the field, and reloaded.

It seemed like the fighting would go on forever. Tissot breathed heavily for a moment, blood up, preparing for the next assault. When it did not come, he sought the safety of one of the earthen barricades dotting the field. The French artillery continued its assault on the enemy, whose army seemed to multiply as the battle wore on. There was a reason the Prussians were reputed to be unstoppable.

He spat the grit from his mouth and wondered, *For what noble cause were they fighting*? Malmaison was five miles west of their crucial defense at the heights of Fort Mont-Valérien. The fort overlooked the lush woods of the Bois de Bologne, where the drawbridge at Porte Dauphine opened into the avenue de l'Impératrice. Tissot's house was steps from the gilded gates.

Just beyond one of the earth barricades in the field, Tissot saw a man hit, struck down hard. "Regnault!" he shouted. Tissot rushed to him. "*Regnault!*"

Tissot recoiled to see that the celebrated young painter had taken a bullet to the head. The wound was a gruesome sight. Bullets whistled over them from both sides, but Tissot gripped Regnault's right hand and stayed with him.

"I will tell your father," Tissot said.

Regnault raised his other hand slightly, with difficulty, over the silver buttons of his blue Guard tunic, and Tissot watched as Regnault pointed to his breast. His eyes made a desperate request before they fell to the side in death. Tissot unbuttoned his tunic several inches and found a card pinned to the inside. On it, Regnault had written the name and address of his fiancée. Tissot shook his head, slipped the card into the pocket of his own tunic, and crossed himself. Before he could scramble to his feet to rejoin the battle, he stumbled back, his neck and arm burning. It felt as if he'd been hit by a heavy rock. It took him a long moment to realize he'd been shot, somewhere between his collarbone and shoulder. Tissot tried to maintain his footing, keep his head, stay alive.

He heard a low, familiar whistle in the smoke. *Le petit* – d'Hurcourt – was down, lying near him with a bloody leg. The Prussian shells were hissing over them, minute by minute, and one had exploded into the roof of a nearby farm house. Orange and black flames shot from the windows and soon the field, littered with the corpses of men and horses, was on fire. The wind was blowing the stinking flames in their direction.

Tissot breathed in the heat and leaned over the kid, protecting him in the only way he could. The flames spread so quickly that soon they were only forty or so feet away. The flattened, dry grasses in the field crackled and reflected the eerie red glow almost in anticipation of being consumed.

"Monsieur d'Hurcourt, you never should have run away to join the Guard."

Le petit struggled to turn his head and speak, Tissot was holding him down so hard. "Actually," he managed to shout, "they sent their blessing, after all."

"Not so you can die like this." The sweat ran down Tissot's back. Over the hiss of the fire and the screaming artillery shells, the whizzing of bullets increased, and a bomb exploded, sending up a shower of dirt and rocks. He tried to lift *le petit*. D'Hurcourt was small enough to have crawled past Prussian sentries more than once, but he was too heavy for James in his wounded condition.

Determined to get him to safety, Tissot looked up and saw the dark bulk of a helmeted Prussian soldier pivot his gun toward them. The bayonet was fixed, and the Prussian soldier stepped toward them, straight-backed and inhumanly tall in his steel-spiked helmet.

A bullet whistled past the band of Tissot's kepi hat, and time seemed to stop for a moment as he and *le petit* heard the sound disappear. His breath caught in his throat. The Prussian leaned over and dropped in a stout heap.

Tissot was able to move d'Hurcourt twenty or thirty feet toward the road, but there the boy fell from his grip. He lost his footing in the pitted bank and dropped to his side. The cross-fire had gone on for three hours, and it was a lurid thing to listen to numberless wounded men moaning across the undulating fields.

"After your leg heals," Tissot said softly, "go home to protect your parents."

"*Non*," d'Hurcourt said, "The worst sin would be to desert the Guard."

"*Général* Ducrot has sounded the retreat!" shouted Berne-Bellecour. "*Tirailleurs, retreat!* Spread the word!"

Tissot waved him over through the chaos. "Help me with *le petit*! Over here, the kid!"

Berne-Bellecour easily raised d'Hurcourt to his feet and carried him back to the shattered rampart where they all had left their knapsacks. The sharpshooters and infantry began falling in, dusting off their blue tunics and picking debris off their shoulders and red kepi hats. Tissot stood and grasped his aching shoulder. He saw the blood stains on his uniform and checked in the pocket of his tunic to be sure the card with the name and address of Regnault's fiancée was not stained.

৯৯৯৯

A bizarre sound rose behind them, on the crest of the hill among their silenced artillery. When he glanced up, Tissot was astonished to see the American flag and the white banner with the Red Cross. Two dozen voices were belting out a cheerful rendition of "Marching through Georgia."

It was the volunteer corps, manning five rattling ambulance wagons from the American field hospital headquartered in front of Tissot's new home and studio in the avenue de l'Impératrice. The Americans trailed down into the lurking blue smoke of the valley. *Général* Ducrot and his staff saluted them as they passed, and the *Tirailleurs de la Seine* sent up a rousing wave of cheers in an echo of the cheers from the French gunners. Berne-Bellecour saw to it that *le petit* was placed comfortably in the first wagon.

Tissot, no longer shooting at the enemy, relaxed his stiff muscles, set down his rifle and lifted the leather visor of his wool kepi hat. He ran his hand over his mustache and surveyed the devastation.

Berne-Bellecour returned, removing straw from his beard, and took a seat off to Tissot's left. Armed now with his pencil rather than his *chassepot*, Berne-Bellecour hastily sketched everything he had seen that day. Gentlemen in uniforms and spats, wielding sleek rifles past demolished stone walls and farm houses on fire. The straw-fortified earth barricades among the charred, ruined fields. The rounded shapes of the stinking, dark smoke that choked them. A *tirailleur* steeling his nerves, lighting a cigarette. All complete compositions, rendered in minute and truthful detail, so that only color needed to be added. His work was unlike all conventional battle-pieces Tissot had seen, always depicting a soldier in the foreground just about to run a bayonet through the enemy, everyone posing heroically as if it were all an entertainment at the opera. Berne-Bellecour was recording the horror, with the optimistic intention of returning to his elegant studio up in the rue Legendre, to illustrate his experience for posterity.

To Tissot's right, lay Joseph Cuvelier.

Tissot tossed his kepi hat to his feet and thrust his hands through his damp hair, digging his fingers into his scalp. He and Cuvelier had become close over the summer. He had visited Joseph's studio several times, to watch him show Degas how he twisted wires on a wooden plank to make the framework for wax models of horses and jockeys. Cuvelier was tenacious, calmly obsessed with movement, making endless, numbered pencil sketches of horses and ponies at the Longchamp racecourse in the Bois, up the avenue from Tissot's house.

When Cuvelier had fallen from the rampart, his body had spiraled down the curving rocky footholds until the toes of his brown leather boots caught against a rocky ledge. He landed face down in the dirt, with his hands thrown to the side. His knapsack was still strapped to his back, his kepi still on his head, as if he might raise himself at any moment.

Tissot trembled and lit a cigarette. Lowering himself down on a rock, he smoked for several minutes. He stared for a long while at Joseph Cuvelier's lifeless body, sitting with it longer than it took to smoke the cigarette. Then, as if by mere reflex, a contraction of muscles that were alive and working, he pulled his small sketch pad and a pencil from his knapsack and sketched his dead friend in conscientious detail, right down to the pool of the sculptor's rich, dark blood. When he finished, he signed his name and wrote, under it, "The first killed that I saw."

Berne-Bellecour, a trim cigar between his long, expressive fingers, strolled over to inspect Tissot's work. He laid a hand on his shoulder.

"It was too, too terrible," Tissot remarked.

"Evil days," said Berne-Bellecour. He packed up his sketch book and pulled his knapsack onto his back. "I think I'll go check on *le petit*."

While the ambulance corps filled their wagons with wounded men, Tissot's comrades slung their precious *chassepot* rifles over their shoulders and started back for Paris, trudging two by two on the rocky seven-mile country road past the windmill on the hill before Fort Mont-Valérien. The sun was setting, the woods were growing black, and they would not reach the city gates of Porte Dauphine until late in the night. Though they wore the

Guard uniform, the sentinels would interrogate them by the orange light of flaming torches before they would be allowed over the drawbridge with their wounded. Then the crowds of mothers and children and old men would press in, pulling at them, crying and demanding news of sons and husbands.

Without Cuvelier, Tissot walked alone, his pierced shoulder throbbing and bleeding through his grimy blue uniform tunic. He didn't need to take up space in the ambulance, but he would go straightaway to the American hospital, where the surgeons had such recent experience treating gunshot wounds from their own war. He was sure to find Regnault's father there as he often was, using his scientific knowledge to improve the heating and ventilation for the patients in the white canvas tents. *How will I dare tell him that his son was killed?* And Regnault's fiancée must be told. He stepped so quickly in his anxiety that he overtook the artillerymen.

"Tissot?"

It was Degas, along the road, smoking the end of a cigarette. He'd been working on the coast but came back to Paris to fight. When his blurry vision prevented him from serving in the infantry, he was assigned to the artillery, with Manet. Tissot embraced them.

Manet, bedraggled but bright-eyed in his huge gunner's greatcoat, said, "Tissot! You are covered with the glory of the battle." He took Tissot's *chassepot* in his hands and admired it.

Degas glanced around and gestured with his right hand. "Where is Joseph?"

Tissot set down his knapsack and pulled out his drawing pad. He leafed through several pages and offered the drawing of Cuvelier to Degas.

Degas' features twisted in grief, and he shoved Tissot so

hard that he stumbled backward into another soldier.

"What savage thing is this?" Degas growled. He threw the drawing pad at Tissot.

Tissot, in agony from his wound, shrugged. "Reality."

Degas was indignant. "*Mon dieu!* You did not carry him back? What kind of man are you?"

Tissot's mind reeled. There were so many corpses. Regnault...just this summer – four months ago! – Regnault had won the gold medal for his great shimmering painting of *Salomé*. He had, like God himself, created a real flesh and blood woman from color and shadow, and he was hailed throughout France as the future of art. He had come back from painting in Spain and North Africa to defend Paris. The dead-cart would retrieve him and the others in the morning, just as the ambulance wagons would return again and again for the wounded left behind.

"Manet and I are prepared to die for *la France*. If you saw my dead body before you, you would sit there and pull out your pencil?" Degas turned on his heel and stormed ahead, his head held high. "It is not human!"

Manet handed Tissot back his rifle with a furtive glance of sympathy. "In this bitch of a life, one can never be too well armed."

Degas raged, "And *why* is the National Guard defending the *front line*? It won't get us back Alsace and Lorraine..."

A reporter approached the column of men stumbling along the road back to Paris. "*New York Times!* How many killed and wounded?"

Someone guessed one dozen, another snapped, "Twice that!"

Tissot shrugged and pushed past the man. The *Tirailleurs de la Seine* started as a company of sixty men, and he did not want to think of the dozen or more killed or wounded. Or taken prisoner.

He took a swig from his water bottle and noticed a blonde man with a high forehead striding toward them in his caped greatcoat and cap. In the deepening twilight, he thought he recognized the energetic gait of his friend from London, the journalist Thomas Gibson Bowles. "Tommy?"

Tommy Bowles steadied the binoculars swinging over his neck. "Ah, James, you're safe!"

"Alive, at least."

"Everyone says the Parisians fought splendidly."

"An army of trained soldiers couldn't have done better for France." Tissot feared that if he stopped walking, he would drop.

Bowles fell in at his side. "An artilleryman just told me the Prussians took two of your cannons?"

"*Impossible.* The cannons were behind us the whole time," said Tissot, cranky and absolute. "In fact, we took four of their cannons."

"What's that you have?"

He showed Bowles the sketch pad poking from his knapsack.

"Good Lord, that's not...Cuvelier?"

"I want people to know, this is what was done to Joseph Cuvelier. This quiet sculptor of race horses and jockeys, lying in his own blood."

"It's a memorial, James. A powerful image. Say, could you do more drawings of real soldiers? I'm putting together a book on this ghastly siege. If you could provide illustrations, just a half dozen, it would show the world what has happened here."

"The world should see how brave the least of these men are."

Tommy handed back the drawing of Cuvelier. "Better draw them alive, James." He lit a cigar and offered a drag to Tissot. "*Vive la France* and all that, you know."

Chapter II

Siege of Paris, 99th day
Grand Hotel, Christmas 1870

It was a joke of God, perhaps, that his career took off at the same moment that war broke out in Paris; who can fathom the will of the Almighty? At just thirty-four, James Tissot was earning well over seventy thousand *francs* a year. Almost as soon as he had built his English-style villa and studio on the broad and prestigious new avenue de l'Impératrice, between the Arc de Triomphe and the lushly wooded pleasure grounds of the Bois de Bologne, the Prussian army attacked and completely surrounded the city. Now he was just one of two million Parisians attempting to defend a capital that was almost entirely cut off from the outside world. Fort Mont-Valérien, on the crest of the hill across the Bois from Tissot's house, was their strongest defense and best hope.

Tissot wore the silver-buttoned blue tunic and red trousers of his Guard uniform with pride and accepted his pay of thirty *sous* a day like every able-bodied Parisian. But even so, he was still a working artist, treating a patron and friend to Christmas dinner at the finest café in the city, in the new Grand Hotel. He had paid his tailor four times the going rate to take in a suit of his evening clothes, since Tommy Bowles had a slighter physique. The tailor, frantically filling orders for officers' uniforms, performed sentry duty in the Guard every four or five days, as he could.

Bowles wore his sleek blonde hair neatly parted back from the center of his high forehead, and his thick mustache and beard were neatly groomed though longer than usual. Tissot studied Tommy across the table. "You are famous, and not even thirty yet! Everyone is talking about you, and how you manage to smuggle regular letters to London."

Tommy laughed. "So far, my editor has received them by hot air balloon, carrier pigeon, and even in the pocket of a Vatican ambassador's vestment." He made flying gestures with his fingers. "But some of the letters haven't made it. I've kept copies of them all, so my book will be a first-person account of the siege based on the daily letters published in the Post as well as the rest."

A spindly man in his seventies dragged a clubfoot toward them. They watched him carry steaming hot bread and red wine to their table, and he set them down on the tablecloth and opened the bottle. Tissot tasted the wine and held it in his mouth for a moment. He raised his eyebrows at the waiter and said, "*Parfait*." Perfect; the old man was visibly pleased.

"Monsieur Tadema is to join us," Tissot instructed him. "Please show him to our table as soon as he arrives."

"*Bon, monsieur*." The man bowed, leaving them to scan the menu at their leisure.

Tommy Bowles took a long sip from his glass, then flashed Tissot a smile and asked, "You brought the illustrations?"

Tissot gestured toward his feet. "After dinner." It seemed unnatural to have carried a thin leather portfolio on the way, rather than his knapsack and the nine- or ten- pound *chassepot* rifle. He ran his hand over his drooping mustache and leaned back into the velvet-upholstered gilt chair. The dining room was unheated, but the men were used to wearing plenty of woolen underclothes.

"I haven't eaten since breakfast," said Tommy. He shivered slightly and sounded both exhausted and energized by his adventures. "Bread and jam with the troops on the front line at Drancy. We could see the Prussian soldiers walking back and forth in their trenches – and they could see us." Tommy's light blue eyes sparkled, and he spoke with a passion for truthful reporting that James admired. He had kept his greatcoat when they entered the dining room, and now he draped it over the shoulders of the evening suit.

"The steeple of the village church was so riddled by gunfire, it looked like a kitchen colander," Tommy continued. "The soldiers are going through the village with hatchets, searching for window frames for their fires, since the doors have all disappeared...Good Lord!" he cried, struggling to read the menu by the light of the dining room's few candles. "Elephant *consommé* and roast camel? And is '*Civet de Chat aux Champignons*' what I think it is?"

"Cat," Tissot translated, cool as always, "with mushrooms. That means the zoo animals are almost gone." He was aware that his English was halting and heavily accented; Tommy's French, on the other hand, was quite impressive.

"No matter," declared Bowles. "Nobody thinks of asking

one to dinner in these times." They both knew that the option was sewer rats. That's what Degas was eating, when he wasn't on sentry duty. "I think cat tastes rather like hare. Dog is like mutton. How people continue to eat pigs, I cannot imagine."

Tissot did not like to say so, but rat tasted like frog. He signaled their waiter and ordered antelope *terrine*, to start. The waiter appraised them and confided, "You gentlemen may wish to know, we have a very fine pike in the kitchen, caught in the lake in the Bois. It's quite dear, for it is the only one, you know."

"Yes, pike," Tissot told him. The restaurants had raised their prices twenty-five percent, a small increase for those who could afford it. He and Tommy had given their pink ration slips for the day's meat to Sylvain, Tissot's manservant. Sylvain had stayed loyally at Tissot's house and daily managed to procure food for the two of them, and now Tommy. He had sent his wife and children into the countryside with the *bouches inutiles* – the useless mouths.

The waiter pivoted on his good leg and made his way back across the room. James turned to Tommy and winked. "The Prussians announced early on, they'd respect the Grand Hotel as neutral territory."

"They've probably got shares in the company," Tommy quipped.

"If so, they will regret it. Those little rooms upstairs that used to rent to a traveler for a small fortune are now packed with three, four, five wounded men each, and no fresh air. The French hospitals are a scandal, Tommy."

"Since I've been at your house, I have seen how clean and efficient the American tents are. I haven't talked to a French soldier yet who hasn't said that is where he wants to be taken, if he is injured."

The dining room was not exactly crowded, and in no

time, the waiter returned with their *terrine* on china plates rimmed in a filigree of platinum and cobalt blue. Tissot held up his wine glass in homage to his friend, and took the first bite of the antelope. It was earthy and gamey on his tongue, delightful.

He raised his eyebrows. "Thyme?"

Tommy pushed the tines of his fork at the layered *pâté* for a moment, then ventured a taste. "Like venison."

The men ate in companionable silence for a few minutes.

"It seems odd that it's only been a year since we first met," Tissot observed.

Bowles brightened. "Yes, I was in Paris and heard that you had drawn some rather wicked political cartoons of European "sovereigns." Burnaby had just lent me the money to start *Vanity Fair*. If I was going to publish as a weekly, I needed to lay my hands on a good supply of caricatures of eminent people. Your wit is popular in London, James."

In that same year Tissot had proved himself to his prosperous father. Even a skeptical seaport merchant had to be impressed with a son who had won a prestigious award at the Paris Salon, the showplace of French art. He chuckled. "I was surprised to get your letter asking for more, so soon. What a lark, to stay with you in Hyde Park and draw all those dignitaries and men-about town."

"Yes, you definitely caught the knack – we mock them, but it's all in good fun. But the best thing you've done, truly, is the portrait of Gus Burnaby."

The waiter delivered plates of steaming pike. Tommy put his face over his dish and breathed in the aroma. In the absence of butter and cream, the fresh fish had been poached to perfection in white wine, garlic and fragrant rosemary. Tissot thanked the old man, who bowed and left them to enjoy their meal.

Tommy told him, "I never expected to meet you that day at Malmaison."

"No offense, Tommy, but you were the last thing I was thinking about, on the front line."

"Thank you for this, James. You are a true friend. I owe you."

"Not at all. I need this as much as you."

When they had finished every bite of their fish, and the waiter had cleared their plates and removed the breadcrumbs from the tablecloth, Tommy leaned back in his chair and flashed his white smile. "Now do I get to see the illustrations?"

"*Oui*, I have made seven drawings for you." Tissot reached below the tablecloth to retrieve his art portfolio. He had every reason to be confident in his abilities in Paris, and the Burnaby portrait that Tommy had commissioned him to paint while in London had made a splash in certain circles there. But in truth, he felt a bit nervous now, realizing how influential Bowles was quickly becoming. "I hope these are what you had in mind."

Tommy carefully leafed through Tissot's detailed and grimly realistic pencil portraits of actual soldiers, with captions identifying their regiment as well as the place and date. "Powerful stuff," said Bowles, finally. "These are the sights I should like to keep for the princes and rulers who delight in war. It is when one finds oneself face to face with the individual man that the misery of the thing really comes home. Five hundred thousand soldiers in Paris alone."

"Some are boys, but there are old men, too." Tissot leaned forward, grateful that his contribution could make a difference. The elite sharpshooters, the *Tirailleurs de la Seine*, had experienced heavy casualties.

Tommy lingered over one drawing, a portrait of a

rifleman in a heroic pose, completely cloaked in his blanket – not a debonair soldier, but a wretched, starving ragamuffin at the edge of a barricade thrown together with earth, straw and shutters ripped from an outbuilding behind him.

"It's been so cold," Tissot commented quietly, "dozens of soldiers have frozen to death at their posts. It was twelve degrees that day."

Bowles closed the portfolio and tapped it. "This book will be the talk of London. I'll have your drawings reproduced as engravings."

Their waiter ushered Tissot's old friend Lourens Tadema to their table, and the gentlemen rose to greet him. Lourens seemed to bring in the icy wind with him but was as bright-eyed and hearty as ever as he hugged James, seemingly relieved they both were still alive. "Happy Christmas! Sorry to be so late. I got rather caught up, having a bit of free time to paint for a change."

Tissot introduced his two friends, inviting the short and portly Dutchman to join them for dessert. "The chef offers a choice of *Begonias au jus*, or *Plum-pudding au rhum et à la Moelle de Cheval.*"

"Hmm...flowers or pudding with horse?" joked Lourens, gamely brushing snow off his dark woolen coat. His French wife had died of smallpox last year, and his young son before her. Tissot was glad to see that, with two small daughters to raise, Lourens had regained the youthful humor that was natural to him. "Gentlemen, I am afraid I have to maintain some of my prejudices: I cannot eat horse."

Tommy nodded. "Horse just tastes like horse."

"I was thinking, heartless as it sounds," Lourens suggested to them, "of celebrating Christmas by finding something at the *Comédie-Française*?" His engaging, childlike smile spread over his face. "Care to join me for a patriotic lecture, or a recital of selections from *La Traviata* played on the harmonium?"

Tissot held out his palm. "I know they are trying to keep up some programs in the theatre, but I have helped carry too many stretchers into that foyer. One of the wounded men had died before we undressed him and was still clutching his water bottle to his lips. Sorry, Lourens, I can't feel festive there."

Lourens winked. "How about stopping in for a gossip at *le cirque de l'Impératrice?*"

"That is what you are calling the Red Cross hospital, a circus?" Tissot chuckled. The American ambulatory hospital was set up in over a dozen airy white canvas tents flanking a large round one in the center, all just down the avenue from Tissot's doorstep. "Do you know, that was just a weedy building lot. The Prince and Princess de Bauffremont donated it. They used to lend it for the dog show." *That is how I met Angelique.*

In an aside to Tissot, Tommy said, "Your neighbor, Dr. Evans, is sending a fortune to his hospital when he can get the money through. Smart of him to stay in London. I hear he's found a suitable house for Empress Eugénie and the Prince Imperial at Chislehurst. It's said to be nearly a château and quite secluded, considering it's only twenty minutes from Charing Cross Station."

Tissot gave them a sly look. "For an American dentist, *Le Beau* Evans had uncanny good luck speculating in Paris real estate. Every time he bought a parcel of land, a new avenue was being cut through it."

"Agreed then?" Lourens grinned amid the laughter. "Pumpkin pie, backgammon and piano duets with the nurses?"

"A bit too lively, Lourens," Tissot said. He loved the

nurses, when he was alone. "Come back to my house? Tommy is staying with me."

Tommy nodded. "When I first came down to Paris on the mail train from Calais, I had assumed my acquaintances all had fled. I was quite amazed to find that I could rent a splendid suite of apartments, ten white and gold rooms, with a long balcony overlooking an elegant boulevard, for only six *francs* a day. Even so, *chez* Tissot is far more agreeable!"

"Alas, no cheerful *américaines* for the holiday!" Lourens Tadema made a face of mock regret and ran his eyes over two ladies entering the dining room with an older man. "And it is too sad, to see the *parisiennes* that remain, dressed like housemaids. The prospect is now the hopeless one of merely waiting for the end of the food." His eyes gleamed in his blocky, odd face, rimmed by thick whiskers. "I am leaving for London, while I have the chance."

"Lourens!" exclaimed Tissot. "Tommy will go home, and only Degas and Manet will be left."

"I have always had a great predilection for London," Lourens told them, "the only place where my work has met with buyers. I've arranged to rent a house and studio already. I can give painting lessons until I'm on my feet. I'm leaving Paris behind, forever."

"London, truly, is nothing to Paris," sighed Tommy Bowles, "dirty and foggy, dull and disgraceful at night, though the only place worth living."

"London is charming," said Tissot, rubbing his hand over his long mustache. "I love its smell of coal smoke, the way the streets shine in the rain –"

"Come with me! Why stay?" Lourens said, tapping his friend's shoulder, but Tissot shook his head.

Tommy opened wide eyes at James. "What will you do?"

"Stay with the Guard and defend Paris." Tissot reached

into the pocket of his blue tunic and pulled out a generous stack of *franc* notes. "Paris may fall," he told them, paying their waiter, "probably *will* fall, but every day that she resists raises the strength of France, and that is enough to make us hold out to the last." He echoed the words of *le petit*. "The worst sin would be to desert the Guard."

Tommy assured them, "I am out and about all day, every day, and I can tell you that not a word of capitulation is breathed."

Lourens ran his eyes over Tommy Bowles, as if assessing his character. "Take good care of James. He is that rarest of things, an honest man and a sincere friend."

"I would trust him with my life," Tommy replied, but he didn't appear so certain he'd escape this thing himself.

"Come, let's at least see Lourens off well," Tissot said, moving toward the entrance to collect his Guard greatcoat, hat and gloves for the long dark walk up the Champs-Élysées and under the Arc de Triomphe for home. The gaslights had been out for a week, and the streets of Paris were almost deserted after dusk now.

"Sylvain will build a roaring fire in the drawing room, and I still have plenty of excellent wine and cigars." He teased them, "If you are entertaining enough, I will have him serve an English plum-pudding. We can do our best to spend the evening like civilized men."

"A good night's sleep wouldn't hurt," Tommy observed. "Especially in a clean, warm bed ...and *who*," he brightly asked his companions, "would ever have imagined Paris reduced to occupying itself with anything more serious than pleasure?"

Chapter III

64 avenue de l'Impératrice, Paris
May 30, 1871

There is no God. Tissot had sworn it to them, just six weeks ago.

For that, he was as damned a man as Courbet, now. He bent to retrieve a gilded crucifix bearing a carving of Christ that had fallen from its place on the wall into the debris on the floor. His red drawing room, once the tidy, refined scene of so much witty conversation among dear friends, had been utterly ransacked.

James slipped the crucifix inside the torn pocket of his blue National Guard tunic. "To think, I used to revere you as one of the greatest men of our time."

Courbet wore filthy street clothes, stinking of beer, sweat and piss. His gut hung over his thighs when he shifted his buttocks on the immense onyx-topped mahogany table. He swung his feet and chortled over a handbill bearing the proclamation that the president of the new government had issued two days ago: *"To the inhabitants of Paris: The French army has come to save you. Paris is freed!"* He crumpled the announcement over his head and tossed it to the floor. *"Order, work and security will be reborn,"* he laughed sarcastically. "Meanwhile, all over Paris, they are slaughtering men like us as political criminals, Tissot."

"Like *us*? You made it pretty clear, I could swear allegiance to the Commune or face your death squad." Tissot's head reeled, thinking of all that had happened since the Prussians defeated Paris. He had come up from Issy the minute he heard of the armistice. "I should have fled with Tommy Bowles and Manet in February."

Tissot had been as bitter as anyone to have fought so hard and endured months of suffering and near-starvation. And for what? A peace that required Parisians to surrender Fort Mont-Valérien to occupation by German troops, who were accorded a victory parade in return for shipments of food! He had supposed his life would resume some kind of normalcy, only to watch in horror while Courbet and a hundred other radicals seized the opportunity to inflame the restless anger of the working class. By March, they rose in arms against the provisional French government, which quickly relocated west to Versailles. But the war had moved to the streets of Paris, and even the American field hospital staff evacuated from the avenue de l'Impératrice.

"We needed the Guard to defend us," Courbet spat, "from the traitors who handed all of us over to the Prussian army. How did you feel, standing on your balcony while the Prussian troops paraded right past your house and through the Arc de Triomphe?"

Tissot looked at Courbet in his greasy long hair, the caliber of man who until two days ago had held control of the most elegant and cultured capital in all of Europe. He shot back, "When the *gendarmes* found Porte St. Cloud unmanned, when they got through the city wall – everyone out here welcomed them with open arms."

"If you think the past two months have been a nightmare," Courbet said, "the coming months will be even worse." He laughed at Tissot's expression of fury and fear. "Almost everyone in Paris can be suspected of having fought for the Commune. Anyone with a gun. Even those who had not actively supported the Commune in some way." He held the wine bottle upside down to be sure he'd drunk the last of it, burped, then called out, "Sylvain! Another bottle!"

Even those who had not actively supported the Commune in some way. Tissot reluctantly nodded to his manservant. Sylvain had stayed all these months to protect his house, if he could, from looters and Commune confiscation. He now disappeared for the cellar. Tissot ran his hand over his mustache and turned his eyes back to Courbet. "You are in a much worse position than I am."

"I have always lived in freedom," Courbet tried to get one last swig from the bottle in his dirty hands. He raged, "Let me end my life free! When I am dead let this be said of me: 'He belonged to no school, to no church, to no institution, to no academy, least of all to any régime except the régime of liberty.' "

"I fought for Paris, for France – not for you, Courbet. I joined the Guard when I was nineteen, and when Paris was attacked, all you could do was show up too drunk to enlist."

"Oh, hurrah! You would have shot your own mother if she'd tried to harm your house. That's what it was."

Tissot hurled himself at Courbet, fists first, throwing him off balance and knocking him to the floor. "This is everything I have, you crazy bastard!" He smashed his right fist into Courbet's face and his left one into his fat gut, then dragged him over the veined checkerboard of white and black marble tiles in the foyer to the great double doors. "Courbet, the great leader of the revolution! Go introduce yourself to the *gendarmes*."

"Tissot, no!" Courbet's eyes flashed with cowardice as Tissot threw him out the front doors, where the government's soldiers patrolled the streets.

"If I had my *chassepot*, you'd be a dead man," Tissot said, turning the key on the brass lock.

Courbet howled from the steps, "Be damned, then!"

Tissot leaned his back against the entryway and compressed his dry lips, fuming with a useless rage for only a few seconds. Then he grabbed the railing of his sweeping staircase and took two steps at a time to the landing. Beams of jewel-colored sunlight filtered through the stained-glass window just as they had on the models in several of his paintings. He raced along the corridor. Doors hung open from the rooms he had given over as lodging to surgeons from the American field hospital in the avenue. A wicked smile crept onto his face as he recalled the effect of his suggestion that the nurses were welcome to his rooms as well. There had been one or two who did not request official permission.

A Prussian bomb had shattered the floor-to-ceiling windows in Tissot's bedroom. He used to stand on the iron balcony to enjoy the lively view of the promenaders, fine horses and open carriages. Now the avenue was littered with the dead. He dragged some of the larger pieces of wood and glass to the edge of his room. Under the crumbling cornices of his ten-foot ceiling, the jacquard fabric draped over his sleigh bed was covered in plaster dust and glittering bits of glass.

Tissot stripped off his tattered, muddy National Guard uniform, staring for a moment at the blood stains on his silver-buttoned blue tunic before wadding it up and hurling it in a heap in the corner behind him. *What I wouldn't give for a wash!* He picked through his wardrobe. It was dusty but intact, and he dressed himself as if he were stepping out into the boulevards. His black frock coat hung on his shoulders, now that he had lost so much weight.

After brushing his thick black hair and mustache, he pulled out his leather valise, then remembered his father's crucifix in the pocket of his uniform. He considered it a powerful talisman of protection, and he was tempted to take it with him. Instead, he lay it on the disheveled covers of his bed, the figure of Christ facing upwards toward Heaven.

Tissot took the stairs down with aplomb. Out of habit, he reached to pull up the brass weights of his tall antique clock, which had long since stopped. A year ago, he had had two successful pictures in the Paris Salon exhibition and was likely to be married. He should have been enjoying himself at the Salon now, with Angelique de Bauffremont on his arm, but there was no exhibition, no idea of art in this horror. He did not know where Angelique had gone.

Gazing across his drawing room, he picked through the debris. Under a cushion that had been ripped open, feathers drifted over the back of a picture frame. It was his portrait of his mother. He had painted her expression just as it was, businesslike and solemn, but when she cast her eyes on her favorite son, her gaze always softened. It was she who sent him to Paris to prove his talent. Her portrait was the first painting he had ever exhibited in public. She had been dead ten years now. The inheritance she had left him helped him build this villa, and she had not lived to see it. He removed the canvas from its heavy frame and rolled it, to take away.

"Those cursed fools," he muttered. Tissot knew Courbet through Degas and Manet, and knew he had always had radical aspirations. Tissot had always considered Courbet misguided in his politics but had tried only to think of him as one of the leading artists in the nation. He had personally killed Romanticism and invented Realism, and they had all been so young, so in awe of him and his thumb to the nose of their elders.

Sylvain appeared and shuffled around among the leather-bound books strewn on the floor. He straightened and handed a stereoscope and a half-dozen ivory-colored cards to Tissot, who searched through the cards for the one he wanted and placed it in the device's slot. When he peered through the lenses, two side-by-side photographs merged, showing his English-style villa, designed to his exact specifications with fanciful half-timbered gables and diamond-patterned brickwork.

"I found this set for sale at a vendor in the Bois," Tissot idly informed Sylvain. He could not stop staring through the stereoscope at the vivid, three-dimensional image of his house in its glory. Even now, its rooms had the smell of new wood, plaster and paint. James forced himself to pull the card from the slot, but he grasped it tightly and murmured, "We all felt we were witnessing the end of the old world, and the beginning of a new, modern world."

"I would have boarded up the windows," said Sylvain. He was a short and muscular man who could have managed to climb to the highest parts of the house to do it, if every possible scrap had not been burned for heat during the winter.

Tissot felt some satisfaction knowing that his house would be looted by Frenchmen rather than Prussians. He nodded, slipped the stereoscope card in the pocket of his frock coat, and wandered through his drawing room, running his callused, lacerated hands over the sculpted white marble mantelpiece. Less than six months ago, it had been lined with blue and white Chinese porcelain vases and bowls. The tall windows that opened to frame the small English garden in fine weather still were graced by his damask draperies. But the artillery shocks had broken out the glass, and now the wind whipped through.

"I will see if they've left anything that is edible," Sylvain said.

Until the events of last fall, Tissot's splendid Oriental studio was the talk of the *chic* set, visited by all the princes and princesses. He stood in the wide threshold to it and sneezed from the dust. He'd given drawing lessons for several months to young Prince Akitake Tokugawa, from the Japanese delegation next door, who called him "Chi-so." His carved *japonais* ebony bibelot stands and enameled cloisonné cache-pots littered the floor.

Yesterday, Tissot had ventured outside the city fortifications at the end of the avenue, only to see *gendarmes* executing National Guardsmen by firing squad and then tossing their corpses, like rubbish, over the high stone wall. On his way home, after watching the massacre, he had seen a number of shops shut up, still bearing their signs reading, "Closed due to service in the National Guard."

Throughout the war and its aftermath, Tissot kept a small notebook with him. In these past bloody days, in a fury of disbelief, he had been recording in it the atrocities of the new French government against its own citizens. He had sketched yesterday's massacre as he had seen it, later tinting the bloodied bodies at the foot of the wall with watercolor. Now that it was dry, he signed and dated it 'Paris, 29 Mai 1871.' The image he had recorded prior to that was of the execution of two *Communards* by the Versaillais *gendarmes*, at the barricade in the rue Saint Germain l'Auxerrois, between the Louvre and Pont Neuf.

He laid his series of watercolors, his mother's portrait, some drawings from the American field hospital and more of his sketchbooks and canvases, flat in his slim valise. Against the wall were several large, framed oil paintings. They represented months of work, and he could have sold each of them for a small fortune – before this madness. If he had fled Paris earlier, he might have been able to take them. They were covered with plaster dust.

"Dried peas, *c'est tout*," Sylvain called out, from the back of the house.

Tissot went to the kitchen, and he and Sylvain each ate half of the small bag, swallowing the peas without thought of how they caught in their throats. They could hear rifles firing down the avenue. Tissot tasted the bitterness of France's triple defeat, by the Prussians, by its own bloodthirsty rebels, and by its new government. He spied the bottle of wine that Courbet had been expecting and chuckled. Sylvain found two glasses, stabbed the cork with his pocket knife, and they savored one of the most expensive wines that Tissot had acquired.

"Where will you go?" he asked Sylvain.

"South, to my parents'. I want to see my wife and children again."

Tissot paced back into his drawing room and gazed at all he had achieved. He spotted a small, familiar drawing pad in the corner, down on the floor, and flipped it to the page he knew so well. His eyes ran over the drawing of Joseph Cuvelier, and the tears slid down his face. '*The first killed that I saw*,' Malmaison. He remembered how determined Joseph had been, developing his talent by becoming an expert in melting and casting bronze, copying masters in the Louvre. Fame had eluded him, but Cuvelier persevered.

When Tissot left the Jesuit schools at nineteen to study art in Paris, he'd moved into rooms in the bohemian Latin

Quarter, painting portraits of pretty housemaids for forty *francs* each, and making friends everywhere he went, never imagining how far he would climb and never, never dreaming it would end like this. He'd lived and painted and prospered in Paris, for fifteen quiet years.

He swiped the back of his hand over his eyes and opened a drawer. From it, he pulled out his meticulous records, albums with photographs of every painting and sketch he'd made, and his *carnet* – his notebook of sale dates and prices. His official Red Cross armband fell from an album. Tissot shoved it in his pocket. The esteem for the symbol might save his life.

Outside, Tissot could hear shouting, and the rifle fire was increasing and growing closer. He heard two loud shots, then *gendarmes* crashing their fists and weapon butts into his locked front door, "Tissot!"

Tissot's heels clicked hard on the marble floor tiles as he leapt down the hall. The outsized ceramic pots holding two desiccated potted palms in his foyer rested on wheeled brass holders. He pushed one palm, then the other, in front of the door and yanked the filigreed carriers out from under them. The trees veered into the doors in a mound of soil, brittle fronds, and broken pottery.

"Tissot! Come out, *Communard*!"

He flew toward the back of the house with his valise and albums. Sylvain was in the butler's pantry using his booted feet to scrape back the shards of china and crystal that remained of the dinnerware that had fallen from the cupboards. It crashed against his ankles as he created a heap off to the side, clearing the floor under the wide wooden counter. Tissot leaned in and dug his fingers into the edge of a wall panel. When he managed to swing it open, the force sent a large copper dough basin on the counter ringing in echoes across the stone flooring.

Out front, the *gendarmes* pounded on his door. Tissot swiftly rotated the combination opening the vault and pocketed the deed to his house. All that remained of his cash was three hundred twenty-five *francs*. He pressed fifty into Sylvain's palm and crammed the photo records and *carnet* into the vault, fumbling to replace the panel hiding the safe. Sylvain's hands shook, but he gathered up the wobbling copper basin and some cooking pots that had been too heavy for the looters. He assembled them in a haphazard line on the counter before they slipped out into the back garden.

They heard the front door smash in and heavy furniture topple in the front of the house.

Tissot stood on a gravel walkway and stamped his feet on the spot where he had buried his *chassepot* rifle yesterday, along with his set of antique English dueling pistols he had left with Sylvain.

"As Bowles said when he decided to cut and run, if provisions can get in, I should be able to get out."

He embraced Sylvain, steeled himself with a deep breath that filled his hollow lungs and left through the trampled tulip beds of his back garden. His glance lingered on the blank stone eyes of the sculpted nymph frolicking at the gate of her routed Eden. James swallowed hard and swung toward the avenue with his valise.

❧❧❧

The Bauffremont's villa had been burned to the ground.

Down on the other side, at the corner of the avenue de Malakoff, Tissot saw that Dr. Evans' villa, Bella Rosa, seemed undisturbed. During the Prussian bombardment in January, the Parisians had constructed an earthen ditch and a formidable crenellated stone barricade before Bella

Rosa for their cannons, and another enormous barricade and ditch between this and the Arc de Triomphe. Along the grass on each side of the roadway, the ground had been honey-combed with pointed stakes. The American field hospital had gone about its business in the middle of it all. Tissot, wearing the official Red Cross armband assigned to him, had carried stretchers of wounded to them until they could accept no more.

Tissot felt a pang as he recalled Dr. Evans, who played it safe and stayed in England with the Empress whom he had smuggled out. He sent money to his field hospital whenever he could get it into Paris, until the surgeons and nurses pulled out at the end of March.

Turning in the opposite direction, Tissot darted across the dirt of the deserted avenue, toward a third barricade closest to the gates of Porte Dauphine. He had wielded a pickax himself to build this one, loosening stones from the avenue to pile high and secure with mortar. It was broken now, and the dead clung stiffly to it.

The sun glinted across a sky of pure blue. Had it not been for this war, the three broad cobblestoned lanes would be jammed with separate parades of carriages, horsemen and pedestrians. The throngs of gay Parisians might have glimpsed the green and gold barouche of the Empress Eugénie as she and her aristocratic friends headed for the Bois between the rows of stately shade trees, for an afternoon of boating on the lake. Angelique would have been taking her Pekinese for its morning walk.

Up on Mont-Valérien, the tricolor of the German Empire snapped over the fort.

James slipped through the back garden of the American Embassy. Its windows were broken out when the Versaillais troops invaded the avenue, searching for *Communards*. The golden yellow trumpets of narcissus waved as he skirted the pale crumpled corpses of four women and three old men who had probably been dead since the Prussian bombardment in January. There were spots of rot on their bloodied skin, and the maggots were feasting where their eyes had been. Tissot put his hand over his nose, tripped over a heap of household garbage, and kept running.

Miraculously, there was no sentinel at Porte Dauphine, its ornamental gilded gates thrown into the earthen mounds of the banks. Tissot waited and watched to be sure it was safe before he cut across the rough wood planks making a drawbridge to the bank beyond the heavily shelled city wall.

He headed straight west, into the Bois de Boulogne. The most intense fighting had swept in an eastward direction through the city in the past week, and he felt that his best chance of evading capture would come once he reached the gravel paths and the circuitous carriage road in the Bois. The thick woods of firs, oaks, beech and cedar trees had been reduced to a desolate landscape of pointed stumps extending a half mile from the wall, interspersed with the decayed carcasses and bones of horses and oxen butchered for their meat.

The lake was as sparkling as ever, and a breeze blew across it at Tissot's face and hair like the ghosts of fashionable crowds and frolicking children.

Do I dare look behind me? he thought. It was bad luck, but he did it anyway and was relieved to see no one. Without his *chassepot* rifle he felt more vulnerable, but free somehow. Tissot knew only that he must get to Calais, to the English mail steamer. Tommy Bowles' odyssey from Paris to London – normally an eight-hour trip – had taken nearly two days. Tissot believed that if he could get three miles out, to Courbevoie by evening, he could head due north. *Tommy!* He would try to send him his picture of the National Guard massacre, with a note.

Just ahead, a gaunt civilian meandered on the path, gathering kindling in a basket strapped to his back. At the sound of Tissot's foot steps behind him, the man spun around and shouted, "*On ne passé pas,*" – Go away! – a habit from his sentry duty.

"Degas!"

"Tissot? You're leaving?"

"*Oui.* For London." Tissot bent to catch his breath. His heart pounded against his ribs.

Under his hooded lids, Degas warily eyed Tissot's valise, then looked into his friend's face. "Even if you make it alive, you will have nothing there. Manet's studio was half-destroyed, but he has hidden his paintings where they will be safe. *He* is staying. Britain is where the Commune leaders are flocking."

Tissot shook his head. *Manet stayed in France, yes, but he had left the danger and deprivation in Paris in February, before the Commune.* "Whistler is there, and Millais. And Tommy Bowles will open doors for me."

"You should have known better than join your fate with those hacks and insurance agents, the *Communards –*"

"*Mon Dieu!* The worst fighting was on my very door step! The only other choice I could have made was to flee long before. *Non.* I fought for my country and I fought for my life. Everything I have in this world is tied up in that house, and it has survived – so far. I can stay and be killed, if you like, by the French government troops rather than the Prussians or the *Communards.* I prefer to take my fate in my own hands, *mon ami.*"

"You could have left your great house, you know, and come to any of us. To me. How can I do without you?" When Tissot made no answer, Degas added, "The Royal

Academy exhibition rejected the paintings of Monet and Pissarro, and the critics are ignoring their work at private galleries. The English are not going to fall at your feet, *James*."

"I do not expect them to, Edgar." Tissot felt a pang of regret, but the ties of affection were a luxury he could not afford just now. He headed toward the road to Courbevoie. "But who is left to buy art here?"

"Too bad for you, Tissot," Degas growled, turning his back. "They never will accept you. You have thrown away your chance to be a serious artist."

Tissot tapped his top hat and called back, "Come see me, in London, you and Manet."

Chapter IV

Millais' studio, 7 Cromwell Place
South Kensington, London, June 19, 1871

It was raining out, but it was one of those delicious, soft London mists that would turn to sunshine by tea time. Tissot strolled the few blocks from Tommy's secluded courtyard street at Hyde Park Gate and passed the modern red brick buildings that housed the school of music, the school of cookery, and the Royal Horticultural Society. The International Exhibition being held there was attracting a great many visitors. He waited with a crowd of pedestrians attempting to cross the Cromwell Road. Regardless of the palatial residences, the omnibuses, carriages and carts clattered by in a steady, deafening stampede. Tissot was adjusting still to the narrowness, dirt and congestion of London's streets, and he squeezed his parcel tightly under his arm to keep it safe. He was relieved to see that Cromwell Place was a quiet cul-de-sac.

The Millais' maid left him in the front hall to find her

mistress. Tissot quickly read and pocketed the invitation put into his hands on his way out of Cleeve Lodge by Tommy Bowles' manservant. It was Monday afternoon. His friend Ouida, the Society novelist, asked him to come to her *soirée* at the luxurious new Langham Hotel on Wednesday evening: *Meet my circle of friends and show them your drawings. It will do you good to be among influential people – military, political and literary. I'm giving you a chance to do something to control your own destiny. Don't sit back and just wring your hands and say the world is terrible.*

Effie appeared and greeted him effusively, leaning into him on raised toes to kiss him on each cheek while he grasped her small hand in his to steady her.

"James! How wonderful to see you again. Do come see Everett."

When their man took away Tissot's hat and gloves, James stood with his paper-wrapped parcel behind his back and admired Effie's afternoon gown. She was as striking and vivacious as when he'd met her and Millais six years ago. The two artists had been brought together to illustrate a book of ballads for Tom Taylor, whose play the American president had been watching when he was assassinated that year.

"*Madame* Millais, you are *très chic*, charming..." James was tense, out of practice at making social chitchat. "How are you faring, with your children? Are there six now?"

"Eight," she said, laughing. "Models for my husband's pictures, you know." She took him by the hand and led him down the hall. His face turned toward the smell of bread and bacon lingering behind the door of the dining room.

The slaughter and destruction in Paris, and his harrowing escape to England, was not even three weeks behind him. James caught his reflection in a hall mirror: he was still gaunt and his eyes betrayed his exhaustion.

"The people of Paris have much to answer for," Effie said gently.

"*Oui, madame.*" He could not pass the London shops without looking at the grisly photographs for sale. The images haunted him: the Tuileries and the Hôtel de Ville had been burned and the Place Vendôme destroyed by Courbet and his madmen. And now he was ruined. James lifted his head, trying not to stoop. He had arrived at Tommy's with less than one hundred *francs* in his pocket. He had lost everything, everything – his fortune, his home, his career, his peace. Degas had even written, to say he was worried for him. Tissot dreaded the thought of having to return, like the prodigal, to his severe father.

Effie knocked before entering the studio, beaming, "Everett, look, it's James!"

Millais was touching up a painting, wearing a smock over his clothes and a plaid wool deerstalker on his head. Though deep in thought, he set aside his palette and pipe and embraced his friend, stepping back to run his eyes over James' attire.

Tissot held his breath.

"How well you look, as if you hadn't been through – well, British black suits you!" Millais returned to the high wooden stool near his easel and draped an arm around his wife's narrow shoulders. "How is Tommy Bowles?"

James stepped toward the bay window and gazed out over the shaded greenery of Millais' lush perennial garden. The azaleas were in bloom. "Splendid, splendid. He cannot do enough for me." He clutched his parcel behind his back and sauntered around the artist's neat studio, remembering his drawing-room studio in the avenue de l'Impératrice. It was so opulent, decorated in the latest Japanese style, that it was written about in all the papers in

Paris as a sight for visitors to the capital.

When he had sent word that he was in Calais, Tommy insisted he stay with him in London for as long as it took to get on his feet. It had taken James a week to stop breaking down, in private conversation with his friend. Under the care of Tommy's housekeeper, he could eat like a man who had endured four months of starvation. It was at least a week before he was able to sleep through the nightmares. He was used to being shelled awake. Even at Tommy's, he had not been able to eat enough, to sleep enough. Buying the French newspapers for sale at Albert Gate, Tissot had cried more than once, not just for himself, but for his friends and for Paris.

He rearranged the pigment jars on Millais' painting table and glanced up to find Everett and Effie observing him. Breaking into a wry smile, he said, "Tommy is under pressure to turn a profit with *Vanity Fair* and is still trying to adjust back to his office routine in the City." Tissot gestured toward the large, finished picture on Millais' easel. "So I wished to see how you are doing. But! Before everything, a gift for *madame*."

Effie gleefully unwrapped layers of heavy brown paper. Over a light piece of paperboard lay an elegant pencil drawing of a young soldier he had drawn during the lull before the battle at Malmaison: it was d'Hurcourt, the brave kid who had run away from home to volunteer for the National Guard, posing with his *chassepot* rifle. James was aware that it was an odd present for a lady, but he had nothing else to give her at this time. He bowed his head toward her and said, "I recall how you complimented my line drawings from *Songs of Brittany*."

She read the inscription, " '*à la Malmaison le 21 Oct 1870, à madame Millais, souvenir affecteux, James Tissot*.' James, how good you are! After I have shown it to all my friends, I shall give this pride of place in my sitting room, and Everett will have to bear the competition." Effie gave James a girlish hug. Millais' long legs dangled like a boy's from the stool. He crossed his arms and exchanged an amused glance with Tissot. Behind him, a stag's head and a mounted salmon were hung high on the wall. None of his painting awards were displayed, and none of the rebelliously experimental Pre-Raphaelite masterpieces of his youth were on view.

From the back of the house, sounds of a childish ruckus arose, and Effie shook her head. "Excuse me." She slipped out with Tissot's drawing, closing the door softly behind her.

"You are fortunate to have such an assistant in your wife." James moved toward Millais' canvas, a depiction of an Elizabethan boy, spellbound by the exotic tales of a sailor. He ran a hand through his hair, trying to recall the last picture he had done that had not been of the war.

Millais said, "She sewed the costume for Raleigh here; that's my young Everett, and George sat for the other boy. It's because of Effie that I can focus on my art." He nodded toward *The Boyhood of Raleigh*. "Tell me, does my painting look all right to you? Do you see anything wrong?"

James bent to scrutinize Millais' brisk brush strokes, so different from the laborious, polished detail of his earlier pictures. "*Parfait*," he laughed, turning with his hands clasped behind his back. "How can you ask? You have been painting as long as I have been alive. You were a legend even in Paris for exhibiting your first painting at sixteen." He quipped, "I was only a boy of ten then, drawing the ships docking at Nantes."

"I love a fresh eye on my work!" Millais, still blonde, grinned like a school boy. "After I married, Ruskin condemned my new, looser style as 'Catastrophe,' " he said, stuffing his pipe, "but I find that I can sell 'em as fast as I can paint 'em."

"You will never please him," Tissot shrugged, relieved that they would never mention his sudden appearance in London nor the reasons behind it. He sank into the deep cushion of a low armchair near Millais' easel and let its curved arms enfold him. *Surely Ruskin could never forgive Millais for taking his wife.*

"I don't bother about him now." Millais airily waved the thought away. "But Effie always will pay the price. No matter that it's been fifteen years. The Ruskins painted her as mentally unstable, and worse. However –" he lowered his voice, "she may have saved a young girl from a similar marriage. Effie received a letter out of the blue, in October, from the parents of a girl who has been the object of Ruskin's fascination since she was ten years old. Effie replied quite frankly that he was an unnatural husband, and incapable of making a woman happy." He offered Tissot a cigarette and a light.

"Ruskin is beyond reproach?" *The man who did not consummate his marriage was not punished by Society, but his innocent young wife was?* Tissot settled back in the tufted armchair and crossed his legs, inhaling gratefully from the cigarette.

"Sir Oracle, they call him," Millais replied. He slipped his pipe between his lips. "His support saved my reputation, back in the days of the Pre-Raphaelite Brotherhood."

"He is just one man." Tissot began to relax in Millais' company. The studio took on the odor of cherry pipe tobacco.

"Don't underestimate him, James. He's an Oxford professor and a sell-out on the lecture circuit, plus he has his own magazine. I was out of favor with the public for three whole years due to Ruskin's dislike of some of my paintings. It's not worth it."

"How did you survive? You had a family to keep."

"We had our lean years when I was lucky to earn thirty shillings a week. But this is the age of reproduction –"

"Editors pay well for book and magazine illustrations." Tissot thought a moment, and added, "But did you not feel...that you had come down in the world? Easel painting is a higher form of art."

"I feel no need to play the mysterious artist," Millais winked. His shoes pushed against the rungs of the high stool, forcing his knees outward. "The public is eager to decorate their homes with engravings of popular pictures – what greater acclaim is there? As for the paintings themselves, when I finish a picture, I am just like a hen who has laid an egg. I say, 'Come and take it away!' Then I start upon another one. My dealers tell me they can sell as many replicas of my paintings as I can produce, as well."

At this, something of James' old enthusiasm returned. He leaned forward and said, "It seems to me that the British are more modern, more open to new ideas in art than the French. And with the new wealth from your industry, there is great potential for patrons."

"Keep in mind, the English like their romance," Millais told him from his perch. "Pictures of purity and heartbreak are perennial favorites with the public. Remorse for moral failure always goes over well with the critics here."

James took another drag on his cigarette and chuckled uneasily. "My paintings of women slipping out of the confessional were snapped up in Paris."

"You may want to tone down the sexual innuendo, just a bit." Millais held the pipe in his hand and gestured with it. "The type of thing they love you for in Paris – like the one you did with the soldier leering at that rather bold girl –" he laughed aloud. "Just a suggestion: Suicide even sells better than sex here. Simple stories, easy to make out, you know."

He slid the pipe back into his mouth and spoke with his teeth clamped on the stem. "Last year, I painted the first and last nude of my career – *A Knight Errant*. A chivalric rescue of a damsel in distress. Oh, it wasn't salacious at all, but it shocked Mrs. Grundy, don't you know –"

"*Pardon*, but – Mrs. Grundy?"

"British public opinion. Everyone was so offended, or pretended to be. I can't get it off my hands, since no one dares to buy it. I hung it in my drawing-room."

"Consider me warned," James said. "At any rate, Tommy Bowles can probably keep me busy indefinitely, doing illustrations for his magazine."

Millais beamed at him, as if Tissot were on some jolly adventure. "With your credentials, you'll be invited to join the Royal Academy before too long."

"Do you really think so?"

Millais looked astonished at Tissot's apprehension. "Yes, why not? I can put in a word for you if you like. It's too late to exhibit this year, of course, but next summer?"

"*Oui, oui.*" Tissot straightened in the armchair, tapping his temple with his forefinger. Whistler had been in London for a decade and had not made it into the Royal Academy. James could hardly think of what lay ahead, but he strained to sound as if he had already put considerable effort into ideas. "I mean to pick up where I left off, painting beautiful women wearing the newest fashions."

"Be careful about that. Veer toward clothes that won't look outdated and ugly to everybody eventually. Historical scenes are a safe bet. How long since you showed your work in London?"

"Seven years," Tissot answered ruefully. *Seven years since the Royal Academy hung my painting down at*

56

crinoline level. "I could have lived happily forever, painting aristocrats and gentlemen from the private clubs during the day, and attending operas and balls at night."

"You'll find success again," Millais assured him.

"*Oui*, and I'll have to find it faster, that is imperative," murmured Tissot. He brushed a hand over his mustache, inhaled sharply and rapped his knuckles on the arm of the chair. "The battle of life..."

"As for myself, I may step away from the battle for a while and concentrate on doing society portraits. I get endless requests for the things, and I never refuse work." His deep blue eyes were resolute. "All I want is to live like a gentleman and earn enough to spend every fall hunting and fishing."

"All *I* want is to earn enough in London so I can never be ruined again," James admitted.

They heard a double rap on the door, and a white-haired gentleman of about forty stuck his head in. "Interrupting?"

Millais set his pipe in a clay dish fashioned by childish hands and greeted him. "Joe, you know James Tissot? He won a medal at the Paris Salon when he was a mere boy of thirty, and he's come to London to show us all up!"

Tissot obligingly sprang to his feet. He crushed his cigarette out, irritated to have to share Millais' time.

Joe Jopling, with obvious distaste, shook his hand. "Tommy Bowles has told everyone about you. That reminds me, I owe him a watercolor for *Vanity Fair*."

"Joe won the Queen's Prize at the National Rifle Competition back in '61," Millais boasted. "He's a crack shot!"

Joe raised his slouched shoulders proudly under his ill-fitting frock coat. He asked Tissot, "Do you shoot?"

"Not for sport."

Millais raised a quizzical eyebrow at Jopling.

Tissot smoothed his frock coat over his wide shoulders and tried to control his temper. Now he recollected seeing a cringe-inducing watercolor of Joe's when he was in London several years ago. It was of a girl cuddling a kitten in her lap while her pet parakeet watched from her shoulder, and he called it *The Three Friends*.

Jopling sidled up to Millais and clapped him on the back. "You shoot so well in Scotland, why don't you come to the competition this year? I expect great things of you there."

Tissot had imagined that Millais surrounded himself with more distinguished and clever men, even if he was no longer close with his Pre-Raphaelite brothers, Holman Hunt and Rossetti. He resented it that Millais liked everyone, even obsequious hangers-on with few artistic credits. It unnerved him, this humiliation. He peered at his pocket watch with a cool detachment.

Effie rustled into the room with a creamware urn of lilacs and set it on a table near the window bay. She lingered near Tissot, then took him by the arm. "James," she said, "I'm taking my son to Paris in a few weeks – I want him to see for himself the results of war. We'll be staying at the Grand Hotel. May I check on anyone for you?"

"*Non* – that is, my friends are fine," Tissot replied anxiously. He tucked his watch away. "But would you be good enough to check on my house, my studio?"

Effie gave him a concerned look. "What a dreadful time you must have had of it."

"But let us not speak of that now," he continued. James would have told her anything she asked, but Millais and Joe Jopling had joined them and were scrutinizing him as well. He was unwilling to lay his heart bare in front of a man like Jopling.

"What do you think of London?" Joe inquired of him, as if expecting Tissot to find fault with it.

"*Merveilleux* – marvelous." Tissot directed his reply to Millais. "A subway train under the Tower and the opening of the Royal Albert Hall by the Queen! You must catch me up on *tout ces choses.*"

"You did know that the Princess Louise married...in March?" Millais said, embarrassed to have mentioned such an occasion, coinciding with Tissot's ordeal.

Effie grasped James by the hands and cried, "Oh, and won't you come with us next week to see Tom Taylor's new play at the Queen's Theatre?"

Joe explained, "Tom writes the art reviews for both *The Times* and the *Graphic,* so you should get to know him."

James fixed his eyes on Jopling. "As a matter of fact, I do know him – quite well. He sought me out some years ago, well before the prices for my paintings skyrocketed."

Joe cleared his throat and appealed contritely to Millais.

Effie's cheeks reddened. She gave Tissot's arm an empathetic squeeze. "You may be sure that Everett and I will see to it you are invited everywhere."

Chapter V

Cleeve Lodge, Hyde Park Gate
September 21, 1871

When they had changed into their black tie for the evening, Tommy and James met up in the large central hall upstairs that Bowles used as a reception room.

"You look very British," Tommy said, and he put a glass of wine in his hand. "We'll get you back in order, James."

"*Mon ami.* You have rejuvenated me with your beef, butter, and brandy." James held up his glass to him. He was profoundly grateful for the opportunity Bowles was providing to him tonight. "To the success of your book, *The Defense of Paris: Narrated as it was Seen.*"

"And to its illustrator! You'll be established in the capital of Great Britain in no time." Bowles toasted James as his manservant led three florist's men up the central staircase with their delivery of six cut-glass vases filled with yellow roses, white lilies and a profusion of lacy greenery. Each attendant held two vases aloft, and the fragrance of the flowers trailed past Tommy and James.

The room's muted blue silk panels and creamy pilasters exuded the quiet taste of a bygone era. With the addition of several potted orange trees, Tommy was content to leave it as it was when he moved in.

"Yes, dear old dad has done right by me, fixing me up with this tenancy at Cleeve Lodge and a steady government job," Tommy observed. "It wasn't his fault that the position didn't suit." He grinned at his oil portrait over the mantel. Tissot had depicted him holding his cigar in his crossed arms and leaning against a desk spread with his magazines, books, and binoculars. "It almost makes me look legitimate!" he said.

Bowles turned to the table beside him and lifted the lid of a large wooden box with a flourish. "Gus Burnaby is still in Odessa, but somehow managed to have them sent expressly for tonight's book party."

James selected a cigar, and Tommy offered him a light. "When I resigned to start *Vanity Fair*, it was Gus who lent me two hundred pounds and suggested the title. He helped me on, and I'm happy to help you." Tommy held a match to his own cigar, puffed at it a moment, and raised an appreciative eyebrow.

"You really are amazing, Tommy. Thanks to you, I have sketched thirteen members of the House of Commons." Drawing weekly full-page caricatures for Tommy provided Tissot with a steady stream of income while he painted straight from his morning coffee to his afternoon tea.

"Purely selfish motivation on my part," Bowles beamed. "You've been fundamental to the magazine's success. You're the best I've got. The most meticulous work, above and beyond, every time. To repay you the favor," he said, hooking his thumb in his waistcoat, "I may have pulled off a surprise visitor for you."

Tissot gave him a quizzical look.

"How would you like to meet the man who could make you in Society?" Tommy's expression was, for once, solemn.

"Who could you mean?"

"Gus Burnaby is a friend of the Prince of Wales."

"You are joking." Tissot was thrilled and yet terrified. He smoothed his thick hair in a tall pier mirror while Tommy admired the reflections of the candles in the wall sconces.

Tommy's wealthy young neighbors in the circular street arrived first, and he introduced everyone to James Tissot. They were polite to James but clustered around Tommy Bowles as he regaled them with stories from his coverage of the Siege. James bided his time, content to listen and assess potential patrons. Tommy, with his blond good looks, radiated pleasure at being the center of attention.

The gathering grew ever larger and soon included Millais' white-haired friend, Joe Jopling. He had grown out his side-whiskers, and his mustache twitched under his ugly nose. "It's lucky you weren't shot, Bowles!" he cried.

Tommy's blue eyes sparkled. "No, but I was once jailed for an hour or two, by a French captain, for being a Prussian spy."

"On what grounds?"

"Oh, the worst – having an accent."

"And did you really eat elephant and rats?" Joe's great side-whiskers flapped as he shuddered. "Unimaginable!"

Tissot rolled his eyes, set his empty glass on a side table and turned toward the great Palladian window. He puffed at his cigar and savored the moment of silence.

Bowles' house sat on the edge of Hyde Park as Tissot's sat on the edge of the Bois de Boulogne – but more safely. He had heard from Degas that his Paris house was still standing, and there was a rumor that he wished to sell it.

God only knew what would become of it. James sighed, pulled out his pocket watch, saw with annoyance what time it was, and slipped it away again.

Tommy approached him, accompanied by a very tall man who carried himself with supple dignity. "James, come meet Henry Irving," Bowles said, gesturing toward him. "His play last year at the Vaudeville ran for three hundred nights, and now his success with *The Bells* has turned the tide for the Lyceum."

Tissot tamped out his cigar and shook Irving's hand gratefully. "I have seen your play twice."

"We have had a run of a hundred and fifty nights with it so far." Irving's voice was deep and resonant.

James' face lit up. "I first saw it because I was intrigued that you had based it on the recent French play, and I saw it the second time because I wanted to hear the bells ring at the daughter's wedding again."

"Ah, the mysterious sleigh bells!" Henry Irving's thick dark eyebrows rose and fell over his expressive eyes. "Now tell me, who will you lampoon next in *Vanity Fair*?"

"Charles Darwin!" answered Tommy.

Tissot lowered his voice to a dramatic, conspiratorial whisper. "I have drawn Darwin looking quite satisfied with himself and fit – though barely – to survive."

"And the caption," smirked Tommy, rubbing his hands together, "will be 'Natural Selection.' " Irving gestured a salute toward Tissot. Bowles, amid their hilarity, boasted, "He's drawn twenty cartoons so far, and now great men are teasing me for the honor of being satirized by Tissot. I told James, you may draw anyone but Dickens."

Joe Jopling joined them, interjecting, "Dickens has been dead for at least a year, Tommy!"

Tissot's lively mood evaporated, but Tommy made a wicked face. "Death is the only explanation for why that publicity hound hasn't pushed to have Tissot sketch him."

The hum of conversation and well-bred laughter grew as gentlemen continued to arrive at the reception. Jopling collared Henry Irving, and Bowles pulled Tissot over to a quiet spot between his oil portrait and one of the potted orange trees. He flashed his white smile. "Having a good time?"

"*Oui*," Tissot lied, and adjusted his gloves, trying not to look as dejected as he felt. So far, it did not seem to him that more than one or two of Tommy's guests had opened his book. "I like Henry Irving very much."

Oblivious to his friend's perceptions, Tommy ran his eyes over the chattering black-tie crowd of journalists, lawyers, politicians, military officers, and aristocrats. He was highly pleased with the success of the evening so far. "Thanks to my book and your caricatures, everyone will be talking up *Vanity Fair*. Just wait until the Prince arrives."

"What should I say?"

"Good Lord, you'll be lucky to get a word in edgeways."

Tissot assumed a mask of easy sociability and continued circulating in the candlelit reception hall with Tommy, shaking hands and listening more than he spoke. His eyes darted at the mantel clock under its sleek glass dome. It was nearly nine; the Prince of Wales would likely make them wait at least another hour. *Where the devil was the man?*

"Tissot!" His old friend, the Dutchman Lourens Tadema, entered the blue drawing room and zigzagged among the shoulder-to-shoulder crush toward the drinks. He was as portly and cheerful as ever and had just returned from his honeymoon on the Continent. He thrust out a hand as he passed them, "Is it true you will paint Chichester Fortescue?"

"*Oui*, Lourens. Another commission already!" Tissot

replied, sipping another glass of wine.

Tommy Bowles did his bragging for him, as Tadema reached toward the man with the tray of filled crystal glasses. "Eighty-one Irish MPs, bishops and peers have commissioned James to commemorate his term as Chief Secretary for Ireland with a full-length portrait, as a present to his wife."

Tommy winked and said in a low voice to Tissot, "The Burnaby portrait did it."

"You were right to advise me to start by painting portraits of men."

"Less amusing than women," Tommy grinned, fingering his blond mustache, "but it is the best manner of proceeding in London."

James replied, "It took me nearly ten years to build my career in France, and I am prepared to spend another decade of hard work in London if I have to."

There was a sudden commotion out in the hall, and Tommy's valet appeared, bowed, and whispered to Tommy. Bowles gave Tissot a significant look. "I believe you will succeed far sooner, and in the cream of society." He excused himself, and Tissot noticed a slight hush had fallen over the gentlemen assembled in the sparkling drawing room.

James straightened his shoulders and took a deep breath to steady his nerves. Then he recognized the much-photographed face of the Prince of Wales, who loudly and cheerfully apologized for being late. Tommy joked with His Royal Highness and led him through the parting crowd and around the flower-filled drum table toward Tissot. As the so-called First Gentleman of Europe crossed the room with his cigar in hand, Tissot studied him with a level gaze. He was dressed in a debonair suit with a winged stand-up white collar, and he stroked his trim Germanic goatee. He was fatter than he appeared in pictures from his wedding to Princess Alexandra of Denmark, Tissot thought. *That explains the English craze for leaving one's waistcoat unbuttoned at the bottom.* His lip curled as he suppressed a wicked idea for a *Vanity Fair* caricature.

"Ah, the man who captured our dashing Gus in paint." The Prince gave Tissot a crushing, dominating handshake without meeting his eyes, and said, "Brilliant, spot on."

Tissot checked his grip, lowered his eyes and bowed, saying, "*Merci*, Your Highness." The heir to the British throne was younger than he had expected, Tommy's age, with a self-satisfied air remarkable in a man who had not yet proved his worth. Tissot recalled that the year before war broke out, newsboys were selling papers covering the Prince's scandalous involvement in the divorce of a Member of Parliament.

Joe Jopling made everyone laugh by lounging on one of the Chippendale settees with his ankles crossed, imitating Gus Burnaby's devil-may-care pose from Tissot's portrait, and mocking Burnaby's elegant loose-fingered grip on his cigarette. Tissot laughed as well, but it irritated him.

Bowles seized the moment. "Tissot recognizes an intrepid soldier when he sees one. His drawings during the sorties outside Paris brought my book to life."

"I enjoyed the sketch of Tommy with his binoculars," the Prince said, " 'a Special Correspondent.' Very good." The guests circled around him but were careful to keep a deferential distance from the man who would someday be their king.

James maintained his habitual demeanor of outward confidence and exerted himself to make a favorable impression. He not only had a more muscular physique, but he was much taller than the Prince. His Royal Highness eyed Tissot's fastidiously English evening suit, lifted his chin and puffed out his chest.

"You must sit for a caricature by Tissot, Sir!" cried Tommy, with a hand at Tissot's back.

"Indeed," the Prince replied. "Perhaps when he has run through the House of Commons." He drew on his cigar and exhaled.

Tissot comprehended that the Prince of Wales, under his urbane poise, viewed him with deep suspicion. He was momentarily indignant, realizing that some of the elite present also suspected him of complicity with the Commune. *Do they believe I ran away from Paris in disgrace, with blood on my hands?*

"Tell me, Mr. Tissot," drawled the Prince, through his cigar, "how did you manage to survive in Paris as long as you did?"

Tissot felt the dead silence, and the eyes of some of the most influential men in Great Britain waiting for his reply. Tommy Bowles nodded encouragement to James.

"You see, Sir," Tissot coolly told him, "My money ran out before my luck, rather than the other way around."

Tommy laughed, and the Prince seemed appeased. Tissot made a crisp bow and moved away from the light of the glittering chandelier in the center of the room. He passed a group conversing privately in the corner behind him, by the fireplace, and overheard one of them murmur, "...Communist? The ones who weren't made a rush for the Channel boats at the start...follower of Courbet...in prison now..."

Tissot grasped his hands behind him and moved to the front of the reception room to look out the Palladian window over the tranquil, dark street below. He could feel the heat rising in his cheeks and glanced over his shoulder at the uniform mass of men in the room. Tommy was encouraging his English Society connections to commission portraits from a Frenchman while simultaneously struggling to persuade them that Tissot was a man of good character. Tissot was mindful that Tommy left Paris after the first week of February, so he wasn't there when Courbet and his *Communards* took over the city – and his house. Bowles, a true friend, accepted Tissot's reputation on faith and had never asked for an explanation.

Lourens Tadema exchanged friendly words with the Prince of Wales and made his way toward Tissot. He stopped to greet Joe Jopling. "Hello, Joe! Where is Millais tonight?"

"Family life, no doubt," Jopling replied. "We should all be so fortunate."

Tissot, from the edge of the room, arched an eyebrow.

Lourens asked, "Joe, have you met James Tissot?"

"Yes, at Millais' studio," he answered, automatically shaking Tissot's hand. "We both do illustrations for Tommy." Joe's small white mustache flickered as he silently appraised the French artist, dismissed himself with an opaque smile, and joined the conversation in the corner.

Lourens grinned at Tissot and gestured over his shoulder at Jopling. "Joe's a crack shot, you know!"

Tissot had had enough of Joe Jopling, and snapped, "He is living off the glory of one bulls-eye at the rifle range, ten years ago." A nearby gentleman in spectacles gave Tissot a hard look and turned away. There was an awkward silence, and Tissot asked Lourens, "You are to become a naturalized British subject?"

"Yes, and changed my name to Lawrence Alma-Tadema, so be forewarned. My buyers may now find me under 'A' in the exhibition catalogues. I'm getting ten thousand pounds for my pictures here." He patted his round stomach. "*Vive* Great Britain!"

Tissot ran his hand over his mustache. Even with Bowles'

assistance, he was not doing so well as that, yet, but he had just had a letter from Degas: *Tissot, why the devil do you not send me a line? They tell me you are earning a lot of money. Do give me some figures...give me some idea of how I could profit from England.*

"I need to consider what to paint for the Royal Academy exhibition next spring." He inclined his head cynically toward the Prince. "Your paintings are admired by everyone, *Lawrence.*"

"Hm, everyone but Ruskin. Here, he is prophet and Pope." Lawrence mused, straightening his spectacles. "Still, there's a golden thread here, to exploit."

Tissot inhaled and squared his shoulders. "Will you be happy here, Lawrence?"

"I should think so," he replied, his eyes twinkling in his blocky face. "Laura's parents allowed me to make her my wife before she turned eighteen, and she's simply wonderful with the girls. You must visit us at Townshend House as often as you like, James. I'll speak to Laura. A party would be just the thing."

Tissot studied the swarm of men vying to capture the notice of the Prince of Wales. "They think me a Communist, here in exile," he murmured, drawing on his cigar.

"He who is not a victor must be a traitor?"

"Others fled...Monet, Pissarro, Sisley. Why should they suspect me of being a radical, just because I kept fighting for my country until there was almost nothing left?"

"You know how the English can be about the French. They look at you and see the Marquis de Sade and the *guillotine* and – now, this recent business."

Tissot was growing angrier than he could allow himself to be. He lowered his voice. "*La France*, it is too complex to explain. It is a...restless, simmering soup, not a placid cream like England."

Lawrence gave him his engaging, childlike smile and rocked on his heels. "Bide your time, James. Be the shrewd man of business you are. You have to adapt to their ways, prove yourself anew, but you will." He nodded toward the crush of black-suited Englishmen. "Become them."

Chapter VI

Whistler's studio, 2 Lindsey Row, Chelsea
November 16, 1871

When Tissot reached the top of the noisy metal-covered steps to the second story and stooped to clear the doorway to the back room, Jimmy Whistler strode to him and clapped him on the back.

"James, just in time for breakfast!"

Tissot stood near the Japanese-style screen which created a small foyer by the door of Whistler's painting studio. The old house Whistler rented overlooked the River Thames, and the noon light spilled in from the two tall windows, brightening the grey and black walls.

"I told you I'd have a dandy surprise for you," Jimmy said, in his high-pitched drawl. He skimmed a hand over his unruly black hair, with its white curl swirling over his forehead. "Allow me to introduce Mrs. Romer!"

A young woman rose from a bamboo chair. Under her small, tilted hat, her lively dark eyes met his. "You have taken the afternoon off from working, *monsieur*?"

"*Enchanté, madame*." Tissot raised her hand to his lips. He had been exasperated to receive Whistler's cryptic, urgent message while he was deep in his *carnet* of sale dates and prices, making an accounting of his deposit for the bank. Now, as this tall, striking creature seated herself, he gave Whistler a secret look of amazed gratitude.

Jimmy positioned his monocle in his right eye and took two strides back from them to better observe them together. "Louise has been painting for only five years, and had three pictures hung at the Royal Academy Exhibition this summer – one on the line!"

"I am honored to meet the woman whose pictures I admired." Tissot ran his eyes over her face. She wore a short fringe of dark hair curling over her forehead, and her gentle expression softened her square jaw. "I beg your pardon for not seeking your acquaintance during the exhibition."

"Jimmy tells me you rarely socialize during the day."

Whistler screeched with laughter and rolled down his shirt sleeves. "Tissot can't paint and talk at the same time!"

"*Oui*," he said, giving Jimmy a pointed glance. "I regret the *discipline* it takes to paint. And since I have missed you in the evenings, tell me about your painting, Mrs. Romer." Tissot lowered himself onto the couch across from her.

Mrs. Romer appeared flattered to be asked, and replied, "What I know I chiefly learned on my own: genius comes from hard work. To succeed, an artist must be able to see, to feel, and to have the courage to express what is there." She smoothed her skirt below her knees and eyed her companions mischievously. "And perhaps, to be a man."

"Ha! ha!" Jimmy guffawed and explained to James, "Louise was not invited to the Academy's annual banquet. Nor is she allowed to observe live models."

74

"But," she said, "since I am at my best painting domestic scenes, no matter." She was aware that Tissot was staring at her, and she cast her eyes down with a small smile.

Despite the fact that they'd been invited for breakfast, there was only a small black lacquered tray of American oatmeal cookies. Next to it on the low trestle table between them was a bottle of golden muscatelle with two very small glasses. Louise helped herself to one of Jimmy's cookies.

Willing himself to remove his eyes from her face, Tissot only now noticed a girl of fourteen or fifteen at the far end of the sparsely-furnished room. Behind a life-sized portrait-in-progress of a beautiful woman in profile, the fragile red-haired girl stood with her hands clasped behind her back, on a wooden crate. She wore a sweeping, pink gown and was preoccupied scrutinizing the brushwork of Jimmy's large, very grey portrait of his mother.

Tissot rose to look at it as well.

"Go on now, Maud," Whistler said affectionately. He stood against the tiled fire surround with his thumbs under the lapels of his yellow waistcoat, as if posing under the exotic purple orchid arcing gracefully on the mantel. "Take care with that gown, and bring it to me on your way out!"

The girl reached behind her to gather up the delicate train that puddled in liquid folds of silk on the floor. Tissot helped her to drape it over her forearm, and she made him an elaborate curtsey and left the room.

Jimmy whispered in his nasal way, "She's standing in for my portrait of Mrs. Leyland. She aspires to be an artist herself. I suspect she's spying on me with a view to stealing my compositions!"

Tissot wandered over to a table by the window, saying, "Perhaps she has her own ideas." He sifted through a portfolio of Jimmy's drawings.

"Painting is so difficult," Louise mused, "it discourages

me dreadfully – besides, I hate being a woman. Women never do anything."

"Don't feel slighted by the Academy, my dear," barked Whistler. "I don't! In fact, I achieved real fame," he paused dramatically, "when I was rejected by both the Royal Academy and the Paris Salon in the same year!" He began to follow Maud out of the room, but stopped to tease Tissot with a comical expression in his piercing eyes.

"James, I knew you'd want to take a gander at my drawings of the Thames. *Punch* loves them: 'A Whistle for Whistler' – ha! ha! And, if you saw *The Times* the day before yesterday, then you know their critic Tom Taylor has bowed in my direction. Now even Ruskin, that babbling British Buddha, will have to extol my greatness. Those etchings are selling like hotcakes at Agnew's gallery in Old Bond Street, so take note!"

Tissot ignored Jimmy's boasting and closed the portfolio. "Where is your mother, Jimmy? I had hoped to see her."

"She'll be disappointed to know she missed you," Jimmy replied, standing in the doorway. "Seeing as you've become one of her particular favorites, right up there with Leyland."

Louise said, "Your portrait of her is a remarkable tribute."

Tissot brushed a hand over his mustache and admired her tact. *It will not lead to many sales for Jimmy.* The portrait, as austere as a picture of a Dutch merchant's wife, showed the old lady in profile against a grid-like background.

"Yes, one does like to make one's mummy just as nice as possible," Jimmy said softly.

When Whistler had finally left the room, James turned to Mrs. Romer. "*You* are remarkable, *madame.*"

"I am seeing so many splendid pictures," Louise replied,

coloring. "My work falls so short of my ambition that I always wonder, will I ever do anything better?"

He took his seat on the low couch across from her. "You are just beginning; don't be discouraged. My mother was a strong woman like you, and very successful in business." Since Mrs. Whistler was out, it was quite possible there would be nothing more to eat than what they saw before them. He leaned in and poured her a glass of muscatelle from the trestle table between them. Their fingertips touched as he handed it to her. "You will find your sea legs among your friends."

"I sometimes feel as if I were in a dream, and all that happened in Paris had never been. Life is made up of such strange incidents." She took a sip of wine, then gazed up at him with a sort of defiance. "Do you know, today is my birthday."

He tapped his glass against hers. She clearly enjoyed his attentions and pushed back the fringe of dark hair curling softly over her eyebrows.

"I remember your last picture in Paris, of the girl adrift in the little boat," she asked, "is it true she was waiting for her lover to row it for her?" Louise Romer exuded more than just the alluring confidence of a married woman, it seemed to him.

Tissot chuckled. "People are always looking for meaning in paintings. I leave it up to you, *madame*." He was captivated by the way the pale colors of her tailored suit echoed her creamy complexion, with its rose tints, all like a canvas for her large brown eyes.

She met his scrutiny amiably and began to speak in French, conversing with him about the dreadful ruins in Paris and about prominent people they knew there before the war. They discussed Manet's audaciously modern paintings, and Louise looked impressed when Tissot told her that Manet had taken Berthe Morisot under his wing.

She replied, "His portrait of her is so luscious; he must be in love with her."

"Manet is married." He lied to her, "He is just doing what he can to help Berthe's career along."

Tissot had to admit, her French was far better than his English. He noted the ring on her left hand and eyed her figure down to her slim booted ankles. He had known Manet to have numerous affairs and didn't like the subterfuge, the constant oppressive danger inherent in betraying the spouse. He did hope to see Louise again and could only attempt the impossible – to offer his friendship to a married woman to whom he was deeply attracted, and who seemed equally attracted to him.

He needed to mind his reputation in London. But he did not care to inquire after the absent husband.

Maud returned, stepping with impish majesty, the gown draped over her outstretched arms. Her heel caught on the rush matting covering Whistler's floors, in lieu of carpet, and she stumbled forward.

"The dress!" Jimmy flew into the room with buttermilk biscuits, lovely silver spoons, and blue and white china on a tray with a pot of hot coffee. He briskly set it on the table between them, adjusted his monocle, and fussed over the folds of fabric that nearly engulfed him. "This is an artist's original!" He held up the appliquéd ribbon rosettes for them to admire while Maud sat on the floor and rubbed her toes.

Tissot said, "You made the dress?"

Whistler gaped at him as if he were mad. "It had to match the apple blossom wallpaper in my drawing room! James, just help me get this folded away properly – Louise, excuse us a moment. If this is ripped, we might as well all clasp hands and hurl ourselves into the Thames!" But to

Maud he made a gallant bow, "Come back Monday morning."

She scrambled to her feet. "What about my pay?"

"You're learning to paint, isn't that enough?"

Maud flashed him an impertinent glance. "You said I could have some things to draw with."

"Take some pencils, but not too much of that paper!"

Tissot was used to Jimmy, but Louise suppressed her merriment and poured herself a cup of coffee.

Tissot followed him through the doorway and across the hall, where a great blue ship with full white sails was painted on the upper wall. Jimmy had painted the woodwork below gold, with chrysanthemum petals fluttering all the way down the stairway. He whispered urgently, "Mrs. Romer is enchanting. It is a tragedy for me that she is married."

"Evidently, it's a tragedy for her, too," Jimmy whispered back, and Tissot wished Jimmy understood the concept of whispering. "She was only seventeen when she married Frank. He became Private Secretary to Baron Rothschild in Paris. After a few years, the Baroness Rothschild recognized Louise's talent and arranged for studio training. So far, so good. But Romer was sacked by the Baron two years ago, and even though Louise was building her credentials at the Salon, he brought her back to England." Whistler nodded possessively in her direction. "She *is* a discovery."

At the end of the hall, Tissot saw that since his previous visit, Jimmy had painted his dining room blue and had glued a few purple Japanese fans to the walls and ceiling. The furniture was haphazardly arranged in the center of the room and covered with sheets. It was no wonder, Tissot thought, Jimmy didn't sell enough of his work to pay his bills. If his saintly mother had not moved in, he would still be getting into street brawls and would produce even less.

"I know what you're thinking, James," Whistler said in a severe tone.

Tissot tried to keep his expression neutral.

"You're working every day, all day, so you can establish your own residence and studio address as soon as possible," Whistler chided him. He reached upward, the sensitive fingers of his hand like a hypnotist's. "An artist is not paid for his labor but for his vision!"

"I built a villa near the Arc de Triomphe by my labor," Tissot replied dryly. "The bank would not have accepted a 'vision' for the downpayment, and neither would the architect or the builder."

Jimmy responded with a hearty, "Ha! Ha!"

Reentering the studio, Tissot stopped to admire Whistler's large Japanese-style screen, embellished with a sumptuous gold moon he'd painted against a deep blue sky. Whatever Jimmy did paint was astonishing. Original ideas welled up within him. *He paints these breathtaking daubs without any forethought, without any idea of making money.* He had been in debt since their student days in Paris, but somehow he survived.

The portraits of Mr. and Mrs. Leyland were commissioned, but Jimmy's monochromatic, linear portrait of his mother was an experiment. He had been working on it for over a year, along with a portrait of himself in a round hat, holding his paint brushes. It was styled after of one of Rembrandt's self-portraits.

Tissot occasionally envied Jimmy's carefree nature, so opposite to his own. Still, as he smoothed his frock coat and considered Whistler's career in London, he decided not to paint anything remotely controversial for the Royal Academy exhibition, to play it safe – at least for now. He had in mind one historical scene, and one sentimental picture of lovers parting. Both would show off his technical virtuosity, relying on typical British subject matter.

Whistler inspected the coffee that Louise had set out for each of them on the table between the couch and her bamboo chair. He laughed when he saw James transfixed by his screen, in spite of himself. "That's Battersea Bridge across the top and Chelsea Church beyond. I painted it for Leyland but decided to keep it for myself. Like it, do you?"

Tissot began, dreamily, "I had a screen that size, in my house..."

Jimmy snapped up a buttermilk biscuit with his long fingers. "And what did you do with all your Oriental art and *objets*?"

"I am afraid it...was left behind." James lifted his coffee cup and began to drink.

There was an uncomfortable silence, until Jimmy, in his way, came to the rescue. He leaned against his pagoda cabinet and plucked at the oversized silk bow at his narrow throat. "Just as well! After you painted practically your whole collection, I remember that savage fellow writing that it matters little whether you painted 'young ladies looking at Japanese objects or Japanese objects looking at young ladies'!"

Tissot laughed, but his collection of Orientalia had been his pride and joy – and he had earned it all by his own effort over years of hard work. *How dare Whistler deride me – and in front of Louise?*

Mrs. Romer must have read his thoughts. She tenderly asserted, "Yes, Jimmy, but I also remember the critic who wrote that a picture by Monsieur Tissot will be enough for archaeologists of the future to reconstitute our epoch."

"My *dear* Mrs. Romer," he declared in his Yankee twang, "You know, I only remember my friends' *bad* reviews!"

❧❧❧

Chapter VII

Aboard the *Aphrodite*, Port of London
River Thames, January 8, 1872

Tissot leaned over the rail and looked out over the heart of the British Empire as the steamer arrived, rocking with the waves. He felt a thrill jolt through him with the wind that buffeted his face. London was twice as big as Paris, and its port was the busiest in the world. Canals like streets opened into the river, and the steamer entered a boulevard of industry filled with hundreds of vessels. Keels scraped, steam hissed, gulls cried overhead, and dockers and watermen shouted in a cacophony of voices bringing spices from Java, ice from Norway, and rubber from Siam to the cargo-handlers at the wharves.

Holding onto his cap, he took a deep breath and let the bracing winter air fill his lungs. It smelled of smoke and tar, rust and beer. Amid the spectacle of three-masted ships from every corner of the world, it was hard to remain dejected. To him, there was no more fascinating place than the Thames at the London Docks.

"*Mon Dieu*, I love this!" he said to himself, gripping the icy rail.

Tissot had come down on the steamer from Chelsea with his sketching materials, several times after seeing Whistler's success with his etchings of the Thames. It was an overcast day and though the water before him was murky and rough, the river in the distance had a bright sheen.

He raced down the gangplank past the other passengers, grinned and pulled the brim of his cap low. The river life swirled around him as it had throughout his boyhood in the port at Nantes. With his pencil he deftly sketched in the spider-web of ships' rigging in the background; study after study, they filled his small notebook as they filled the stone-grey sky before him.

You have given up any chance of being a serious painter, Degas had sneered at him when he fled Paris. Now Degas was impressed by the prices his paintings were fetching in London, but he had Jimmy Whistler denigrating his work as trivial. *I can out-paint all of them!* He just wanted to find subject matter that would please the British critics, especially this man Ruskin.

Tissot pocketed his drawing pad and strode along the docks. His eyes took in every detail, and his brain considered every possibility. He had no chance to become a sensation in a crowded art market unless he did something immediately, before the Royal Academy show opened in four months. Tissot felt himself struggling to stand out in London. *If I do not establish myself as a "British" painter soon, I will be pigeonholed as just one more small-time foreigner*. He needed to attract a great deal of attention quickly – or to make a great deal of money, which would accomplish the same thing. He would have to establish a residence of his own soon, and launch himself in style. After six months as Tommy Bowles' houseguest, Tissot knew he was perceived as a mere hanger-on, just another part-time illustrator for *Vanity Fair*.

Strolling past produce vendors and meat carts, Tissot tried not to think of Louise Romer. Whistler told him that her husband had secured a post as secretary to a Member of Parliament. He and Louise had taken an apartment in Bayswater, where she made the front drawing-room into a studio. He could not visit her, but heard of her through Whistler.

Tissot shoved his hands in his coat and watched the dockmen, soldiers, prostitutes and pickpockets. What a scandal, if he painted what was really here – the drunks and whores, shoeless errand boys or even the sweating, impoverished working men who did their best to earn a living moving cargo. *I could be the Manet of London*, he thought wryly. But he was not out to shock, just to get back on his feet.

He had come down to the London Docks, the first time, with the thought of painting scenes similar to those Jimmy Whistler had etched. He exchanged his starched collar and frock coat for warm clothing and shoes appropriate to protect him from the bone-chilling winds. Wandering the riverside, Tissot observed the activity until he finally decided to paint the romance of it – the towering masts, the jungle of rigging. *Oui*, why not draw some things as they really are? He threw his cigarette down into the river. *Millais paints Britain's glorious past, but I will paint its present*. What could be more British than its enterprising, cosmopolitan seamen?

On his next sketching trip, he had made it his business to talk with ships' captains. Lumley Kennedy had seen him sketching and conversing and had sent out a man to invite him on board, where he arranged for Tissot to spend a day on his ship in its berth.

Now Tissot took the gangplank and gave his name to a dogsbody who disappeared to find the captain. He leaned over the gunnel and watched as a sailor emerged from a dockside pub with a whore on each arm. The women argued over him and one slapped at the other, but the sailor pulled them to his sides and shouted, "Ladies, there's enough for both of you!"

When they heard Tissot chuckle, one of the women called up to him, "Oh, *there's* a gentleman! Come on, now, make it a proper party!"

Tissot waved, enjoying the absurdity of it.

Captain Kennedy appeared and bellowed, "Clear out, you sluts! I want none of that near the *Aphrodite*. He laughed at the irony and murmured to Tissot, "Gives the ship a bad name to the emigrants. Those folks are scared enough already." He quickly shook James' hand and pushed him along. "It's cold enough to freeze the balls off a brass monkey."

"It has been awhile since I have heard that said."

"Been awhile since it's been this cold," the Captain observed. "Have a bite to eat? Margaret and John have arranged to be onboard all afternoon."

Kennedy guided Tissot before the mast to his private quarters and introduced them to his attractive younger sister. Soon a knock-kneed cabin boy appeared with a tray.

"Hot cider," Captain Kennedy nodded, plunking down a pewter tankard near Tissot on the long table. "You left Paris after the war?"

"Don't pry, my dear." The captain's sister, Margaret Freebody, reminded him of his ladylike Aunt Arsène. She sat down to a mug of cider with them, and her manners were easy and amiable.

With his large, square hands, Captain Kennedy cut thick slices of bread for each of them. "That's all right – I'll tell you about the *Aphrodite*. With her, we have made a good living taking emigrants to America."

"Poor, broken things, they always look so sad to leave England –" Margaret observed, uncovering a wedge of cheese.

"– and so optimistic when they arrive in New York," said her brother. There was a blast of cold air, and he sliced more bread, saying, "Ah, here's John."

Lumley Kennedy was a hefty, short man with a full red beard and mustache. His sister's husband, John Freebody, was slim, blonde and a head taller. Both men wore their gold-buttoned blue captains' uniforms and expressions of worldly-wise, good-humored contentment.

They put Tissot at ease and asked him at length about the war. Margaret and Tissot asked each other to repeat a phrase from time to time, until she grew more used to his thick French accent and he to her Irish lilt. With her alert eyes and ready laugh, she offered her friendship as much as her husband and brother did.

Freebody, captain of the *Warwick Castle*, asked to look at Tissot's sketchbook and flipped through approvingly. "Look at the way he's drawn the bends at the belaying pins. And the cleats and the way that buntline is tied – only a seaman could know that much about ship rigging and fittings."

"I grew up in Nantes," James replied, "and spent every minute I could on the ships in port. I could step right on to them from our dock at my father's shop."

"I had taken you for the son of an aristocrat," observed Captain Kennedy, settling back in his red armchair. Behind him were two framed etchings of early paintings by Millais alongside some photograph cards of New York City.

John Freebody refilled their cider mugs, and Margaret rose with a small key and brought out carefully wrapped dishes of nuts and Turkish Delight from a polished cabinet.

"*Non*, my father was in trade. He built his wholesale and export business from a linen-draper and dry goods shop. He became alarmed when he saw how interested I was in the calicos and muslins and trims. I used to sketch from the fashion plates always on the counter." The bread and cheese were fine, and Tissot washed them down with a long sip of cider. "If I was determined to draw, my father sent me outside to watch the constant arrival of merchant ships instead."

"He is unhappy you are a painter?" Margaret suggested gently, taking a piece of the sugar-dusted candy before her. She wore her brunette hair parted down the center and pulled back simply, as his mother had.

Tissot leaned over his mug and answered her frankly. "My eldest brother was in the Navy, before he became mayor of the town where my father bought a château. *Non*, my father cares nothing for art, but he would be mollified to know I can make money from painting things that he considers important, such as ships."

Tissot was used to fraternizing with people who were the center of everyone's attention – Tommy Bowles, Whistler, Manet in Paris like Jesus among his disciples. But the Freebodys, who were his age, encouraged him do most of the talking, and he enjoyed being a source of fascination to them.

Margaret proved the most inquisitive. "What did you paint in Paris?"

"Women, mostly. In my house."

"Relatives, you mean?"

Tissot cracked a walnut. "*Non, madame*."

Captain Kennedy and his brother-in-law as well as his

sister burst out laughing.

"You Frenchmen are all the same!" the Captain said, while John patted him warmly on the back.

Tissot laughed, too. "In Paris, art is supposed to portray history or mythology, or Biblical scenes. But I made a name for myself painting modern life for people of fashion...before the war. I will never regain my standing in France," Tissot confided to them. He gestured toward Kennedy's sextant displayed in its case, "So it is crucial for me now to calibrate my pictures to please the British public. I must cater to Ruskin's likes and dislikes."

Seeing their blank faces, he explained, "John Ruskin – *the* Oxford professor of art."

"I know who he is – 'I paints and paints, hears no complaints...then savage Ruskin sticks his tusk in and nobody will buy.' That's from *Punch*," Captain Kennedy said. "But we've heard him speak, haven't we, John?"

"Bloody nonsense," John agreed, "and the way he flaps around in his academic gown! Rather mad, isn't he?"

Tissot was stunned. "You have attended Ruskin's lectures?"

"Went up to Oxford last week," Kennedy replied. "He doesn't teach or give lessons or exams. Just these lectures when the mood strikes him. It was quiet as a church, though there must have been six hundred people. We had to stand and wedge the door open for over an hour, didn't we, John?"

John swept up the shells from the walnuts he had consumed and disposed of them. "He's an awful prig, though – wants to take anatomy lessons out of the art school –"

Tissot's eyes widened. "How can anyone paint who has not studied the human form?"

Margaret looked from one man to the other, openly

enjoying the conversation as high entertainment.

Kennedy shrugged gamely. "I know nothing about it, just that Professor Ruskin said, 'If you want to know anatomy, go to an hospital and cut dead bodies to pieces 'til you are satisfied...then come to me, and I'll teach you to draw.' "

"The Prince of Wales was even there," said John. "He and Ruskin looked thick –"

"But *why* did you go?" Tissot scratched his chin. He was chagrined to admit, "I have never met the man, or even seen him."

The captain reached into a low cupboard and slapped two magazines down on the table. Tissot flipped through them and shook his head at Ruskin's claim: " *'My readers may trust me to tell them what is well done or ill...'* You read Ruskin's magazine?"

John Freebody laughed. "He means it for 'the working man,' but he writes rather above the laboring class. Yes, I am well situated, and we fancy a bit of art for our walls. It's just that I don't want to be taken in. I want to know something about it all, you see."

Captain Kennedy said, "I saw a painting once, at the Royal Academy, of polar bears eating a man. Tearing him to pieces, actually."

"I have seen it," Tissot began. "It is by one of your most famous painters –"

John waved that off. "I wouldn't want it in my house."

"Bad luck," Margaret said, shuddering and pulling her paisley shawl tighter. "I'll tell you what I like –"

"You always do," her husband teased her.

She ignored him and continued, "Pictures of beautiful ladies, pictures that look real. I want to see the fur and grass and metal pop off the canvas."

"I agree with my wife there," John said. "But none of that stiff Shakespeare stuff, nor naked babies flying 'round strange women. And no sermons, either. Something of the life around me, that my eyes don't tire of looking at. Something that amuses me."

Tissot looked from Captain Kennedy to his sister and her husband uneasily. Then he clasped his hands behind his head with a mischievous gleam in his eyes. "What amuses us may not amuse John Ruskin."

Freebody turned to Margaret. "Do you know, I fancy some art for my cabin."

"Your cabin? First, for our *home* in South Bermondsey. I need something to look at besides my four new walls while you're away, my dear. And I'd rather our money went to our friend James, here, rather than some London dealer."

Tissot suddenly remembered Degas growling, *Art should not be made available to the lower classes.*

He tapped at his mustache, envisioning numerous possible scenes of shipside farewells, bittersweet partings – and even, if they were game, compositions onboard with the two men and the pretty young woman, which could be slightly *risqué.*

"Will you pose for me – all three of you?"

They readily agreed, but John Freebody said, "Only on the condition that I am allowed to purchase the first painting." Margaret raised her eyebrow at him. "For my wife, of course."

Tissot rubbed his hands together and pulled out his pencils and sketch book. He could hardly wait to paint precise nautical settings and men in uniform, and he could see the commercial possibilities. "I can make studies to use in future oil paintings... I can think of a great number of scenes aboard the *Aphrodite.*"

"Like what?" said Captain Kennedy.

Tissot thought for a half minute. "When I was a boy, I was often collared to listen to long, boring stories by some retired salt who would spread out his maps and relive his sailing days. He would take no notice of my yawns and as there was usually no chance of escaping him, all I could do was say, 'How interesting! Tell me more!' It would be comical to paint a pretty woman in that situation with an old seaman."

They all laughed, Captain Kennedy the loudest of all. "Now that's a picture I would want!" he said.

James chuckled and flipped his drawing pad to a blank page. He could earn real money, independent of illustrations for Tommy's magazine, painting for 'self-made' men like Kennedy and Freebody. He was grateful to have their friendship.

By the time he disembarked the *Aphrodite* for the bracing air of the bustling river port, alive with its smells and sounds, Tissot felt like a boy again. Unencumbered by a household, passing his time with sea captains on their ships, James felt more himself than ever. He drew a deep, invigorating breath, ready to take on London's art world as his own man.

Chapter VIII

Wilton Crescent, Merton Park
February 23, 1872

Tommy Bowles threw himself into an overstuffed red velvet armchair and draped a leg over the side. He was completely at home in his father's household.

"My sister is so excited you're painting her portrait," Tommy said. "Just wait until you see her – you'll love Sydney as much as I do. Of all my father's children, she is my favorite."

The sofa beckoned, and Tissot perched on the edge of it. His head ached; not only had he caught a bad cold on his last jaunt down to the London Docks, but he had the worst hangover of his life. Last night, Tommy had found four bottles of champagne on his doorstep, accompanied by two boyhood friends. They had what Tommy called "a big drunk as of old in Duke Street," bingeing on oysters and the remains of Tommy's liquor cabinet until one of his companions finally vomited. Tommy put his friends in a hansom cab around four this morning, oblivious that he and James had an appointment at eleven o'clock – eight miles south at Merton Park, near Wimbledon.

After Tissot stumbled to his room and passed out, Tommy snatched a few hours of sleep, wrote two articles for *Vanity Fair*, and rode to Fleet Street to deliver them, paying an ostler to hold his horse until he was ready to ride home. Tommy finally had the magazine back on its feet after his absence reporting on the Siege of Paris.

Tissot leaned forward to set his sketchbook on the table and blow his nose. He could not tell, but he hoped to God his trousers did not smell of oysters and Scotch. "Tommy, you make me feel old. I cannot keep up with you anymore." James spoke quietly, trying not to sound as ill and out of sorts as he felt, while they waited in the Milner-Gibsons' serene drawing-room. *Why are highborn women always so heedless of time?*

Tommy just laughed and bounced out of the armchair to pick out a few notes on the shining upright piano near the door to the foyer. "It's one way for me to keep up with the gossip for *Vanity Fair* between house parties. The Prince of Wales now is such an avid fan that I had to issue a statement denying that His Royal Tum-Tum has become part proprietor!"

"I never met anyone who could get by on so little sleep," James said, yawning. The time had come for him to move into his own lodging. He could not be productive with the constant distractions at Cleeve Lodge. Besides the frequent late-night parties, there was Tommy's well-meaning help to contend with.

As they waited, Tommy's light blue eyes danced. "Once you begin to paint girls like my sister, word will get around, and you'll have more commissions than you can find time for. You'll be the next new thing."

"I am looking forward to painting her," James assured him, his headache hammering the spot between his eyes. He rubbed at it, and a vague memory of Tommy chasing his rooster around his back garden drifted through his brain. He gave way to temptation and sank into the sofa, tossing aside a stiff horsehair cushion behind him and leaning back as far back as he could. His eyes closed and he stretched out his legs to their full length.

Tommy spoke often of Sydney and had commissioned James to paint her portrait as a present in honor of her twenty-first birthday. While Tommy's mother, Susannah Bowles, had been a servant in his father's household, Sydney's mother was the daughter of a baronet. It would be a *coup* indeed for Tissot to exhibit a portrait of the aristocratic young daughter of a Member of Parliament at the Royal Academy.

"It will be like my portrait of the Marquise de Miramon in Paris, six years ago," James murmured. He opened one eye and glanced around the quietly refined room, imagining different backgrounds and poses for Miss Milner-Gibson. And, he thought, John Ruskin's opinion would not matter, once aristocratic ladies learned of Tissot's skill at depicting their beauty. If he sold nothing else but Society portraits, he could become immensely wealthy.

At the click of heeled shoes on the staircase, Tommy leapt up and flashed his white grin. "Here she is!"

James stood, squared his shoulders, and smoothed his frock coat.

"James Tissot, allow me to introduce my adorable sister, Sydney Milner-Gibson, a regular reader of the wittiest magazine in town and a *particular* fan of your cartoons."

Sydney curtseyed, and James' heart sank. Tommy was so blonde and irresistibly handsome, Tissot had assumed his looks ran in the family. Although composed and ladylike, Tommy's half-sister was a heavy girl with all the grace of a butternut squash.

Sydney raised her eyes sweetly to Tommy's French friend. James bowed and kissed her hand, and she giggled. She wore a skirt of tiered muslin ruffles and carried a handkerchief which she twisted nervously between her short fingers.

A wave of nausea hit him. *Less than four months before the Royal Academy exhibition – what else can I submit?*

Tommy whirled Sydney around and complimented her dress. "How are you, my dearest girl?"

"Very glad to see you, and quite overcome by the idea of having my picture done." She caught her breath, turned her doughy features to Tissot and smiled shyly under her too-short fringe of frizzy, reddish-blonde hair. "I have never sat to a painter before." Her voice had a hint of a baby's lisp. "Must I stay entirely still for hours and hours?"

"Not for hours and hours, but sometimes," Tissot replied, through a mask of professionalism. "I shall need to arrange several sittings with you." He strolled to the other side of the room and blew his nose, inwardly cursing the commission as a waste of time.

"Speak with mama. She arranges everything for me."

"*Bon.* For today, let us decide on the pose."

"Stand her before the mantel, gazing at a vase of white roses," said Tommy, taking charge and tipping Sydney's double chin up at a jaunty angle.

A mottled red blush spread over her pudgy cheeks. "You mustn't tease me, Tommy!"

"That is a lovely composition," James nodded, fighting the raw feeling in his stomach. *Why did I have to get as drunk as Tommy's old schoolfellows?* "However, I think *mademoiselle* should look more at home, more relaxed.

Perhaps in this chair, with a book?"

Sydney took a seat, and her hips filled the width of the velvet armchair, squeezing her skirts out at her knees. James strained to devise some pose that would minimize her ample proportions. When he suggested she seat herself on the arm of the red velvet chair, she dropped awkwardly onto it. He courteously assisted her in adopting a more artistic posture, casually leaning over the chair's arm and resting a hand on the other side in a way that sent her hips into shadow. As he ran his eyes over her, he grew alarmed by her expression of open admiration.

"Sydney," Tommy said, beaming, "James plans to exhibit your portrait at the Royal Academy!"

"Oh...I think not," Sydney confessed, looking up from under her heavy eyelids. She struggled for balance while James arranged her layered skirts. "I would not wish my likeness to be exhibited. It really is not something an unmarried lady ought to do."

"Nonsense! It will be an honor to make your *début* twice – once before Her Majesty, and once at the Royal Academy." Tommy gazed fondly at his half-sister as Tissot began to sketch her. "And it will be wonderful for Tissot to begin his London career by honoring you. All the most exclusive Society women will seek him out."

Sydney insisted, "I am sorry, Monsieur Tissot. I am delighted by my brother's generosity, but I confess that I do not wish my portrait to be shown in public. It's not something a young lady should allow. I am not distinguished, nor a great beauty, and I'm afraid it will seem like an advertisement for a husband."

James, biting his lip, feigned furious concentration leafing through his drawing pad to begin.

Tommy kissed her fringed forehead. "There's a thought! Shall I print an etching of you in *Vanity Fair* with a caption, 'Wanted, one prince of a man to marry adorable sister of publisher?' It would be up to me to interview them and select the perfect husband for you!"

"You really mustn't tease me," Sydney pleaded in her baby voice. Her load-bearing arm wavered, and she snuck a guilty peek at Tissot while adjusting her position across the red armchair. "I'm likely to die an old maid."

"Not at twenty-one!" Tommy told her. He folded his arms over his chest and stood at Tissot's shoulder, watching his preliminary outlines. "You have such a tender heart, Sydney. I should like to see you marry a man who deserves you."

James hid his panic. And he hardly wished to exhibit this as an example of his portrait painting skills. "*Mademoiselle* Sydney must have her way, Tommy. Is she not of age to make decisions for herself?"

Sydney and Tommy exchanged a knowing look. Tommy took a seat on the sofa, crossed his legs, and explained, "My father and stepmother will likely decide who is worthy of my sister. Then the poor sod will have to endure the *ghastly* ordeal of a three- or four-year engagement, a Scotland Yard investigation into his finances and a thorough check of the mental stability of all his relations going back to William the Conqueror."

Sydney broke into self-conscious, hiccupping laughter. While Tissot made diligent pencil studies of her, she and her brother entertained him with silly characterizations of Society courtship and marriage rituals.

"I just hope they settle on someone from Suffolk," she said in her little lisp, "rather than someone they meet this summer when we go abroad. I would so like to stay close to Mother."

Tommy winked at her. "You know she is more likely to be in Paris at any given moment." He added, to James, "My stepmother encourages me to marry a lady of my own station, but I am not entirely sure what that is."

Tissot was amazed by Tommy Bowles, who had told him during the Siege that he was the bastard son of a Liberal MP and a servant girl. His father readily acknowledged him, and it was his stepmother, the Liberal hostess Arethusa Susannah Milner-Gibson, who told everyone, "This is Tom Bowles. Be civil to him – or leave the house."

Sydney clucked her tongue. "Tommy! Shall I look about for a wife for you?"

"Yes, find me a wife who loves you as I do, and who indulges me as you do." He turned to James. "Tissot, you handsome devil, why are you not married?"

James smoothed his black frock coat as Tommy and Sydney watched him expectantly. He ran a hand through his hair and gave them a sly smile. "My friend Degas once told me he could never bring himself to marry. He said, 'I would have been in mortal misery all my life for fear my wife might say, "That's a pretty little thing," after I had finished a picture.' "

Sydney giggled, and Tommy reached his hands out to haul her up from a pose she could barely maintain.

For Tissot now, the only woman in the world worth having was taken. Whistler told him that Louise Romer had moved out on her two-timing gambler of a husband, who then left for New York. From there, he was attempting through his lawyer in London to empty Louise's bank account while his family pressured her to "be a good wife."

Tissot longed to paint Mrs. Romer's portrait, and he intended to ask her to sit to him as soon as her situation settled down. The art critic Tom Taylor and his wife had taken Louise under their wing. Though Tissot longed to see her, he did not wish to set tongues wagging. He thought of her beauty and earnest artistic ambition, and he anticipated how quickly *she* would grasp how he wished her to pose, how professionally they would work together.

He bowed to Sydney and thanked her for her time, and Tommy embraced her with extravagant pleas to visit him at Cleeve Lodge. A little black dog trotted in, and she grabbed it up into her frothy ruffled arms and began whispering into its ears. It yapped at Tissot, who restrained his impatience until Tommy was ready to depart.

ॐॐॐ

In the chilly railway carriage on the new line at Merton, Tommy draped a boiled wool lap rug over his trousers and said, "Sorry about the Royal Academy, James. What a disappointment for you."

"You do too much for me, Tommy." Tissot set his top hat on the seat next to him and sneezed. "Your hospitality will be repaid with privacy soon, as I have arranged to lease my own house next month."

"I haven't driven you out of Cleeve Lodge, have I?"

"On the contrary – you have earned an open invitation to my new home."

"Shall we be neighbors? I understand there is a house shortly to be available in Queen's Gate."

"*Non*, it is just west of the Regent's Park. St. John's Wood reminds me a bit of the Bois de Bologne, and a number of gentlemen artists have formed a colony in the area." James pulled the stereoscope photograph card of his villa on the avenue de l'Impératrice from his breast pocket and gazed at it.

Tommy hung onto the leather strap in the swaying wooden train carriage and glanced over at his friend. "Hmm. There are other 'suburbs,' if that's where you're determined to set up. Funny thing to say to a Frenchman,"

Bowles observed, "but you *do* know what St. John's Wood is known for..."

James checked his watch and yawned with a pleasant expression.

Bowles gestured insinuatingly, "...shaded footpaths, private gates... kept women..."

Tissot merely chuckled, "Then you must promise never to ask how I get on there."

Chapter IX

Opening of the 104th Exhibition of the Royal Academy of Arts Burlington House, 49 Piccadilly, May 31, 1872

Just as the Salon had always been the event of the year in Paris, the Annual Exhibition of the Royal Academy of Arts was one of the highlights of the London season. A crush of carriages and pedestrians were arriving, crunching over the gravel courtyard. Tissot and Millais, jostled by people on all sides, made their way through the entrance to Burlington House.

In addition to the crowds, they met with a great deal of confusion and congestion from the construction. The government had moved the Royal Academy of Arts from the National Gallery at Trafalgar Square, where Tissot had exhibited when he was still in his twenties, to Burlington House in Piccadilly five years ago. The government had acquired the Palladian mansion, a private residence built in the seventeenth century, and the east and west wing expansions were due to be completed next year.

A lady's feathered hat floated over the heads around her, and she sailed past Tissot on the arm of her elderly male escort, who left a waft of a fine Scottish whiskey. From the silk top hats to the trailing skirts, everyone was dressed to be seen. Anyone who could not pay the shilling fee could visit free on Sundays. Tissot paid Millais' entry fee as well as his own, and purchased them each an exhibition catalog. It was a rare opportunity to spend the day with his English friend, and Tissot found Millais a reassuring presence at the first Academy exhibition of his work as an expatriate.

They joined the stream of visitors flowing through the main vestibule into the long, narrow corridors to view the thousands of pictures selected for the floor-to-ceiling display on the walls.

Tissot brushed the construction dust off his new black frock coat. He had grown used to the display at the Paris Salon, where paintings were hung in four or five rows, in alphabetical order by artists' names. At the Royal Academy, the paintings were hung floor to ceiling, in a jumble of gilded frames arranged with little logic except to fit the various size pictures together like puzzle pieces. Here, the work of the most prominent artists was hung "on the line" – at eye level – with others displayed near the floor or toward the vaulted ceiling. Like the Salon, the Academy rarely accepted paintings that were very different.

"Come look!" cried Joe Jopling from the *mêlée*, like a meaty fish jumping up from a foaming river current. He laughed and waved them toward him. "Whistler's been skyed!"

Joe led as Tissot and Millais pushed their way through the cramped Exhibition galleries. They found themselves struggling to pass through the throng convulsed with laughter at Whistler's *Arrangement in Grey and Black:*

Portrait of the Painter's Mother. The Academicians had accepted the picture – and hung it up near the ceiling over an entryway, out of sight.

"Didn't know Whistler *had* a mother!" Jopling was so overcome with hilarity he had to squeeze Millais' shoulder to steady himself.

Millais clasped his hands behind his back, and his fine straight features radiated only benevolence.

"Jimmy likely will never again exhibit at the Royal Academy," Tissot said, folding his arms over his chest. He could be angry at Whistler occasionally, but who was Joe Jopling to mock Jimmy Whistler? Jopling gave himself airs about being an artist while shuffling documents in the War Office. It was because the Salon had rejected Whistler's *At the Piano* that he had left Paris years ago. The Royal Academy had accepted *At the Piano* the next year, and Jimmy began to make a name for himself in London.

"He should stay the course, really," Millais replied soberly. "Especially after Sir William threatened to resign if the portrait were not hung."

Jopling's small white mustache twitched. "They say, 'If only Whistler behaved himself...' "

Tissot retorted, "Exactly why they disgust him."

"The Academicians are good enough old fellows." Millais shrugged, and a charming smile played over his mouth. "In any case, one must have genial relations with them."

"Can't wait to hear Ruskin's verdict," Joe said, smirking.

Tissot took a deep breath. It was hot and airless in the galleries, which smelled of varnish and the various hair pomades and perfumes of the passing visitors. He adjusted his waistcoat, enjoying the perfect fit of the suede gloves he'd just bought, and leafed through his catalog.

Listed under Joseph Jopling was one picture: *Extensive Highland Landscape with Cattle.*

Joe saw Tissot looking him up and raised his shoulders proudly. "You'll see it in the next gallery. I spent three winters in Rome, studying the Old Masters."

"Oh, *hang* the Old Masters!" Millais shot back merrily. "I prefer the young mistresses."

Joe reached up to clap Millais on the back. "Only you would dare to make a remark like that!"

They drifted with the flow of visitors into the next gallery, where Jopling pointed out his insipid landscape, hung on the line. If ever Tissot had wondered whether London was the right place for him after he fled Paris, this was his answer. If men like Joe Jopling could compete in the crowded London art market, then Tissot knew he could exceed even his own expectations. He had submitted only two paintings to the Royal Academy and was gratified that both were accepted. His portraits of Gus Burnaby and a modern businessman in a railway carriage already were on display at the International Exposition at the Royal Horticultural Society in the Cromwell Road. In London only a year, he had taken pains to ensure his work was displayed in the largest possible public venues. It unnerved him to read a critic's pronouncement in the *Illustrated London News* that he had "more skill than the unlearned public is ever likely to appreciate." He was anxious about the reception of his Academy pictures today.

Millais paid profuse compliments to Jopling's depiction of grazing cattle and assured him it would be noticed by all the critics. Tissot finally interrupted by pointing out Lawrence Alma-Tadema's picture, wedged in a corner, of an Egyptian widow.

"Lawrence, Lawrence..." Millais clucked his tongue. "His paint always looks so rough and dry."

The three men continued through the crush of visitors in a forced march along the hot, dimly-lit corridor. As Tissot scanned the gallery, he saw a great many portraits, historical pieces, rural landscapes, maritime scenes and pictures of horses and dogs, along with a few depictions of the plight of the urban poor, numerous Shakespearean dramas and endless variations of sweet English girls with flowers. Vain about his Parisian art training, Tissot could not help dismissing some of the work as no better than *efforts* at art. Then, high on the wall, he glimpsed Louise Romer's *Queen Vashti Refusing to Show Herself to the People.*

"Ah, the queen who was divorced for refusing to obey her husband's command," Millais commented lightly. "And now Louise must stay away and mourn her husband's death, though they'd been estranged for years. Mr. Romer, one hears, could not be persuaded to take her art seriously."

Joe Jopling, planting himself between them, just shook his head.

"Mrs. Romer is exquisite," James murmured, running his gloved hand over his mustache.

"Admire her, do you, James?" Millais grinned like a schoolboy. "She has told me, you know, that by marrying again, she would be cutting her own throat as far as her profession goes..."

"Widows and lady artists are the very devil," said Jopling.

"She has a refreshing *esprit*." Tissot's mind dwelt on her, and he studied her painting more closely. He still yearned to paint her portrait, but for propriety's sake, he would have to wait for a proper interval to pass before he could ask her to sit to him. He could hardly wait to see her again, now that she was not bound by marriage. His gaze wandered down the hall. "Millais, look – there!"

Leaning languidly against the threshold into the next

gallery was the president of the Royal Academy, Frederic Leighton, his aristocratic profile framed by his long, curly blonde locks and jutting beard. Had his shoulder given way, he looked as if he would slide down the wall and onto the floor. Tissot pulled a slim cloisonné notebook from his pocket and captured Leighton's essence in a dozen surreptitious strokes of his enameled pencil. "Tommy will want this for *Vanity Fair*!"

Jopling nudged Tissot's shoulder. "But look, while you're lampooning Leighton, Alma-Tadema is courting him."

Tissot looked up only momentarily. "As I am. It is not malicious."

Millais was entertained by Tissot's sketch. "If he is not properly flattered, he still will relish the publicity." He gestured to his friends. "Come, let's have a look at the Reynolds show."

Joe Jopling checked his pocket watch and told Millais he needed to get back to the War Office. "Meet me at the Club for a drink before you head home," he said, excluding Tissot as he took his leave.

Tissot breathed a sigh of relief, and he and Millais quickened their pace. Both were eager to view the collection of pictures by the Royal Academy's first president, Sir Joshua Reynolds, being shown along with the Exhibition.

Millais modeled the romantic costumes of his sitters on depictions of eighteenth-century clothing from Reynolds' pictures. "One never tires of them," he reflected. "Unlike those ugly pictures of people wearing whatever goes today, they are timeless."

It was, Tissot reflected, English native art. Exactly why he had drawn on it for both of his Academy submissions this year. But in Paris, he had received the most acclaim for his provocative portrait of a confident, modern woman in a trendy red *bolero*, trimmed in pompoms. It was that bold move that won him the Salon prize that year, propelling him to the top of his profession and ultimately enabling him to build his house and studio in the avenue de l'Impératrice. *Do not look back*, he told himself.

Proceeding along the wall of paintings, Tissot was surprised to encounter Degas in the crush. He embraced him warmly and introduced him to Millais, who greeted him with a buoyant welcoming eagerness in his deep blue eyes.

"I've just seen Whistler's painting," Degas told them. "He should paint with his tongue, then he might be a genius."

Millais responded with a hearty laugh, but Tissot asked, "Why did you not write that you were coming to London?" He, Degas, and Millais formed an obstacle in the corridor that the ceaseless stream of visitors flowed around.

"Whistler did not tell you?" Degas grumbled. "I want to see what business I can drum up here. Jimmy is put off with me for telling him he should follow your example, Tissot, and paint more."

Millais and Tissot turned to each other and burst out in a shared guffaw at the idea of Degas rebuking Whistler.

"Why do you laugh?" Degas growled at Tissot, eyeing James' new frock coat and his stylish top hat. "You are the epitome of French success in London."

"I am?"

"*Oui*," insisted Degas, almost accusingly. "And I have talked to Manet's new dealer, Durand-Ruel. In Paris, he has sold a few of my ballet and racecourse scenes. Everyone is talking about how he bought almost every picture in Manet's studio on the spot in January, but in his London gallery, he tells me he will not stock much Franco-realist inventory," Degas complained, fiddling with the brim of his old top hat. "The only French artist of our age that English dealers will buy and sell is *you*, Tissot. Your William Agnew won't touch work by Manet or Whistler." He added wryly, "I am going to imitate your style – so I can sell my work in London and grow rich like you."

"I have seen your pictures in the gallery in New Bond Street," Millais enthused. "They are far superior to everything there."

Tissot stood stupefied at what Degas had said. He tried not to think back to the days when his paintings displayed in Goupil's gallery windows drew crowds of fascinated Parisians. "Rich I am not, yet – the house is merely leased – but I am setting up my own household at last."

"So I hear." Degas stared at Tissot's shoes, then his own worn ones.

The gleaming new shoes that Degas envied were pinching Tissot's feet, and he fidgeted in them. He wished there were a place to sit and have a cup of tea – or better yet, a cold glass of champagne.

"How long are you in town?" Millais asked Degas. The crowd pushed impatiently at them, though they had tried to move off to the side of the narrow corridor.

"I've seen all I need to see," Degas declared. "Manet also is interested in selling his work in London. He asked me to make inquiries for him, but he is going to have to produce something that can sell here first." A lady bumped into him, and he made her a curt bow and squeezed farther against the wall. "In the meantime, my mother's family in New Orleans is urging me to spend the fall and winter with them. They just may make a fortune with their cotton business, now that the Southern states are rebuilding."

"Dine with us," Millais insisted. "We're not likely to meet again soon, and I want to hear more about your work. There is a real invasion of French art in London these days." He grinned and added, "Effie would like to see you, to hear about Paris. You must come too, Tissot."

"I am staying at the Hotel Conte in Golden Square. Send a note if you wish." Degas pulled a handkerchief from his pocket, glared at Tissot and said, "I hope you understand how fortunate you are to have left. Those of us who stayed in the ruins and ashes were rewarded with a Salon determined to showcase not art, but French patriotism. They are doing their part to further our national humiliation."

Degas' nostrils flickered as he grew heated. "Courbet, from prison, submitted two paintings. They were rejected, but he won great public sympathy. Monet and Pissarro have returned to Paris but refused to submit their work, as did Cezanne and I. Renoir submitted two paintings, which were both stamped with a red *R* on the back and returned," he ranted, gesturing with his handkerchief crushed into his fist. "But our persistent friend Manet submitted an old painting of an American naval battle during *their* war, and though the Salon officials have always said he possesses no talent, they accepted this picture as somehow 'patriotic.' Among two thousand shitty paintings embarrassing France, *Manet's sinking war ship* is considered the most interesting thing at the Salon!"

Degas wiped the sweat from his wide forehead with the handkerchief and abruptly bowed and turned away.

Millais winked at Tissot, who wryly observed, "The Americans will love him."

On the way back to the main exhibition to view the crowd's reaction to their own paintings, they found their way blocked by an imposing gentleman in mutton-chop whiskers. His wrinkled face was grey and severe, and he was trembling as he clutched the middle of a long cane.

Tissot studied his face, which seemed familiar though he had never seen him. The man scrutinized Tissot from head to toe, but it was Millais who attracted the malevolent gaze of his almost colorless eyes. After a tense moment, the man drew himself up defiantly, then reversed direction.

Millais shrugged and commented, "That, my friend, was John Ruskin."

"Ruskin! He is still angry with you for marrying Effie?"

"Not because of that." Someone's elbow collided with Millais's arm, and he tipped his tall hat, begged the man's pardon and continued. "It's that girl I was telling you about – the young one who has obsessed him since she was ten or eleven. Her parents opposed the match after they received Effie's letter, and the girl won't marry him. Ruskin is evidently suffering the most acute mental distress, and he blames Effie. And me, it would seem."

"He looks dangerous," Tissot said, "as if he would have horsewhipped us both."

"He may thrash me if he wishes, as long as he leaves Effie alone." Millais was silent and subdued until they reached his large painting, hung prominently at eye level.

"They said it couldn't be done – that I could never paint a modern triple portrait as well as Reynolds in his day." His face glowed as his many friends called out compliments to him. In Millais' cheerful company, Tissot soon forgot Degas and Ruskin.

Hearts are Trumps depicted the three daughters of a wealthy British merchant in Reynolds-inspired gowns, though their throats were encircled by black velvet ribbons in the current style. Millais shook hands with those gathered around the picture, pronouncing it a sensation for overcoming the stumbling block of contemporary fashions. Tissot looked beyond the young beauties that the canvas advertised for marriage and, instead, nodded approvingly at the Japanese screen painted behind them. Millais, though not a connoisseur of Orientalia, understood that it was all the rage and had relied on Tissot's taste to select the screen as a backdrop for this lucrative triple portrait commission.

Down the corridor hung Tissot's *The Farewell*, a scene of two young lovers – a dandy and a woman who might have been a governess – holding hands through a tall iron gate that separated them, while the man's horse waited. The picture had been placed just below the line. Tissot watched as a thin woman in a grey broadcloth gown that shone from too much starch crouched besotted before it.

"Really, I think Monsieur Tissot must consider reproducing his pictures," she sighed to the freckled girl she gripped by the hand. "I can never be happy until I have at least a small copy of this to look at."

"I don't like it here, Nanny," whined the little girl. "Everyone is pushing. Take me home now."

"It is so tender, it makes me want to cry," the lady in grey said, tearing herself away. "And the finish is flawless, like satin…Tissot's brush leaves no mark at all."

Tissot chuckled quietly and made Millais laugh with a discreet show of bowing. When the woman and her young charge moved down the wall, Millais approached the picture and bent his golden head to admire his friend's brushwork at close range.

A raspy male voice behind them sniped, "Look, it's Tissot, that plagiarist painter from France. He's done Whistler's docks, and now he's doing Millais!"

"Tissot has out-painted Millais," another visitor contradicted him, in passing. "It's not everyone who can wash up on shore and paint better than Britain's best."

Millais burst out laughing and threw a convivial arm around Tissot's shoulder.

Tissot leaned into his ear and said, *"Je suis arrivé!"* I *have arrived.*

Chapter X

17 Grove End Road, St. John's Wood
March 20, 1873

Only you would be capable of drawing money out of this crowd of cotton dealers, Tissot. I saw an engraved illustration of one of your London pictures in the newspaper! You are getting on like a house on fire! 900 pounds for your painting – but that's a fortune! I hear that you have bought a house – my mouth is still open. Ye gods, it is really time one thought about marriage.

Tissot grinned and set Degas' letter from New Orleans on the mail tray on the carved pier table in his newly-papered entrance hall. He enjoyed the tranquil life of St. John's Wood so much that he purchased the leasehold on a Queen Anne-style villa, built of red brick with white stone ornamentation. It had the added advantage of a large garden, which James was looking forward to improving this spring. And he had been thinking of marriage.

In the meantime, between his many social invitations, Tissot wished to fill his new home with friends just as he had in the avenue de l'Impératrice. Among his new neighbors was a small clique of gentleman artists, but Tissot had his own circle. The first guests to arrive for Tissot's dinner party were Lawrence Alma-Tadema and his young artist wife, Laura. She looked pale under her cloud of golden red hair, but Lawrence was as hearty as ever, offering up a magnum of champagne cradled in each arm.

"Housewarming gifts – one from each of us," he said, with his engaging, childlike smile. "And already chilled!"

James greeted Lawrence and Laura heartily and handed the bottles off to the butler, who set them aside to help the guests with their coats and hats. The Alma-Tademas lived nearby, in the Regent's Park across from Laura's parents, but James had not seen them in several months.

"How did you enjoy Belgium and Holland?" he asked Laura. She had been ill much of last year, and though Tissot did not know the details, he suspected she was having trouble carrying a baby.

"Lawrence took me to meet *all* his friends," she replied.

"Yes," said Lawrence, his blocky face beaming, "and Laura made Christmas gifts of her drawings and impressed everyone with her talent and originality."

James lifted her gloved arms and admired her new beaded gown. Lawrence liked to spend his money on her. *"Très chic, madame."*

"Oh, it was exciting!" she said, following Tissot into the drawing-room, recently furnished in English antiques and rich fabrics. "But I did miss Ann and Laurens and was glad to return."

Lawrence put a possessive hand around her slim waist

and kissed her on the forehead. "Laura is a wonderful stepmother." She gave him an indulgent look and headed for the fireplace to warm herself.

Tissot anxiously checked the foyer, then clasped his fidgety hands behind his back. *It is a long drive up from southwest London. Did she decide, after all, not to come?*

Ouida, Tissot's novelist friend, arrived next. A squat woman, she always wore her hair piled in thick twists over her head, held in place with a narrow tiara. When Henry Irving, the actor, appeared, he towered over her and everyone.

Tissot embraced his friends and introduced them to each other. As soon as Ouida learned that Lawrence was Dutch, she began to tell him and Laura about her latest novel, *A Dog of Flanders.*

"And our friend, Tommy Bowles?" asked Henry Irving. His resonant voice was a joy to the ear.

"Tommy sent his regrets. He is dining with Sir John Hibbert." Tissot had scheduled his party for a Sunday evening to accommodate Irving, since it was the only night he was free from *Richelieu* at the Lyceum.

"Does Tommy Bowles have his eye on Hibbert's daughter?" Ouida called across the room. People always said that Ouida had a voice like a carving knife, and Tissot chuckled to himself as she tried to gather information for her weekly Salons. "I understand she will inherit the family estate in Warwickshire."

"*Non*, Tommy is taking Sir John to the Criterion in Piccadilly in the hope of ferreting out some publishable gossip from Lady Hibbert's dinner last week. To earn his confidence, he plans to ply him with champagne and promise I will draw him for *Vanity Fair.*"

The doorbell rang, and Tissot tensed and smoothed his mustache. But it was Jules Benedict, the conductor of the

Monday Pops Concerts at the new Royal Albert Hall. Unlike Tissot, Jules cared nothing for clothes, and under his greatcoat, his dinner jacket was as rumpled as ever. Tissot loved the man for his mischievous sense of humor and made him an exaggerated, deferential bow. "*Sir* Jules!"

Benedict grinned and slapped at Tissot's shoulder. "*Ach*, stop! It's been two years now." He wore his usual toupee, edged with a fat sausage curl that wound around his shiny bald head like a misshapen laurel wreath.

Tissot asked him, "Will you play your new symphony for us tonight?"

It did not take Sir Jules long to find a seat at Tissot's shining piano under a floral burst of calla lilies, dogwood blossoms and pussy willow. Lawrence was in his element and not only enjoyed every moment of the music, but was conversant on every opera, cantata and oratorio that Jules Benedict had composed. Tissot ran his eyes over the room, checking that everything was perfect and waiting for one more, special guest.

"Ha! Ha!" Whistler exclaimed, from the foyer, "Only, would you be so kind as to send your butler out to the cab with the fare? I seem to have forgotten to bring any money!"

Tissot nodded to his butler with the grace he could only have mustered this evening.

Whistler took no notice but sought out the hall mirror to preen before encountering the other guests. He fluffed his oiled black curls and teased up the white tuft of hair near his forehead. Then, smoothing his clothes, he took a final look at himself and exclaimed, "Amazing!"

"Forgive me for being unable to invite Maud," Tissot told him. Jimmy had taken his teenage model as his mistress, though they were careful around his mother.

"I left my pupil in her bath," Jimmy slipped his thumbs

in his bright yellow waistcoat and loudly whispered back, "but I suspect she jumped right out and will spend the evening painting at the easel she borrowed." He fixed his monocle and exclaimed, "My *dear* Ouida! Dandy to see you!" He strutted into the drawing-room, where his screeching voice joined hers.

James glanced up and drew in his breath. Mrs. Romer stood inside his door, framed by the high arch of polished wood. He had not seen her in nearly a year. Her small square face was unchanged, and her sparkling eyes greeted him in a wordless smile. "*Madame*, I am so glad you could accept my invitation." He felt flustered and added, "Shall I pay the cab driver?"

"How kind, but that's not necessary," Louise said, turning her head away from him. She quietly handed the fare to the butler, who stepped out in the chilly night air to handle the transaction for her.

Determined that she would not feel as awkward as he, Tissot helped her with her wrap and muff and waved her into the drawing-room. Her scent was intoxicating – some perfume so light, one had to be close to her skin to detect it. Louise was gradually emerging from the expected period of mourning for her husband, and she looked youthful and radiant in her fitted white gown and long kid gloves. Before the evening was over, James planned to ask her to sit for a portrait. But the whole evening was for her, really – a ruse to show her his home. His spacious sanctuary lacked only one thing, and he constantly envisioned Louise Romer sharing his growing prosperity. Even Millais had begun advising him, "I would immensely like to see you married like myself and anchored."

"Please – make yourself at home," he told her.

The seasoned old butler, who had come highly recommended by Tommy Bowles, balanced delicate glasses of champagne on a lacquered tray. He served them in the soft candle light that bounced off the red oblong. Louise turned her face languorously toward the windows, outside of which Tissot's garden was hidden in the shadows.

She gazed about, absorbing the multitude of elegant furniture and exotic objects Tissot had collected. He watched her supple figure move around his drawing-room as she admired his new home and the effect of the flower arrangements he had placed everywhere. Near her, on a small oval table covered with an embroidered yellow shawl, stood a cloisonné pot holding a half-dozen Japanese scrolls. Louise traced her fingertips over the pot's enameled edge and murmured, "Stunning..."

As he attended to his duties as host, Tissot's eyes followed Louise Romer. For a moment distancing herself from the other guests, she seemed grateful to sink into the comfortable sofa. She tilted her face toward the gardenias on the side table and gently inhaled their fragrance.

Why should she live and paint all alone in those pokey rented rooms overlooking Brompton Cemetery? Tissot thought. He was keenly aware that Millais and Lawrence had happy households filled with children, and that Laura painted while raising her two stepdaughters. Even Maud Franklin painted, under Whistler's tutelage.

James brought Louise a velvet hassock trimmed in gold fringe. She smiled warmly and pressed the toes of her soft leather shoes against it.

He sat across from her and initiated a lively conversation with her in French; she was far more fluent than any of his friends. Delighting in her contralto voice, he once or twice leaned in to catch her fleeting scent. He wondered what her intimate life with Romer had been like, if Frank had been a brute. He imagined he might be the first to show her joy in bed. He ran his eyes over her pert bustline, so clearly delineated by the tailoring of her bodice.

Idly, he asked, "Do you hear much from your friend in Paris, the Baroness Rothschild?"

"Yes, she's been kind enough to encourage all her family here to support me." Louise's face lit up. "And – I've just met the great Millais, who has taken an interest in me. His friend, Joe Jopling, is to help me improve my watercolor technique."

Joe Jopling? Tissot thought. He wondered how much Louise could possibly learn from Jopling's weak daubing, but he folded his arms over his chest and replied, "I am happy that you have the chance to practice."

"I'm sure one does what one has to, to survive," Louise mused.

Whistler and Lawrence and Ouida were entertaining each other with anecdotes, each more ridiculous than the other, keeping Laura, Henry Irving and Sir Jules in stitches. Irving and Sir Jules had their own stories of theatre people and gossip, and soon the only active listener was Laura. When her face was red from laughing, Ouida spied Tissot and Louise Romer in their *tête-à-tête*. She detached herself from the group and made her way over to Tissot, her short, stiff train rustling behind her.

Ouida's round *décolletage* was filled with an assortment of necklaces and chains, and a black velvet ribbon with a heavy locket encircled her bare neck. She took in Louise's delicate features and vulnerable beauty, and when she opened her mouth to speak, Tissot's heart pounded. Ouida's prominent eyes had a serious gleam, and her wit could be sarcastic. But she only said, "Mrs. Romer, you and I have something in common."

"In addition to our friendship with Monsieur Tissot?"

"We are women who must earn our own way in this life, me by selling my novels and you by selling your pictures."

In her sharp voice, Ouida added, "So few of us do something to control our own destiny."

"I confess I find it difficult to price my work," Louise replied. "There is no income so fluctuating as that of an artist, and with studio expenses and the price of paints and canvases, the uncertainty is overwhelming." She smiled and added, "But I have too keen a relish for the bread of independence *ever* to exchange it for the trinkets of dependence."

Tissot cleared his throat and stood. It was just the time to invite his friends into his temporary studio to show them his nearly-complete work-in-progress, a large unframed canvas displayed on the easel.

"It is called *Too Early*, for, you see, our unfortunate *nouveaux riches* have committed a *faux pas* in their eagerness to arrive at the great ball on time." It was an idea that had come to him last year by way of the *Illustrated London News*, where he saw a comical engraving of a nervous young gentleman sent into a rich man's drawing-room by a supercilious butler.

Whistler adjusted his monocle and cackled as he inspected the young women in their off-the-shoulder gowns of cascading flounces, looking as if they wished to melt through the floor, and the servants laughing at them from a door at the back of the empty room.

"Very good theatre," Henry Irving intoned, sweeping his hand in an arc past the picture. "A comic tragedy."

"The pianist in the background," Ouida said, turning to Sir Jules, "would not happen to be you?"

Sir Jules, nearing seventy and no more than five feet tall, beamed and patted the small grosgrain bow at his throat in place of a cravat. "I am now an artist's model!"

"Good thing Tissot paints faster than I do," observed Jimmy. "If you modeled for me, you'd have to quit composing and conducting! I am painting the portrait of the little daughter of a London banker, and I have threatened to require a hundred sittings if she doesn't stand still!"

But no one paid Jimmy any attention. Laura observed Tissot's depiction of the mortified hostess with her back turned, speaking to the pianist. "I have never seen anything like it. It is like a situation in a Jane Austen novel."

When his wife moved back to take the picture in from a distance, Lawrence moved in to scrutinize the brushwork. "You have out-Tissoted yourself," he said.

"Why!" Louise cried, "It is a new departure in art, this witty representation of modern life! It will make a great sensation!"

"My dear *madame*, it already has." Tissot raised her hand and brushed his lips over her fingers; Louise repressed a smile at the touch of his drooping mustache. The little group of British artists living in St. John's Wood struggled to earn an income without recognition from the Royal Academy or the critics, but James had thrown them into the shade. "You can be sure I will show it at the Academy exhibition, though the dealer Agnew bought it, and has sold it to a London wine merchant."

"That sherry importer from Upper Tooting who buys Millais' pictures?" Alma-Tadema sounded rather put out. "He paid over a thousand, I hope?"

Tissot chuckled. "One thousand, one hundred and fifty-five pounds."

Whistler groaned and threw himself backward into a cushioned armchair in the corner. Startled, he sprang up and grabbed the thing he'd sat on, holding it up in alarm. It was the stuffed tiger skin Tissot sometimes used as a prop in his paintings, its preserved head attached.

Jimmy threw it over his black curls and roared, "Ha! Ha!

Look, I'm John Ruskin!"

"If only Ruskin were that vigorous," Lawrence chortled. "He is in a sad state over that girl who rejected him." Laura patted his arm in an attempt to quell his fondness for gossip.

"They say the girl has gone mad," Ouida chimed in, "and Ruskin is nearly delirious with despair over losing her."

Whistler tended his curls and drawled, "That hasn't stopped his vicious critiques of my pictures or yours, Lawrence."

"Yes, Jimmy, the only critic in Britain or Europe who does not love my paintings is John Ruskin." Lawrence pulled a frown, but his eyes twinkled as he straightened his spectacles. "He is *definitely* mad."

"How can any red-blooded man," intoned Henry Irving, "not love paintings of women in togas, lounging around ancient baths?"

"They are *too* popular," Laura observed ruefully, amid the gales of laughter. "In fact, to foil the forgers, Lawrence is now assigning a number to each painting, writing it under his signature."

"Each of my works is now inscribed with an 'opus' in Roman numerals," explained Lawrence. "I dare anyone to try to pass off a fake now. I have just completed a watercolor, 'Opus CVIII' *On a Roman stair-case*."

"Your career has shot up like a meteor here, Lawrence," Tissot said, with some envy.

"Who are you to complain?" barked Jimmy. "The critics fawn over you, and the public sales of your steel engraving must have bought you this house!" Laura Alma-Tadema looked a bit shocked at this, and Jimmy told her, "I can say these things, ill-bred American that I am!"

"The critics have been very kind," Tissot grinned, "as long as I paint English subjects."

Ouida told Tissot, "I see your engraving of *The Farewell* for sale in every shop. I admit, I bought one myself."

"So did I!" Sir Jules Benedict confessed, with an expression so guilty they all laughed.

Louise sheepishly told them, "So did I, and as it was the last in the shop, I considered myself quite lucky for the rest of the day."

Tissot ran his eyes over Louise's delighted face and thought, *Mon Dieu, she is radiant.*

"I will never exhibit at the Royal Academy again," said Whistler, "after what they did to my *Arrangement in Grey and Black*. But don't you know, an eminent neighbor came to me to have his portrait done as *Arrangement in Grey and Black, No. 2.* You see, Lawrence – I shall start numbering my pictures, too!"

After a hearty dinner of *coq au vin* served on blue and white porcelain, the butler brought out Tissot's silver coffee service. Ouida took her cup and saucer and drifted over the piano. She asked Henry Irving about his next production at the Lyceum while Jules Benedict played his *Andantino*, and Whistler and Alma-Tadema debated whether John Ruskin's opinion mattered anymore, really.

"He hasn't affected my sales!" Lawrence laughed, rocking on his heels.

"That's because you're in with the President of the Royal Academy," Jimmy snorted. "If only Leighton were *my* biggest supporter!"

Tissot felt he would not be missed and invited Louise to view his garden.

She accepted his arm and inquired, "Will you have a formal French park or romantic English flower beds?"

"I prefer your perennials, but I may plant a backdrop of green shrubbery as in the French parks. I also have a notion of constructing a colonnade like the one in the Parc

Monceau, around an ornamental pond."

Before they stepped outdoors, he removed his dinner jacket and placed it over her shoulders. "I plan to add a studio, leading out the garden, and a conservatory for exotic plants." He gestured off to the side of the house, wondering how long he could hide his feelings for her. "There are kitchen gardens too, and I plan to expand the greenhouses for fruit and vegetables as well as flowers."

"It will be wonderful..." Louise's soft brown eyes met his.

Tissot gazed at her, then took her hand and brushed his lips to it. "I would very much like to paint your portrait, *madame*," he said, "perhaps in my garden, when the azaleas bloom."

"I would like nothing more." Louise glanced up at him, and she added, "But I'm afraid I really must wait." Her square jaw set, and she shivered. "Two full years are expected, though perhaps Mrs. Grundy would not be so very shocked if I set aside my mourning this summer."

"Of course," he replied, smoothly hiding his disappointment. "I completely understand." Tissot soon guided Louise back inside, where the Alma-Tademas, Ouida, Irving and Sir Jules began to thank him.

He called for his butler to bring their coats, hats and gloves. Sir Jules offered Irving a ride home in his carriage, and the butler hailed a cab for Mrs. Romer. While Jimmy Whistler dallied within earshot, Tissot wished Louise a good night.

"Thank you for your hospitality, Monsieur Tissot," she said. "It was a delightful evening."

Only after Louise Romer was gone did Whistler collect his coat, hat and cane. Approaching Tissot at the door, he cleared his throat and made a dramatic disclosure.

"You might wish to know, Mrs. Romer has been speaking about you behind your back."

"Have I offended her? What did she say of me?"

"Well, let me think," Whistler dodged, preening about in his short coat and silk scarf. "I believe it was 'a charming man and very handsome.' "

"What else? Do not play with me."

"That you look 'like a prince.' " He put on his top hat and headed out the door. "And, though I don't think you deserve it, she claims you're a snappy dresser." Whistler, who never wore a necktie in the evening, wavered in the door jamb. He made to leave as the chill breeze blew past him into the house. "And – oh, and something else..."

"Come, Jimmy!"

"Well...oh, yes!" Whistler clucked his tongue. "But remember, having been married to Frank Romer, she held you to a low standard – she called you 'extraordinarily clever'!"

Tissot stepped out into the black night and looked off in the direction Louise's cab had gone. "She told you all that?"

"I might grossly exaggerate, but I never lie!"

ॐॐॐ

Chapter XI

Kew, on the River Thames
June 26, 1873

Tommy winked at James, removed his shoes and socks, and rolled his trousers up to his knees. Tissot secured the wooden oars, and he, Louise Romer, and young Jessie Evans-Gordon laughed as Tommy heaved their row boat through the pungent shallow water toward the emerald river bank. Tommy was wearing his blonde sideburns quite long now, and he looked dapper in his straw boater and white linen suit. The reeds buzzed with dragonflies and water bugs. He tied their rented boat to a birch tree, and Jessie handed him their wicker picnic hamper. He grasped it in one hand and helped her disembark.

In contrast to Louise's billowing summer frock and parasol, Jessie was attired more practically, in a high-necked, long-sleeved gown, sturdy shoes and a wide-brimmed straw hat tied firmly under her chin. She handed Tissot one of the waterproof canvas picnic cloths over her arm. "So we won't spoil our clothes."

Tissot chuckled at Tommy's choice of companion for their day trip along the Thames. Women from his stepmother and stepsister to actresses, war nurses and housemaids, always had found Tommy Bowles irresistible. Jessica Evans-Gordon was the granddaughter of a renowned Presbyterian minister. Her father was a Lieutenant-Colonel in Her Majesty's Army, who recently had been promoted to Governor of the Royal Military Hospital at Netley, near Southampton.

"How I love the river!" James breathed in the fresh smell of green growth and offered his hand to Louise. She gathered up her tiered muslin skirts and stepped lightly from the wooden boat they had rented after taking the steamer from Chelsea to Kew Bridge. Under her tilted straw bonnet, her clear square face was more arresting than ever.

"Tommy, help me find a spot for the mineral water," Jessica said, pulling pear-shaped glass bottles out of the hamper in his hand. They were the latest thing everyone had to have. Tommy set the hamper at his feet and repositioned some stones along the river's edge to set the bottles securely in the cool water. Then he screeched, and Tissot was astonished to see Jessica holding a blinking green frog up at him.

"I'll get you back, Jess, I swear it!" he said, flashing his toothy grin.

She was not a beautiful girl, but James took in how her gentle good humor softened her pinched, angular features.

Tommy sat on a large rock, rolled his trousers back down and donned his socks and shoes.

"Jess – come, let's explore the bank." Bowles gave Tissot a significant look: he had promised to stay away from him and Louise for at least one hour.

"And I am going to sketch *la belle anglaise.*" With the canvas picnic cloth draped over his left arm, Tissot casually collected their sketching materials from the boat's bench. Passing Tommy on the way back up the bank, he fastened the top buttons of his sporty double-breasted coat and whispered, "Today is going to be one of the happiest days of my life."

He had fallen in love with Louise Romer the moment he had met her at Jimmy Whistler's studio, never dreaming that her husband would die and that she could become his. For a year and a half now, James had bided his time, thinking only of how complete his life would be with Louise at his side.

Tommy and Jessica meandered away through the white and pink wildflowers, talking as easily as a long-married couple.

Louise watched them disappear beyond the rise and said, "Your friend seems to admire Miss Evans-Gordon a good deal."

"She is just what Tommy needs, no-nonsense and active, but she has a sister Tommy's age who has long been the object of his interest." As far as Tissot understood, Tommy was showing Jessica a good time while she was in London visiting with her oldest brother's family. "Jessie's older sister has managed the family since their mother died several years ago, and even though the two youngest boys have been at Cheltenham College for a few years, I am not sure that Tommy has a chance with her."

"We don't always see what is best for us, do we?"

"*Non,*" James smiled at her. But he knew what was best for him – Louise. He was grateful that Tommy agreed to his suggestion of a river jaunt, and that he had brought another woman along to make a party.

"He seems to think of her as a little girl," Louise bit her

lip to keep from laughing. Jessica was so methodical, and Tommy had such boyish high spirits, that she actually seemed older than he. "She's of age, isn't she?"

"*Oui*, but Tommy has known her since she was a small child," Tissot said absently, leading the way through some tangled vines amid the grass. "She has five brothers, and Tommy used to sail with Henry, the eldest, at Southampton Water. Jessica is only here to visit Henry, who married a few years ago into a Society family. They keep a Chelsea house during the Season."

Tissot had no interest in a conventional marriage or the rituals for binding himself with a Society woman. He had fond memories of growing up in a family bound by real love and affection, friends with each other. He had no desire for a stiff, formal marriage with a wife who wanted his house and his income, who would spend her days dressing to pay calls and whose parents would expect him to order his life to suit their demands.

In fact, James reflected, he had everything he wanted – now that his London career was taking off – except someone who loved and appreciated him. He was looking about the serene river bank, not for subject matter as Louise thought, but for the perfect spot to propose.

"Oh, yes – I've met the Evans-Gordons," she replied, picking her careful way behind Tissot through the meadow. "Isn't Henry in banking? His wife is a beauty painted often by Leighton. She's from a famous theatrical family. That's just the sort of patron I dream of."

Tissot found a high, grassy spot with a view of white swans floating on the rippling, sparkling river and spread the canvas cloth for her.

"How lovely!" Louise began to organize their sketching materials and glanced up at him. Her brown eyes were softly evasive as she untied her tilted bonnet and set it carefully aside. "Oh, *why* do I not paint landscapes instead of being a portrait painter?"

James was thrilled to have her alone, away from the drawing rooms and polite conversations, to have her all to himself. Her skirts swayed in the breeze, revealing her slim ankles in their smooth buttoned boots, and her faint perfume wafted past him. Reaching for her hands, James moved his lips toward hers and kissed her with all the pent-up passion of the past year and a half. After a moment of indecision, she responded, and he pressed her close to him and brushed his lips along her cheek and throat.

As his desire mounted and his hands began to trace the outline of her corseted figure, Louise pressed her palm against his chest and turned her head away from him. Then she looked into his eyes with something like fear. Her square jaw appeared set. "James, I'm going to be married. To Joe Jopling. In January."

James was speechless.

"I wanted you to be the first to know, after Millais. Once Jimmy Whistler finds out, it will be his news to tell."

James shook his head, and they both laughed, embarrassed. *Dear God, I have never asked you for anything, until this*, he thought. With his hands in his trouser pockets, he paced toward the river, watching a duck land and disturb the swans with its raucous call. He kept his back to her while he grappled with his disbelief. *Joe Jopling, that self-taught, Sunday painter*. He had a mad desire to call Jopling out, if for no other reason than to crush his ridiculous reputation as a "crack shot."

Louise took a lighter tone. "I had promised Joe I would give him a sitting for my portrait today, but when I received your message to come sketch, I wired him that I was called out of town on business." Her face tipped toward the sun as she followed a fast-moving cloud across the blue expanse of the bright June sky. "I should have said, 'for pleasure.' "

James leaned against a tree, crossed his arms over his chest, and searched her face. *Wire Joe again and tell him you have decided to marry me instead*, he wanted to say. He could change her mind. They were silent for a long moment, until he finally remarked, "He's more than a decade older than you."

"About the difference between Tommy and Jessie?" she countered, with an indulgent look. "Joe is very supportive of my career. He has never wished for a large family. We are well suited."

"Are we not more suited? Louise, you know I love you."

James waited, and when she offered no other response, he sighed and sat by her.

Louise made a melancholy smile at the sky.

He ran his hand over his mustache and lay his arms over his bent knees. "So the two of you will paint together?"

"Oh, I don't think so. Joe enjoys his watercolors. He doesn't consider painting his career."

Tissot tried to sound calm and rational. "You will need more income than Joe can provide, working in the War Office."

Louise brightened. "It's really my art he likes to speak of."

"Paint with me!"

"There cannot be two great careers under one roof, I suspect. And I know whose will suffer."

"When my mother accepted my father," he said, "she owned a hat-making business. She and my Aunt Arsène were partners, and they continued to run their company after she was married. And she managed my father's shop at the same time." He was afraid this made his mother sound like a workhorse for her husband, and he explained,

"He was a wholesale dealer of fabrics, for retail and export, in Nantes. Both businesses did so well that they eventually purchased a country estate, a château by the Loue River. They achieved their success by working hard, together."

Louise reclined on her elbow at his side and toyed with the ribbons on her bonnet, lost in thought. "My father was a railway contractor in Manchester. I was one of nine children, and both my parents died before I was seventeen. I watched my mother...with children coming every second year, where would be my time or strength for work?"

"Louise...I could help you." When he envisioned the new studio he planned to build, he intended it to have space for Louise's easel side-by-side with his.

"James, we must always wish each other well, and help each other if we can." A breeze rustled the trees around them, and when he slid his arm around her, she accepted the warmth he offered. "Millais has taught me so much, helped me improve my work."

"Did he bring about your engagement to his friend?"

Louise put up a hand to shade her eyes and looked into his. "You know too well the time and concentration art requires. You would...distract me."

"I would make you happy." He traced his thumb over her cheekbone.

"I will not be buried under Joe's career."

A sailboat slipped along the river, and the sounds of muted laughter reached them. He recalled the laughter at his dinner party, the first in his new home. Louise had said to him, *"I'm sure one does what one has to, to survive."* James lay back on the grass, and they watched the clouds drift past. Their hands touched, and he interlaced his fingers with hers in her lace mitts. *She believes I would consume her.*

"Truly, Louise, you have so much to offer." James

wanted to consume her.

She sprang up, away from him, and held out her hands toward the wide sky. "There's so much I want to do! Do you know, I published my first story when I was fifteen?" All her enthusiasm burst out. "I want to write, and perhaps, some day, to teach – to have an art school where girls can go, to draw live models. I hope to somehow make it easier for other women than it has been for me."

"Just paint," he said, patting the cloth at his side. "Show them the way."

Louise folded her skirts beneath her and sat near him again. "If I am to succeed in this, I need to gain more notice at the Academy than I have so far. I want to exhibit something that results in a deluge of portrait commissions! Then I will need a studio smart enough for the set I want to cater to. Something in Chelsea."

James felt choked by sense that he had waited too long, given her too long to mourn the undeserving Frank Romer. Was he destined always to be unlucky in his dreams of marriage?

"I intend to earn my own income," she said, in her measured contralto. "And you need a woman who can devote her attention wholly to you."

They lay, side by side, the tips of their fingers brushing in the grass. He thought of all the things Louise had told Whistler about him. She had to have known that Whistler would tell him everything. It was all he could do not to pull her toward him in a full embrace and leave her breathless with the strength of his feelings.

"My friend Degas says we must devote our passion to our art," he told her, in French.

Louise whispered, into the shaking tree limbs overhead, "Art requires sacrifice."

Tommy and Jessie Evans-Gordon returned, arm in arm,

in giddy harmony under the shimmering afternoon sunlight. "Jess and I are ready for our picnic!" Tommy called, too loudly, as if warning James and Louise of their approach.

Louise sat up and tied on her bonnet. She called back, with a cheerful rapidity that suggested Tommy had interrupted something, "And what wonderful things did you see?"

"Butterflies!" cried Jessie, now wearing a daisy chain around her neck. "Everywhere! Tommy and I saw a Painted Lady."

James jumped to his feet and brushed the grass from his trousers.

Tommy's blue eyes sparkled as he asked, "And to what have you two been drawn all afternoon?"

Tissot wished he had the wit to banter with Tommy, but his heart had broken. "Wonderful news!"

Tommy raised an eyebrow and scanned their faces.

"Mrs. Romer plans to marry again –" James announced. "One of your best *Vanity Fair* illustrators – Joe Jopling."

Jessie kissed Louise's cheek, and in that moment when the women could not see, Tommy made a dumbfounded expression to James, who merely shrugged.

"Now our picnic will be a celebration!" Jessie told them, "I've brought *pâté* and cherries and bread," as if it were the greatest of feasts. "Tommy, I even have a small loaf of the brown bread you like, but you must go fetch the water bottles first. They should be good and cold by now. Louise and James look quite faint."

James reflected that the sense of self-sufficient contentment Jessica radiated made her very attractive indeed, and that Tommy would be a fool to continue to pine after her older sister. Tissot wished he had seized his happiness much sooner.

He grasped Tommy's shoulder and said, "Stay here, and let me retrieve the water bottles." The sky was bright blue between the clouds, and he inhaled the fresh meadow air, forced a smile and told them all, "We shall drink a toast to the happiness and success of the future Louise Jopling."

Chapter XII

17 Grove End Road, St. John's Wood
October 7, 1873

Tissot stood before the vast canvas on his easel, feeling more alive than he did even in the heady crush of his evenings at the opera and the theatre. The English art market was endlessly stimulating, and the competition to predominate was fierce. *The battle of life.*

Alone in the painting room, absorbed in his craft and the sharp odor of poppy seed oil and paints, his ambitious vision emerged. He needed to follow up the dramatic success of *Too Early* with something even more modern and exceptional to show at the Royal Academy next year. Always looking for inspiration, he had gone to view Degas' paintings on display at Durand-Ruel's London gallery. Tissot wanted to return to painting scenes open to interpretation, though part of the reason Degas' work did not sell here was that ambiguity defied convention in England. Still, Tissot felt compelled to do something this daring and had no doubt it would create a sensation.

He put the final touches on the web of ropes from the ships' masts in the background of his picture, copied from Captain Kennedy's ship, the *Aphrodite*. Now he was ready to add the central figures in the foreground, and he had invited a trio of sisters to his studio to model today. Dozens of multi-colored silk flags – every nation's he could buy – hung from the ceiling to replicate a festive ship equipped to fly a courtesy flag when entering any foreign port. The picture would showcase his skill at rendering precise nautical detail as well as the most current fashions women wore at yachting galas such as the annual sailing regatta off the Isle of Wight. But there would be no clear story. He also was taking a risk by using bright, bold colors on a large canvas that would stand out in the sea of thousands of paintings and portraits. In every way, Tissot intended this picture to be the most show-stopping thing on the wall at next year's Royal Academy exhibition.

Out in the entrance hall, the tall case clock chimed over his working silence. Tissot ignored it for a long moment, then sighed, put down his brushes and stepped back to examine his morning's progress. He wished each day had twice the hours, and that he did not need nourishment or sleep, that he might paint and paint regardless of time, distractions and obligations.

His butler knocked softly at the pocket doors and slipped into the studio with a slight bow. "Sir?"

"They are here?"

"The ladies are enjoying iced champagne in the small parlour, sir."

Tissot chuckled. "Let them wait a quarter-hour, and then show them in."

"Very good, sir." With the air of a practiced conspirator, the butler removed Tissot's breakfast tray.

James saw a stray hair that had clung to his canvas, on the figure modeled by his friend Margaret Freebody, Captain Kennedy's sister. He pulled up a stool and carefully lifted the hair embedded in her black lace fan with his palette knife. He dipped a fine brush in poppy seed oil and smoothed the silken surface of his creation.

Girlish giggles, maternal hushes, and the rustle of stiff silk trains signaled the arrival of his models for the figures of his shipboard guests. Tissot straightened his back, inhaled, and forced himself to set down his paint brush. He checked his black frock coat in the looking glass by the door. *Spotless.* He never wore a smock.

The butler opened the pocket doors to Tissot's studio with a flourish and a self-satisfied smile. He tipped his head toward the window. Tissot followed his glance to the back garden, where one of the young footmen was wielding an ostrich-feather duster over each leaf of the shrubbery.

"So *elegant*," whispered one of the sisters to another.

Tissot bit his lip, knowing it would not take long for word to spread of the decadent pleasures of his household: *A servant in silk stockings polishes his shrubs!* It would double his client base. He made an aristocratic bow to the wife and three daughters of a prominent Sheffield steel magnate. Raising *Maman*'s hand to his lips, he ran his eyes over the wasp-waisted figures of her daughters as their mother introduced each to him. The two eldest wore new sailing dresses for the occasion. The youngest – a sweet thing with heavy eyebrows and a little pug nose – wore tiers of pink and red ruffles. Perhaps sixteen, she was enthralled by the exotic silk flags hung from the studio ceiling. They billowed in the slight breeze created when the butler slid the pocket doors closed. She stood beneath the center of the tent-like effect and turned in a slow circle, face raised.

"*Très chic*," he nodded at *Maman*'s gown, and she beamed as if her taste had been blessed by the Pope himself. Her figure was not bad for a woman of her age, but her careworn face indicated she had not always belonged to the leisured class to which her husband's industry and good fortune had raised them.

Truth be told, James found the wives and daughters of the *parvenus* much more fun to paint than women from the British aristocracy. Though high-born women wore only the most expensive fabrics, they favored dark, unadorned gowns. The fun for Tissot was in painting the colored and intricate ribbons, ruffles, ruches, bows and trimmings worn by people like these as they displayed their newfound wealth – and collected his paintings.

Maman appraised his furnishings, seeming to make a thorough mental inventory to replicate in her own prosperous household. The elder girls *oohed* and *aahed* over his pictures on display and the garden through the painting room windows.

The eldest daughter, who flaunted a diamond engagement ring worn over her kid glove, asked, "*Monsieur* Tissot, do you really have a villa in Paris as well?"

"*Oui, mademoiselle.* Here is my *carte-de-visite.*" His calling card bore the address of his house near the Bois de Boulogne as well as his new home near the Regent's Park.

The middle daughter snatched the card from her sister and ran her eyes over the photograph of Tissot printed on it. She tapped the toes of her little high heeled boots, humming some song in her head, then abruptly said, "*Maman*, it would be a fine thing if *Monsieur* Tissot could paint a portrait of us, for father. He could put it in his library."

"Nonsense!" said *Maman*, seizing the calling card for

herself. "He would put it in the drawing room, so everyone who calls can admire it!"

Tissot asked the humming girl, "What is it that you like in my pictures?" It was not ego, but research to ensure he understood what most appealed to these new female clients.

The girl fingered her varnished bamboo parasol handle and gushed, "*Si...charmante.*" Her older sister elbowed her at the absurdity of trying to impress *Monsieur* with her limited French. She moved to the window to admire his garden and sighed. After ascertaining that *Maman* was preoccupied running her hands over the carved cabinet on the far end of the room, she leaned forward against the window ledge, revealing her ankles. Tissot smiled and looked away.

The youngest daughter smiled shyly and ventured, "I liked your painting at the Royal Academy, *Too Early*. It seemed very real." She looked him straight in the eye and confided, "It is hard to know how to fit in with Society, how to wear the right clothes and do the right things. I feel I will never get it right."

"Oh, yes you will!" put in *Maman*. "I will see to it. And your father has high expectations. You must attract a husband of the proper station." Conscious she had said too much in front of *Monsieur* Tissot, she blushed. Her elder daughters turned away, mortified.

Tissot took no notice, but gestured toward the pug-nosed girl. "*Mademoiselle*, sit here. You shall be the first to pose."

He adjusted her position, moving her and then her sisters with a light touch on the shoulder, arm or chin as he worked out the picture's composition. They did not hold their poses well, but chatted and giggled while he sketched in their forms.

"You must make your face blank," he instructed them,

"like this." He imitated the bored, vapid look affected by women of fashion.

"Remember that, girls," said *Maman*, caressing Tissot's embossed wallpaper. "It does not do to appear too eager or interested."

Their three faces turned to her, incredulous at her hypocrisy. *Maman* continued on, wholly ignorant of having transgressed, "Though for the life of me, I can't see *how* they could be bored when there are such shops in London!"

James brushed a hand over his drooping mustache and gave her a sly smile. "Would you like to know what is *au courant* in Paris?" The girls nodded emphatically and fluttered around him. Tissot seated himself and produced a notebook. He made a show of sketching several entirely different gowns, and as he deftly completed each, it was plucked from his hand by one or the other of them to take to their London dressmaker.

"This is what Worth is showing for visiting. This one is for walking. Go to his salon in the rue de la Paix. He will show you fabrics and tailor them to flatter your figure." Tissot was in his element, drawing energy from their excitement. "He dressed the Empress, you know."

Maman looked at her daughters and back at Tissot, intimidated. "What if...he turns us away?"

"But you are special," Tissot assured them. "Ask for one of his sons. Here, I will write their names with the address. Tell them the painter James Tissot has sent you." He directed a wicked little wink at the daughter with the engagement ring. "Worth designs wedding dresses and nightgowns as well."

She cried, "*Maman*, when can we buy my *trousseau*?"

"Can I go as well?" the middle girl said, blushing. "Next season, when it is my turn to look about for a husband, I want to be done up right." She turned coyly to Tissot. "Why are you not married, *Monsieur*?"

"Because I am always in my studio, at my easel." James chuckled as he turned back to the preparatory study for his painting. He worked rapidly, outlining their figures and faces with red-brown paint. Perhaps he should just take a wife, but...what kind of woman? For him, there was no one but Louise.

It crossed Tissot's mind that he might never marry. Or, perhaps he should marry – anyone, just to marry, and he would learn to love her. When he looked up, the middle daughter was gazing at him and humming to herself.

The butler appeared and murmured, "If you please, sir, Mr. Bowles." His entrance sent the ceiling tent of colorful silk flags rippling, to the delight of the youngest girl, who reached up toward them.

Tissot set down his brushes and held out both his arms. "Tommy!"

Tommy, more handsome with each passing year, stepped toward James, then stopped, gaping out the window. The liveried footman had worked his way around the garden and was still in sight, dusting Tissot's shrubs.

Tissot winked and shook his friend's hand. "*Un moment*," he said to the ladies, and stepped to the far corner of the room to converse privately. "What brings you here? My house full of eligible young women?"

Tommy did not laugh, and he shook his head when the butler reached for the hat and gloves in his hands. "Tissot – shall we speak in the library?"

Tissot asked the butler to bring tea and biscuits for his models, and as much champagne as *Maman* would allow. "*Pardon*," Tissot excused himself, amused to see that the daughters could not take their eyes off Tommy Bowles, "but please enjoy the garden until I return." He whispered to the butler that the footman polishing the shrubbery could return to his household duties.

He led Tommy to the library and closed the double doors. "What is it?"

"James, I've just come from Jessica Gordon's brother's house in Chelsea." Tommy's expression was grave as he stood before Tissot and set his gloves inside his upturned top hat on a chair. "Henry tells me the Prince of Wales is commissioning an official portrait from 'the finest painter he knows.'"

"Millais, of course."

"No, that would not be such terrible news," Tommy said. He idly sifted through an assortment of magazines on the center table.

"Terrible news?"

"His Royal Highness has commissioned a French painter."

Tissot crossed his arms over his chest and scrutinized Tommy's blue eyes. "If you mean that the Prince of Wales will be difficult to paint –"

"Tissot, look. You are the most accomplished and successful painter in London, outside of Millais. The Prince can't ask *him*, because of Effie and Ruskin – the annulment, you know. But the Prince has commissioned Bastien-Lepage."

James took in this news, shook his head, snorted, and lowered himself into an armchair. He had socialized with the Prince of Wales at numerous functions. It was a slap in the face. In France – *before* the war at any rate – artists were respected as professionals, like scientists and writers. Here, one could be nothing more than a court painter...or a businessman.

Tommy fingered the yellow chrysanthemums in the vase before him and slowly said, "In aristocratic circles, you are considered a political exile –" He forced himself to say it straight out. "A radical, a *Communard*. A murderer and arsonist."

James' instinctive response was to wonder if that was the real reason Louise kept her distance from him, marrying Joe Jopling instead. He remembered what Louise said, at his dinner party: *I'm sure one does what one has to, to survive.*

His thoughts were confused, and he rubbed the arms of the chair rather than let Bowles see his fingers tremble. "No, I am not a murderer, Tommy. No one who did not live through the Commune, who did not witness it, could possibly...the worst thing I did was to document, in little watercolor paintings that I have never made public, the week of blood when the new government butchered its own citizens."

Tommy drew a breath and looked away.

They both were silent for a long moment, until Tissot said, "*Bastien-Lepage?* He was a fat young postal clerk who had enlisted in the sharpshooters, was wounded early on and spent most of the war in the hospital. He went to the countryside to convalesce with his family. The last I knew, he was painting villagers and had been unable to find work as an illustrator. His paintings are not worth shit."

"It was evidently his little painting of his grandfather in his garden that won the Prince's favor."

Louise had been on Tissot's mind all day, and thinking of Louise reminded him of something: her Paris benefactor, the Baroness Rothschild. Tissot raised his chin, gave Tommy a sharp look, and strode to the towering, antique secretary across the room.

"The Rothschilds gave considerable funds to my American neighbor, Dr. Evans, for his hospital. During the war, I drew several illustrations at the Red Cross Ambulance on the avenue de l'Impératrice for Dr. Evans."

Tissot fumbled from drawer to drawer and finally held out a book to Tommy Bowles. He just published this –"

"Yes, *History of the American ambulance established in Paris during the siege*," said Tommy. "What follows?"

"It was Dr. Evans who smuggled the Empress from Paris to London. She is living at the estate he found for her, at Chislehurst." James had grown so agitated that he began to feel short of breath. He rifled through various drawers and sorted through his sketchbooks until he reached one nearly at the bottom. The drawings it contained, as he flipped through its pages, included the military infirmary under one of the white canvas tents of the "cirque de l'Impératrice," several drawings documenting the appearance of wounded men at the time of their discharge, and one of Dr. Evan's villa, Bella Rosa – before the war.

"When I left Paris, I took as many of my drawings and paintings as I could fit in my valise. I will send Dr. Evans my drawings of the American hospital, and ask him to arrange an interview with the Empress in Chislehurst. She will know me; I painted her friends in better days. She knows I am no traitor."

"It's badly done, James, that's all there is to it. It can materially harm your chances for portrait commissions, if not general sales."

Tissot shook Tommy's hand, trying not to succumb to his terror of being ruined a second time. "I must get back to the ladies. These new people, they do not know of the gossip. They are not accepted in the circles that whisper against people like me. I need them."

"You need *him*, too, James," Tommy reminded him, putting on his top hat. "He and his friends could undo you here any time they wish, and then where would you go? You'll put yourself in a precarious position, gambling on social climbers."

Tissot folded his arms across his chest. "Are you asking me to grovel?"

"I do; one has no choice." Tommy lay a steadying hand on Tissot's shoulder. "I'll write to the Prince and suggest it's time for his cartoon to appear in *Vanity Fair*. Perhaps I can persuade him to allow you to draw him for the magazine, and the sooner, the better."

Chapter XIII

Arts Club, 17 Hanover Square, Mayfair
January 14, 1874

Tissot nestled into a deep leather armchair in the dim light of a kerosene lamp in the smoking room of the Arts Club. As the wind rattled the tall windows, the fire in the grate hissed and threw off a welcome heat in the drafty second floor chamber. He sipped brandy, let it warm his insides, and idly considered whether he should peruse the stack of reviews on the table at his left elbow. Instead, he leaned back, stretched out his legs, and breathed in the rare quiet.

Not even three years! In less than three years, he had built a life in London: a successful career with regular showings at the Royal Academy, a fashionable home that reflected his prosperity, and friends to share it with. Tissot had not yet been made a member of the Royal Academy, but he was sure that honor would soon follow. He knew everyone, he was invited everywhere, and he had been asked to join the Arts Club, *the* club to belong to, last year before he'd turned thirty-seven. Everyone from his composer friend, Sir Jules Benedict, to Henry Irving was a member – except Laurence Alma-Tadema. Jimmy Whistler had proposed Tissot for membership, and Millais had seconded him.

Now London's most distinguished art dealer, William Agnew, was on his way to meet Tissot at the Club. Degas had written from Paris, intrigued by what he had heard of Agnew and urging Tissot to put in a good word for him, adding, *Here Durand-Ruel assures me of his devotion and swears he wants everything I do, but scarcely sells anything I send to his new gallery in London. Manet, always confident, says that he is keeping us as the tasty little tidbits.*

Tissot thought he might eventually speak to Agnew about Degas' work, but he wanted to start by introducing Agnew to the more celebrated Manet. In the meantime, he had sent some rich American women, whom Tommy Bowles had met on a train, to see Degas' studio. He was not in a position to ask many – if any – favors of William Agnew, yet. He swirled the amber liquor in his glass and smiled to himself. The artist he really wished to call Agnew's attention to was Louise Romer – now Louise Jopling.

Outside the smoking room door, Club members took the creaky stairs to and from their private quarters on the upper floors. Amid the clamor and laughter, Tissot heard Agnew's urbane voice on the landing, and he sat up straight and listened.

"Four hundred guineas is a fair price," Agnew said. "It's a wonderful picture, Joe. I want more like it."

Joe...Jopling? Agnew was soliciting Joe Jopling's work? Mon Dieu, the man could sell anything. For the love of God, the man's latest work was a watercolor of a life-sized girl holding a dog: Fluffy!

From his armchair, Tissot strained to hear the conversation, but could not make out what Joe replied. Then he heard Agnew again, saying, "Mrs. Jopling's work speaks for itself."

It was Louise's painting that Agnew was admiring. *Joe has positioned himself as his wife's manager?*

Tissot was startled when the doorknob rattled, and a gentleman peered through the open door, backed out, then popped his white head back in. "Oh, sorry. Hello! Anyone seen Millais?"

Because William Agnew was standing just outside the door, Tissot made a special effort to be cordial. "Joe!" he called, rising and setting his brandy on the side table. "Come, sit."

"Can't, sorry." Joe Jopling's small mustache twitched under his ugly nose. "I was hoping to talk with Millais before I leave, but, well, gentlemen...I am off on my wedding trip with the loveliest woman in London."

Tissot paused only momentarily, before raising his glass again. "To your happiness, *mon ami.*"

Joe waved and, from the sound of his heels down the stairs, took the steps at least two at a time.

Agnew joined Tissot by the fire in the grate and offered him a hearty handshake. "James, I hope I haven't kept you waiting."

"Not at all, *monsieur,*" Tissot said, looking down upon the center part in the thick hair of the Establishment powerhouse.

In London as in Paris, younger dealers were moving into the burgeoning art market. The flashy Marsden had aggressively pursued Tissot, taking him to dinner and revues, spending money he did not have to convince Tissot he could represent him from his rented Bayswater apartment better than an established dealer with high overhead. Tissot did not mind selling some of his small watercolors and etchings through Marsden, but regardless of the commission, it was a coup for Tissot to have attracted Agnew's interest.

Tissot poured him a glass of brandy, and Agnew held it up to him. "You are the man of the moment, James. No English painter can touch your style, not even Millais." Agnew was well-fed, with a voice like buttercream. "*Too Early* really broke new ground, and now I am receiving more inquiries than I can believe – from MPs, industrialists, and our favorite sherry importer. Let me see *The Ball on Shipboard* the minute you finish it. If you continue to paint these witty takes on the leisured class, I can sell them for at least twice your present price."

"*Bon.*" Tissot meant to be cool and businesslike, but he could not suppress a chuckle. He and Agnew were going to get on. He had made preparatory studies already for two more pictures – one, a satirical look at an eighteenth-century man and his bored wife, and the other a candid observation of an elegantly estranged British couple standing on the portico of the National Gallery in Trafalgar Square. The first sketch was Millais-like in its quaint historical costumes, the other pure Tissot.

"It's a competitive market, James. You'll have to make some decisions. How do you want to style yourself?" Agnew gave him a pointed glance and set down his nearly empty glass. "You don't want to paint this and that. Are you a French artist or an English one?

This was the aspect of working with a middleman that Tissot disliked, and he bristled. "I am *un Londonien de Paris.*"

"A Londoner from Paris, precisely the problem," Agnew said, twisting his straight mouth and appraising the artist's suave demeanor. "You will confuse the public. And the critics, Ruskin especially. Do yourself in with him and you might as well go back to that mess in France." He pulled a cigar from his pocket and lit it. "I'll tell you the straight truth, I only want your most ambitious paintings in the English style. Modern British girls at fashionable amusements, jaunts on the Thames – that sells. These pictures you do of girls running up the French flag – don't bring them to me."

"They are not –" James was insulted, but he knew enough to stifle his indignation.

In Paris, before the war, he had sold his own paintings. Or rather, his paintings sold themselves, especially after the Salon had awarded him the honor of exhibiting any painting he wished, bypassing the jury entirely. But this was London. And dealers had become essential even in Paris, after the war. Still, with each of Tissot's large canvases selling for upwards of a thousand pounds, it infuriated him to feel that Agnew would censor his work. He drew a deep breath and took a seat.

Agnew puffed at his cigar as he circled the room, causing the floorboards to squeak under the thick Persian carpet. "This 'new' French style is increasingly self-indulgent and bizarre, James. You want to make sure you are not seen as part of that crowd of madmen. I won't touch that experimental or political stuff for one simple reason: the English won't buy it, not the old money or even the self-made men."

Crossing his legs, Tissot tapped one foot nervously and set a forefinger to his temple in thought. He would deliver *The Ball on Shipboard*, sold or not, to the Royal Academy exhibition in a few months. While he fully intended his enigmatic, modern picture to be a showstopper, defying convention posed a risk if Agnew was to take him on. If the critics – if Ruskin – did not laud it, would Agnew drop him? Being dropped by Agnew would be worse than not having the benefit of his influence in the first place. Word would get out, and the London art world would consider his career over as soon as it had begun. He could feel his heart pounding. *I cannot be ruined again.*

Tissot was well aware that Degas' dealer, Durand-Ruel, was eager to represent the most innovative new French artists. When the Prussians marched on Paris, the young picture dealer escaped for London, where he met the expatriate artists Monet, Pissarro, and Sisley. Durand-Ruel held regular exhibitions of French artists at his New Bond Street gallery. A bolder sort than Agnew perhaps, he was risking his reputation to promote their careers. He had even exhibited several of Whistler's paintings.

"Understood," Tissot replied smoothly, taking the plunge with Agnew. "Still, I would like to talk to you about my friend, Manet, sometime soon. I have known him for nearly twenty years, and what you may have heard of him is untrue. He is a distinguished gentleman, truly venerated as a leader in the Paris art world." He leaned forward and added, "You must have heard – immediately after the war, Durand-Ruel visited Manet's half-destroyed studio, and when he saw all the paintings unharmed, he bought them on the spot for 50,000 *francs*. And both of Manet's pictures were praised as sensations in last summer's Salon exhibition."

Tissot regretted that bit of exaggeration, as Manet's portrait of Berthe Morisot was denounced by the critics, one of whom referred to it as "a confusion defying all description."

"You're a true friend, James," Agnew replied. "Another time, perhaps. The next time I'm in Paris, you know, if I have an hour to spare...it's your career prospects and

personal reputation as a gentleman that I want to discuss."
He perched on the edge of a desk and looked Tissot straight
in the eye. "They say you're a *Communard*, James. That
you fought for the Commune and then ran away."

Tissot felt his throat constrict with panic, but in a
moment he squelched it, mustered all his *sang-froid* and
laughed. " 'They' can speak to the Empress Eugénie at
Chislehurst. She has commissioned me to paint her with
the Prince Imperial in honor of his twenty-first birthday in
March." He reached into his breast pocket, steadied his
hand and held out a small folded paper as if it were a life
insurance policy. "You may read it for yourself: '...we
anticipate the pleasure of sitting for a portrait by our loyal
friend, Monsieur James Tissot.' "

Agnew flashed him an admiring smile and gestured that
he did not need to read the letter. "You do know, you're
considered a fugitive from French justice. I understand the
Prefecture of Police in Paris maintains a dossier on your
activities during the war."

Tissot was stunned. "I did not know."

Agnew snuffed out his cigar in a crystal dish, and James
rapped his knuckles on the arm of the chair. After
everything, to be done in by this! *Besides, all the public
records in Paris were destroyed when the Communards
torched the Hôtel de Ville.*

Outside the door, Club members had congregated over
some fraternal hijinks that involved repeated thumps on
the walls and stairs, as if they were tossing billiard balls.
Their raucous laughter filtered through the sitting room
door, and the smell of toasted bread crept into the room.

William Agnew patted his stomach and glanced at his
gold watch. As if Tissot's time were up, Agnew observed,
"What you need now, perhaps, is to become a naturalized
British citizen like your Dutch friend, Alma-Tadema."

James sunk his head into the chair back. *Am I cursed?* Fighting on the side of the *Communards*, even briefly, was so necessary at that time, under those circumstances...he recalled Courbet damning him to hell. *I was an elite soldier, defending Paris from the Prussian invaders!* He was French, through and through. He just wanted to be clean – completely free from it all, forever – if that were possible.

"I will have to hazard a trip to Paris," he told Agnew, "and speak to the *Préfet de Police* – if I can."

"Take that letter with you, my friend. That may be the most important commission you'll ever receive – as a Frenchman." Agnew shook his head. "But the gossip here is what concerns me. These things take hold in people's minds, you know. Watch your back."

꙰ ꙰ ꙰

Chapter XIV

Paris
March 18, 1874

Tissot had been detained nearly two hours in a cold antechamber, waiting to speak with the *Préfet de Police*. As the *Communards* had burned the Hôtel de Ville – City Hall – the *Préfecture* was now housed in the Luxembourg Palace. Tissot was forced to endure a series of interviews by underlings, who strung him along while insisting that the *Préfet* was tied up with various obligations. Rain spattered Tissot from a leaking window, and he was unnerved, trapped in the Luxembourg, a building used as a prison during the first revolution in France.

He pulled his elegant cigarette case from his coat, fumbled for one, then lit up.

Boots clicked on the stone floor of the corridor, and a uniformed functionary entered the chamber repeating that *Monsieur le Préfet de Police* was delayed.

"What is it, this time?" Tissot demanded, tilting back in

his chair. His terror during the morning's solitary wait was turning to anger.

"The *Préfet* is taking his coffee."

Tissot crossed his legs and kept his top hat on his lap, ready to spring up and leave as soon as possible. At his side was his leather valise, containing papers, books, and a parcel he meant to deliver to a friend, if all went well.

When the *Préfet* finally initiated the interrogation, Tissot sat in the narrow chair before his desk and offered in his defense numerous letters from his fellow sharpshooters who defended Paris from the Prussians in the months between September 1870 and January 1871. They included newspaper clippings mentioning Tissot's prominence and devotion in the city's defense, and the wounds he suffered in battle. He presented the *Préfet* with a copy of Tommy Bowle's book, *The Defense of Paris*, citing specific instances of Tissot's courage as a soldier, as well as Dr. Evans' recent book on the American Ambulance, with a testament to Tissot's contributions as a Red Cross stretcher-bearer.

Monsieur le Préfet de Police barely glanced at these items. Instead, he took in Tissot's fashionable attire, his cane and top hat and gentlemanly demeanor. "*Monsieur* Tissot, all of Paris admires Dr. Evans and his staff for saving so many lives at his hospital. But it was *after* the Americans evacuated that spring, that you were complicit with the *Communards*."

James swallowed his fury. *After the public records burned with the Hôtel de Ville, who compiled complaints against him?* "Might I at least review this dossier?"

The *Préfet*, a man as still and cold as a steel pole, clasped his hand over the green file.

"What is the evidence against me?" James demanded, "Where is this slander coming from?"

Monsieur le Préfet pushed the dossier to the side and clasped his hands on his desk, savoring the authority to adjudicate Tissot's case. "Numerous witnesses have testified that you fired on the *gendarmes* entering the avenue de l'Impératrice. That you were using a government-issued *chassepot* rifle."

James was not going to let this bureaucrat see him shudder. "If I am incriminated by hearsay," he insisted, "then I must be exonerated by it as well." He did not have permission from the Empress Eugénie to use her informal letter for this purpose, but he took the risk. *She may never know.* James stood, pulled it from his breast pocket, and handed it over with some bravado.

The *Préfet*'s lip curled under his over-waxed mustache. He ran his thumb over the Empress' seal and merely scanned the letter before handing it back. "You got rich off the Empire, *Monsieur* Tissot. You ruined yourself by throwing your lot in with the Commune, and now you crawl back to Paris, to save your hide."

"I *earned* the money to buy that house with my own hands. And, before the war, the imperial government helped us, gave loans to artists and writers so we could build those houses in their new suburb – what reason would I have had to hate them? I am a painter, not a dissident...I was one of the first to join the National Guard! I fought *for* the government!"

"You cannot deny that you helped build barricades that spring against the new provisional government at Versailles, then shot at them – your own countrymen?"

Tissot, standing at his full height over the seated *Préfet*, struggled to control his fury. "Those incompetents let the Prussians have peace on their own terms! After how hard we fought, it was an insult to allow their victory parade under our Arc de Triomphe – past my house, which they had bombed just months before. The *Versaillais* sold us out. We starved and suffered and saw our friends die." He threw his arms out. "I did join in the rebellion that resulted. It wasn't enough to be loyal? You demand blind loyalty?"

"Then you ran away."

Tissot laughed at this. "I did. The *Communards* started out as brave fellows, full of good intentions. No one could foresee the direction the insurrection would take. A lot of us in the Western suburbs were glad that the *Versaillais* found their way through Porte St. Cloud to put an end to it. Then I watched our new government massacre its own citizens, even its National Guard. I saw them with my own eyes, and *I* am the criminal?"

The *Préfet* pursed his lips. "Spare me the intellectual speech, Victor Hugo: 'I accept the principle of the Commune; I do not accept the men.' "

"Let me ask you this: what about all the Parisians who boarded boats and ran away to England at the first sign of war, draft dodgers and Socialists –" Even this livid, Tissot would not name names: *Monet, Sisley, Pissarro...* "And the men who fled to the countryside to stay safe and well fed while we fought for Paris? The ones who refused to defend Paris were better men?"

"They were nobodies, you arrogant son-of-a-bitch."

"If there is anything in that dossier," Tissot said, spreading his wide hand over it, "arrest me now, or burn it."

The *Préfet* tapped his fingers on his desktop. "You should consider yourself lucky to be alive."

"What about you, *Monsieur*?" Tissot asked. "During all that time, you killed only Prussians?"

The *Préfet* scrutinized James' face with hatred. Then he called for the guard.

Tissot inhaled and braced himself.

The *Préfet* ordered the guard, "Strike a match." He held the file to the flame, and the three men watched it reduced to ash. The *Préfet* seemed deflated. He turned his back and looked out the grimy windows. "Now get out, you traitor."

James pushed his books and papers back into his valise and clutched it and his parcel under his arm. He took long, echoing strides down the corridors and then the stone steps into the rue de Vaugirard. *It is all behind me now.* They had nothing on him, here. The threat now was in London, where invisible and continual gossip could undermine everything he had achieved. He put on his top hat and adjusted his cravat under his frock coat. Atop the cupola overhead, the immense allegorical statues of Eloquence, Justice, Wisdom, Prudence, War, and Peace loomed as the clock struck two.

It had stopped raining, and a weak sun was glistening on the wet streets. He hailed a hansom cab to take him north of the Seine. Tissot was determined not to walk Paris.

The steam packet from London to Calais had been filled with tourists chattering about viewing the ruins of the Quai d'Orsay, the Tuileries, and the Hôtel de Ville – and the cemeteries where thousands of Commune sympathizers had been massacred by the French. The cab hurried him into and past the heart of the destruction, and James tried not to look out the window. Still, he could not help but see what was, in place of what used to be. The charred ruins were unexpectedly beautiful, bearing a haunted majesty. He felt hot tears stream down his cheeks and rubbed them off with his fist as he did when he was a boy and his father made him leave his mother to go away to school.

Tissot felt his heart would break. *I want to go home.* He knocked on the cab roof with his walking stick, and at the next wait in traffic, he shouted to the driver, "Take me down the avenue de l'Impératrice."

"It's not that anymore! The new government renamed it. You mean the avenue du Bois de Boulogne." James closed his eyes and shook his head.

❧❧❧

James gave the cab driver directions to Edgar Degas' modest but pleasant stucco house up in the rue Blanche, toward the skating rink.

He reached the top of the steep, narrow staircase at the back of the house with his paper-wrapped gift under his arm. Degas' familiar, cramped studio was more like a mechanic's workroom, heated by a small coal stove and filled with everything from a dented zinc bathtub to dusty wax sculptures of horses. Tissot's eyes fell on the portrait that Edgar had painted of him, looking rather the dandy, in better days.

He held out his hand to greet his friend.

But Degas, in his shabby painter's smock and crushed felt hat, regarded James' debonair tailoring and shining black leather gaiter shoes from under his hooded eyes. Heavier than in the old days and graying, he held his head high and moved his charcoal-smudged hand behind his back.

"My dear Tissot, so you have not forgotten me entirely. I am curious to hear what you are doing. Are you returning to Paris for good? That sounds nice, to me."

"*Non*, but let us talk about it later." Tissot set aside his cane, hat and gloves and took a seat behind Degas at his easel.

Degas glanced over his shoulder and saw Tissot taking in the clutter. "I'm glad to say I haven't found my style yet. I'd be bored to death."

164

James leaned forward to admire his friend's latest pastel pictures of jockeys and dancers. "Deepen that shadow there," he advised him off-handedly. "And the ceiling should be lighter when reflected in a mirror. How are you, Edgar?"

"As well as I can be, considering my brother's business debts have nearly bankrupted the family. Once my father's estate has been settled, it is likely I will have to part with my house. Now, for the first time, I must sell my own art for *income*."

"Can I be of any assistance to you, perhaps –"

"Pauline!" Degas shouted as a young woman in a rain-soaked hat stole up the rickety wooden stairs and through his half-opened door. "You are late! But at least you turned up, this time. Over there!" He pointed her to a dim, dusty corner far from the coal stove.

Pauline was a dainty undresser, and Tissot found himself amused as she folded her damp jacket, skirt, petticoat, bodice and gloves into precise squares that slowly grew into a pyramid-shaped stack.

"If not for the war, I would still be painting at the racecourse," Degas said. "I submitted a drawing to the *London Illustrated News*, but my art doesn't translate with your success." Degas flung around a number of reworked, small canvases into a pile near his stool, then pulled one of them up on his easel. It depicted a dancer in close up, the sort of thing that inspired James' cropped views of fashionably dressed women.

"Do you want that? Take what you like," Degas said. "If it's here, it hasn't sold."

Tissot always had admired Degas' brilliant compositions and his passion for depicting movement. He rummaged around and was struck by an oil sketch of several ballet dancers rehearsing onstage, cropped and angled in a manner he had never thought of. He set it aside, near a trio of prancing horse sculptures, and watched Pauline from the corner of his eye.

"*Écoute*, James!" Degas held his head high. "Renoir and I are organizing a private showing of modern art, independent of the government's Salon – the first exclusive show of new French artists."

Tissot sat sideways in a hard chair and rested an arm along its back slats. His friends had been discussing an independent exhibition as long as he could remember.

"Look here, my dear Tissot, no hesitations, no escape. You positively must exhibit at our Realist Salon. It will do you good – for it is a means of showing yourself in Paris from which people said you have run away – and us too." Degas continued, "I am determined to include paintings of all our colleagues whose work is of Salon standard and will be well-received by the public such as...you, James."

"Oh?" Tissot was offended by such a grudging compliment.

"Nadar will let us use his photography studio on the Boulevard des Capucines next month. He won't charge us anything, even though the lease is nearly bankrupting him. It is as good as anywhere. Have you seen it?"

"His premises are superb," Tissot had to agree. "All those windows up to the ceiling, the cast iron pillars. The skylight." He would have been envious, if the whole proposition were not so misguided. Especially since the war, the Salon was the only market for those who could afford to collect art.

Degas was more excited than James had ever seen him. "For our exhibition, Nadar says he will dress entirely in red robes, and he has painted all his studio walls red, too – to make a contrast to the paintings. I tell him we must maintain our dignity, but Nadar argues that it is a brilliant plan to draw attention to our work. He says by letting the public see it for two weeks before the official Salon opens with only the paintings that inbred crowd approves of, they will understand what we are trying to do. The Salon jury rewards those who paint what is dead, not what is alive!"

Tissot's attention was distracted by Pauline's glorious *décolletage*. He crossed his legs and asked Degas, "Do you really think this is the best way to attract favorable notice by the critics and the Salon committee?"

"*Pauline!* If you do not disrobe this minute, I will –" Degas clapped his hands and his housekeeper, a matron in her forties, appeared.

"Monsieur Degas, you expect me to lay my clothes on this dirty floor?" Pauline shot back.

Degas waved his right hand toward the housekeeper. "Tear her shift off!"

The older woman wiped her hands on her apron and deftly removed Pauline's undergarments, unlaced her muddy leather boots and rolled her stockings off.

Degas gestured toward the nude girl, and asked Tissot, "Quite fresh and pretty, isn't she? A real find. With a first-rate back. Come now, Pauline, show your back."

She made a petulant face, saying, "Could you ask your housekeeper to add more coal to that stove?"

"Only if you want the cost deducted from your pay," Degas growled. "Don't worry, my eyes are too weak to see your goosebumps." He waved the housekeeper out.

Tissot watched Pauline as she executed a recalcitrant *pirouette*. But now, as she struck one of the off-balance poses that Degas demanded, he felt only pity for her. He ran his hand through his thick hair and leaned away. He rarely asked his models to disrobe.

Degas kept his left hand in the pocket of his trousers and sketched Pauline impassively with his ground-down charcoal, commenting to Tissot, "Women can never forgive me; they hate me, they feel I am disarming them. I show them without their coquetry."

Pauline looked over her shoulder and stuck her tongue out at him; Degas could not see her.

Tissot did not react to her, but ran his eyes over Degas' familiar studio, littered as always with unfinished paintings and wasted canvases showing models in numerous variations of the same pose. He missed his well-ordered painting room in the leafy serenity of St. John's Wood.

Degas began to sketch his model, to freeze her diagonal pose in time. He continued, "I am getting really worked up and am running the thing with energy and, I think, a certain success." Preoccupied with his canvas, he said, "You and Whistler must send several of your biggest pictures to Paris immediately. Exhibit anything you like and have it all delivered through Durand-Ruel's as soon as you return to London."

Tissot tilted his chair back, crossed his arms and humored his oldest friend. "Have you written to Whistler?"

"*Oui*, and I will tell you what I told him. Durand-Ruel is unable to fund us after all. Perhaps Whistler and I shall both achieve wealth, at the moment when we no longer need it. For now, each of us must make a deposit of sixty *francs*, and may exhibit as many pictures as we wish. When the exhibit has closed, we will tally the profits from admission fees and sales, deduct the operating costs, and divide what remains."

There will be no profits to divide! Though Degas did not see Tissot's derisive expression, Pauline did. Still, James asked, "Who is with you?"

"Monet, Pissarro, and Sisley. Renoir, of course. Others. Renoir and I are determined to gather everyone we can, even my Italian friend. Some of the others think his work is shit, but he is respectable, at least."

"And Manet?"

"Not him. Manet is busy being revered for his genius. He seems determined to keep aloof, and he may well regret it. I definitely think he is more vain than intelligent. He keeps telling me, 'the Salon is the real field of battle.' Really, he is appalled at our defiance! His *protégée* Berthe Morisot believes her future is with us, though."

Tissot was not about to tell Degas what he thought.

Degas tapped at his high domed forehead, smearing charcoal on his face. "I do agree with Manet that Cezanne is a disgrace, but Pissarro and Monet argue that we can't object to Salon rejections while rejecting each other. Manet thinks Renoir is a just a decent chap who took up painting by mistake, but he said he would *never* commit himself with Cezanne. To tell you the truth, I would not invite Monet or Renoir to my house, and I am not crazy about Monet's pictures. Those reflections in the water hurt my eyes. But we all must stick together."

Degas turned his shrewd eyes to Tissot. "They all are pressing me to get Whistler, but I told them it's your reputation we need. Your success will rub off on us a little."

Tissot straightened in his chair and murmured, "Edgar...I am *un Londonien* now."

"Stay with your country and with your friends."

As if I would ever consider Pissarro and Monet my friends! James dodged, "I have too many commissions to fulfill in London. It is not possible."

"I assure you that the whole thing makes more progress and is better received than I would have thought...Our style is simple and bold. It may be that we will fall on our faces, as one says. But the merit will still be ours."

Tissot shifted in his seat and pressed his fingers to his temple. "What you want is a sponsor..."

"You think I want your money! We have a patron. I hounded the man. He is too new at painting to exhibit with us, but he just inherited a fortune." Degas turned his face toward his model. "Pauline! You pose so badly that you will make me die of rage!"

Pauline stood, stretched her neck once in each direction, raised her arms to the ceiling, then tried to recreate her awkward stance. James smiled at her, and she rolled her eyes and stared intently at the back of Degas' canvas.

Degas rubbed out the lines he had drawn and began again. Under his breath, he muttered, "My last good years are passing in mediocrity."

"They will see your genius eventually, Edgar. The Salon must soon relent, and accept your paintings, along with the others." *Making a show of their independence would only hurt each of them in the long run.*

"Come now! We need you, James. You should be honored."

"I wish you the utmost success, Edgar, but –" The higher he climbed, the more he feared that someone or something would topple his precarious new career in London. Or ruin his chance of being made a member of the Royal Academy. Tissot gave way to temptation and blamed his dealer. "Agnew would never countenance it. I must please him if I am to flourish in London."

"You are a traitor *and* a coward, you know, Tissot," Degas retorted, pointing his charcoal stump at Tissot for emphasis. "For you, it is just the money and the fame. Never the art."

James felt keenly how preposterous the situation was. It was because Tissot was successful and well-known that Degas was seeking his credibility, for those who were not. He inhaled and said, sharply, "I am not inclined – yet, perhaps – to 'upset the apple cart,' as they say in England."

Degas offered only a sniff in response. "Pauline, take a rest."

Pauline ventured behind Degas' easel, tipped her chin up at Tissot, and inspected Degas' work so far. "Is that my nose, Monsieur Degas? My nose was never like that!"

Tissot was startled when Degas threw the canvas he'd been painting to the floor. He yelled, "*Out!*," pushed the naked girl through his door, and slammed it on her.

Pauline banged her fist against the wood, and Tissot could her muffled screaming, "You old maniac!"

Tissot leapt to his feet and watched his friend rush to the corner of his studio, grab up Pauline's neat stack of clothes, and hurl them in a heap at her head, leaving her to dress on the little landing at the top of the stairs.

"And what about my pay?" she shouted.

Degas opened the door again and threw Pauline's shoes down the steps; they clunked down several treads at a time, until they hit the bottom with a *thunk*.

"*Maniac!*"

"Protestant bitch!" Degas turned away from Tissot and kicked the upside-down canvas on the floor, muttering, "I am disgusted with everyone, and especially myself!" He pulled off his felt hat and ran a hand through his thin hair, leaving it sticking up at odd angles amid black charcoal and perspiration. "Ah, if I had my old eyes."

James rubbed his mustache and shook his head. Edgar Degas had been one of his closest friends for fifteen years. He simply had too much to lose and nothing to gain by associating himself with this melodrama.

He collected his hat, cane, valise and the painting Degas said he could have. Handing Degas the parcel he had brought for him, he said, "Before I go, a gift for you."

Degas ripped off the string and loosened the heavy brown paper wrapping until it fell to his feet. He stared at

Tissot's pencil study of a British girl pouring tea and flipped it over, reading James' inscription, "*À mon ami Degas*" on the backing. "Have you not tired of plagiarizing the English?"

James said, "It is a copy of a picture I painted after I arrived in England, for the International Exhibition that year. It was one of my first successes in London." *Placid, businesslike London.*

Degas fished roughly around the floor for a relatively blank canvas and perched it on his easel. He turned his back and grumbled, "Go back and be a big shot, *James.*"

Tissot was as hurt as Degas intended him to be, but he let Degas have the last word, as always. When he reached the street, he drew a breath to clear his head.

He would check up on his house like the prudent man and property owner he was. He would ensure that the repairs had been well executed, collect the rent, and then call on his old neighbor, Dr. Evans at his villa, Bella Rosa. He hailed a cab to take him to his house – in the avenue du Bois de Boulogne. It was largely due to the American dentist who had smuggled the Empress Eugénie to London that Tissot now would be able to return to Paris in safety.

If he wished to.

Chapter XV

17 Grove End Road, St. John's Wood
August 3, 1874

Tissot had set up his easel under one of the old chestnut trees in his garden, amid the orderly profusion of flowering shrubs and greenery. He sat at his camp stool and appraised the work pinned to his easel, then sipped lemonade and supervised the working men with their carts and stacks of red bricks. The workers were making great progress framing the conservatory to the side of his new studio, and the wide steps that would lead down into the garden. It was a fine, warm day, and they had torn out the back wall of his house. But the noise from the construction, and the men's talk, was a distant buzz as Tissot tried to quell a terror that he would lose everything, once again.

William Agnew had snapped up *The Ball on Shipboard* as he had *Too Early* last year. He had paid Tissot a huge sum and sold it for an even larger one, yet the English critics turned up their noses in seeming unison at his shipboard gala at the Royal Academy exhibition.

He had expected the critics to laud his close observation of British contemporary life, but he was shocked by the reviews. The *Athenaeum* writer declared that his fashionable scene of a shipboard gala featured "no pretty women, but a set of showy rather than elegant costumes, some few graceful, but more ungraceful attitudes, and not a lady in a score of female figures." Other critics chimed in, offended at his portrayal of the *nouveaux riches* making a mockery of a Society regatta. Meanwhile, the *Art Journal* critic wrote that he searched in vain for some "distinct and intelligible meaning" to the "frigid" picture.

James had to take the critics seriously. *Strange, though, this silence from Ruskin.*

The breeze tugged at his hair, and Tissot continued to paint, proud of his facility in depicting foliage with a deft swirl of the brush. He was earning more than any artist in London outside Millais, and he was being put in his place. He smoothed his hair and folded his arms over his chest.

"Dandy!" Whistler's high-pitched Yankee twang announced his presence over the sawing and hammering. "I'm glad to find your door is open, Tissot! Or rather, your wall!"

James' heart sank, as he had intended to paint all day.

As Jimmy took the makeshift temporary wooden steps from the house to the garden, he slipped and fell. Tissot leapt to his feet. The workmen in their loose smocks and leather aprons helped Whistler up. They sniggered a bit at the foppish little man in his fitted short coat, wearing patent leather pumps rather than boots.

"Did you hurt yourself?" asked Tissot, straightening the potted pink fuchsias and yellow lilies. He kicked the debris of nails and wood bits aside for Whistler.

"No," Jimmy said, "but curse your damned teetotaler

architect!" He paused to adjust his monocle. Tissot, aware that Jimmy did not drink but hoped to be quoted by the workmen, shook his hand and motioned him toward the shade of the chestnut tree.

Whistler handed over a copy of a magazine he clutched. "You are such a swell, your extension is featured in *The Building News*."

"*Oui*, soon I will be able to look out over my garden through walls of windows." Tissot resigned himself to the interruption and reluctantly gathered up his brushes and paints. While his pictures had been exhibited at the Royal Academy, Jimmy Whistler had staged a one-man exhibition at the Flemish Gallery in Pall Mall, defying convention like Courbet had done twenty years ago, and Manet before the war. "Are you satisfied, challenging the Royal Academy?"

"Ha! Ha! I stuffed nearly every letter box in Chelsea!" Whistler crowed, gesturing with his manicured hand. "I didn't sell any pictures, but it was a great satisfaction to have the gallery all to myself."

Tissot's butler brought out a tray with more tall glasses, a fresh pitcher of lemonade, and some biscuits. Tissot poured him a drink. "You scandalized London."

"Yes, but if only the gallery staff had been reasonable – they would have agreed to dress their guards in livery that matched my paintings!" Whistler strutted along the edge of the pond, peeped at Tissot's work, then removed his monocle. "People will forgive anything but beauty and talent. So I am doubly unpardonable."

"It is your titles they find unpardonable."

"I know that many good people think my *Arrangements* and *Nocturnes* are shocking and that I am eccentric. The vast majority of English folk cannot and will not consider a picture as a picture, apart from any story which it may be supposed to tell." Whistler picked an orange poppy and paused for dramatic effect. "Just as music is the poetry of sound, so is painting the poetry of sight, and the subject matter has nothing to do with harmony of sound or of color."

Jimmy scanned Tissot's painting of his garden and observed, "The imitator is a poor kind of creature. If the man who paints only the tree, or flower, or other surface he sees before him were an artist, the King of artists would be the photographer. It is for the artist to do something beyond this, to capture a mood or atmosphere."

Tissot threw out his hand in exasperation. "What about capturing the imagination, with wit or skill?" He and Whistler were so close, as students. Now it seemed they were each going their own way. Whistler, notorious and increasingly in debt, appeared enchanted with himself, persuaded that he was moving forward while Tissot stuck with the old way of painting. "The English critics say you are not fulfilling your early promise, Jimmy."

Whistler slipped the poppy into his button-hole and quipped, "Who has, except you?" A brief look of hurt and fear crept into his face. He sipped at his drink and took in the workmen in their straw hats and leather aprons, laboring over the enlargement to Tissot's large house, and his expression became sardonic again.

"I do not know that I have," James replied slowly. "When I painted that model in the racy red *bolero* jacket, I was hailed as the future of art. That was ten years ago."

"Regret not going in with Degas? Do you feel left out?"

"Not really," James told him. "It was a disaster."

"They knew they were taking a big risk," Jimmy said. "The Paris Salon attracted hundreds of thousands of visitors, and their 'Realist Salon' drew only a few thousand even though Nadar had advertised it in something like fifty newspapers and kept it open until after dinner –"

Tissot nodded. "A lot of those visitors were probably in their circle, if they were willing to pay the same fee as the Salon. Or people who just came for the spectacle. It is no surprise that they sold almost none of their paintings, and their deposit money along with the admission fees couldn't keep it open more than a month." He put his hands in his pockets. "They went out of business, really."

"Well, the show pulled them together," Whistler said. He slapped his knees and cackled. "And they have a name now – 'Impressionists'!"

"Degas is so disappointed," said Tissot. "The Paris critics were merciless. But he tells me he intends to force the group to exhibit together again. They will hate him. Degas is very trying."

"Degas is brilliant!" Whistler said fiercely. "His drawings are more beautiful than anything, and, by Jove, he is modern! They will never succeed without him. He said one review referred to them as 'pioneers of the painting of the future.' "

"Powerful incentive for them to persevere," Tissot admitted. "The strange thing is that Manet is being given the credit –"

"Blame, you mean."

"*Oui*, the 'King of the Impressionists,' " Tissot said, with a twinge of envy for Manet's effortless ability to be the center of attention. Everyone who knew Manet loved and praised him, but he persisted in painting pictures that shocked rather than sold.

"He probably wishes he *had* spurned the Paris Salon, after all that trouble to get just two paintings accepted, and then to have them vilified," Whistler retorted.

"Manet is an optimist," said Tissot. "He always says, 'Everything arrives.' "

"Everything but money and fame," Whistler chortled. He hitched his thumbs under his lapels. "I should be flattered that Degas is angry with me for refusing to go in with them. They needed you more than they needed me."

"Degas is having a hard time of it," Tissot said, toying with his watch chain. "I sent him two American women, daughters of a rich real estate investor in Manhattan. Tommy Bowles had met them on a train. Degas was unhappy with me at first, because he had no money to escort them around Paris. But one of them bought a ballet picture of his, a pastel, for 500 *francs*. He was badly in need of it, to put toward the rent."

"His first American patron," cackled Jimmy.

"She evidently was not sure she liked it or not," Tissot chuckled. "She expressed a belief that it takes special brain cells to understand Degas." He added, "Quite honestly, I feel more guilty than I should, spurning his Realist Salon. Degas, Manet and I drew inspiration from each other. There is always something in their constant experiments with subject matter and composition I find challenging."

"I thought that was why you needed me!"

"What did you think of *The North-West Passage*?" Tissot parried. Millais had huge popular and critical success at the Royal Academy with his picture of an old seaman confident that the British could conquer the dangerous sea route around North America to the Pacific Ocean. The legend under the painting read, *It might be done, and England ought to do it*. He added, "I saw grown men weep in front of that picture."

Whistler could be flippant, but never about art. "Art should be independent of all claptrap," he observed, "should stand alone, and appeal to the artistic sense of eye and ear, without confounding this with emotions entirely foreign to it, like devotion, pity, love, patriotism. Don't tell me you feel *inspired* by Millais' work?"

"No one can out-paint Millais."

Whistler snorted. "Bah! And do you aspire to paint pictures arousing British patriotism, or moody native landscapes?"

"I am committed to painting the life around me, the truth of our age."

"Courbet's influence was disgusting! All that damned Realism...there are much more beautiful things to paint than objects."

Tissot was growing angry, but he was not going to let Whistler provoke him. Jimmy Whistler was well received when he first arrived in London. But this solo exhibition established him as *the* artist in London to ridicule. The most important reviewers ignored his show, while lesser magazines mumbled briefly about it, not knowing what to make of it. The critic in the *Academy* merely noted that Whistler's one-man show was justified due to 'scanty welcome at the hands of art's official censors.'

"When you first moved to London, the critics lauded you," replied Tissot evenly. He rubbed a hand over his drooping mustache, afraid he might say too much. He valued his friendship with Jimmy Whistler, but in truth, he was impatient with him, painting so beautifully but persisting in antagonizing everyone and digging himself deeper in debt. Tissot feared nothing more than being ostracized, as Whistler was, in London. "Perhaps it is inevitable – now I am in for some bad reviews. After all, there was a time when Ruskin hated Millais' work, and for at least three years, he could sell nothing."

"Yes, and then what?" demanded Whistler. "He began painting tripe and was rewarded with mammon. What do you want?" he pressed. His long, slender fingers were like a hypnotist's. "Do you still want to be the future of art?"

Tissot shrugged uncomfortably. He had struck a gold mine after completing *News of Our Marriage*. Set in a riverside tavern, his oil painting showed an eighteenth-century man poring over his newspaper while his bored and neglected young wife gazes at the ships outside the bay window. The painting was so popular that a large printing firm contracted with James to make a steel engraving and was selling reproductions to the general public as fast as they could be published. Agnew was able to sell the original oil at a significant mark up, to a banker in his native city, Manchester.

But deep down, Tissot admired the foolhardiness of Degas' venture, the sheer crazed bravery of what his friends, including Whistler, were doing. As much as James considered a lot of their work self-indulgent and faddish, he had to admit that he envied their originality, their bold modernity. They could afford to experiment and fail, but he did not have that luxury. He feared losing his *avant-garde* edge in London.

Whistler badgered him. "Admit it, Tissot – keeping William Agnew interested in your work will kill you. An artist can die and never even know it."

Tissot, stung, said nothing for a long moment. He stood well away from the chaos of the workers, carts, and stacks of lumber and inspected what they had accomplished so far. After the framers, the glaziers would come to do the windows, and then the masons and the trim carpenters to finish the exterior. He had been assured that the extension would be completed by the end of the year. His house would be a showplace, the envy of every artist in London, even Millais.

"Perhaps fighting for the Commune was my last act of defiance," he murmured to Whistler. Then, keeping a close watch over the workmen near the house, Tissot shouted,

"*Un moment!* That is not where the second bay window is to be. Look at the plan! You must measure again, tear it out."

The head workman pulled off his straw hat and rubbed an arm over his sweaty brow. "Start over, you mean?"

"*Oui*, begin again. You have a plan – follow it!" Tissot shook his head at Whistler, who winked. Tissot murmured, "The battle of life."

"Battle," Whistler corrected him, "is the *spice* of life!" A breeze cropped up, disordering Whistler's feathery white forelock. He pulled his curl over his eyes and struggled to keep it in place. "It's not easy to start over, my dear Tissot. No one knows that more than we do. But you are a better man than Millais. They just can't admit it."

Tissot wasn't sure, but he thought this might be the first real compliment he had ever received from Jimmy Whistler, at least since he had lived in London. Deep down, he and Jimmy were still each other's best friend and most loyal supporter.

"Gentlemen!" boomed a voice from the hole in the wall. The familiar, blocky form of Lawrence Alma-Tadema appeared. He had spent the summer on the Continent with his wife, after her father passed away in May. Tissot had not realized he was back and inwardly cursed the lost day of work, then greeted Lawrence as he charged across the green lawn, straight through the construction and the arguing workers.

Tissot heard one of the construction men complain to his mate, "I hate these damned suburban jobs."

Lawrence looked exceedingly smug. "What do you say! I have just received the most intriguing commission – from the Prince of Wales!" He handed Tissot a jeroboam of champagne.

Lawrence is not even a member of the Royal Academy!

He has been so preoccupied remodeling Townshend House that he has earned a reputation as an artist who hurries his paintings to completion. James recovered his *savoir-faire* quickly enough to enthuse, "Wonderful news – but not for Millais." His butler brought flutes and disappeared with the earlier tray and glasses.

"No," Lawrence laughed. "Millais would not be up to this one. Are you ready?" he asked, rocking on his heels.

Whistler fixed his piercing eyes on Alma-Tadema and drawled, *"The Apotheosis of the Philandering Prince?"*

Lawrence clapped his hands with glee, ignoring Whistler. "The Prince would like me to paint a series of pornographic scenes for his private chambers."

"Bingo!" Whistler howled with high-pitched laughter.

"And just how much is His Royal Highness paying for that?" inquired Tissot, hiding his disgust.

"I should make some pennies out of it," Lawrence gloated, as he polished his spectacles on his coat sleeve. "I'm not allowed to say, nor am I allowed to show the pictures to anyone. I will have to bar Laura from my studio through at least the end of the year!"

Tissot popped the cork, dumbfounded. Lawrence exhibited two paintings in the Royal Academy, *Joseph, overseer of Pharaoh's granaries* and *A picture gallery in Rome.* His well-researched and highly detailed paintings pleased the public and sold quickly.

"Just in time, too," grinned Alma-Tadema. He held up a glass in each hand for James to fill. "My dealer has commissioned over forty pictures this year alone, and I am running myself ragged, portraying his whole family and all his business associates. But now they will have to wait." He offered a flute to Whistler.

Jimmy declined champagne and remarked, "What a relief, to devote yourself to nothing but the Prince's naughty whim." He put a fist to his hip and threw a sardonic glance at Tissot. "No one can paint naked women like Lawrence Alma-Tadema!"

Regardless of the demands on his time, Lawrence's studio was filled with ever more daring oil sketches like *Exhausted Maenads after the Dance*, attracting a great many of his gentlemen friends to call. Tissot forced a smile and touched his glass to Alma-Tadema's. "What man would not want to see pictures of naked women sleeping off a night of music, dancing and wine?"

Lawrence pulled his sketch pad from his frock coat. "Since Laura is spending the day with her mother, I'll show you some of my ideas." He raised his glass toward the bright summer sky. "*Vive* Great Britain!"

Tissot gazed into the distance, deep in thought and increasingly resentful and anxious.

"Ha! Ha!" Whistler exclaimed. "So this is where the money is. And how did it come about, some trusted equerry dispatched with a discreet request? A pretense at anonymity?" He shrieked with laughter and affixed his monocle.

"Not at all. The Prince was at my house, and though we were quite drunk when he suggested it, he had sobered up by the time we shook hands on the arrangement."

Tissot was incredulous. "Jimmy Whistler the Yankee entertains aristocrats, and *Lourens Tadema* has become an intimate of the heir to the British throne!" He gamely clapped Lawrence on the back. "It was worth it for you to become an English citizen."

"What's stopping *you*, James?" Lawrence ran his eyes from the well-established kitchen garden off to the west side of the house to the cast-iron colonnade curving along the east edge of the pond. "You're planning to remain in London, aren't you?"

Tissot studied Lawrence's expression for a tense moment. "I am French." He tried to picture himself back in Paris. It would never be the same as in those heady days before the war. *It would be impossible to reclaim my success there. I would be caught up in the new painters' fight, forced to choose between them and the Salon, where I had earned the right to exhibit anything I wished. If I were to fall from grace now, I would be ruined both in Paris and London.* For a serious artist, there was nowhere else.

His friends awaited his further response, and James threw them a dubious look.

How long before the Royal Academy will confer membership on me, now? And why is Ruskin taking no notice of my work? Tissot felt an irrational fear that "Sir Oracle" intended to completely ignore him, as if he did not warrant a mention. He had climbed nearly to the top of the London art world, but his foothold was still precarious.

Tissot was determined to make his name as the equal of Millais in the eyes of the British. "Gentlemen, for next summer's Royal Academy exhibition, I will paint something so remarkable, so modern and so British, that even John Ruskin will have to acknowledge my standing at the forefront of art here."

Whistler beamed proudly and raised his glass of lemonade. "To the future of art!"

ﾐﾐﾐ

Chapter XVI

Lord and Lady Coopes' townhome, Kensington
March 27, 1875

Tissot stood in evening dress in a deep, paneled threshold of Lord and Lady Coope's opulent London home. It had taken him long enough to gain admittance to a fortress like this. The candlelight of the enormous crystal chandelier was multiplied by the floor-to-ceiling mirrors. He glanced in the gilt-framed edge of the nearest one, anxious that the cut of his tail coat had the proper British reserve. The men wore white tie, but Tissot chose to wear the new style of black tie with the stand-up, turned down collar that the Prince of Wales was sporting.

"Come, James, let me introduce you around," said Tommy Bowles grandly.

"*Oui*," Tissot murmured, squaring his shoulders. "The hunt is on." He had just over a month left to produce a large-scale picture to suit Agnew – and to meet the deadline for the Royal Academy's summer exhibition. His pride still was stung by the criticism of *The Ball on Shipboard* as filled with vulgar women and lacking in meaning. He needed to depict some story, and this time, it needed to involve upper-crust subjects rather than the daughters of industrial barons.

Behind him, crowds of the fashionable streamed down the curved stairway from the upper rooms. Those who could find no room to sit or stand in the reception hall seated themselves on the steps, where they could look through the filigreed iron railing. It was almost like the old days in Paris, when he was a carefree *boulevardier* enjoying a *soirée* at the Marquise de Miramon's luxurious drawing room, sipping champagne. But Tissot felt keenly that he was a guest, not an intimate. Not an equal – yet. He bowed and made charming small talk with the women, though it was difficult to hear amid the loud conversations of the many guests.

Tommy Bowles was in his element. He had a gift for remembering names and faces, and he had something new and different to say to everyone. Boyishly handsome with his blond hair and mischievous light blue eyes, Bowles was followed by the gazes of the women as he moved through the crush.

Tissot supposed he never would see so many Worth gowns in one room again. He noticed some of the older women looking at him and whispering among themselves and also to the men accompanying them. They all inclined their heads politely while casting suspicious glances at him.

In his three and a half years in London, James had found it easy to assimilate with the artistic circles in London, especially with the help of his friends like Ouida the novelist, Irving the actor, and Sir Jules Benedict, the composer. He continually received invitations to dine with friends, and to attend the theater, symphony or opera.

But Society was a different matter, exclusive, and he had not found an *entrée* – until tonight. Even Sir Jules Benedict had not been able to wrangle an invitation for him. Despite being a distinguished conductor at festivals throughout Great Britain, Sir Jules was here tonight in a working, not a social, capacity; he was Jewish. Tissot reflected that even Sir Jules would not be here tonight except that he was Madame Wilhelmine Neruda's regular accompanist at the Monday Popular Concerts in St. James's Park. Tissot had seen the celebrated lady violinist from Moravia in the quartet at the Monday Pops and wished to hear her in this private solo performance. *As soon as I am made a member of the Royal Academy, all doors will open.*

It was Tommy Bowles, in the end, whose family connections and personal charm had resulted in an engraved invitation sent by messenger just this morning to Grove End Road. Tissot was amazed.

Tommy Bowles was a tireless conversationalist, and he also was campaigning. He had declared his candidacy for Parliament, as a conservative in Darlington. This amused James, since Tommy held rather Liberal views and often fumed about the "accursed idea of sacrificing everything to the making of money."

But he knew how to craft his remarks to his audience. With every guest they pushed through the crowd to meet, Tommy could talk about any number of his other passions, including amateur dramatics or sailing – he owned a yacht he called *Billy Baby* and was working toward his master's certificate in navigation.

Yet as Tommy glad-handed, James felt all eyes on *him*. He sensed the presence of enemies. The heat rose in his face as he watched a group of people whispering. *Are these the people still gossiping that I am a Communard in exile?*

When one elderly gentleman looked him up and down, James sensed a confrontation. The man wore military medals on his sash. Tissot straightened, summoning his dignity.

The old man finally said, "Say, you're not that Whistler fellow, are you?"

James laughed with relief and offered his hand. "I am a friend of Lord Carlingford." *No need to add that I painted Carlingford – before he was raised to the peerage last year – when he was merely Chichester Fortesque.*

The man's wife flicked her fan open and said, "Lord and Lady Coope *never* would invite Whistler *here*, dear."

A sleek woman struggling to cross the room bumped into Tissot from behind. "How clumsy of me!" She laughed and snapped her fan shut.

"Are you quite all right, *madame*?"

"Yes, please forgive me!" She introduced herself, more flustered than she need be, and James grinned at her guile. As she flirted with him, her eyes darted to a nearby man who was likely her husband. He excused himself before they drew his attention. James' affairs had never been adulterous, but it was tempting to think he could get away with making love to a few married women in Society, the discreet ones with charm, humor and intelligence who were merely neglected. In an ideal world, he would have been settled, like Millais with Effie at his side. *It would have been different, with Louise...*But now, Louise was going to have a baby, Joe Jopling's baby.

While Tommy collected gossip for *Vanity Fair*, James turned to the gentleman on his right, wishing he could have an intelligent discussion about art, music or even Ouida's latest novel.

"Was Sandy's party not the most amusing evening of your life!" the man sniggered. "Deuced if I can remember, wasn't it *his* cook who fluttered up like a game hen to be thanked for her salmon what-d'you-call-it?"

"I am afraid I cannot tell you," Tissot apologized.

The man threw him a disparaging look and quickly moved away.

Tissot turned to Tommy, "Did I say the wrong thing?"

"Oh, that one – he's such a boor!" Tommy whispered, "but then, in this crowd, anyone who speaks for over six seconds at a time is considered a boor."

James cast his eyes over the people around him, uninspired. *I must produce something ambitious to amaze these people.* He had just over a month before the Royal Academy show. If he could not find something in this *soirée* to impress Agnew and lay his claim to being in the front rank of painters in London, then what?

"Tedious, after all, isn't it?" Tommy said. "The trick is," he said in mock-conspiratorial voice, "to say something pleasant, without meaning anything and to look at them as if they are important, without appearing to care."

Tommy blithely introduced him to a prodigious *grande dame* in black lace who peeped at him through her lorgnette. "I have seen your paintings," she said to Tissot, with her double chin fully extended. "You must stop painting those ugly, purse-proud girls! The more you encourage outsiders, the bolder they grow. They must not be encouraged to think they can just *buy* their way into Society."

Tissot bowed his head with polished affability. "*Enchanté, madame.*" *Frumpy old porpoise!* Still, he wished he could be introduced to such people with the distinction of being a member of the Royal Academy.

A footman closed the gold damask draperies under the double swags and lit two tall tapers on the piano.

"How wonderful that Sir Jules could be here tonight,"

James enthused to Tommy. "His stamina is astonishing."

Tommy Bowles led James through the crowd to the side of the room, where they stood near the wall, allowing the ladies to have the seats. The gallant gesture allowed both men a view over the women's *décolletages* as well as the bare flesh of their shoulders from behind. The scent of roses drifted toward them from the women's upswept hair.

Sir Jules winked at Tissot before he seated himself behind the grand piano in the corner. Then Madame Neruda glided into the center of the room to tune. She wore a pale-yellow Worth gown, surely a gift from the Coopes.

James and Tommy were riveted. The other guests continued to talk among themselves, heedless; the *débutantes* and eligible men were not necessarily music lovers. The only others prepared to listen to the concert were two Chinese diplomats, who had pulled their upholstered chairs up to the piano and leaned forward.

James looked out over the crowded reception room and chuckled. *"Un moment!"* He handed Tommy Bowles his drink and extended his gloved forefingers and thumbs to frame the scene before him. "Look!" he said to Tommy. "My next painting."

Tommy shrugged apologetically, and James prodded him, "Pretend it is a photograph. What do you see?"

Bowles grinned as he understood. "A Society *soirée*. Lady violinist preparing to play. Everyone dressed to the nines, bored and discontented."

"Exactement! And look – only the Chinese diplomats are interested in the entertainment."

Lady Coope tapped her fan and whispered, "Hush!" Once the clamor around her let up, she nodded, and Madame Neruda gently began to play Beethoven's *Romance in F.*

Tissot's gaze was captivated by the lithe brunette, holding the gleaming violin. Her bare throat was encircled with a black velvet ribbon, and another narrower one graced each slim wrist.

He was intrigued by the exotic Madame Neruda, who had left her husband and come to London with her two young sons. She pursued her career with such energy that she was inspiring girls like the daughters of Millais and Alma-Tadema to take up the violin when it always had been considered unladylike. "She is a marvel!" he whispered. "Look at her arms..."

"She is Catholic, unable to divorce," Tommy teased him. "Does this mean you're over Louise Jopling at last? Who knows, the right girl may be here tonight." He stood on his toes to view the possibilities. "What you need is –"

Tissot held a finger to his lips. He ignored Bowles and drank in every sweet note, watching Madame Neruda and Sir Jules perform in perfect unison. Both played with an understated passion that made their art look easy. He knew what it was like to be self-made, to be born with a determination to use one's talent to create a life independent of family position.

During the polite applause after Madame Neruda's performance, punctuated by the noisy enthusiasm of the Chinese delegation, James devised a concept for which William Agnew would pay handsomely. He would write to Lady Coope tomorrow and ask her and all her friends to pose for a large-scale Royal Academy picture commemorating her *soirée* and comprising dozens of portraits of her exclusive set.

He rubbed his gloved hands together. He would lose no time telling Agnew.

❧❧❧

A fortnight later, Tissot sat on a revolving piano stool in

his elegant new studio before his latest painting-in-progress. It was early afternoon, and clear northeast light spilled into the large, open space. He felt too deflated to continue. He set his brushes down, took a deep breath and scrutinized the ghostly forms roughed in on the wide stretched canvas before him.

A sharp rap at his door interrupted his mood. "Thought I'd stop in," Tommy said, his boots clicking across the new oak parquet flooring. "Good Lord, James! Are you ill?"

James turned an anxious face to him. "Lady Coope has curtly declined 'the honor' of sitting for a portrait to be exhibited at the Royal Academy. Her phrasing negates the possibility that a portrait of her, or her friends, ever would be painted by anyone other than 'our dear English artists.' "

"Why should you kowtow to that empty-headed bunch?" Tommy wandered over to the sketchy picture. "Do you want me to pose for you?"

"*Merci*, but that defeats the purpose, *mon ami*," James explained. "I have told William Agnew that I will paint Lady Coope's *soirée*, complete with portraits of all her Society friends. Agnew cannot wait until I have finished! He offered me twelve hundred guineas. He is convinced that if Lord Coope does not snap the picture up, the others will fall over each other to buy it."

"But they won't cooperate."

"*Non*." James felt his hands shaking. He crossed his legs and interlaced his fingers over his knees. "What will I tell Agnew?"

"So..." said Tommy, tapping his blonde mustache with his long forefinger, "Paint 'a' *soirée*. You know, it doesn't have to be *hers*." Tommy's blue eyes sparkled. "It's just a concert, in an elegant private home, with Madame Neruda performing."

"Unfortunately, the fair Madame Neruda sent word that

she does not wish to be portrayed in any way that might embarrass the Coopes. She was kind and thanked me."

"Sorry about that. They must have warned her off."

James' face fell as the implications of that awakened his worst fears.

"That is it, then. I must get something to the Royal Academy in less than three weeks. I will send just the lady with the lilacs. It will sell, but it will not be the talk of the town."

Tissot folded his arms over his chest and stood before *The Bunch of Lilacs.* The sophisticated beauty of the woman, the details of her white afternoon gown, the immense carved Oriental birdcage amid exotic greenery, the gleaming ceramic tile of his conservatory floor...he had put all his mastery into every brush stroke. *Not groundbreaking, or witty. Not "British," not ambitious enough.*

Tommy Bowles examined Tissot's *Lilacs* for a moment. "It's a *tour de force*, James, the very definition of grace and leisure. But I understand. It's the same with my magazine – you're either gaining momentum or losing ground." He took a turn around the room, lost in thought. One side of it opened to Tissot's new conservatory, where etched and leaded glass screened a profusion of botanical specimens punctuated by bursts of red and orange blooms.

As Tommy glanced out the tall windows overlooking the garden, pond and iron colonnade, a sly twist occurred to him, and he pivoted toward James. "Paint 'a lady violinist.' In fact, there are so many amateurs, thanks to Madame Neruda, that it could be someone's daughter trotted out to entertain the guests. Think about it, James! It actually is quite funny – this elegant Society party, everyone is bored enough with each other, and then the hostess foists off her marriageable daughter as the *pièce de résistance*."

Tissot ran his hand over his mustache. "Everyone who sees the painting will know it is Madame Neruda. Sir Jules would have no qualms about posing –"

"Yes, he was quite vain about being 'an artist's model' in *Too Early*."

James chuckled and turned Tommy's idea over in his imagination. "I could get my friends to pose, and I can paint the gowns and the room well enough from memory. Ouida would love to be in on the joke, but she is off in Italy now. Margaret Freebody will pose for me, I am sure."

"I met her onboard the *Aphrodite*, talking to her husband and Captain Kennedy about my yacht as you suggested. He had some excellent ideas to refit it. Yes, his wife is marvelous."

"She is willing to sit for any length of time, and she has such fine hands," Tissot said. "I can always line up a half-dozen professional models." He looked at the prepared canvas, at the sketched-in forms of the Chinese diplomats leaning in to hear the music over the social cacophony. "I did want to include them."

Tommy grinned, remembering how bizarre their enthusiasm for music seemed in that setting. "The Prince of Wales is off to tour India. Why don't you make them Hindus in extravagant turbans?"

Tissot rose and clapped Tommy Bowles on the shoulder. "You are brilliant!"

"Please, you take the credit!" laughed Tommy. "I don't want to be blamed!"

"They will hate me for this."

"That just means you can sell it for a fortune." Tommy clapped James on the shoulder. "Back on top of the world?"

"I am in your debt, *mon ami*."

"Good," Tommy said on his way out, "as there is one small favor I'd like to ask –"

"Anything."

"Paint my fiancée into your picture, won't you?"

"You are...?"

"You must include Jessie Gordon's portrait as well, since we are engaged!"

Tissot offered his friend sincere congratulations. "She will make you so happy."

"I am the luckiest man alive! She was right in front of me the whole time, but I was too pigheaded to realize it until...recently." Bowles grinned and popped on his top hat. "James, you need to find a girl just like Jess."

"Tommy, you never cease to amaze me."

Bowles had not let the circumstance of his illegitimate birth deter him in any endeavor. At thirty-four, he was campaigning for Parliament, his magazine was thriving and now sold for a shilling rather than sixpence a copy. Tommy was printing it on larger, more expensive paper, and the popular full-color caricatures of everybody who was anybody had never looked better. Plus, he was to marry a woman who openly adored him and whose respectable family had long ago welcomed him.

Tissot was happy for Tommy but very anxious for himself. He was going to offer a painting to the Royal Academy that he was sure would make a sensation – perhaps the more so because Lady Coope did not wish him to paint it. *Agnew will certainly be able to sell it, but how much of a* faux pas *am I committing?*

But he would do it anyway. *So much for my Society début.*

Chapter XVII

17 Grove End Road, St. John's Wood
July 20, 1875

Tissot covered his paints and smoothed his thick black hair in the mirror near the door to the hall. It was a clear summer day, and the breeze through the open windows cooled his sunny studio. He checked to see that the gardener, an elderly Englishman who lived on the property with his wife, had ceased his work in the perennial beds and moved his cart off to the kitchen garden before Monsieur and Madame Manet were announced. They were in London during their wedding journey, and he wanted them to see how he had vindicated himself after fleeing France.

Degas' painting, the one he had brought back from Paris and hung over his mantel, was crooked. He adjusted it and stood back to ensure it was level. The ballet dancers fairly leapt off the canvas into Tissot's studio; Degas had painted them from above, at a steep angle, to bring their movements to life. Tissot looked at the picture often, to remind himself to maintain his edge, as if he still were among the most innovative artists in France. *If not for the war...*

Degas wrote hardly at all now. Manet, almost never – but then, he was struggling, championed by the intellectuals of Paris while rejected yet again this year by those he disdained as "old fogies" at the Salon.

When the butler ushered in his guests, Tissot greeted them like old friends.

He drew in a breath to see Berthe's face again. Her dark eyes were as intense, her lips as sensual, and her air as melancholy as the days when he would discreetly leave each time she called at Manet's studio in the rue Guyot.

Dressed in high style, Eugène Manet looked remarkably like his brother. He had the same red-blonde hair and beard, but he lacked Édouard's charm and confidence. He also, clearly, lacked the passion of the stunning Berthe. He threw himself onto the sofa, lounging with one leg upon the cushion, as if she had dragged him along against his will.

Berthe was dressed in crisp black taffeta and wore a jaunty, high-crowned top hat bunched with veiling atop her careful *coiffure*. She was more slender than he remembered her, her cheekbones more pronounced, but her bearing was as aristocratic as ever. *Could one expect less, from the granddaughter of Fragonard?* And yet, because Berthe had stayed in Paris with her prominent parents during the war and the Siege, this *femme fatale* had eaten rats and encountered corpses every time she left her family's luxurious apartment in the rue Guichard.

Berthe sauntered around Tissot's spacious studio, peering into the exotic profusion of his conservatory, taking in the view of the extensive gardens from the bay window in back, passing the handsome mantelpiece and lingering at the bay window to the side. "You have copied the colonnade from the Parc Monceau!" She turned to him with an amused and accusatory expression. "James, you are set up like a king!"

Eugène roused himself to inspect Tissot's premises. He drawled, "I would rather spend my life in a boat without a single material possession," but nevertheless picked up the blue and white Chinese porcelain jars from Tissot's mantel to examine them closely. He barely looked at Degas' painting.

Tissot waited while they wandered about his studio. He was pleased by their dumbstruck awe. After several minutes, he nodded, and his long-limbed, liveried footman brought in a bucket of iced champagne for *madame* and *monsieur*.

Berthe raised an eyebrow as she accepted a crystal flute emitting a haze of pinpoint bubbles. "Do you keep champagne at hand?"

Tissot smiled as if it were nothing. "My clients enjoy it. And word gets around that my studio is *the* place to be painted."

"Ingenious," Eugène muttered.

James thought he meant the champagne, but happened to look out the back window into the garden. His footman had silently slipped off to the garden and was stepping from shrub to shrub, polishing the laurel leaves in a highly visible, thoroughly self-conscious effort to impress his employer's Parisian guests as if they were clients. In his silk stockings and tailcoat, the manservant was a vision of splendor from the court of Versailles. James held his fingers to his mustache; it was all he could do not to burst out laughing at the sight.

When the butler brought the tea-tray, Tissot gestured Berthe toward a wicker armchair filled with soft cushions.

She seated herself, her posture so ladylike that both her feet rested on the Oriental carpet. *How few men Berthe Morisot would treat to a glimpse of her ankles!*

James truly was glad to see her again, but one never knew the right thing to say to her. "I saw some of your pictures when I was in Paris last spring," he remarked, resting a hand on his mantelpiece. "They are charming, and you have made a name for yourself as an 'Impressionist.'"

Berthe's lips moved as if she were tempted to ask him which paintings in particular he liked and why, but she was too mannerly to corner him. Instead, she said, "Those who did not call me 'delusional' – or worse – were kind enough to say I lent 'prestige' to the show."

Eugène gulped the rest of his champagne and remarked to Tissot, "So your defection did not matter after all."

"You forget," she said to her husband, "Édouard did not participate, either."

There was an awkward pause, and James took a seat across from Berthe, inquiring, "What did you think of the Royal Academy exhibition?"

Berthe forced herself not to stare at the footman outside. She accepted tea from the butler, but waved away the tray of biscuits with some repugnance. "I did see your picture of the lady violinist, if that is what you are asking," she replied. "You are using lighter colors and looser brushwork."

"It looked less English," sniffed Eugène, pacing about the perimeter of the studio with one hand behind his back.

"*Merci.*" Tissot drew a deep breath. Though he tried not to let Eugène rankle him, he could not help himself, nor could he help feeling defensive. "Agnew bought it for twelve hundred guineas, sold it immediately, and arranged for it to be lent to the Royal Academy show."

Eugène did not conceal the trace of a sneer. "You are a

real money-maker, are you not! A painting machine. At the Hôtel Drouot auction in March, Berthe's pictures – the ones that sold – fetched 250 *francs*."

"Yes, we so admire your pretty little things. And since you are cozy with William Agnew," Berthe smoothly interrupted, "surely you can persuade him to buy Édouard's two new paintings. He is counting on you." She sipped her tea with fastidious restraint.

"I am afraid that Agnew has no interest in representing French artists," Tissot replied. He rested an arm along the back of the couch. "I tried to speak to him on Manet's behalf, but it did not help that both pictures were rejected by the Paris Salon."

Eugène looked personally insulted and remarked, "They are calling you an 'outsider.' "

"*Pardon? Non*, that is Lawrence. Alma-Tadema. He is Dutch, you know."

"They refer to Alma-Tadema as 'another outsider,' " Berthe repeated, a sly challenge in her innocent expression. "What does that make you?"

Tissot said tersely, "It is their Oxford University art professor, John Ruskin, who writes these things."

Eugène sniggered, "Ruskin says that your Dutch friend seems to hold it his heavenly mission to portray the Bacchanalian frenzy of Rome."

Tissot folded his arms over his chest. He never did care for Édouard's brother. "An explosion on the canal nearly destroyed his home, Eugène. Lawrence is busy trying to get back on his feet, if only for the sake of his wife and daughters, and Ruskin suddenly has taken a savage dislike to his work. He has no pity, no human feeling." Tissot found it hard to believe Ruskin could be so coldhearted. It was rumored that the love of his life had just died, from brain fever, though she was quite young. Tissot could still see Ruskin's angry, pathetic face in his mind, that day when he had stood before Millais in the corridor at the Royal Academy exhibition.

James tried to explain how it was here. "In Paris, there is a cacophony of critics, vying to be heard over each other. In England, there is one critic who actually has the power to undo a man's entire career. They call him Sir Oracle. He publishes his reviews of the annual Royal Academy Exhibitions..." He could see it was futile to make them understand. "No matter," he observed, crossing his legs, "as long as the Prince of Wales admires Lawrence. And he does."

"They are calling you the painter of the *parvenus*," mused Berthe, "social climbers and husband-hunters." She sat upright, habitually poised, but even with the black silk scarf wound around her throat, her open white blouse was tantalizing. Tissot could think only of the picture Manet had painted of her, reclining on a couch as if she had just made love with those long, tapered fingers. *He* had revealed her ankles, for all to see.

"They do not consider you a serious painter, like their Millais," remarked Eugène. He continued to stroll idly around the studio, picking up Tissot's things to examine them.

"Millais is a British institution. No artist can compete with him here. But I assure you that I sell my work as rapidly as I can paint it," James said genially, "and my printer makes reproductions of my large paintings that sell out as soon as the shops get them in." He found it humiliating – and infuriating – that the Royal Academy continued to withhold membership from him.

Berthe lay her cup and saucer on the carved mahogany side table, balancing her spoon on top to indicate that the footman should remove it now. "Édouard is making plans to paint in Venice for several weeks, if you send him a buyer," she said, "as you promised."

"*Oui*, I intend to go with him, but he has told Suzanne that the whole trip depends on me and my collector."

At the mention of Édouard's wife, Berthe's chin tipped up. She added, "He has so great a talent, and so much courage despite the constant rejections..." She cast a sideways glance at his brother, her new husband. "We all endured so much, during the war and the Siege."

"Good thing you were not wounded or disfigured with the smallpox," quipped Eugène. He stood behind her wicker chair, toying with his blue silk cravat. "That would have been a shame, for I would feel lonely without you. I would miss your chatter and pretty plumage a great deal."

Berthe colored, and rose to look out at Tissot's pond and garden. Her figure was stunning, but under her rather severe hat, her face was anxious and unhappy.

Tissot felt some anger that she had married Eugène – anger at Manet, whose infrequent letters from Paris to James had hinted at this solution. Once Berthe reached thirty, she had to appease her mother, who ceaselessly reminded her that her charms were fading and her paintings were not selling.

"Mind if I take a turn around your garden, Tissot?" Eugène drawled. "English drawing rooms make me restless."

Berthe did not glance after him, but seemed glad for a respite from him. Tissot invited her into the garden with him. She lingered at his cast iron colonnade, wrapping an arm around one of the columns as she admired his shimmering pond.

"I have spent these weeks painting at Cowes, while Eugène was off sailing," she said, and paused. "Édouard has encouraged me to go to Venice to paint. But now that

Maman is all alone, I cannot stay away much longer."

"Perhaps next year," Tissot said.

She was nearly as tall as he was, and looked into his eyes. "Paris still gives me nightmares," she confessed, fingering the black chiffon scarf at her throat. "But I have been so inured to war, I feel I can endure anything. And all I want to do is paint. Gone are my days of trysts..."

James realized that she was beseeching his discretion, and he offered his reassurance.

"*Madame Manet*, there is much that should be put behind, for all of us." He made her a little bow.

"You deserve all the compliments I have heard of you, James," Berthe said, taking in the splendor of his studio windows overlooking the garden. "Édouard always has said that success in the form of money is the key to any kind of freedom."

James felt keenly that, even as Berthe Morisot was impressed by his prosperity, she found him rather vulgar and would forever disdain him as the son of a seaport shopkeeper. She always made him feel like a country bumpkin. He offered her his arm and walked her back up the stone steps to his house.

A high breeze tugged at her *chapeau*, and before she could secure it, it was blown away by the wind. Her chestnut curls loosened and spilled over her lovely neck. "Please, can you chase it?" she begged James, breathless. "It puts Eugène out when my hair is disordered."

Sure enough, Eugène materialized in his crisp fawn-colored jacket and blue trousers, scolding her, "Am I to have a wife who is a lady, or did I marry a slattern?"

Tissot suavely hid his astonishment and fetched her hat. He murmured to her, "Come, use the mirror in my studio."

The personal life is one's own business.

When they finally took their leave, Tissot craved the

fresh air of the Regent's Park and stepped out for a walk.

The English air was moist and wonderful; he savored the cool breeze on his face. As he strolled toward the park, he was captivated by a slim woman who was skipping along with a little girl. The child might have been three or four; the woman was perhaps twenty. She wore an afternoon dress in cornflower blue muslin and a light paisley shawl. The small oval of her face, defined by a wide ribbon to the side of her chin, was exquisite under the arc of her straw bonnet.

She held the hand of the girl, who bounced at her side as they spoke in low, happy voices. The little one let go, chasing pigeons on the path, and called back, "Mama! Come here!" She picked up a pebble and tried to get the attention of the most preening bird, boldly approaching her.

"Violet, be kind, darling."

"He's going to bite me, Mama!"

"So am I!" said the woman, grabbing the little one and covering her face with kisses as she wriggled and squealed.

James did not realize he had stopped walking. He was listening to the intermingled peals of laughter floating away on the wind, like the gentle, far-off chime of chapel bells.

❧❧❧

Tissot closed the windows in his library; it was only mid-September, but the weather had turned, and mornings had become chilly. He took his coffee and *brioche* at his desk as usual and attended to his correspondence. Today, it was imperative that he wrap up all outstanding business prior to leaving for Venice with Manet. He had persuaded Marsden, the aggressive young art dealer in Bayswater to whom he sold his smaller pieces, to buy Manet's two new paintings.

With his *carnet* before him, he entered the handsome sum he had received for painting a wealthy financier who owned a printing ink factory outside Paris and was in London looking for investment opportunities. The latest portrait commission he had completed, now ready to be framed, was of Sir Henry Keppel, Admiral of the Fleet, who had commanded the British naval brigade in the Crimean War as well as naval forces in China. James composed a letter to the Admiral's secretary, arranging payment and delivery, as well as a note suggesting sitting dates for a pencil portrait of Jessie Gordon, as a wedding gift for Tommy Bowles. He also confirmed to the dealer Durand-Ruel that he would exhibit a number of his etchings at his gallery in Paris next year.

Tissot strolled toward the red kiosk on the corner to post his letters. The blue sky belied the temperature. He secured his top hat and watched the clouds, lush and pearly white.

And there she was, *La Mystérieuse* – the mystery woman. He had not set eyes on her in the two months since he had first seen her out with her little girl, though he had taken to strolling in the neighborhood much more frequently.

She was dressed simply but elegantly in black, with a pleated cape over her shoulders. As she leaned forward to post her letter, he glimpsed her slim, booted ankle under her fluttering white petticoats.

"*Bonjour,*" he bowed. As easily as he conversed with women, standing before her now reduced him to a provincial schoolboy.

"Good morning, *Monsieur* Tissot." Her voice was unexpected, a rich contralto.

He was transfixed. "How do you know me?"

She broke into peals of laughter. "You *are* rather famous."

James cursed his stupidity. He stood there and gazed at *La Mystérieuse*, a very real and straightforward woman with a light brown fringe of hair over her forehead.

"I'm sending a letter to my brother, Freddie, in India." Her voice had the same gentle quality as Louise Jopling's.

Tissot made no response, and she waited, seeming to find him comical. After another moment, she gamely informed him, "He's an army officer."

He inquired about the book tucked under her arm, and when she held it out to him, he laughed. It was the new French translation of Edgar Allan Poe's *The Raven*, illustrated by Édouard Manet.

"*Pardon!* I am – would you consider modeling for me? For my painting, that is." James was conscious that his English was imperfect, that he sounded like a "foreigner" – and yet, *La Mystérieuse* had an accent as well. She sounded *irlandaise* – Irish. "I am looking for – for someone, just like...that is, your face would..."

"Alone, do you mean?" She shivered and drew her cape closer.

"Oh, not at all. You may bring your husband..."

"Who would refuse to sit for *Monsieur* Tissot? I can call as soon as you wish. I have no husband."

"Then I shall send my footman for you this afternoon," he said, puzzled. If she were a widow, she could have replied that her husband had passed. Perhaps it was too recent, and too painful. Her black attire could be mourning, but James recollected Bowles' comments on the amorous secrets of St. John's Wood. "May I tell him where?"

"I live with my sister, Mrs. Hervey, at 6 Hill Road. Just round the corner."

If she were currently someone's mistress, she could hardly be living with her sister. But what man would cast off such a creature? Were both sisters kept? Who was the father of her child?

Tissot bowed and suggested one o'clock. The Admiral's portrait could wait to be framed. As they parted, he turned. "Your name, *Madame*?"

"Mrs. Newton."

ৡৡৡ

She arrived, heavily bundled against the damp autumn chill and accompanied by an elderly woman dressed in layers of rust-colored knife pleats. "My sister has taken the children to the menagerie and did not need their nurse today, so I have brought Nanny."

He hid his disappointment and offered *La Mystérieuse* the use of his library to change into the costume he had selected for the picture. He pointed the way to his studio, where she and the nurse could meet him when she had dressed.

Under a leaning oak tree, at the end of the reflecting pool in his colonnaded garden, he had instructed his footman to lay out one of the Oriental carpets from his studio.

It was to be his first painting executed entirely out of doors. He busied himself arranging the scene: in the picture's foreground, a wicker *chaise longue*, and on a small carved mahogany table behind it, he set out a silver tea service, two china teacups, and a domed almond cake. He carefully removed a wide slice from the front to reveal its tender interior.

"Your garden!" Mrs. Newton stood at the top of the steps to the lawn, clasping her hands with a delight that few women of his acquaintance were artless enough to express

– much less feel.

She was dazzling in the loose white gown with a yellow ribbon running down the front. He asked, "You will be happy to pose for hours, then?"

"Hours and hours. It's like...Paradise."

The footman stood behind the nurse, and after an awkward moment of wishing the old lady would disappear, Tissot gallantly instructed him, "Bring a wicker armchair for Nanny, and place it just there, behind the tea table."

"Mrs. Newton, this is for you." He gestured for her to recline on the *chaise*. The gown was a few inches too long on her, and he held her arm as she drew it up a bit to cross the lawn. She perched on the edge of the *chaise longue*, then stretched out beneath him.

James held her face and gently leaned her head against a cushion. He stood back to study the effect and drew a breath as she gazed up at him, serenely awaiting his satisfaction. *Delicious, almost more than a man of flesh and blood can bear.*

The nurse observed his movements and bundled her shawl closer. He did not care what she thought.

"*Un moment!*" he cried. He took the stone steps two at a time up into his studio and reappeared with a white, bobble-fringed shawl for Mrs. Newton. This he arranged around her shoulders, which he held longer than was strictly necessary. Her exquisite oval face was inches from his as he made a pretense of examining the folds of the shawl over her bust and, finally, letting its loose end drape down the side of the *chaise*.

He situated Nanny, surveyed the combined result and, on a devilish impulse, asked his footman to bring out another wicker chair. On it, he placed his hat and cane as if an unseen man were visiting them – or watching them. He ruffled the edge of the carpet, then moved to Mrs. Newton's *chaise* and pulled the fabric of her gown downward over the ankles and extended toes of her supple leather boots.

Her eyes followed him, amused and patient. "Put your right hand under your cheek, like this," and he moved her fingers, "yes, as if you are resting on it..." Despite his efforts, he could not tell if she were wearing a wedding ring. "Nanny, you look out at me as I paint. *Bon.* How still you both are! When you ladies tire, I will order a very large tea."

He sat on his camp stool and began a casual conversation as he roughed in his composition. "Mrs. Newton, are you from a family of artists, who have asked you to model before?"

"Not at all. My father was an officer with the East India Company in Agra."

"And he lives here, in London?"

"No, in Yorkshire."

"He is fortunate, to have his daughters and grandchildren close."

She made no answer, and from this, he surmised something about her.

"And you, *Monsieur*? Tell us about your family in Paris."

"But you must call me James."

"*Zhames!*" she giggled. "Your mum gave you a very proper French name!" Her peals of laughter were irresistible.

He chuckled and set down his palette for a moment. Then he laughed more deeply and told her, "Mrs. Newton, you disarm me. I was christened Jacques-Joseph, and took the name when I was a student. I have always loved all things English."

"And are you from a family of artists, James?"

"My father was a merchant, who built a very successful dress fabric business in Nantes. He thought my childish interest in drawing would pass, and he was fairly disgusted when it only grew." James sketched out the composition of his picture in red-brown paint as he talked.

"He was not a stern man, just pragmatic, and a Christian of the old-fashioned sort. When I was twelve, he sent me to a Jesuit boarding school, at Brugelette in Flanders, and then another school in Brittany, and to another in Normandy. Living in these ancient towns only inspired me to sketch the architecture, and he was disappointed that I did not want to design buildings."

She yawned, and her mouth was as delicate as a kitten's. "I'm so sorry – please, go on."

"I was just going to tell you of my mother," Tissot grinned. "She had been willing, as my father had not, to look at my endless drawings of gowns from the fashion plates on my father's counter. After all that schooling, she proposed that they should send me to Paris, pay just a few years more for me to receive the education of a proper artist. My father agreed – *if* the Académie des Beaux-Arts would accept me, and *if* I would work hard, respect the advice of my instructors, and not waste his investment in me on 'Bohemian nonsense.' And so, the first painting I ever exhibited was a portrait of my mother."

James realized how much he was running on and looked up; Nanny nodded toward Mrs. Newton, "Mr. Tissot, I'm afraid she's asleep."

He caught the nurse's expression and turned his eyes on Mrs. Newton's figure. Wife or widow, *La Mystérieuse* was pregnant.

༔ ༔ ༔

Chapter XVIII

Venice
October 9, 1875

Giulia rustled in the bedclothes and turned to him; James was awake, listening to the sounds of dawn in Venice through her open windows. She buried her face in his warm skin, eventually opening bleary eyes to the church bells, pigeons, vendors' musical voices, and the lapping oars and cries of the gondoliers. James smiled, but Giulia did not seem to recognize him – until he kissed her.

"You want more?" she laughed, with strands of hair over her moist pink cheeks. "How do you want it?" She snuggled into him, then rolled on top and straddled him, pressing her breasts into him in the same way he remembered. "What do you want?"

"I have missed you," he whispered. He had lingered in the street where he used to meet her, when he was a student touring Florence and Venice. How surprised he was to find her again, now a widow. He made love with her again, reveling in her full figure.

She fell asleep in his arms, and he stroked her hair. Giulia would ensnare him, if he were not careful. She was Catholic, but she would hardly meet the approval of his father at the château in Besançon. *Still, if I chose to marry her, bring her back to London...*

He slipped out of her bed to dress, finding his way to her tall armoire in the early morning light. Her maid must have hung his clothes, and he wandered through the interconnected apartments to another chamber, which might have belonged to her late husband. He found his shirt, but the trousers were too small to be his, and he could not find his frock coat.

James glanced at the man's photograph on the chest: he was years older than Giulia, and of hefty proportions. He opened some of the drawers below and saw more trousers, and in a large bottom drawer, a shaving brush, razor, and mismatched cufflinks rattled around as if hastily stored. Under them, turned over, were a half-dozen *carte-de-visite* photographs, calling cards of different, well-dressed men. With a moment's clarity, he knew that she had lied to him.

Giulia stood behind him, holding her beribboned dressing gown closed and offering him his frock coat. "You have done well for yourself, James. I am glad you have come back to me."

He dodged her caress and buttoned his coat, then turned for the door.

❧ ❧ ❧

Tissot wound his way through the gnarled alleys between the decaying stucco *palazzos* back to his hotel, prior to meeting Manet at the Café Florian.

The early morning sun shimmered pink on the water

lapping in the canals. When James came to Venice as a student, he had stayed near the Fenice Theatre, but the Villa Igea had just opened near the Accademia galleries, with the new exhibition devoted to the works of Michelangelo.

The Villa Igea was a pretty little place with green shutters and flower boxes, right off the San Marco waterfront. James hastened through its sunny yellow lobby, his boots echoing over the diamond-patterned stone floor and up the stairs to his room. His windows overlooked a serene square from which rose the Renaissance façade of the Church of San Zaccaria, with its paintings by Tintoretto.

He braced himself on the window ledge and leaned out to smell the sweet air. If James was dismayed at Giulia, he pitied her life as a widow, without fortune or family to rely on. His thoughts wandered to young Mrs. Newton. He would not want to see her reduced to that.

Tissot washed and changed and soon was strolling along the narrow streets over two bridges. In a few minutes reached the Café Florian in St. Mark's Square. Under a vast, cloudless blue sky, masses of Venetians and travelers savored their coffee and pastries at tables spilling into the *piazza*. A slender woman caught his eye. *Of course it is not her!* He must be half-crazed, to dream that Mrs. Newton had followed him.

Manet, as blonde as a god in the clear sunlight, was waving his top hat at him. Tissot made his way past the orchestra that played Verdi, through the laughter and conversation to his friend.

"And where did you sleep last night?" Manet teased him, brushing dust from his impeccably-creased trouser legs. "Will she let you paint her without her clothes?"

Tissot took a seat. "We paint different things, Édouard."

"If you had paid attention to your anatomy studies, you

would not have to waste so much time on your costumes."
As he spoke, Manet's keen eyes moved over the crowd,
always searching for something livelier.

"You may be right," Tissot replied, "but whose work is
selling?"

"Your genius has always been as a wheeler-dealer."

Despite their bond of affection, James had long ago tired
of Manet's lordly disparagement. Manet's father had left
him a small inheritance, enough to live on, but not enough
for luxuries like this holiday. He crossed his arms and gave
Manet a look as if to say, *You would not be in Venice, were
it not for my assistance.*

Édouard flashed his crooked smile at him, as he used to
do when they were students in Paris. "Everything comes
easily to you, James." He made a charming bow over the
café table. "I thank you for selling your young dealer my
two paintings. Of all of us, you have been the only one to
achieve fame and fortune. Don't let it go to your head."

"Let me see what you paint in Venice." Tissot chuckled.
"Perhaps I shall buy something as a souvenir." It was
impossible to stay angry at Manet.

"Will you?" Manet said. "Pretend to be mad for my
pictures and unable to decide which to buy. In Paris,
insults are pouring down on me as thick as hail. I try to
keep seeing things from new angles, but the attacks have
broken the spring of life in me." He held his hand to his
heart in a mock despair that did not hide his real
despondence. "People don't realize what it feels like to be
constantly insulted. The only place my paintings are hung
is in my own studio. Well, no matter. There is always the
next Salon..."

Tissot searched his friend's face momentarily, then lit a
cigarette. He had, from the day they met, felt a certain awe
and envy at Manet's renegade attitude. Even as James'

reputation grew, in those heady years before the war, it was Manet who was worshipped by the intellectual crowd. Tissot could never say so, but he believed that Manet was wasting his life. He basked in the adulation of influential writers who crafted a myth around him, defending him to the Establishment as he continually sought to offend public opinion. Still, compared to Manet, James always felt less than talented, and less than famous.

"*You* make no false steps," Manet remarked. "What are you going to do next?"

"I have written Durand-Ruel that I will exhibit my etchings in his Paris gallery show," Tissot hesitated, then added, "...and I am painting an outdoor scene, of a woman, in my garden."

"Who is she?" Manet taunted him. When Tissot gave him a barely perceptible smile, Manet said, "Don't be such a dead fish! Let me guess – she is married."

James waved his curiosity off. "She will remain *La Mystérieuse*."

Édouard idly swung his cane back and forth. He squinted and pointed it across the lagoon, toward the Benedictine Abbey. "They say Casanova enjoyed frolicking with the nuns over there. *Ah, Venice* – and its handmaidens." He felt around in his pocket, forgetting where he had put something. "Before I left Paris, Degas gave me an address where I can buy a large number of condoms. He said we should only bring back good things from this trip. Enough said."

"And how is Degas?" Tissot asked.

"As fierce and witty as ever," Manet replied, quoting him, " 'Woman is the desolation of the righteous.' "

Tissot chuckled. "He must be mad with joy that a collector from Brighton bought a half-dozen of his pictures from Durand-Ruel's London gallery. I hear it is likely to close at the end of the year. Durand-Ruel cannot sell anything by Monet, Pissarro, Renoir, or Sisley. Degas was the first and only of his modern French artists to find a British buyer."

Manet rolled his eyes at the orchestra with the air of a Paris street urchin. "My God, how bored I am here."

"But how wonderful, to enjoy this music in the open air!" Tissot recognized the piece from its premiere at the Royal Albert Hall in the spring and found it restoring his spirits.

But Manet, swinging his cane, insisted, "Let us walk about before my wife finds me."

James exhaled a stream of smoke, crushed his cigarette, and reluctantly joined him in a stroll through the square. Manet was limping a bit, favoring his left leg, but when he spied a stunning young woman in the crowd moving ahead of them, he nodded for Tissot to follow him. He clutched his cane and hurried his pace in an attempt to overtake her.

Dieu, how the women here carry themselves. Tissot saw the beauty acknowledge Manet's interest, slowing her steps and swaying her hips. He cast his eyes around the crowd and murmured, "Do you not expect *Madame* Manet any moment?"

Manet whispered to Tissot, "Everything is forgivable, if one maintains appearances."

Suddenly Suzanne caught up with him and said, "There! I've caught you this time." She was a corpulent Dutchwoman who moved as if every pound of flesh was a drag on her feet.

"Well, that's funny!" Manet greeted her with a suave bow. "I thought it was you!" Suzanne gave him a fake laugh and reminded him, "You told me to wait for you near the pastries at the café."

Tissot always had found Manet's marriage hard to believe. Suzanne, once the Manet family's piano tutor, was so talented a musician that his friend and patron, the composer Chabrier, had dedicated his *Impromptu in C Major* to her. She often visited the poet Baudelaire after his stroke, to play Wagner on the piano in the nursing home. Suzanne's younger brother, who was now nearly twenty-four, had lived with them throughout their twelve-year Protestant marriage. Suzanne and Édouard were the boy's godparents, and had doted on him ever since Tissot had first moved to Paris as an art student.

James had always felt she had a kind heart – but she *was* very hard on the eyes. When Manet had her pose naked for some of his early pictures, he had painted on another woman's head. But when Degas painted Suzanne, Manet angrily ripped the canvas, saying Degas had not done justice to his wife.

Tissot greeted Suzanne and asked, "Is your husband bringing you to hear Madame Gerster at the Fenice tonight?"

Manet quickly answered for her. "No, she prefers German music, Wagnerian noise."

Suzanne's dull expression hid her disappointment. "Édouard never has cared for music," she mumbled to James, who used to sit near her at the piano when he called on Manet.

"How is it possible," mused Tissot, "for an artist not to be sensitive to beauty in all its forms?"

"No one can be a painter unless he cares for painting above all else," Manet said.

"Another pleasant evening apart?" Suzanne complained, putting a plump hand to her neck.

Manet turned to his wife, instantly in a dark mood. "You get that from your father," he burst out. "The attitude of the Dutch burgher, surly, grumbling, stingy, and incapable of understanding an artist."

Suzanne did not raise her voice, but observed, "He is no worse than your mother, who allows me to entertain our guests but treats me like a servant when I am not at the piano."

Turning to Tissot as if she could not hear, Manet declared, "Unable to suppress love, the Church wanted at least to disinfect it, and it created marriage."

When they were finally gone, Tissot raised his face to the pink-tinged Venetian sun and thought, *I may marry some day, but never to have it turn out like this unholy mess.*

☙☙☙

Manet had come to Venice to paint and spent much of his time sketching, planning pictures, and attempting to capture the light and color of the Grand Canal, the gondolas and gondoliers.

James, who spent so much time indoors, wanted only to enjoy the airy splendor of this place. His father had worked all the time and never stopped doing business, except on Sunday. Tissot had never had a holiday in all these years of building his career in Paris, fighting and starving in the war, rebuilding his career in London.

Numerous artists in London now were imitating Tissot's paintings of fashionable women, especially after he exhibited *The Bunch of Lilacs* at the Royal Academy this summer. All these artists – younger, less accomplished and many from his own neighborhood – reprised his work purely as pretty images of the gowns, the interiors. But Tissot prided himself on the superiority of his pictures. Only he hinted at mood, humor, sexuality – the complex mind at work – in his figures, his women even more so than his men. Female buyers loved his work, perhaps seeing themselves in it as more attractive, more interesting, more cosmopolitan than they were.

Finally, he felt he had made enough of a mark in London to rest up before taking on the next challenge. *What will it take to be made a member of the Royal Academy?* He would speak with Millais upon his return. Here in Venice, he wanted only to play the tourist and stroll the winding streets, shop and take in all the art and music and theatre he could.

He meandered north and west of Piazza San Marco, to the Mercerie shopping district. He wandered in and out of the textile shops, where merchants who took him for an Englishman touted their sumptuous silks and brocades on ancient wooden looms. He bought fabric to have made into draperies for his house and some silk for his London tailor to fashion into waistcoats.

As he ran his fingers over antique fabrics, expensive laces, silk velvets, beaded and embroidered cloth, it struck him that he might offer a present to *La Mystérieuse. Would she accept a token from him in appreciation for posing for his picture?* Just to be sure, he selected some expensive fabric for her nurse as well.

Back at the Villa Igea, James stopped at the desk to collect his mail before dressing for an evening out. He had tried to persuade Ouida, his British novelist friend, to meet him in Venice. She had left London last year for the thermal waters and seclusion of Bagni di Lucca, to the west. Ouida had recently published another novel, *Two Little Wooden Shoes*, and wrote James that she expected its success to satisfy her creditors but was unable to make the trip at this time.

James loved his friends, but more than a few of them seemed unable to look after themselves. *How do they survive at all — what would have become of me, if I were not entirely self-sufficient?* He dreaded the thought of being in debt, of owing anything to anyone.

After the theatre and a late supper, Tissot returned to his hotel. On the Villa Igea's rooftop terrace, he took a seat under the glimmering stars in the wide-open sky. He ordered a *prosecco*, lit a cheroot and gazed out over the immense pink marble complex of the Doge's Palace.

Madame Etelka Gerster had created a furor at the Fenice, singing the part of the overprotected, cursed Gilda in *Rigoletto*. Verdi had discovered the Hungarian soprano in Vienna and recommended her to the theatre manager. The twenty-year old *prima donna*'s voice was brilliant, pure, and powerful. The tiers of theatre-goers leaning from the gold and blue Rococo balconies became worshippers, rising in five separate waves of ovations, each deserved. James believed he had witnessed the launch of a career.

It was, however, another woman of about that age, with a much more vulnerable voice, who obsessed his thoughts. A woman, however beautiful, with one child and another on the way. *Whose children?* He tapped at the cigar and rocked it in his fingers. One explanation that seized him was that she had left her husband. *Had the man been a brute to her? Or had he taken a mistress?*

James exhaled his cigar smoke into the night air and leaned forward anxiously, draping his hands over his thighs. Across the lagoon loomed the silhouette of the distant basilica of San Giorgio Maggiore, and its towering campanile.

Who would be in Venice, thinking of being elsewhere? James swirled his sparkling *prosecco* without tasting it. He felt restless to see her again, *La Mystérieuse*.

Chapter XIX

17 Grove End Road, St. John's Wood
March 31, 1876

"A little lower, I think," Tissot instructed his silk-stockinged footman, "That's it."

Once *Blue Venice* was hung over his studio mantelpiece, Tissot stood back to admire Manet's painting, a dazzling dream version of their sunlit days along the canals. The light and the water and the air all seemed to move. Manet had been bedeviled by how to capture the gondola and gondolier and was beside himself when James offered him the modest sum of 2,500 *francs* for it.

Tissot felt sure he could show it off to Agnew and other English dealers and collectors to Manet's advantage. *Blue Venice*, he could tell Agnew, was the best of the new French art: beautiful in the vibrant, modern colors now available, and without the notorious nudity and coarseness that so offended British morals.

The footman balanced the heavy framed canvas, then

stood down from the stepladder and began to fold it. "The enquiries you wished –"

Tissot's eyes met his. "*Oui?*"

"The housekeeper confirmed that both ladies have husbands in India, while they raise the children in London. Their father is a Civil Service accounting officer who retired to Yorkshire." He cleared his throat. "Mrs. Newton has delivered a son, as I understand."

James ran a hand over his mustache. "I am going out," he murmured. "I will take my dinner at the Club."

The footman carefully set aside the painting that Manet's had replaced, Degas' picture of off-kilter ballet dancers. "Very good, sir."

৵৵৵

Tissot strolled around the neighborhood. He found himself on Hill Road, before a semi-detached yellow brick house fronted by a wrought-iron fence and small garden. One of the ground floor bay windows was fitted with a Wardian case, an airtight glass box in which several pink orchids were thriving, despite the outdoor temperature, amid a profusion of Japanese ferns.

James recalled Tommy Bowles joking that there was a reason that the views through the parlour windows of St. John's Wood were obscured by potted palms. He paced down the block, then back again, loitering near a gas street lamp a few houses down to consider his approach. He was a neighbor, like any other, so it would be perfectly appropriate to call. He was not sure what he would say to the sister.

When Tissot had returned from Venice, he called with his gifts of fabric for Mrs. Newton and the nurse who had posed with her in his garden in the fall. As an afterthought, he had bought a piece of lace for the sister as well. Mrs. Newton's sister, Mrs. Hervey, had come to the door. Older by a few years, she was less attractive and had an air of reproof even as she accepted the parcels. Down the narrow hall, in the back parlour, he saw Mrs. Newton stand and acknowledge him. Her figure was full with the child she was carrying. Later that week, she sent a graceful note regretting she was unable to receive at present. She added, *I hope to thank you in person, come spring.*

That had been over four months ago. James was overcome by the desire to see her again and mounted the steps up to the arched front door. Behind it, he heard Mrs. Hervey's voice call out, "Children!"

The maid who answered the door bobbed when he asked to see Mrs. Newton. After a moment, a boy and three little girls scrambled up the stairs, gaping at him through the balustrade as if he were a pirate. The maid tittered and led him to the parlour in the back of the house.

"James! We were just taking tea. Please, sit." Mrs. Newton's self-possession struck him as both odd and challenging.

James could hear an infant crying. Mrs. Newton looked very tired and apologized. "Cecil is colicky around tea-time."

Tissot was completely disarmed by her demeanor. She was not dressed for callers and wore a simple flowered cotton gown. But since she was not self-conscious, he seated himself in the chair opposite and glanced at her things on the side table – the *Illustrated London News*, her black onyx rosary beads, a child's drawing.

"Shall I bring you some books?" he asked.

She laughed, "Yes, please do! I have the newspapers, but I've read everything else in the house."

Cecil's cries sounded increasingly urgent, and the nurse

appeared with the baby, handing him to his mother and slipping away. Mrs. Newton kissed his tiny red mouth.

"He needs to be nursed."

"*Pardon!* I will take my leave –"

"No, I wish you to stay," she replied, draping a shawl over her shoulder.

James set his elbow on the chair arm and leaned his face into his hand. She was engrossed in her baby, and he could observe her exquisite profile, the curve of her nose coming to a perfect tip, her eyes and mouth tending to curve downward in repose.

"You're watching me, James," she said, serene and aware of the absurdity of entertaining an elegant gentleman in this way. "Why don't you wait until I'm getting more sleep?"

He rubbed the bridge of his nose, and rather than chuckle, he began to laugh out loud so hard his stomach hurt.

Then she trembled and flashed him a dubious look. "My husband is not in India." Her voice broke as she told him, "That is, he *is* in India – he is no longer my husband. I am divorced."

James could not ask her to explain. For a woman to obtain a divorce in England, her husband had to be found guilty of cruelty – or bigamy or incest – in addition to adultery.

"I am glad you are not married," he replied in low voice, "or I would not be able to ask you to be my wife."

She broke into peals of laughter, not as if he were comical, but as if she were a bit frightened for his sanity.

"Kathleen, marry me!" The words surprised him, but he did not regret them. Just a few months ago, he had attended the Presbyterian wedding of Tommy and Jessica Bowles in Southampton. Amid the gaiety of bagpipes and

Jessie's high-spirited younger brothers, James saw them off on their wedding trip: a fortnight alone on Tommy's yacht, calling at ports as they pleased. James had envied their happiness and optimism.

"James, you must go." Kathleen was not upset. She merely stood, indicating their visit had ended.

Tissot gathered his gloves and hat, and softly asked her, "Why must I go?"

Cecil began to cry, and she gently rocked him. "Because I am living comfortably with Polly, and although I have two children to care for, I am free."

James and Kathleen looked into each other's eyes for a long moment, before he quietly made his way to the front of the house and closed the door behind himself. St. John's Wood had a clique of small-time painters, and two of them passed him, one tipping his hat. The other stared at Tissot as if he were a wild man or some exotic zoo creature not often on view. He stood there momentarily on the Herveys' front stoop and looked out at the neighbors walking along Hill Road without caring what they thought.

Another joke of God? James had grown rich and famous not once but twice; finally, at forty, he had found a woman he wanted enough to marry – an adorable Irishwoman who needed him but would not have him.

❧ ❧ ❧

Tissot sat on the piano stool in his studio, feet planted on the oak parquet floor, swiveling one way and the other. It was raining, a grey, dreary day, and he could not concentrate on the painting fastened to his easel. The Royal Academy Exhibition pictures were due in a few weeks. In addition to the outdoor picture he had painted of Mrs. Newton and her nurse in the fall, which he called *The*

Convalescent, he was close to completing *The Thames,* a river scene that depicted a naval officer leaving the London dockyards on a pleasure jaunt with two lady friends, a picnic hamper and champagne. It was similar to his other shipboard paintings, and he again left the picture's meaning ambiguous and provocative by giving it a title that did not hint at its subject. The expressions on his figures looked cold, but he could not help himself.

Tissot leaned over with his face against his fist. He had proposed marriage to a divorcée. If she *would* have him, respectable people would no longer be able to call on him, or invite them to their homes. They would be unable to appear in public together. He had sought the approval and praise of the British art establishment for five years, and he had achieved his success without changing his citizenship like Lawrence Alma-Tadema.

Would I truly give everything up for this woman – any woman? Surely it is just as well she refused me. He flinched inside at the memory of his youthful, ambitious engagement to the Prince de Bauffremont's daughter, Angelique, whom he met and fell in love with along the avenue de l'Impératrice.

The butler bowed just inside the door. "Sir, Mrs. Newton wishes to see you."

"She has come in the rain?"

She let the butler take her wet coat, but she was agitated and clearly intended to stay only a moment.

"Please, come sit by the fire..." James offered. He held his hand lightly at her back.

"I cannot accept this," she said, returning the new George Eliot novel he had sent to her house. "The flowers...you must stop sending me things, Monsieur Tissot..."

She was shivering, not just with the weather, but with

anger, and yet her eyes met his with something else. "I can't marry you, so please just stop this."

"If it is nothing to me, why will you not agree?"

"James!" She was unnerved in a way that he did not understand. "Cecil is not weaned..."

"Can a wet nurse be engaged? I could –"

"Truly, I prefer living with my sister, on our own, rather than..." She coughed hard and began again. "Polly hates India – the cholera that killed Mum, the heat, all of it. Colonel Hervey sends money to the bank, and she says it's plenty. Polly says you're just sniffing about."

James gasped, stupefied.

"Monsieur Tissot, I am twenty-two and already have been discarded by three men – if I count Dad. I have two children to raise. I want some peace."

James crossed the room and wrapped his arms around her. "That is what I want as well." She felt cold, and he tightened his embrace.

She pulled away and went to the far end of the room, where glass-paned doors led to the garden. "Since you haven't yet heard it from others," she said, resignation replacing her impatience with him, "Dr. Newton divorced *me*. For adultery."

Tissot's legs felt weak. He lowered himself into the wicker armchair and waited.

She spoke to James in a familiar way, as if she always had known him. "Dad had a long career with the East India Company. We grew up in Agra – near the Taj Mahal, can you imagine!" She coughed and blotted the remaining rain drops off her face with her handkerchief. "And then Mum died, and Dad retired and brought Polly and me to Isleworth, to be educated at Gumley House Convent. Freddy was an officer and stayed in Lahore, and Polly was engaged to Colonel Hervey and went to live with his parents in Camden Town."

He scanned her face, trying his best to absorb what she meant to tell him. "Freddy is your brother?"

She nodded and tried not to look too curiously at all the paintings in his studio. "Dad was courting a widow, and he complained that it was costing him twenty-eight guineas a year to keep me at the convent school. The sisters saw to it that I was not spoiled by vanity or affection." She pressed her palms together and laughed grimly. "Believe me, I learned the meaning of submission to authority. Fraternization between the girls was not allowed, except during our morning break. I spent the days praying, reading. After nearly five years, Dad wrote that he was sending me back to India." Kathleen stopped before the fire, finally, and rubbed her hands near its warmth. "I was excited to travel, to see Freddy, and my childhood friends, but –"

"Freddy had found me a husband, as Dad had told him to." She cleared her throat. "Freddy wrote me that Dr. Newton was 'a decent chap, but lonely.' He was a Civil Service surgeon, whose wife had recently died of typhus, and I was to marry him. I felt *dead*, like my life was being lived for me by others...until I met a man on the ship, and for the first time..."

James propped his elbow on the wicker chair arm, and when it slipped off, he ran his hand through his hair. Outside, tree branches rattled against his house and rain dribbled down the window panes. Kathleen turned her back on the fire – and on him – and stared out into the dreary garden.

"After my brother introduced me to Dr. Newton and we had talked a bit, I prayed with my confessor in Lahore. He advised me to speak with my intended husband as if I were standing before God..."

James leaned forward. "And what did you tell him?"

She threw him a dubious look. "Dr. Newton was over fifty and it was so difficult, so unnatural to speak to him, that I could not manage it. After the marriage ceremony, before we were to spend our first night together – this was just two days after the New Year; I had just turned seventeen..."

James watched her run her hands slowly along the table edge and over the calla lilies from his conservatory. His thoughts were racing, but he did her the courtesy of hearing her out.

"You will think it foolish, but I did expect my husband to forgive me, once I'd confessed my shipboard romance with Captain Palliser and begged his forgiveness. Dr. Newton seemed to remain calm. He questioned me: 'Did he touch your breasts?' 'Did he lay his eyes on them as well?' Yes to both, I answered, but that was all."

There was a pause before James said, "Go on."

"My new husband struck me in the face and called me a whore. He pushed me out the door and told me he would file for divorce immediately."

"What did you do?"

"Freddy lived in the officers' quarters, but he tried to find someone to take me in." Kathleen's voice broke, but she folded her arms over her chest, turned to James, and took a deep breath. "His colonel's wife had no wish to cross Dr. Newton. English women in India are tough old birds." She shuddered in distaste. "And anyway, the British are too ambitious to risk their reputations. By this time, it had grown dark –"

A light tapping at the door signaled the return of the butler.

"*Oui?*" Tissot said angrily.

"If you please, sir, Mr. Whistler has sent word that he

wishes you to 'fly like a bullet' to see –"

"*In the rain?* Send word back that I am indisposed!" Tissot thundered, then softened his tone. "See that I am not disturbed. Tell Cook to leave supper in the larder, and you both may take the evening off."

"Thank you, sir."

Kathleen perched on the edge of the window seat near him and twisted the handkerchief she held in her lap. When the outer hall was quiet, she shrugged and continued in her low voice, "Freddy sent me in a rickshaw, to Captain Palliser. He quickly moved me to the home of a friend of his, in town, and agreed to pay for my passage back, but he said it would be several weeks before another ship was to sail for London. He visited me often, begged me to show that his love for me was returned...he said he could not marry me until he proved himself in his new posting, and was able to return to England and speak with his family in Brixton."

"When I arrived back in London, I stayed with Polly. But I was carrying his child, and Polly had her children to consider. She said Dad would have to keep me in Yorkshire. Violet was born in December of that year, the same day the divorce decree came through. Dad wanted to marry again and said it would be best if Polly keeps me in London as long as Colonel Hervey continues on in Lahore."

Tissot squared his shoulders and looked quizzically at her. *The new baby?*

"It is true I have sinned once, and God knows I love that one too deeply to sin with any other." Kathleen lifted her chin at him, and her voice shook just a bit. "Captain Palliser paid me a surprise visit last year, during his leave. He missed me so dreadfully, and said we were meant to be together. I introduced him to Violet, but he could not stay long, just one night. He told me his mother had come round to our marriage, but his father would not allow it – insisted he is in no position to marry yet. He returned to India. I am sure he will write any time now."

Tissot leapt from his seat and pulled her to him. "Kathleen, marry me."

"You don't know him like I do! Do you think I would have – if I hadn't been persuaded of his deepest love? I am sure he will manage things soon, now that he knows we have a son as well as a daughter..."

She stood, and shook James' hand in a businesslike way. "You are very kind to take an interest in me, Monsieur Tissot. But I have Violet and Cecil to think about now. I am a divorced Catholic; I can never marry again, but...in trying to make amends for my sins, I believe the right thing to do is wait for Captain Palliser."

Tissot rose as well. *She thinks I am shocked and disgusted.* He shook his head and laughed ruefully. Her face reddened, and he strode across his studio and folded her in his arms, "You didn't do anything wrong!"

"God forgive me." Her eyes filled with tears, and he held her until she angrily pushed away from him, saying, "I wish you would leave me be."

James caught her up by the waist and kissed her, and she responded with a warmth and tenderness that he had not anticipated. He craved her so that he could not let her go. When he could stand it no longer, he held his finger to her lips and led her up the staircase to his bedroom.

ॐॐॐ

"Now I am doubly ruined," she murmured, her voice partially buried in his chest.

James ran a hand over her light brown hair, playing with the loose waves that fell over the luminous skin of her shoulder. He tipped her face towards his and murmured, "*Non*...Kate – you are no more ruined than I am. March 1871 did not destroy either of us."

She flashed him a radiant smile.

"You must agree to marry me." He intertwined his fingers in hers and kissed her lips. "I love you beyond anything."

"James, you're mad," she said, in her quiet contralto. She tried to add some levity to her tone, but it fell flat. "Look at you! You need an elegant Society lady, or the beautiful daughter of some famous British painter –"

He pulled her to him. "Why would I want to live in that constricted way, with a wife who wants only my house and the Society life?"

"James...I am not, I am not able to, really...manage all the servants, your household," she said softly. "If I were to marry you, would I be *Madame* Tissot, overlooking the menus and the beating of the carpets, settling the arguments over which maid gets Thursday evenings off?"

He grasped her hands, looked her straight in the eye, and mouthed, "*Stop.*"

Kathleen looked terrified, for both of them. "To marry a divorcée – an *Irish* divorcée, and the daughter of a civil servant at that." Kathleen ran her eyes over his face. "You know that in the eyes of God, I am still married to Dr. Newton."

"Then have your things brought here," he suggested, simply. "There is no need to sneak around behind the neighbors – and worse, the servants. You can model for me, be my muse."

Kathleen rolled her eyes. "The Census-takers will like that!" Her expressive face mimicked a dour bureaucrat absorbed in taking notes, and she deadpanned, "Number 17, Grove End Road...one butler, one cook, two footmen, three maids. One muse."

James looked at her, taken aback, and she burst out in a peal of laughter that provoked him to join in. *She is so alive!*

"Would I have to hide from your clients and guests? Should I scurry upstairs if I see your friends at the door? What about Violet and Cecil, James?"

"Do you know how rich I am? I can do as I please! What do I care about the opinion of a few gossiping neighbors?" He took her in his arms and brushed her hair away from the small oval of her face. "My household staff are capable and discreet. My house is my sanctuary – the garden, all of it, can be our...oasis."

He added, "I cannot be happy without you in my sight, every moment of every day. *Belle irlandaise!* My friends will love you as I do."

❧ ❧ ❧

Chapter XX

17 Grove End Road, St. John's Wood
August 15, 1876

When Tissot finally emerged from his library, and the front door had closed on William Agnew, Kathleen peeked out from the small family parlour. For the duration of Agnew's call, Kate had confined herself to the back of house, pasting Violet's drawings into her memory album.

"Can I come out now?" she laughed. She wore the gold silk at-home gown he had ordered from Paris for her, and she had not yet dressed her hair.

James strode down the hall toward her, cursing. "Here is something for your scrapbook." He slapped a stack of newspapers and magazines down on her work table. Several of her own papers fluttered to the floor.

Kate cast him a wary glance and retrieved her clippings. "What did he say?"

"That my 'naughty nautical' has shocked public morals." James continued, trying to think how he had offended so suddenly, merely with one painting. He unbuttoned his frock coat and threw it on the bentwood rocker so hard it set the chair in motion. "*The Thames* is not my first picture of a man alone with two attractive women – just the first one I have shown at the Royal Academy."

He had read the reviews Agnew brought him: *The Athenaeum* called *The Thames*, "thoroughly and willfully vulgar...ugly and lowbred women." *The Times* reported that Tissot's picture was "questionable material" for ladies visiting the galleries, "a pleasanter thing in reality than on canvas..." *The Graphic*, "Hardly nice in its suggestions. More French, shall we say, than English..." *The Spectator* referred to his two women as "undeniably Parisian ladies."

Tissot stripped off his waistcoat and cravat as his brain absorbed the storm of outrage, and he concluded, "My sins consist of vulgarity, painting ugly women, *being French*, and daring to paint as well as Millais and Alma-Tadema."

Kathleen made a wry face and remarked, "Imagine that." She set his frock coat neatly aside, folded her gown beneath her and sank into the bentwood rocking chair. "Except that you paint what one sees in London, every day."

"Precisely," James said, unbuttoning his stiff shirt collar. "And Agnew will not take it. He says that gentlemen may buy 'this kind of thing' in droves, but not from *his* firm. He said at this point in my career, I should be 'cheek to jowl' with Millais in terms of my reputation."

"You can't be surprised, James," she remarked, quietly. "What will you do now?"

"I am going to do – what I want!" He pulled her up from the rocker and swung her around. "There is always Durand-Ruel, Marsden...I will find new dealers up north and sell my own paintings, too. I will sell more reproductions of my paintings – prints – everything."

Kathleen took in his exhilaration and looked alarmed. "You don't need them?"

"*Non.*" He kissed her. "I need no one but you."

"What about – were any of those reviews by that man Ruskin?"

"Ruskin?" he said dismissively. "He behaves as if I am beneath his notice. But at least *he* has written nothing against me. I am a nobody to him, thank God." He ran his eyes over her, always amazed at her fresh-faced beauty. Her hair spilled in waves down past her shoulders.

James wrapped his arms around her and kissed her. She ran her slender fingers up into his hair and pressed against him, and he was aroused knowing she had nothing under her quilted silk gown. She lowered her eyes as he ran his lips along the side of her neck, pushing the golden fabric toward her shoulder. Sliding his hand under the gown, James caressed her silky skin, and she responded instantly. He moaned with desire, and Kate drew in her breath.

"How long do we have before Polly brings the children?" he whispered.

He was shocked to hear a man's voice in the room.

"James? I knocked, but –"

Lawrence Alma-Tadema stood before them, holding two bottles of wine meant for Tissot's little dinner party tonight.

Kate was suddenly motionless, as if she were Lot's wife, transmuted into a pillar of salt.

Alma-Tadema's eyes ran from Kathleen in her disheveled at-home gown to her work table covered in her albums to the hobbyhorse and doll in the corner. He glared at Tissot, then turned on his heel.

James took after him, putting a hand on his arm. "Come, Lawrence!"

Alma-Tadema shook him off. He was red-faced and pointed toward the street, sputtering, "*Laura* is in the carriage! What if she had – her parents would be horrified if I let her set foot in such a house. It's completely beyond the pale, James!"

Kathleen shrank back, wide-eyed as if she expected Tissot to abandon her on the spot.

James reached into the pocket of his folded frock coat, drew out his cigarette case, and offered one to his friend. These occasional bursts of temper were always short-lived. "We have known each other nearly twenty years now..."

Lawrence, behaving as if the woman in the room were invisible, warned Tissot, "But this is serious, James! I cannot call again, and you know you cannot be welcome in my home. In fact, unless you end this, you will be a social outcast, for *no* gentleman..." Heated, he continued, "Do you know what you're doing, man?"

James lit a cigarette. "I do."

"It's a question of judgment! Openly flouting with –"

Kathleen's face, without defiance or pretension, wore a natural dignity as she stepped toward the hall.

"*Non!*" James motioned for her to remain. The three stood like points in a triangle in the room. Turning to Lawrence, he said, "Mrs. Newton is quite settled here."

Lawrence would not acknowledge her presence. Angled against her, clutching the neck of a wine bottle in each fist, he inhaled and said, "James...this is not *Paris*. We don't do this here."

"I hope I may rely on your discretion, if not your friendship."

"*My* discretion!" Lawrence was affronted. "If this becomes public, no one can stand by you, not Millais, not anyone."

James exhaled smoke and pursed his lips sardonically. "Now you are Mrs. Grumble?"

Kathleen piped up, "You mean, *Mrs. Grundy*, dear." Her eyes darted between Alma-Tadema and Tissot, and then she bit her lip.

"We each have our private lives," James told him, gesturing with his cigarette in hand, "and at least *I* am not the Prince's pornographer."

"I'm not one of those hedonists like Whistler, and your friends in Paris, Manet –"

"And I am not one of those who change their country as they change their shirt!"

Under his spectacles, Lawrence's jovial features were twisted in outrage and frustration. He strode down the hall and slammed the front door.

James turned his head to the back of the house, then took a drag on his cigarette. His hand trembled; he had not felt this terror since the days of the war.

"It is only a matter of time before people begin gossiping," Kate said. She dropped back into the bentwood rocker, and they both were silent for some time. Finally, in a small and fearful voice, Kathleen asked, "What do you want, James?"

"To be happy. To live on my own terms."

"Then we will." She offered him her slim hand. "I am a sinner. I have not lived as God requires. But since I have fallen from Grace, should I not seek all the earthly happiness I can?"

He opened a drawer and ran his eyes over the old stereoscope photograph of his villa on the avenue de l'Impératrice. "*The battle of life,*" he murmured. For the first time, he felt he might not be up to it.

"But I do not wish to cost you your friends."

"There is a price to be paid for everything," he replied. He turned the photograph face down in the drawer, then softly closed it.

"Yes," she agreed, "and it's usually paid by the woman."

"No man has the right to tell me how to live in my own

home." He crushed his cigarette in a tabletop dish. "Do you think Polly and the children would enjoy a picnic in the garden when they come for tea?"

Her face brightened. "There is no one like you."

"We are not like them, are we?"

"You will never be Millais, James," she said, kissing him. "You are French. It is quite unpardonable of you." She kissed him tenderly and gave him a reassuring pat. "And now – your muse is ready to hold a pose."

ले ले ले

A week later, James had begun a large new canvas, depicting a scene that joined two nearly sacred British traditions – afternoon tea and cricket. He gripped a fine camel hair brush and stood back to examine his progress. He was certain the picture would prove immensely popular, and it was calculated to restore his good standing with the critics.

"James, how much longer do you think I can hold this pose?" Kate giggled, bent over in a striped prop gown, pretending to pour cream from a small silver pitcher.

"How much longer until we get some tea?" laughed the handsome athlete who had held an empty cup toward Kathleen for nearly half an hour. He wore the orange- and black-striped cap of the I Zingari cricket team from the Lord's Cricket Grounds around the corner. Tissot had put a red geranium in the button-hole of the young man's linen suit and posed him lounging on one arm on the picnic blanket.

James had invited them and a few of their lady friends for afternoon tea over the course of the week. They did not ask uncomfortable questions, and James was as thrilled to see Kathleen enjoying the company as he was with his picture. It showed a group of good-looking young people in handsome clothes, at their leisure around his ornamental pond. It was a labor of love to paint the details, right down to the four glass mineral water bottles on the picnic blanket. He painted everyone laughing and flirting – and, as a racy twist, showed the elderly chaperone, Polly Hervey's nursemaid, nodding off in the bentwood rocking chair under his chestnut trees. James leaned in to add highlights to the water bottles.

Perhaps it was just as well, he reflected, that he no longer had to sell his biggest pictures through the rigid Agnew and worry about gossip. But he was anxious to maintain his niche in painting modern British life – especially now, with his new living arrangement. In London, Durand-Ruel again had exhibited contemporary French art in his New Bond Street gallery a few months ago. Manet's picture of a couple in a canoe was called "singularly offensive" by Tom Taylor, the reviewer for *The Times*. And though Degas' painting of a drunk woman in a café with her glass of absinthe was called disgusting by the critics even in Paris, a British collector bought four of Degas' innocuous dance pictures at Durand-Ruel's gallery here.

But despite critical hostility to the so-called "invasion of French art" exhibited in Durand-Ruel's London gallery for the past several years, British collectors had bought Tissot's work like mad so far. He scanned his cricket picture, anxious to have it erase any injury to his position from the much-criticized *Thames* painting.

The butler whispered that Mr. Bowles had dropped in.

James leapt to his feet and glanced at Kathleen, who instantly understood the situation. "Where is he?"

"He is in the library, sir, waiting at your convenience."

James nodded at Kate, knowing she would keep everyone merry until he returned. He told them all he would be back momentarily. *But the poses will be ruined, and what trouble it will be to set everyone right again!* Still, what was that compared to the prospect of his reputation being ruined?

"Can we eat these?" teased a cricket player, moving his long fingers toward the bread, cake and fruit spread on the blanket before them.

Tissot had a momentary, desperate sense of everything slipping out of control. He held his index finger up at the fellow. "Better not!"

"James!" Kate shamed him good-naturedly.

He laid a hand on her shoulder. "I will ask the butler to bring some tea and cakes." James strode to the library and greeted Tommy as the butler slid the pocket doors shut on them.

Tommy looked startled by being closed in, but spied the new issue of *Vanity Fair* on the center table and grinned. "James, I feel it's been ages since you've called at Cleeve Lodge. Come dine with Jess and me tonight!" His light blue eyes were filled with anticipation.

James did not mistrust Tommy. He almost wished to confide in him. But gossip was Tommy's stock-in-trade, and if Members of Parliament could be a target of his satire, anyone could. It was a risk James could not take; there was too much to lose. "I regret, I'm engaged for this evening." James folded his arms over his chest and cursed himself for sounding so formal with Bowles. *Mon Dieu, we slept in trenches together during the war!*

"Some other time, then." Tommy toyed with the brim of his top hat. "Now that the baby is sleeping through the night, I'll have Jess send you a note."

"Did you stop in just for that?" Tissot hovered between Tommy and the doors to the hall.

Tommy glanced at him quizzically. "Why, yes! Caught

you at a bad time, have I?"

James ran a hand through his hair. "*Oui – pardon!* I am painting a group of models –" He dared not identify them as cricket players, for fear Tommy would march out to meet them – and learn about Kathleen. "I know you never leave off work for lunch, but I will stop by your office next week."

"Jess will miss you! She keeps urging me to let you know you're welcome any time."

James had a brief vision of Jessie, so sensible and forthright, being introduced to *La Mystérieuse*. It was possible Jess, raised in an Army family and married to the illegitimate Tommy Bowles, would not be as sanctimonious as the Alma-Tademas. But the Bowles were a proper young couple on the rise. "Please give her my best compliments, and forgive my inhospitality." He could not look Tommy in the eye as he made an excuse. "I have more work than I can manage, and I am afraid I have been rather shut in."

"Your *Kathleen Mavourneen* is in every shop window in the West End! I've seen lines stretching out the door. People are calling it a masterpiece."

"The printing press in my studio was in constant use until I contracted the work out." James rubbed the bridge of his nose.

"Say, are you sure you're quite alright?"

"*Oui, oui*...just a bit overwhelmed."

Tommy shook his hand, not altogether convinced, but sympathetic. "I often feel like that with *Vanity Fair*. But there are worse things than being too successful."

"Indeed." James accompanied Tommy Bowles to the front door, and leaned his back against it for several minutes afterward, with a knot in his stomach.

Chapter XXI

Whistler's studio, 2 Lindsey Row, Chelsea
November 9, 1876

Louise Jopling had just stepped up on a raised platform in the corner when Tissot arrived at Whistler's studio. Louise wore a long-sleeved, ruched white gown trailing a black train. Whistler directed her pose, then stood before a canvas taller than himself. Standing yards away from the picture with his brush, he darted toward the canvas with his long-handled brush, dabbed a bit of paint, then jumped back to assess its effect.

And of course, there is nothing to eat, thought Tissot. Whistler's mother had retired to Hastings for her health over a year ago, and though Maud had moved in, she was busy trying to straighten out Jimmy's financial accounts.

"Leyland asked my advice on the best colors to paint the shutters and doors of his dining room to complement his collection of blue and white porcelain," Jimmy drawled. Wearing just a loud waistcoat over his rolled-up shirt sleeves, he clasped a selection of a half-dozen long-handled paint brushes in his left fist. "But while he is out of town, I am transforming the entire room into a harmony in blue and gold with peacocks. You must come see – I am painting every inch of the walls and ceiling with a pattern of peacock feathers! It is really alive with beauty!"

"Jimmy, you sent a messenger to summon me – just to tell me this?" For weeks, Whistler had been engrossed in decorating the dining room of the London house of the Liverpool shipping magnate who had financed his solo exhibition a few years ago. "You may not keep to your studio, but I am trying to finish something."

"As you can see, so am I!" Whistler cackled. He stepped backward to eye Louise and knocked into Tissot.

Tissot was irritated beyond measure, but inhaled and remembered his manners. "*Bonjour*, Louise – *excusez-moi.*"

James pulled up a small caned chair near the window and sat it backwards so he could rest his arms on its back. As his stomach growled, he watched Jimmy dart forward and hastily delineate Louise's left profile with a sweep of thin paint. Her dark hair was arranged elegantly atop her head, interwoven with crimson ribbon, but the portrait was mostly of her costume, from the back. Tissot had not seen her in some time. She was stunning, in the full bloom of womanhood in her mid-thirties.

Whistler wet his finger and gently rubbed the shape that was to be Louise's head. He asked, "Louise, do you approve of being called *Harmony in Flesh Color and Black*?"

"Only if you add, *Portrait of a Portrait Painter*. I am seeking commissions, you see!" The gentlemen joined her laughter, which was brave considering it had gone around town that Mrs. Jopling had won a certain portrait commission paying 150 guineas, but lost it to Millais, who was paid 1,000 guineas for it.

Louise added, "Truly, Jimmy, I do appreciate the attention this will bring. And, speaking of artists looking for notice –"

"Redundant, my dear!" barked Whistler, who lived to see himself lampooned in *Punch* with increasing frequency. James thought it trivialized Jimmy's work, as did Whistler's flamboyant appearance. His white tuft of hair curled over his forehead, and his monocle was fixed in his right eye. "And hold that pose!"

Louise straightened and continued, "– let us pounce, now that we have the ear of the illustrious Monsieur Tissot. James, Lord and Lady Lindsay are opening a gallery, and you *must* contribute. They wish to promote the best contemporary artists in summer exhibitions to run through the London season, coinciding with the Royal Academy show."

James' jaw tightened. *Not another independent show, like the "Impressionists."* Their second exhibition together, this summer, had been as much of a failure as the first. The only good that came out of it was that Degas received some compliments from a prominent art critic. Otherwise: twenty-two pictures, no sales.

He rose from his seat and went to the window, shoving his hands in his trouser pockets. "They think they can compete with the Royal Academy?"

"This is by invitation only, James," laughed Jimmy. While Louise stood perfectly motionless, he painted frenetically, hopping about like a sparrow.

James crossed his arms over his chest and ran his eyes over the pictures against Jimmy Whistler's studio wall. *Nocturnes. Arrangements.* He had shown them at various small galleries in London, but not at the Academy's exhibitions. Nothing with the power of his early work.

James would be cutting his own throat, exhibiting his work with Jimmy's current nonsense.

"It will be remarkable!" Louise spoke from her sideways pose. "Blanche wants elegant, spacious galleries, where all the work can be hung on the line."

"You mean, not all hidden in a jumble of frames up to the ceiling," James said, "or down where the crinolines brush against them?" It was hard to believe.

"Precisely," she said. "Blanche is making a point of spacing the pictures well apart, grouping all the paintings by artist."

Jimmy nodded as he continued to paint. "About time. Now the public will be able to see the artists' style all at once, undiluted with the treacle that forms a backdrop to the *real* art at the Academy shows – because there will be no Hanging Committee!"

Tissot shook his head and held his hand against his temple. Mostly due to his standing at the Paris Salon in the years before the war, he had never had a single picture rejected by the Hanging Committee, although the ugly, unfair reviews of *The Thames* still made him angry. But what Louise described was unlikely – it would mean very few pictures wasting space in large rooms that someone would have to pay for. And with no means of selecting the best submissions, it could be a disaster. He leaned his shoulder on the window frame and turned back to her.

Louise's eyes twinkled. "The Grosvenor Gallery is exactly what is needed in London now. And the Lindsays will be art patrons in the tradition of the Medicis!"

"Weren't some of her watercolor portraits, and an Italian landscape of his, rejected by the Academy last year?" asked Tissot. The whole thing sounded to him like a vanity project by *dilettantes*. He was skeptical about just which aristocratic and royal patrons the Lindsays could ensure.

"Yes, they've quite done with the Academicians, who consider their work to have rather *foreign* qualities," Louise assured him. "Blanche wants space to exhibit her and her husband's work as well as that of their friends. Lindsay feels some of our most distinguished artists are being neglected by the Academy, or feel so hampered that they have stopped bothering to submit their work to the jury. Burne-Jones, Holman Hunt – Jimmy Whistler! They want to showcase pictures worth seeing, with no limit on the number of works each artist can show at once."

Tissot gazed out the window at the river. He had considered himself fortunate to have two or three pictures a year on exhibit at the Royal Academy. But he did fear that after the moral outrage over *The Thames* this spring, the Hanging Committee would be severe on him next year. He was getting a headache. Looking over his shoulder, he inquired, "What is their commission on sales?"

"Just five percent," said Jimmy. "Lindsay intends to charge a shilling for admission and will sell catalogs, to defray his costs. Louise – stand still! The best part is, he'll send his assistants to our studios to pick up the paintings! No more sending the carter bumping my work through traffic."

"No, Jimmy!" Louise laughed. "The best part is, they have secured an address – in New Bond Street."

"You know what that means?" Tissot dropped back into the cane chair and leaned forward with excitement. "Collectors can buy a painting while they're out shopping for jewels and or cigars. Brilliant!"

"Smack during the Academy show, too," Jimmy pointed out, gesturing with his fistful of long paintbrushes that flicked paint onto his face and shirt.

"They have taken on two gallery assistants to solicit contributions," Louise said, "and I told Blanche that I would speak to you both. She's spoken with Millais, of course, since she first hatched her plan."

"Millais!" scoffed Tissot. "He has been a member of the Royal Academy for years – do you really believe he would participate?"

"Oh, yes, he's a great admirer of Lady Lindsay, and he and I have been thick as thieves about it all. He is no snob." Louise smiled broadly. "Leighton, you know, as president of the Academy, told Lindsay that the Grosvenor was unpatriotic."

Jimmy sneered, "For siphoning talent off the Academy exhibition?"

"He calmed down," Louise laughed, "once they assured him that they did not require their artists to choose them over the Academy – and after they promised him space to show as well."

Tissot wryly took in their glee. He leaned the chair back at an angle and murmured, "Still, it is subversive." He asked Louise, "You are contributing?"

"Most definitely. Blanche is making a special point that the Grosvenor will promote female artists, equally. In fact, she'll have a watercolor room for us. She is making a significant investment of her own funds in all of this."

"What will you send?" Tissot prodded her. He wanted to know what types of pictures his would be among.

She shook her head. "You know my husband took *Five Sisters of York* to Philadelphia, and it achieved fair success there. But I must still depend on my portraits."

Joe Jopling, who had been appointed Superintendent of English Art for the Philadelphia Exposition, had been in America nearly all year. James had kept well away from her – or had she, from him? Actually, he had heard that Louise wanted to accompany her husband, but could not bring herself to leave her baby boy.

He set the chair down on all four legs and praised her. "There could be no better advertisement than your exquisite head of Miss de Rothschild at the Royal Academy this summer."

Whistler erupted, "Ha! Ha! A far cry from the days when you served as your own model, Louise. For the last time, *don't move!*" He gestured at her with his long, mesmerizing finger tips.

Louise smiled ruefully.

Tissot tapped a forefinger near his temple and mulled her proposal. Manet's painting of a woman washing clothes in a tub in her garden had been peremptorily rejected by the Paris Salon. Now he advertised his studio open to the public for a one-man show, calling it *Faire Vrai, Laisser Dire* – Do What's True, Let them Talk. His studio, a former fencing gallery overlooking the Place de l'Europe, was spacious and bright. And though it was frequented by actresses and courtesans, Manet exerted himself to polish his image as a hard-working, respectable *bourgeois*. He had become a celebrity in Paris. A pamphlet was even published a few months ago, extolling his genius.

James tugged at the ends of his mustache. How much more advantageous it would be, after last year's criticism, for the reviewers to see his work hung as a body! And if the Hanging Committee meant to chastise him for *The Thames* – well, he had no intention of courting the humiliation of a public rejection. With Kate living in his house…perhaps this was the moment to move away from the Academy, toward something altogether more progressive.

"Solo shows are expensive," Jimmy remarked, running at the canvas with a loaded brush. "But this – this has all the advantages of a one-man show, with none of the risks."

Tissot asked Louise, "Will my work be relegated to the 'Foreign Art' wing?"

"James! What nonsense!" Louise looked hurt, and James felt momentary shame for directing his bitterness at her, of all people. "What Lord Lindsay would like to do is emphasize the international participation of the enterprise." To Tissot's pessimistic expression, she said, "He wants to make your work *more* prominent. Jimmy's, too. He expects great things of you both."

Tissot had to admit to himself that there was something monumentally fortunate in the Lindsays' timing, considering his relationship with Kathleen. In Paris, he believed he made a start at reestablishing his name by exhibiting his prints at Durand-Ruel's gallery. Durand-Ruel featured them at his gallery in London as well. James had taken pains to locate new venues, exhibiting pictures in North Wales and the Border Counties and even at the Glasgow Institute of Fine Arts. He continued to look out for new dealers. Marsden was a gambler who liked the high life and was always in debt. James could not rely on him to sell his pictures.

James mentally tallied his income for the year to date, including his sales from prints and his payments from *Vanity Fair* cartoons. He was earning more than ever, but if gossip spread about Kathleen Newton...

Finally, he yielded to temptation and bowed his head at Louise. "I will exhibit at the Grosvenor, only."

Jimmy's black eyebrows darted upward. "And leave the Royal Academy high and dry?"

James knew there would be no going back, that he was severing his relationship with the Royal Academy. *They will never make me a member, anyway – to hell with them.* He threw his arms open. "Louise, please tell Lord and Lady Lindsay they have my full support – and that they should reserve plenty of room for Tissot's paintings."

Louise offered him her applause, and Jimmy held up a

fist in victory. "Good man! I'm in, of course. The biggest showplace calls for the biggest talent!"

"There will be a banquet for the opening of the exhibition," Louise told them, "and you both must come."

Tissot and Jimmy exchanged a quick glance: wives always were invited. They must attend as bachelors.

There was a silent understanding between James and Louise Jopling, that he could no longer invite her to his Grove End Road home, and that she could no longer call. James wondered if she had listened to gossip, or if Joe Jopling did not like her associating with him. In any case, Louise was discreet, and the subject was never alluded to.

Any awkwardness that might have attended Mrs. Jopling's comprehension of their thoughts was interrupted when Whistler began to clean his brushes. At their quizzical expressions, he announced, "That's it! Contrary to critical opinion, it *can* be done!"

"Finished already?" Louise, incredulous, climbed down from the platform to have a look. Jimmy offered a hand with the train of her loose, artistic gown.

Tissot stood and made a joke of consulting his pocket watch. "One hour and a half. Your beauty is quickly observed, Louise!"

Louise shook her head in comical impatience, and gathering up the yards of sheer fabric spilling around her, she said, "And now you must excuse me, gentlemen, for it is time for me to turn back into a pumpkin!"

"Is that what you call it, being a wife and mother?" Whistler chortled.

"No, a painter," she replied, stealing the last laugh.

When she was safely out of earshot, James asked him, "What did she say?"

"She misses being invited to your 'delightful dinners.' Word is out that you're living with a married woman."

Whistler grasped the lapels of his short jacket. "She seems concerned about you.

"No doubt, Joe Jopling is aware..."

"He is a very great friend, so I'll be the first to admit that Joe is an old grey collie dog," Whistler said, giving him an amused look. "But as a husband, he falls under the heading 'be careful what you wish for.' "

"What have you heard?" James asked sharply.

"Oh, you don't know? Joe resigned from his position at the War Department to go to Philadelphia. In any case, his income never could pay for the studio in Chelsea that Louise needs if she is to attract Society commissions. Joe's paintings aren't in high demand even though his watercolor won that medal at the Crystal Palace. Louise must support them both, so she's more than doubled the number of pictures she paints. I'm afraid she's wearing herself out."

And then only to be known as "Joe Jopling's wife"! In his embarrassment for Louise, James said, "I must get back to *la belle irlandaise*." He remembered to ask, "How is Maud? When will she be able to model for you again?"

"The little one is kicking inside her," Jimmy laughed. "Three months left of peace and quiet before the Muse returns."

ॐॐॐ

It was the butler's night off, and Whistler ushered a very pregnant Maud Franklin into the foyer of Tissot's home in Grove End Road. He helped her remove her long military-style ulster coat. Underneath, she wore an excessively frilled maternity dress.

Tissot was surprised that Jimmy had not married her, but he was not one to cast the first stone regarding irregular personal lives. He greeted them and Kate kissed Maud, who was just a few years younger than she.

The two women had made fast friends, and Maud asked, "And how are Violet and Cecil? Do they need more fairy tales?"

"Violet and Cecil come with my sister's children for tea most days. When James can spare the time, he joins us. The girls persist in calling him 'Mister Sir'!"

James watched, pleased, as they linked arms and caught up on their latest favorite novel, *Daniel Deronda*. Kate told him that the lady novelist George Eliot made Dickens' work seem so old-fashioned that she would no longer read it.

"Did you see the *Morning Post*?" Whistler cackled to Tissot, as he arranged his black curls like a woman. "Leyland is rather upset with me."

"You did bring reporters into his house behind his back, Jimmy."

"Of course, so they could see the Peacock Room as a work in progress – and the gold leaf I added to all of his lattice bric-a-brac shelves!"

I would be furious, too, if Jimmy threw a public party in my home while I was out of town. Leyland was a significant patron, and Tissot could hardly believe Jimmy was so careless about offending him. But there was no point telling Whistler anything, especially regarding his finances.

Tissot waved them into his studio. "I have been hard at work as well. Come and see the pictures I have completed for the Grosvenor, so far."

"Are they all of Kate?" Maud laughed.

"Mostly!" Kate grinned. Wearing a flowered cotton dress and simple hairstyle, she seemed to consider it a good joke.

Tissot winked at her. "But no one will ever know. The public will only see a beautiful woman." He kissed Kate's cheek. "This one is called *Summer*, one of a series of the seasons. I am using strontium yellow in my green." He picked up a newfangled metal tube of pigment. "These new colors are pure, and so bright. By painting over white, I can capture the sun in my garden."

"Oh, I like this!" gushed Maud, turning to another picture in a heavy gilt frame.

"This is *The Ball*." He had painted Kathleen in a vivid yellow gown, making a grand entrance at a Society event on the arm of a grey-haired gentleman.

"What else have you got?" said Jimmy, his eyes roving restlessly over Tissot's canvases. He fixed his monocle and stared at one with his usual sardonic grin. "What is this, eh? It isn't half bad."

"This is *Holyday*," said James, smoothly, ignoring the insult. "Since the Lord's Cricket Ground is around the corner, I invited several of the members for tea if they would pose in my garden."

Kate said, "I have never laughed so much in my life!"

"Dandy!" Whistler cried. Tissot knew he was acknowledging Kate's excitement, not complimenting the picture. But Whistler's smile was irresistible, and though Tissot knew better, he tried to convince himself it was an apology of sorts.

Maud drew up close, inspecting every detail of the modern-day picnic among leisured young men and women. "You've captured it all, James, even to the bottles of mineral water. Makes me feel that I'm there with them," she said.

Jimmy pointed to a very different picture. "What do you think you're doing with this heroic stuff?"

"Ah, this is the first in a series, *The Triumph of Will*," James explained. "This is *The Challenge*...you see I have represented Will as a *belle dame* in armor, attended by her servants, Daring and Reserve. She wields her sword against Vice and Temptation – half woman, half tiger."

Kate and Maud both looked at the tiger skin rug that James painted from and exchanged a giggle.

Whistler clucked his tongue. "Pandering? Hardly your style, James."

"They will appeal to Ruskin," Tissot insisted. "A poem in paint in five parts, to include *The Temptation*, *The Rescue*, *The Victory* and *The Reward*."

"Yes, that is just the sort of thing Ruskin prefers. Ha! Ha! I feel morally uplifted already!"

Jimmy Whistler had always spoken of Tissot's art in this denigrating way, but decency prevented James from pointing out how much more successful he was. As always, he just absorbed the blows.

Maud poked her elbow at Whistler. "Jimmy, stop!"

"Ah, but you have provided the antidote," Jimmy said, admiring the prominent, bustled *derrière* of a woman bending over a ship's rail.

"That's HMS Calcutta," Tissot said, now feeling really defensive. "A little flirtation scene – that one will be the first to sell, I assure you."

"*Très risqué*," said Maud. "Your pictures have such wit! If I had the money, I'd buy this one myself."

Whistler ignored her delight in his friend's painting and put his thumbs under the lapels of his short jacket. "Ruskin can't fail to notice my *Nocturnes* at last. He must not have been to the Dudley Gallery last year to see *The Falling Rocket*, but he'll get his chance at the Grosvenor! And I've touched up my *Arrangement in Black No. 3*, the portrait of Henry Irving." He boasted, "The Peacock Room takes all my time, so I have little that is new. But Leyland pays."

James was shocked at his cavalier attitude. "Jimmy, can you not produce some new paintings for the Grosvenor?"

"Why, when hardly anyone has seen my *Falling Rocket*?"

James thought he was making a big mistake, exhibiting at a major venue with so little advance effort. *The Falling Rocket* – what Jimmy subtitled the *"Nocturne in Black and Gold"* – was hideous, he thought, hardly Jimmy's best work. But he valued Whistler's friendship, and only said, "You must be the first artist who has painted the night, Jimmy."

"And James must be the first to paint *through* the night!" Kathleen said, with a peal of laughter. "He is at his easel all day, and if I did not model for him, I would rarely see him."

James slipped his arm around her waist and drew her to him. Then he chuckled. "My father would like to know I am not the lazybones I once was. I never could pay attention to my teachers and was always drawing when they were not looking. I had to take my exams three times."

"And I was expelled from West Point," Jimmy reminded him, "but the two of us will be the most talked-of artists in the Grosvenor Exhibition!" Whistler piped up, "We are redeeming our ill-spent youth, you and I!"

For both their sakes, Tissot could hardly wait for the Grosvenor's opening night. He broke out the champagne.

Chapter XXII

The Grosvenor Gallery
135-137 New Bond Street, Exhibition Opening
May 4, 1877

Once past the traffic of carriages and cabs blocking the street before the Grosvenor Gallery's four-storey Italianate façade, Tissot paused to orient himself in the crush. The foyer was too vast to take in all at once. Its aristocratic murals and inlaid tables, covered with Japanese porcelain, swept past his vision in a blur of modern gas light that reminded him of former times in Paris.

He passed through the turnstile, and an attendant took his coat and hat while another offered him a catalog. James handed over his two shillings, adjusted his impeccable evening suit, and took a deep breath. Kate had not looked like herself when he left, but he attributed her pallor to her overwrought emotions and the sharp words they had exchanged over his outing. Usually so placid, joking more often than not, and hardly self-pitying, her social nonexistence did hurt her. When the hansom cab had arrived to take him away, she had bitterly turned her back on him, crying, "I am a sinner, and they all are saints? Go, dine with the saints, James!"

He rarely left her in the evening, but he really was beside himself with anticipation of finally achieving the recognition he deserved at the Grosvenor Gallery opening. He caught many familiar faces in the tide of VIPs swelling up the stairs to the first-floor galleries. Millais and the Joplings, Sir Jules Benedict and his wife, Tommy Bowles, Prime Minister Gladstone, and Walter Crane, who illustrated some of the fairy tales Kate read to her children. One of Sir Coutts Lindsay's gallery assistants was escorting Madame Neruda, the violinist. Tissot felt his heart pound to see the dealer William Agnew, as well as art critic and dramatist Tom Taylor, whom he had met through Millais years ago and who was now editor of *Punch*.

Ruskin is sure to be here.

Flipping through the catalog, Tissot saw that his paintings were among the first listed – one of the "international artists" whose pictures hung in the East Gallery. He had never felt so conspicuously foreign, so sure to be watched and appraised as one of the few contemporary artists who were not British. Just last month in Paris, Degas and his friends had held a third exhibition of "Impressionist" art, which failed miserably; Tissot feared some guilt by association.

At the top of the broad steps, James joined the queue to greet Lord and Lady Lindsay, and to admire a life-sized portrait of Lady Lindsay playing violin. Lord Lindsay, whom Whistler called "the handsomest man in London," hailed from one of Scotland's oldest families. His wife was a darkly beautiful Rothschild *parvenu* who in her younger days had modeled for both Millais and Holman Hunt, and she gushed kindly over James.

Formalities over, James gave way to his nervous excitement and turned into the East Gallery, racing past his own exhibit to the main gallery behind it. Tissot's strategy was to slip through the large West Gallery as quickly as the social parade would allow – and then double back to spend the majority of the evening near his own exhibit. He was not sure what he would find. Who – besides Millais – might outshine him?

He entered the cavernous West Gallery only to face a huge canvas labeled *Love and Death*. Death, a veiled phantom, loomed over a flowered doorway while Love, a little boy with crushed wings, shrank back, in a terrified attempt to bar the threshold of the House of Life. James stood before it, trembling with an inexplicable terror, as if it awakened a long-buried memory of some nightmare. He shook his head as if to wake himself.

Jimmy Whistler appeared at his side, wearing his distinctive short coat and cackling.

"What a dreadful thing to put on canvas," Tissot said, transfixed.

Whistler patted him on the back and cheerily advised him, "Go. See the other pictures, James. Ha! Ha! More importantly, *be* seen!" He held up his slender bamboo walking stick, now lampooned by *Punch* cartoonists. "I was the first one here, and since all the reporters know me from the Peacock Room," he said, gleefully rubbing his hands together, "my name will be in all the papers tomorrow!"

"Oh, Jimmy!" Tissot exhaled impatiently. *He makes himself more and more ridiculous.*

Lawrence Alma-Tadema stood in a circle of admirers, sipping champagne with his red-haired young wife, Laura. He had recently returned from a holiday in Rome, where he researched archaeological backgrounds for future pictures. Lawrence saw James from the corner of his eye and turned his back. They had not spoken since the day he had burst in on Tissot and *La Mystérieuse*. James scanned his half-dozen paintings as he sauntered past. They ranged from a very small one of Roman girls bathing under a splashing sphinx-topped bronze fountain to the ambitious *Phidias Showing the Frieze of the Parthenon to his Friends*, with its ingenious illusion of a view from a tower of scaffolding.

Alma-Tadema's paintings looked learned and eminently respectable compared to another artist's nearby sly nude, *Eve Tempted by the Serpent*. The life-sized, blue-eyed blonde thrusting her breasts forward had attracted a group of gentlemen admiring the picture's similarity to Florentine masters. More like, *The Serpent Tempted by Eve*, James chuckled to himself.

The long, seemingly endless gallery was hung with scarlet damask. Moving at the pace of the crowd along the wall of gilded frames, Tissot took in five pictures by Millais, who was off greeting everyone possible. Millais had contributed a portrait of the daughters of the Grosvenor Gallery's landlord, the Duke of Westminster. Above these delicate, wealthy ladies hung a smaller picture – a sad, impoverished little seamstress, surely the heroine of some popular poem. James took a deep breath in relief. *Millais' Grosvenor contributions are nothing, compared to the great works that made his reputation thirty years ago.*

Tissot thought the same when he saw the four pictures shown by the legendary Pre-Raphaelite Brotherhood's second founder, Holman Hunt. The third, Rossetti, had refused to cooperate with Lord and Lady Lindsay after they decided to allow members of the Royal Academy to exhibit at the Grosvenor Gallery.

Any fear that Tissot felt about staying on top dissipated.

ॐॐॐ

The crowd parted to make way for the towering Henry Irving, and again even more admiringly for the lady novelist George Eliot, who lived a reclusive life with the husband of another woman.

Tissot shook hands with Irving and wove his way in and out of the groups conversing along the main gallery, standing or seated on the velvet couches. He stopped at the end of the room, where dozens of men and women chattered excitedly. They formed a half-circle around a towering oil painting and a spare, pale man tugging at his straggling beard.

"What is it?" he asked an elderly bystander he knew from the Arts Club.

"*The Beguiling of Merlin,*" the gentleman informed him. "A scene from Arthurian legend – Merlin's infatuation with the Lady of the Lake as she casts her spell over him."

Tissot, unfamiliar with the allusion, stopped before the strangely sinister picture. The woman was all luscious gauze-draped thighs and bare feet.

The man could barely contain his wicked merriment. "A fair admission of the rumors."

"*Pardon?*" said Tissot.

"Of his affair with his model, that lady artist – the Greek." The man snickered at Tissot and pointed. "Further along in the gallery, you will see a portrait of *Mrs.* Burne-Jones – but not by her husband. At least the Lindsays' gallery assistants had the tact to hang it away from this!"

Tissot laughed. "To think, in Paris, the latest scandal is Manet's picture of a courtesan in her undergarments while a man – her client for the evening – waits. It is a scene from a novel."

"That is nothing, compared to this."

People around them were in raptures, exclaiming accolades, "Burne-Jones is the man of the hour!" and "He is like no one else – a poet in paint! Only a Philistine would not admire his genius."

Ruskin will have something to say about that.

Wending his way through the West Gallery, careful not to tread on silk trains, Tissot began to relax. Rather than feeling diminished by any of London's "greatest" contemporary artists, he was increasingly exasperated with the self-absorption of many of the offerings. Someone had painted a portrait of Burne-Jones, and someone else had done a head of the Duchess of Westminster, wife of the Grosvenor's landlord.

The Prince and Princess of Wales entered, with a retinue trailing their progress past the works on display. Everyone was rubbing elbows, making introductions to ramp up careers, or attempting to learn what others thought of the pictures.

But Tissot was satisfied there was nothing exhibited which could overshadow his own work.

Louise Jopling, on the arm of her white-haired husband, waved Tissot over to see her painting. She was spectacular in a crimson and gold gown fashioned from an Indian *sari*. But as James approached, Louise was pulled into the orbit of the Prince of Wales, who was flanked by his wife and his artistic and frail younger brother, Prince Leopold.

Tissot kept his distance; he never had cared for the Prince of Wales though he would have liked to meet Prince Leopold. Instead, he clasped his hands behind his back and studied Louise's painting of a melancholy girl leaning against an artistic screen, in a room filled with blue and white Oriental vases. It was called *It Might Have Been*.

"Ah, Mrs. Jopling," intoned the Prince, "Allow me to

introduce you to my wife, Alexandra, the Princess of Wales."

Louise made a deep curtsey, and Princess Alexandra took her hand and said in her thick Danish accent, "Mrs. Jopling, I like your picture very much. It is charming."

Now Louise's career will take off, James thought. Indeed, the royals' presence ensured the success of the Grosvenor, but Tissot had made his own success. The Prince eyed Tissot over Louise's shoulder and carried on his conversation with Joe.

James tried to maintain an air of indifference as he continued on, but his lip curled as he passed a few of the really dreadful works. Considering there were only two hundred works in the show, by sixty-four artists, Tissot found no surprises, except that Burne-Jones' beguiled *Merlin* was causing such a sensation.

Satisfied that he had seen everything, he slipped away to witness the reaction to his pictures back in the coveted corner of the East Gallery. He had counted, and he was now sure that he was the largest contributor to the Grosvenor's inaugural exhibition, showing ten pictures. He made a point of demonstrating the full range of his abilities. On top of that, he was exhibiting *Portsmouth Dockyard*, subtitled *How happy I could be with either*. After the outrage over the morality of last year's *The Thames*, he had painted this new version that replaced the hard-eyed naval officer with a cheerful, kilted Highlander. He felt certain it would redeem him in the eyes of his critics.

He scanned the room, still hoping to meet Ruskin, then stood back to take a long look at his collected paintings, neatly hung in two rows on the line – for once, all together, and at eye level. He strolled back and forth behind the gathering of admirers, pleased with the overall effect and variety: *The Gallery of the HMS Calcutta, Holyday (The Picnic), Portsmouth Dockyard, The Widower, The Triumph of Will, Portrait of Miss L...* Miss Lloyd was a professional model, but her striking portrait would attract commissions straight away.

When Tissot overheard two artistic ladies deliriously examining the figures in *HMS Calcutta*, he crossed his arms over his chest and listened; he had come to rely on the wives of moneyed men to collect his work.

"She looks so...*real*," said the woman nearer to Tissot. "Look at her flesh showing through the muslin of her bodice!"

The gentleman with them adjusted his spectacles and said, "One feels one could *touch* her."

The lady snapped her fan against his upper arm. "Better not!"

"No one handles paint like *Monsieur* Tissot. He is a virtuoso."

The man said, "You know it's been reproduced as an engraving in the *Graphic*? I shall dig mine out for you, as a souvenir."

"You are too good!"

James smiled and waited until they had moved along, then stood before *The Ball*. The critic Tom Taylor was particularly impressed by it, complimenting the unnamed model in her dazzling yellow gown and fan as "a figure worthy of Worth." James had depicted Kate, as vibrant as the Italian sun, at an elegant *soirée* – to which she never would be invited – on the arm of a much older man.

As much as James missed her tonight, her angry words were still ringing in his ears. It was a relief to be out again, alone. He felt free and masterful, as he used to.

అఅఅ

Farther down the gallery, Whistler by now was causing a commotion, standing on a chair and using his bamboo cane to point out the various merits of his paintings. Tissot shook his head at the sight of Jimmy holding court with journalists before his *Nocturne in Black and Gold: The Falling Rocket*, his depiction of a burst of fireworks raining gold, green and red sparks against the night sky over Cremorne Gardens. Countless nights, Jimmy had stayed out to gaze up into the dark, holding the memory in his heart until he returned to his studio. *Yet he produced this mess?* Tissot was disgusted with him.

Millais seized his friend, Tom Taylor the art critic, by the arm and dragged him past Tissot toward the crowd ridiculing Whistler's canvases, saying, "You must see this, Tom!" The two men affected a straight face as they ran their eyes over the portrait of Louise Jopling that Tissot had watched Jimmy paint in under two hours.

"Poor Louise! *Nocturne* or *Arrangement*, does he call it?" Millais mumbled to Tom, "It's damned clever – a damned sight too clever." They rejoined Millais' group across the room, where everyone but Lord Lindsay seemed to be laughing at Whistler's work. Lindsay looked likely to wring Jimmy Whistler's neck.

The Duke of Westminster joined them. "My dear Millais!"

Tom Taylor held up his wine glass and thanked the Duke for procuring a liquor license for the Grosvenor.

"It is necessary, if one is to appreciate some of this contemporary art," the duke smirked, clapping Tom on his stooped shoulder and with the other hand, patting Millais on the back.

A tall, long-haired university student dressed in a brown velvet suit with many buttons sailed into the gallery like an overgrown page boy. Tissot's eyes widened at the cloud of young followers who accompanied him, eager to hear his pronouncements on each picture.

He assumed a mannered pose before Jimmy Whistler's exhibit and quipped, "Ah, we come now to the color symphonies of the Great Dark Master, Mr. Whistler."

"These two ladies, evidently caught in a black London fog, look like sisters," he drawled in a deep, melodious voice, "but are not related probably, as one is a Harmony in Amber and Black, the other only an Arrangement in Brown." He paused and basked in the gale of laughter from his audience. "These pictures are certainly worth looking at for about as long as one looks at a real rocket," he added. "That is, for somewhat less than a quarter of a minute."

He beheld Tissot and sidled toward him in his knickerbockers with his fingers outstretched. After turning his head this way and that before *HMS Calcutta*, delaying his reaction for dramatic effect, he intoned, "It's rather a picture of her – *derrière*, isn't it? Such a refreshing change from the sentimental pictures preferred by Royal Academy." Amid more laughter from his friends, he took a sip of sherry from his glass, which seemed preposterously out of proportion to his huge, fleshy hand.

Tissot maintained a cool detachment. "She wears the same fashion of every lady here tonight."

The young Irishman gestured in a flamboyant curve around the woman's bottom. "That is why the nude is a form of refinement. This overdressed lady, or woman, I should say, appears to be someone...one could *know*. And she seems to be," he moved his lavender-gloved hand toward them, "*thrusting* herself at us, you see."

James appraised him like an adversary. "She is merely a modern woman at her leisure."

"Quite," the youth scoffed, continuing along the wall with

his entourage. "But an artist, if he wishes to gain immortality, should always strive to paint *interesting* things in an *interesting* manner."

Tissot's gloved hands were clenched in fists behind his back; he had to restrain himself from striking the fellow.

Tommy Bowles called out Tissot's name. James had not seen him since shortly after his son was born. A British handshake would not do; Tissot relaxed his arms and embraced him, even as his eyes followed the ridiculous student down the gallery. "Jess is home with the baby? How is she?"

"As near perfect as a wife and mother can be," Tommy grinned. "An unspeakable blessing, so bright and sweet and wise – a constant motive to be a better man, for her sake. When are you going to marry, James?"

Their attention was diverted by the Irishman in the outlandish velvet knee britches.

"Tommy, who in God's name *is* that character?"

Tommy Bowles laughed, "Oh, never mind Oscar Wilde. He's a promising young man, but now you know why some of his fellow Oxford students threw his china at him."

తితితి

The dancing went on for hours after the banquet in the reception hall on the ground floor. Tissot was mesmerized by Louise Jopling as she waltzed with Jimmy Whistler. Her beaded crimson gown sparkled as she whirred by. He waited for the right moment, then cut in.

Louise's square face lit up. She placed a slender gloved hand on his shoulder as he lightly gripped her waist, twirling her around the room. The embroidered train of her evening dress was caught up at her wrist with a ribbon.

"You look stunning tonight," James told her,

overwhelmed. "The show is a huge success, and you must take some of the credit."

"For the first time, artists got to see justice done to the creations of their brains." Louise was radiant. "Then you are happy I invited you?"

"I am very happy, now." It was like the days of his youth in Paris, staying up all night to drive to a ball and dance until morning. Savoring this moment of pure joy, James whirled Louise around the room until everyone else appeared like a vision through a stained-glass kaleidoscope. He knew they made a handsome pair. "Why do I feel the enemy is watching?"

"Surely not!" she laughed gaily. "But then, I have no enemies. At least I am unconscious of them, so that for me, they do not exist."

Tissot fixed his gaze on her lustrous brown eyes until she could no longer meet his scrutiny. He was aware of Joe Jopling, who had taken a position as an underling at an art gallery down the street, standing at the edge of the dance floor as they spun past him again and again. *Joe looks old enough to be her father*, he thought.

"Your picture," he asked. "*It Might Have Been*?"

"It was sold, for two hundred pounds!" Louise was breathless in her low-cut, corseted gown as he swirled her around. She colored, recalling his passion – and her own – on the river that day at Kew. "We passed some happy hours together." She whispered, "I hope you will forget my frailties...I found a calmer love, an abiding one. I pray for you, James."

From the corner of his eye, Tissot saw that Jimmy Whistler had joined the glowering Joe Jopling.

"Look at my husband!" Louise was giddy. "I am afraid he is giving me a very penetrating look. Does he not have a beautifully curved mouth?"

Joe Jopling stepped across the floor in his ill-fitting gaiters and tapped James on the shoulder.

"May I?" he said, and his ugly nose quivered with a stiff courtesy. He gave his wife a hangdog look and said, "Mole?"

Louise was flustered and made a little curtsey as Tissot gallantly handed her to her husband.

He made his way over to Whistler, who removed his monocle and thrust his thumbs under his lapels. James had never known Whistler to be silent, and he gave him a sidelong glance.

"Hmm," remarked Jimmy. "It's quite possible that Joe did not enjoy seeing his wife in the arms of a man twice as handsome and ten times wealthier."

Tissot chuckled scornfully and scanned the crowd at the edge of the room. Alma-Tadema, conversing with Lord and Lady Lindsay, turned his back. Nearby, *Punch* editor Tom Taylor lurked in a doorway, stooped and pulling at his great white beard. He fixed Tissot with a cold stare.

"Did you know it was I who introduced Joe to Louise?" Jimmy drawled, idly. "She is one of the few women I have ever known who enjoys a spotless reputation."

"You are Mrs. Grundy now?" Tissot had never felt more of an outsider. He swiped his hand over his mustache and murmured, "I must get back to *La Mystérieuse*."

❧❧❧

It was past two when Tissot returned home, still early by Society standards, but he felt exhausted. Moonlight streamed through the leaded glass transom over the front door. No letters on the hall table. He lit the candlestick near the mail tray and headed up the staircase.

On the landing, behind the closed door of the lavatory,

he could hear her sobbing and coughing, choking.

"Kathleen?" He rapped at the door and turned the knob. *She has locked me out.* He had never been annoyed with her, but this was too much, creating this hysterical scene. In fact, this behavior was unlike her. He knocked sharply, hoping that the servants could not hear from their quarters in the basement. "Kate, come to bed."

"Go *away!*"

Her coughing alarmed him; he sensed that she was not upset at him, but in some distress. "Kate! *Kathleen!* Open the door." She was running water; it sounded at high volume in the porcelain tub.

Tissot made his way back to his bedroom by the light of the candlestick and fumbled for a skeleton key. He returned and thrust it into the keyhole, but the key went in sideways and jammed. He managed to yank it out and tried it again, and then burst in on her.

She was bent over the tub, her back to him, and when she turned, he could see the blood stains on the front of her white linen nightdress. There were clumps of blood in the basin and dotting the black-and-white tiled floor. Kate was madly trying to wipe it all up with heavy cotton toweling, which she was rinsing and wringing in the tub. She put her wrist to her lips and was about to speak, but instead her pale features twisted and she uttered a guttural cry of desperation. Her lovely Irish eyes were huge in disbelief and horror.

This is not happening. James threw his arm around her narrow shoulders and held a towel near her chin, helping her to clean herself. "Hush," he comforted her, "hush now."

He wanted to throw his arms around her knees and sob, but instead he carried her back to their bed, arranged all the feather pillows under her head and shoulders, and watched over her until the sun rose.

Chapter XXIII

17 Grove End Road, St. John's Wood
May 10, 1877

The doctor had come and gone once again, and Kate was sleeping fitfully. Her feverish perspiration had soaked the sheets. A maid was stationed at her bedside with instructions to call him when she awoke. James slipped downstairs to the library, where his butler had left the usual pot of coffee and tray of *brioche* as if life were proceeding normally.

Consumption. The very word overwhelmed him with a numbness that would have to get him through the days, while he wept at night. It was a death sentence, allotting her a half-dozen more years at most. He poured a cup of coffee with a shaking hand, sopping up the spillage with a napkin. *Was this Courbet's damnation?* No sooner to have found happiness than to have this innocent woman caught up in a curse aimed at him. He feared this more than anything – being able to do nothing but stand by and watch, as he had his poor, suffering mother. Control over his happiness had been snatched from him by the Almighty, as it had before.

The one thing he could control – from which he had always derived his sense of mastery – was his career, and he tried to concentrate on this as a barricade against despair.

One by one, he scanned the morning papers, anticipating recognition of his body of work on show at the Grosvenor. The public response that he had observed at the gallery opening set his overtaxed mind moving, like a machine, to all the possibilities for sales of replicas, variations and reproductions of his paintings.

He poured himself more coffee and flipped through the small stack of papers on his desk. The critics all seemed obsessed with Rossetti's *protégé*, Burne-Jones. For a man who had shown only two paintings in public since Tissot could remember, he was everywhere being touted as the herald of the "Aesthetic Style" – art for art's sake, without meaning or morality. It made James' blood boil; he did not understand the fuss over a man painting from his strange dreams, unacceptable to the Royal Academy since his picture of a nude man and woman scandalized London several years ago. After the painting was declared indecent and removed, he only displayed his work in his studio.

Nonetheless, he was everywhere being celebrated as practically the reason the Lindsays had created the Grosvenor Gallery. According to the critics, Burne-Jones was "finally getting his long-due recognition." Tissot rubbed his eyes and stretched his legs out before him. He checked his urge to run upstairs and look in on Kathleen, only because she needed her sleep.

He idly unfurled *The Yorkshire Post and Leeds Intelligencer*. It contained the only review of his own pictures James had seen so far. He ran his eyes down the column, absorbing a comment on *Holyday*. The critic referred to the picnic scene in his garden as taking place amid an "unhealthy-looking pool and luxuriant vegetation."

Tissot folded the paper and tossed it aside to sip the last of his coffee. *Once this mania for Burne-Jones blows off, reason will return*. He leaned back in his leather chair, exhausted.

The butler slipped in, and Tissot leapt to his feet, ready to comfort Kathleen. He wondered how she would look this morning, and how soon she would have another fit. How long would he have her?

"Sir, Mr. Bowles to see you."

Tissot froze in a momentary terror. He had declined more than one invitation to dine with Tommy and Jessica Bowles at Cleeve Lodge. Had Tommy come to confront him about Kathleen? *Not today!* In a low voice, he said, "When she awakens, Mrs. Newton will take her breakfast in her room."

"Very good, sir." The older man bowed and, on his way out, tucked her novel under his arm.

Tissot scanned the room, saw her paisley shawl on a chair in a corner, and barely had time to fold it under a cushion before Tommy Bowles strode through the library door. Too late, James noticed that Kate's black onyx rosary fell to the floor.

"James! Glad to find you at home. I am in a state – the Prince is trying to ruin me!"

"Tommy! Please –" James said, gesturing at a seat away from the one hiding Kate's shawl. He fumbled to scoop up the rosary and slip it into his pocket.

"His Royal Highness – Tum-Tum, the Prince of Wales, is upset that *Vanity Fair* reported he sacked his Indian cook and sent him packing back to the subcontinent. 'No ladies will henceforth have to smile approval while the roof of their mouth is being burnt off by the devilish arts of the heathen.' "

Tissot ran a hand through his thick hair and chuckled with relief. *Is this all?*

Tommy gave him a dark look and threw himself into the armchair. "The Prince is pressuring my writer, and I am afraid word will get around. I've just lost a prime source of gossip – a certain aristocratic lady with an ear for news has been found out by her husband – and I don't need to lose writers as well. I sent a deferential note to His Royal Tum-Tum to the effect that I am at a loss to account for the personal animosity he has shown me for the past few years. He even has implied to Gus Burnaby – barely unpacked from Asia Minor – that he would do well to drop me."

"Do you believe he had a hand in the election?" Tissot, distracted, only knew Tommy had been humiliated by his loss after the long Parliamentary campaign a few years back.

"That? Who knows? I have always publicly defended the Royal Family, so I don't at all understand his hostility," Bowles fumed.

Tissot felt the weight of the beads in his frock coat and wondered if they showed. He was at a loss for advice and moved across the room. *I should be up there with her.* It was early in the day, but he offered, "Drink?"

Tommy accepted the glass Tissot poured for him. "Why, only last year, when...certain letters... came to light, His Royal Highness sent an advisor to me. And I did take active steps to prevent their publication." Bowles threw his head back against the chair. When Tissot made no comment, he glanced at him, then continued. "If the Prince of Wales uses his great influence to detach my private friends from

278

me and to deprive my magazine of its writers, he will inflict on me the gravest possible injury. Now that Jess and I are so settled, and we have little George…"

Tissot realized he must make some reply. "But you have been on friendly terms with him for years. Why would he use his position to ruin you? He must have more important tasks before him than such petty revenges."

"These constantly recurring incidents of the same nature seem to point to the painful impression that he is trying to make me a pariah, and I regret to say he has not done or said anything to remove that impression."

James downed his drink and paced to the window, fingering the onyx rosary beads in his pocket. He wondered if God would restore *La Mystérieuse* if he would go to Mass, confess his sins, say a rosary a day…two rosaries, four rosaries? *The battle of life.* He rubbed his forehead and murmured, "You have endured worse things, Tommy."

"I suppose one must make peace with certain realities. Even the heroic Gus must tread carefully."

Tissot stared outside at the bright sky and the well-dressed people out for a promenade in the park. That was just how he had first set eyes on Kate, not even two years ago. He leaned against the window frame, inhaled and glanced over his shoulder. "Don't get cynical, now."

"I *am* cynical, James – that's why people love *Vanity Fair*." Tommy looked at Tissot and abruptly began laughing. "You know, if the Grosvenor Gallery is to become merely an artistic lounge for the worshippers of the Fleshly School of Art, you really should paint Mrs. Langtry."

"*Pardon?*"

"You have not met the most splendid creature that has ever taken hold of London? She arrived out of nowhere – well, Jersey. She says she is in mourning for her brother. Always wears the same sublimely simple black gown. All the artists are scrambling to paint her."

"She is that stunning?" James answered dully. *Kate will waste away before my eyes.*

Tommy gave Tissot a meaningful look. "So far beyond the Pretty with which we are usually more than content that she is like some newer and more perfect creature. The Prince of Wales has been seen riding side by side with her in Rotten Row."

"An official mistress?"

"His first." Tommy said. "And while lesser men hide theirs in the suburbs, word has it that the Prince has introduced Mrs. Langtry to his wife."

He does not know. For a brief moment, James considered telling him. What a comfort it would be to unburden himself to Tommy, perhaps the one friend he had who was capable of compassion. James smiled uneasily. But instead, he tried to offer prudent advice to hasten Tommy's departure. "Do you recall, you once told me that the Prince of Wales could undo me any time he wished? You said I needed to remain in his good graces."

"*Yes,*" Tommy admitted, pulling a face of exaggerated annoyance.

"Write something flattering about Mrs. Langtry in your magazine."

Reluctantly, like the loyal British subject he was, Tommy Bowles rose to do his duty. James patted his old friend on the shoulder and accompanied him to the door, saying, "Then go home to your good wife and give her my kindest regards."

࿇࿇࿇

Tissot concentrated on the painting on his easel set up in his colonnaded garden. With the new tubes of paints, it was easier than ever to paint out of doors, and he was working up a background for a lighthearted painting of the children. They were affectionate to him and each other, and he had grown fond of them as well as Polly Hervey's daughter, Lilian, who was inseparable from Violet.

Kate reclined on the wicker *chaise longue*, with Violet and Lilian alternately chasing each other around the pond and climbing up to hug her. The doctor's prescribed regimen of rest and nourishing food had quieted her symptoms, and her color had returned somewhat. She and James exchanged a smile, and he allowed himself to hope for the future.

Polly's nursemaid dandled Cecil on her knee. She had brought along their new dog, a black Border collie, a gift from James to distract Violet from her mother's ill health. It ran to chase a neighbor's tennis ball that flew over the garden wall.

"Violet," Kate finally called out in the girls' direction, "go now, and play so Mummy can read." She began catching up with a stack of reading, enviously devouring the details of the Grosvenor Gallery's splendor. "*Dublin University Magazine* has a review of the Grosvenor, dear." Under her straw hat, Kate tipped a puzzled face to him. "Oscar Wilde?"

"Oh, not that fool. I wonder how much they paid for his nonsense? What can he have to say?"

Kathleen flipped through the pages. "Let me see... 'Nearly all of Mr. Tissot's pictures are deficient in feeling and depth... he has a hard unscrupulousness...' " She bit her lip and scanned the column, continuing, "Here, he's referring to *Holyday*... 'overdressed, common-looking people...ugly, painfully accurate representation of modern soda-water bottles....' "

Tissot was genuinely surprised. "Members of the I

Zingari cricket team, taking tea after a match at Lord's? It is an old Etonian club! And what does the ugly, painfully overdressed and common-looking Oscar Wilde have to say of Burne-Jones?"

" 'Burne-Jones is one of the greatest masters of color that we have ever had in England... He is a dreamer in the land of mythology, a seer of fairy visions, a symbolical painter: faith, and love, and reverence, the three golden keys to the gate of the House Beautiful.' "

"*Mon Dieu.*"

"Oh, James! Listen to this: 'Then come eight pictures by Alma-Tadema, good examples of that accurate drawing of inanimate objects which makes his pictures so real from an antiquarian point of view, and of the sweet subtlety of coloring which gives to them a magic all their own... very perfect indeed... delightful... wonderful... a world of atmosphere and reality... very cleverly managed.' " Kate drew an irate breath and held the magazine out to him.

James, disgusted, waved it away.

Kate said, "It's because they are British."

"Perhaps, but Wilde has made a point of slighting Millais as well."

A clatter at the back of the house signaled Whistler. He barged through the studio door and down the steps into the garden, kicking the children's toys.

The dog ran to him, barking, and the nurse pulled it and the two excited girls away from the visitor.

"Ruskin!" he shrieked, gripping his little bamboo walking stick like a horse whip. "They all will take their cue from him."

"He thinks we are undermining the Royal Academy?" Tissot remarked, without looking up from the greenery he was painting. *There goes a day's work.*

Jimmy, enjoying being the center of an uproar, was

slapping at the journal in his hand. "He objects to the 'exorbitant prices' which 'degrade the productions even of distinguished genius into marketable commodities'... he particularly objects to my asking two hundred guineas for the *Nocturne* – 'deficient in craftsmanship and labor, and immoral in its neglect of the painter's duty to express noble ideas – ' "

Tissot put down his brush and wiped his hands with some exasperation. The tennis-playing artist next door was friendly enough, but his whole clique of small-time English painters did not need to hear Tissot's business. Kate sat up, intending to greet Jimmy, but Whistler ignored her; he was on a tirade.

"He smears us all as tradesmen, as if we are grocers hawking turnips! He says, 'Sir Coutts Lindsay is at present an amateur both in art and shop-keeping. He must take up either one or the other business, if he would prosper in either.' "

"He calls the Grosvenor 'a shop'?" Tissot, covering his paints, shook his head. "Let me see that." Ruskin praised Burne-Jones, then attacked Whistler. James read the review aloud to Kate:

> *For Mr. Whistler's own sake, no less than for the protection of the purchaser, Sir Coutts Lindsay ought not to have admitted works into the Grosvenor Gallery in which the ill-educated conceit of the artist so nearly approached the aspect of willful imposture. I have seen, and heard, much of Cockney impudence before now; but never expected to hear a coxcomb ask two hundred guineas for flinging a pot of paint in the public's face.*

Whistler, grabbing his journal back, howled, "It is the most debased style of criticism I have had thrown at me yet!" Jimmy looked at Tissot's impassive expression and poked his walking stick toward his chest. "The Grosvenor exhibition was to make my reputation! You know damned well that Ruskin can ruin me – I'll never sell another picture."

Tissot had never seen Jimmy so serious – devastated, in fact. But even the children at their play were more considerate of Kate's peace than Whistler. James was concerned for her quiet even more than his own.

"He has it in for us all, James! He says most of *your* paintings are 'subversive,' and that your subject matter depends 'on a highly unstable form of irony,' 'unhappily, mere colored photographs of vulgar society.' " Whistler made an exasperated sound and affixed his monocle.

"Here – *Monsieur Tissot's pictures require a special notice, because their dexterity and brilliancy are apt to make the spectator forget their conscientiousness... Paintings of vulgar middle-class boating parties, portraits of overdressed ironmongers' daughters and their pomaded swains in brand-new suits* – read it for yourself!"

James felt nauseated: this threat to his career had materialized at last. Why should Ruskin attack him? But Jimmy wanted to rile him into mounting a full-bore defense against a common enemy. *Always spoiling for a fight.*

Another tennis ball flew over the high brick wall, and Tissot caught it and hurled it back toward his neighbor's garden, the dog in noisy pursuit and the girls shouting with laughter and following after it. Kate made room for James at the end of the *chaise longue*, and he sat on the edge with his arm around her.

Whistler ranted on. "Oscar Wilde even gets into the fray! Have you seen the *Dublin University Magazine*?"

"*Oui*," James said wearily, "but they will not stop my pictures from selling." Kate slipped her hand into his, and they exchanged a glance. He realized that his increasingly secluded life with her did, in fact, insulate him from the worst. And now, he cared less. "The bankers and brokers and 'ironmongers' who buy my work do not care what such people think."

"That's just dandy! Bah! *Your* paintings may still sell," Whistler bristled. "It's my own hide that is of concern to me. I'm of a mind to sue the wretch."

James held up his palm. "*Un moment*, Jimmy." He asked the footman to bring tea for Kate and the children, then rose and adjusted Kate's pillows as she lay down again.

She whispered, "Be calm, James, if only for my sake."

"For your sake, I would like to show him the door!"

She kissed him and smiled. "Really... we have so few friends... it would hurt me if you and Jimmy were estranged. Maud could no longer call..."

James took a deep breath, then strolled back to Whistler, took his arm, and drew him off to the courtyard at the side of the house.

"How is your lawsuit against Leyland progressing?" James asked evenly. "I heard at the Club that you broke into Leyland's house and painted two fighting peacocks on his wall."

Jimmy's blue eyes flashed. "One with a paint brush and the other holding a bag of the filthy lucre!"

"He claims you destroyed the antique Spanish leather wall coverings."

"Well, you know, I just painted on — putting in every touch – and the harmony in blue and gold developing, you know, I forgot everything in my joy of it. Even the fact that

I had no business contract." Whistler drew arabesques with his walking stick, then punctuated his words by spiking it into the ground. "Leyland hasn't paid for the confounded thing, yet I have made him famous. My work will live on when Leyland is forgotten. I told him, in the dim ages to come, he will be remembered only as the proprietor of the Peacock Room!"

Tissot folded his arms over his chest. "They say you are seeing his wife."

"Why? Because she happened to let herself in while I was there?"

James shot him an impatient look. "I saw you walking with her at the Lord's Cricket Grounds last Friday."

Whistler thrust his thumbs under the lapels of his short coat and met his eyes. "Is it wrong to speak to a woman who always has been kind to me?" He cleared his throat. "And having counted to ten now, I'm going straight to my solicitor. I will order him to draw up a writ for libel and have it served on Ruskin."

"For how much?" Tissot inquired.

"Why, for what Leyland owes me – one thousand pounds – plus the costs of the action."

"Jimmy, what would that accomplish?"

"They can't ruin a man on a whim! And if they try, I will be carried even higher by the publicity!"

Tissot gazed at Whistler, who was red in the face. The popular press had taken to lampooning Whistler as a glib, racy devil, with his white forelock and monocle and outrageous pronouncements on art. But taking a British institution to court was beyond mad.

"Jimmy, two lawsuits? You are a gentleman. What would your mother say?"

"That her Jemmie should be compensated and his genius recognized by all!" Whistler straightened the loose silk bow at his neck and twirled his walking stick to rest against his forearm. "In a few weeks, I will be commissioning the most *avant-garde* architect in London to design me a new studio on the best street in Chelsea."

Tissot ran his hand through his hair, beside himself. "Can you not wait? You are deeply in debt, Jimmy."

Whistler shoved his fists in his trouser pockets, took a deep breath, and moved his eyes over the breadth of Tissot's home and gardens, from the ornamental pond and black iron colonnade, to the conservatory and studio on the rise above them. "My good Tissot, if it were your livelihood at stake, I doubt you would be so philosophical." He made a mocking bow and added, "You know, I had to take a cab to get here, and the driver hasn't a clue how empty my pockets are just now."

Tissot, disgusted, wordlessly handed Whistler a few shillings.

From a distance, Kathleen quietly watched. After Whistler stomped away and Tissot rejoined her, she said, "James, is there nothing you can do?"

Before he could answer, his silk-stockinged footman brought him a tray. "Telegram, sir."

Tissot opened it. "My brother – my father's heir – has died." He raised his eyes to Kate and said, "How would you like to see Paris?"

కాకాకా

Chapter XXIV

Paris

September 14-15, 1877

The doctor was right – the change of air was doing Kate a world of good.

When James entered the airy sitting room of their suite at the Hotel Normandy, opposite the Louvre, Kate was bounding around in a corset and cage bustle and her new square-toed high heels. She had arranged her light brown hair in a low chignon at her nape and had curled the fringe at her brow, in the fashion set by Mrs. Langtry back home. Dress and hat boxes from the House of Worth, their lids tucked underneath, covered every surface in the room.

"James, you are just in time! I am trying on each and every article, and you are going to fasten me up, starting with the Irish lace evening gown."

"How I have missed you!" James kissed her throat and shoulders until she laughingly pushed him away and insisted he help her into the gown.

Tissot's villa in the avenue du Bois de Boulogne, a shell of its former glory without his splendid studio and conservatory, his English garden, and all the stained-glass, now was occupied by his old friend from the trenches of Malmaison, Berne-Bellecour. He had overseen basic repairs and set up Tissot's former drawing room as his studio. Tissot was too discreet to expect to bring Kate there to stay with Madame Berne-Bellecour and their young son.

James also had no desire to stay when just two doors down, the wife of a famous playwright had built a new townhouse – which she had crammed with every Oriental treasure she could lay her hands on. Since Tissot had almost emptied the import shops before the war to build the largest collection of Chinese and Japanese *objets d'art* in France or England, the looters, antique dealers and curiosity shops of Paris surely turned a profit from Tissot's villa.

He would never get out of his head the bloodbath on the barricades in the avenue de l'Impératrice six years ago, the faces of the soldiers he had killed, the voice of Courbet, cursing him to hell forever...it would be bad luck for him to stay in the villa now.

The Hôtel de Ville and the Palace of the Tuileries were still heaps of ruins. But their hotel was new, close to the Champs-Élysées, and their sunny windows overlooked the River Seine. James arranged Kate's beaded train for her and asked, "And how was Suzanne Manet?"

"She is so very kind!" Kate pulled a long white glove up her arm as he admired her. "We shopped and talked and played piano to our hearts' content. I am glad *Maman* Manet had to go attend her other son."

Tissot could not help chuckling at the little conspiracy to keep Kate with Édouard Manet's wife for the weekend. "*Oui*, though of course we all are sorry Eugène is ill!"

"Did all go well with your father?" She adjusted the fit of her slender fingers in the second glove.

"It is a bitter thing for him, to lose a third son. And Marcel's wife! *Pauvre petit*, she has a son and three daughters to raise."

"And how are you?" Kate asked softly, grasping him from behind and leaning her cheek on his back.

Tissot shook his head. "My father set great store by my oldest brother. Marcel shared his political views, and becoming mayor of Rigney was an achievement my father could only have dreamed of for himself." He interlaced his fingers with Kate's. "My father never believed in me; it was all my mother."

"Why is it a question of what he believes? Your success is real."

"But I can never be *good* enough, as a man, as a Catholic." He pulled away and sat before her, marveling at her beauty.

"Still, he will leave you the Château de Buillon upon his death."

"The house was built near the ruins of a Cistercian monastery...it is as restful as a cemetery near a river." He lay his head against his right hand and gazed at her. "*Belle irlandaise!* Do you know what I want?"

She laughed, "Yes."

"I am going to make love to you and then, we are going out together. Would you like to go to the Opéra?"

"Oh, James, I want to do *everything*!"

He swept her up in his arms and kissed her lips. "Time to unfasten the gown."

❧❧❧

The new Opéra Garnier was an intricate confection of

architecture that produced not only the show onstage. It offered up the spectacle of Paris Society, parading on the marble-and-onyx Grand Staircase and through its vast vestibules and miles of winding corridors and galleries.

Kate, glamorous in her low-cut gown and long white gloves, squeezed Tissot's arm. She greedily took in the massive crystal chandelier, the sculpture, the painted ceilings, and the ornate plasterwork without the slightest pretense of "having seen it all."

When the opera was over, and the crowds streamed out of the layers of balconies and boxes and into the gilded foyer, James recognized Degas and called to him. He was thinner and his hairline more receded since the last time James had seen him.

Degas stopped, flanked by two gentlemen, whom he introduced to James as boyhood friends. "This is Tissot, the London painter."

Tissot nodded and introduced Kate as Mrs. Newton. Degas' friends greeted her politely.

She smiled affectionately and held out her hand to his old friend.

Degas regarded her from under his heavy-lidded eyes. He made her a punctilious bow but eyed James dismally. "I cannot talk with you now. Monsieur Faure, the baritone, is impatient for his pictures. They would have been finished a long time ago if I – no matter. I must devote this fortnight almost entirely to him."

"My brother has died, Edgar. I had no time to wire you."

Degas made an arch expression. "Please be good enough to come to my studio if you wish to talk. Until then." He turned stiffly to Kate and said, *"Bon soir, madame,"* before disappearing into the crowd.

かかか

The next morning, Tissot slipped away to Degas' studio while Kate slept in. She had cried herself to sleep at her cold reception by Tissot's oldest friend, frightening them both that she might suffer a relapse.

"I wanted to meet him so badly," she wept, "because Suzanne Manet told me he is very sad, living all alone and getting older, and that he feels he has organized his life very badly. I thought we would be friends."

"He has made his choices in this life freely," Tissot consoled her. There was no point trying to make Degas behave well toward her.

Now, as he looked out the window of the hansom cab on the way to see Degas, Tissot felt Paris was rapidly becoming something unfamiliar to him. Leaving him behind.

Amid the ruins of the war, there had been a burst of enterprise since James had seen Paris three years ago. The most imposing new edifice loomed overhead as a chaos of white stone and scaffolding on the summit of Montmartre, the highest point in Paris. The Basilica of Sacré-Cœur had been under construction for the past two years, on the site of the Commune's first insurrection, and where *Communards* had performed executions – and had been executed in their turn.

The cab driver waited to turn left into the rue Blanche while horse-drawn omnibuses clattered by, their open top decks filled with people talking and laughing.

Degas rented a studio at the foot of a repellant alley off the rue Pigalle. Tissot paid the driver, who cast a suspicious glance at the well-dressed gentleman alighting in this place.

It might have been picturesque a long time ago, Tissot thought, pressing a handkerchief to his nose. Now it was decaying and reeked of beer and *pissoirs*, rotting vegetables and moldy plaster. He climbed up to the third floor, trying not to listen to the sounds of a woman's shrieks mingled with someone banging relentlessly on metal.

James knocked on the door he supposed to be Degas', and after a long pause, he put his ear to the wood. When he heard Degas singing in his sweet voice, James quietly entered.

Degas sat at his easel with the air of a dreamer. He painted near the window, the only source of light in the gloom. The room was a disgrace, dusty and disordered. He lifted an earthenware jar and held it out to his visitor. "I have paid off all my debts," he said, and shot Tissot a challenging look. "Pay yours. All my callers must give at least ten *francs* toward the Sacré-Cœur. Twenty thousand war dead must be atoned for."

Tissot met his friend's gaze and pushed a hundred-*franc* note into the narrow jar.

"For that," Degas sniffed, "perhaps they will carve your name in a stone." He continued working up a pastel picture of sweating washerwomen.

James shivered; the dampness worsened the cold of the place. "How are you getting on, Edgar?"

"I keep my season tickets to the Opéra to maintain some semblance of my old routine, and I could not part with my art collection, but must otherwise deny myself everything."

Tissot idly scanned the stacks of pictures leaning against the far wall, where Degas kept canvases by El Greco, Goya, and Ingres as well as paintings given to him by Manet and his Impressionist friends. "Your paintings are selling now, are they not? I have heard that your work has become fashionable in progressive circles."

"Faure, the opera singer, paid me three years ago for four

large paintings. I still owe him these two." He waved at the well-advanced canvases behind him, a racing scene and a picture of some dancers rehearsing at the old opera house. "I am forced every day to do something to earn money. Damnable life. You cannot imagine the burdens of all kinds which overwhelm me. I was stuck in Naples all the end of last year, enduring these degrading legal procedures for the estate."

"Could you not paint in Italy?"

Degas glared at him. "You have no idea what a hardship it is, to have your work disrupted. It ground me down. And it was bad weather for the eyes."

James sat near the window and held a forefinger to his temple. He recalled first meeting Degas while travelling in Italy, copying Old Masters in the Uffizi. They had everything in common: both were young men from wealthy, conservative families. He remembered particularly that Degas' father – a banker – was so concerned by "our Raphael's" idleness that he lectured him on the importance of some day being able to earn his living. He told him repeatedly, "The problem of keeping the pot boiling is so grave that only madmen can afford to ignore it."

Against his crumbling studio wall, Degas had leaned a painting, more complete than was usual for him. It showed an elegant man and his two young daughters with their greyhound, in the Place de la Concorde. *Degas captures movement like no one else*, Tissot thought. *No wonder he used to call our drawing master an idiot.* He scrutinized the picture. *How does he capture the ephemeral, that one fleeting moment of experience?* Yet rather than exert himself to sell his pictures, Degas clung to them, intending – one day – to perfect each one.

Degas gave him a sideways glance. "Whatever happened

to your fiancée, Angelique de Bauffremont?"

"I do not know, Edgar." Tissot felt his jaw and neck muscles tense. "Still writing sonnets?"

"It keeps my soul alive."

"The critics here are saying you stand out, that you are the highlight of the Impressionist group, that you should show at the Salon...your reputation is growing."

"Life is too short and the strength one has only just suffices."

James studied his friend's haggard face. He was not insensitive to Degas' fear of blindness nor to the injustice of this atrocious family debt he had taken upon himself as a matter of honor. Under his high forehead and drooping eyelids, Degas' angry features showed something else. Tissot wanted to say, *You are not the only one who has suffered*. Instead, he said, "Edgar, I am sorry I hurt you. I had to leave, and in leaving, I had to succeed."

"A villa near the Arc de Triomphe, a palace filled with servants in the suburbs of London, and next, a château in the French countryside. There is a kind of success that is indistinguishable from panic."

"And how do *you* measure success?" The minute the words escaped from his lips, Tissot realized how cruel they were.

Degas squinted, then rubbed his eyes and exchanged the pastel drawing on his easel for one of the large paintings he was obligated to finish for Faure. He stooped over it and said only, "I had forgotten what a *bourgeois* you are."

❧❧❧

James and Kate had spent the afternoon at the Louvre. He made dozens of elegant sketches of her in her English double-caped coat and straw bonnet, looking at the art, strolling through the galleries, resting in the sculpture hall. Back in his studio, he would make each one into a painting, and they would sell quickly. He had promised her he would take her out for a glass of wine somewhere so she could people watch, and the place she asked to see was the café in all the papers, the Café de la Nouvelle-Athènes.

Tissot would deny her nothing, though Pigalle was no place for a woman like her. But he hoped they would find Manet there at least, and sure enough, there he was, seated outside the glass doors of the café at his easel, squeezing bright colors from his paint tubes onto his palette. Elegantly dressed, he worked with a theatrical swagger that had throngs of idlers orbiting around him as if the blonde celebrity were the sun itself.

"Make him fatter!" called out someone in the raucous group, when Manet painted in the bartender with facile, vigorous brushstrokes. Someone else egged him on, "Give him a red nose as if he has been drinking the profits!"

Kate merrily viewed the show from the edge of the crowd.

Manet joked loudly with the onlookers, just as Courbet used to do. "Shall I paint a few whores at the bar with him?"

"*On* the bar with him!" a man called out, then another man shouted, "No, on *him*!"

Tissot apologized to Kate, who said, "It's like a circus, isn't it?"

Manet caught sight of Tissot and waved. His right leg stuck out stiffly, but even using his cane to rise and join them, he managed to swagger. "Just a touch of the old rheumatism!" he said. Running his keen eyes over Kate, he made her a deep bow, sweeping his tall hat before him. "My wife enjoyed your company immensely, *madame*. Now I see why." He shook Tissot's hand and winked.

Tissot only said, in a low voice, "I saw your picture in the window of a shop on the Boulevard des Capucines the other day."

Manet flashed him his crooked smile and replaced his hat. "When the Salon refused it, I put it on public display myself. Scandalous, is it not?"

"It is causing quite a stir," James assured him. To the public, this *courtesan* undressed before her impatient client was tantamount to pornography.

Manet always was defiant, Tissot thought. When he refused to study law, then failed his Naval exams for the second time, his exasperated father sent him to Paris to study with a Salon professional. The master left his class to itself, and eighteen-year-old Édouard Manet was soon arguing with the models to pose more naturally. After he stalked out one day, then skipped class for a month, his father ordered him to return.

Tissot added, "Degas praises you to the skies."

"Oh, the pig!" Manet replied, as if he were a street urchin. "He says absolutely nothing to me. It serves him right that Faure pays more for my pictures than his!"

"He is so discouraged, and his situation is so degrading that I fear it will damage his reputation."

"Degas lacks ambition and is satisfied with no reputation at all," Manet said, scanning the crowd he had attracted. "Faure came to *me* to have his portrait painted! If I get into an omnibus and someone doesn't say, 'Monsieur Manet, how are you, where are you going?' I am disappointed, for I know then that I am not famous."

James did not laugh, but Kate did.

Manet turned his keen eyes on her. "Have you been in an omnibus, *chère*? The top deck on a breezy day is very stimulating."

Tissot was astonished to see Kate playing the *coquette* to

Manet, who then suggested to her, "I would love you to come to my studio and pose for a portrait. I will paint you on the *loggia*, make you like some mysterious –"

"*Impossible*," Tissot interrupted. He tensed and squared his shoulders.

Kate looked askance at James, then quickly said, "It has been a long day, and I am afraid I need rest more than anything just now." She slipped her arm under Tissot's.

He did not blame Kate; no one – not even Degas – could resist Manet, whose whole persona suddenly seemed menacing.

"*Quel dommage* – too bad!" Manet said, his eyes dancing over her and sporting with Tissot. "You must see my studio. It's marvelous – the windows overlook the Place de l'Europe, and the St. Lazare train sheds. I showed it to some journalists, you know, and they wrote that it is the cleanest studio they have ever seen. " 'Not the slightest trace of revolution in these surroundings,' in their opinion." He broke out into ironic laughter. "I have shown myself to be no more of a threat to public order than any respectable *bourgeois*. For good measure, I told them that I was not even in Paris at the time of the Commune, but miles away in the country with my wife and our godson!" He was laughing at them, all of them.

Tissot felt as if he had been struck in the chest; his heart began to pound, and he slowly lifted his eyes to Manet. "That day I left Paris, I saw Degas in the Bois de Boulogne, and he mentioned that you were back."

Manet toyed with his watch chain and returned a level gaze. "Why, yes. What a good memory you have, James. It is so long ago. Courbet had the Commune's attorney general draw up safe-conduct papers so we could enter and leave Paris as we pleased. But of course, I was not involved in the actual fighting, as you were."

Stunned, Tissot reacted with nothing more than a wide-eyed gape. *Why am I seeing him for the first time?*

"Don't stand there like a cold fish. It all turned out well enough, did it not?"

Tissot fixed his eyes on Manet. "But Édouard, if you were not in Paris during the Commune, how did you draw those famous eyewitness accounts of the barricades and the massacres?"

"Come, you take life too seriously, James!"

Tissot gripped Kate's arm so tightly that she grimaced.

Manet allowed his attention to be diverted by witticisms from his devoted followers, who were helping a bowler-hatted photographer and his assistant to set up a tripod and camera in the street. No one recognized James Tissot, and the crowd that moved in closer to Manet edged Tissot out. Manet slowly turned and flashed a three-quarters view of his grinning face, ensuring that the photographs would portray him in conversation with his admirers.

After a calculated delay, Manet turned back to Tissot and offhandedly elbowed him in the ribs. "When are you going to paint something that will take the art world by storm? You were a Realist, a follower of Courbet who urged us to paint the truths of modern life. You have intellect enough, so use it! Why do you not experiment, use your imagination, do something spontaneous? Are you satisfied being the equal only of your friend Alma-Tadema?"

James and Kate exchanged a long look. They both were ready to go home.

In the cab back to their hotel, James considered his place in the art world. He believed in Realism, and he knew he was one of the most skilled painters in Paris or London. *Mon Dieu, I am more successful than all of them, except Millais!* He wished his friends to be successful and was disgusted by their lack of business sense and application.

But more frustrating was their arrogance toward him, their attitude that their continual troubles elevated their art over his. It was infuriating – he had surmounted exile and British xenophobia to build a second career from nothing. *What is brilliant about living in penury as a "genius" to be worshipped by a few avant-garde intellectuals, and purposely antagonizing those from whom they professed to crave recognition?* His pulse raced.

Kate leaned into him and, though struggling not to, allowed her eyes to close as the horse clopped along the streets of Paris. James put his arm around her and made an effort to calm himself, feeling her forehead. It was cool, and he put his cheek against hers.

Let Manet and Degas paint the lowest side of society. *All the truths of modern life are not ugly and seamy.*

"We will not confine ourselves to the house," he vowed softly to her, kissing her hair. "I will take you outside London – I'll paint you everywhere!"

I will make you live forever, in paint.

Chapter XXV

Millais' studio
2 Palace Gate, Kensington Gardens
February 8, 1878

Tissot was ushered up to the head of the grand staircase, past a splashing marble fountain on the landing, to Millais' immense new studio in the royal suburb of Kensington, at the end of Palace Gate. James, for Kate's sake, had politely declined Effie's invitation to the gala open house for their neo-Renaissance mansion last spring.

Now, as his eyes wandered around the studio, at the tapestries hung on three walls and the center dais for models, James felt his suburban house reduced to a country cottage by comparison. With its parquet floor, great coved ceiling, and trio of electric chandeliers, Millais' studio could be a splendid ballroom. Tissot had not danced since last May, at the Grosvenor with Louise Jopling. He had received few invitations to any social events, and he assumed word had spread about his living arrangements with Kathleen. *Had the gossip reached Millais?*

Millais, his back turned, was painting with energetic brush strokes near the massive white marble chimney piece. The clear north light streamed from his window overlooking Kensington Gardens. Fit as ever in his morning coat and grey waistcoat, he greeted James with open arms, like an English squire, saying, "We must be the only two artists in London who dress like men of business!"

He begged for a few moments to finish the detail that absorbed his attention, and pointed the end of his brush toward the gardens. "There are few parks in England more beautiful than this. I could paint some good landscapes here." Millais winked as he held his palette in the crook of his left arm, with several brushes held at an angle through it. "This morning, I discovered a couple of pheasants in the shrubberies near Rotten Row!" He continued to work, mixing shades of brown while Tissot waited.

James had come in a discouraged mood, and while he did not begrudge Millais his fortune, it did reduce him to a small foreign figure by comparison. Of all the eminent men Tissot knew, it was Millais he most admired. Level-headed and beyond petty professional jealousies, his personal trial – waiting to marry Effie until her marriage to Ruskin was annulled – was long past. The youthful rebel of Pre-Raphaelitism had earned the love of his countrymen, and his paintings now captured the mood of the nation. Journalists described him as "Anglo-Saxon from skin to core," the heir to Gainsborough and Reynolds.

Millais had canvases in various states of completion on several tall easels. Tissot inched over in a wheeled leather chair and ran his eyes up and down the paintings on the two easels nearest him.

One of the pictures was of a Beefeater in his scarlet and gold costume, as Tissot had seen on duty at the Tower of

London. The dignity of the old man showcased Millais' skill capturing character in paint; Tissot thought back to his student days in Paris, when he received an extravagant description of Millais' Courbet-like powers of Realism from Whistler. He folded his arms over his chest, half in awe and half despondent over ever finding such a perfect artistic niche himself.

From the corner of his eye, Millais observed Tissot's face with amusement. "That one is *A Yeoman of the Guard*. I'm sending it to the Paris International Exhibition."

The painting on the second easel near Tissot was a coy little girl in an oversized mobcap, very like a Reynolds masterpiece in the National Gallery – with a heavy dose of syrup. He had depicted the girl with her feet dangling off a fallen tree in the woods, and tiny pink bows on her slippers echoed the floppy pink bow on her mobcap.

"That's *Cherry Ripe*, after a folk song by one of our English poets. It's a commission from the editor of the *Graphic*, who is the girl's uncle." Millais stepped back and appraised his work. "Tell me, what do you think?"

"*Charmant* – charming," Tissot said, stifling a laugh. *How Jimmy Whistler would sneer!* Only Millais could get away with painting something this silly.

"In fact, I'm rather backed up just now," Millais added. "After *Vanity Fair*'s savage attack on Gladstone last month, I've been commissioned to paint *his* portrait. Effie and I have been invited to dine at Downing Street!"

Tissot tried not to chuckle at Tommy's recent portrayal in *Vanity Fair* of the Tory Prime Minister as a champion of nepotism and "a middle-class man who falls down flat on his face before a title." He crossed his legs and mused, "So you have accepted the mantle of 'Painter of the Empire.' "

"Why not? Yes, now that her Majesty is Empress of India, and I've painted the Viceroy." Satisfied with his work for the moment, Millais set his palette and brushes on his work table with his jars of crushed pigment. "It's a little terrifying, staying on top, you know. There are a few commissions I've lost — the Prince of Wales, to that French fellow, Bastien-Lepage. And I could not manage to meet Her Royal Highness Princess Alexandra's schedule — but at this point, I could live on portraits alone."

It is *terrifying*, Tissot thought, but he only nodded. In Paris, before the war, he painted the Princess Mathilde and the Marquise de Miramon and their friends who frequented his stylish "Oriental" studio. Here, while Millais painted aristocrats and eminent personages, Tissot painted the likes of Mrs. Katherine Chappell-Gill — whose husband was willing to pay for James to move in with his wife and children in Liverpool for two months. Kate stayed with Polly during that time, and as much as he disliked leaving her, he could not turn down the opportunity. Mr. Chappell-Gill was a cotton broker who traveled a great deal, and Tissot decided to use his spare time meeting the considerable number of art dealers in Liverpool. Far removed from Society gossip, they speedily accepted the proposition of exhibiting the work of such a well-known London artist in their local galleries.

"It has helped me immensely to exhibit at the World's Fairs," Millais said, observing Tissot's dejected silence. He stirred his brushes in a jar of turpentine. "Are you sending any pictures to the Paris Exposition?"

"*Non*, but I will exhibit my prints at art galleries in Liverpool and Manchester as well as London, and I am looking at Glasgow for good measure."

When Millais' face betrayed some embarrassment, James summoned the bravado to add, "I want collectors throughout Great Britain to become familiar with my work. I also am experimenting with enamels, cloisonné vases..."

"Good, good..." Millais' voiced trailed off, and he began to clean his palette, taking care for his white shirt cuffs. "Joe and I urged Louise to send her *Modern Cinderella* to the Paris Exhibition." At the thought of Louise Jopling, his eyes twinkled. "She is a stunner, isn't she? I've told Joe, if anything were to happen to him, I have my eye on Louise for my second wife! Do you think I would suit, for her third husband?"

Tissot cringed inside, hoping to God that Effie was not within earshot out in the hall – even if Millais were joking. Then, thinking of Louise exhibiting in Paris, he rubbed the bridge of his nose and leaned forward, laughing grimly at his own predicament. "A French artist in London sending paintings to Paris to showcase English art?"

Millais' deep blue eyes fixed on him kindly. "The key is to paint the British the way they see themselves, not the way they are."

"They say that a 'Gallic' artist can never paint the English face," Tissot sullenly reminded him.

"Ah, well! You have been painting a charming face recently."

Tissot tensed and sat up straight.

Millais finished cleaning his hands. He merely remarked, "You may wish to give her a fuller jaw, like Mrs. Langtry's."

He knows. James sat in miserable silence while his friend kept up a breezy conversational tone. "You did see what your friend Bowles wrote about Lillie in *Vanity Fair*? She *is* the most splendid creature!"

Tissot threw his hand over the chair back and groaned. "She sent Tommy a note, rather than thanking him, asking if her brother might try his hand at writing for the magazine."

"You must be the only man in London who doesn't worship the Jersey Lily!"

I must be the only man in London who sees her for what she is. James shook his head.

"She is a clever woman," Millais continued, with possessive pride. "Society always requires some new diversion, and her rise has been brilliant. But, since we are both from Jersey, I am biased!"

Once everything was in order, Millais gestured for Tissot to follow him, and he showed off some of the innovations of his studio. There was a tall door that opened to street level, where large canvases could be loaded directly into a van. He opened a smaller door that led to a back staircase. "The models I hire need never disturb my family. They have their own entrance, dressing room, and even a water closet."

"You have thought of everything," Tissot said, enviously wondering how he could update his own arrangements.

Millais took up his pipe, stuffed it with tobacco, and settled back on the sofa that was among the few furnishings in his vast studio. "Now – tell me about Whistler. *Vanity Fair*'s caricature of him was certainly clever."

"*Oui*, everyone says it is the best they have done, 'A Symphony.' Jimmy loves to see himself in print." Tissot retook his seat in the wheeled leather chair with the half-circle back.

"Whistler grows more bizarre every year," said Millais. He lit his pipe and began to draw on it. "I don't recognize him anymore, he has grown so strange. All the negative publicity around the trial will drive potential patrons away, and as for this business with Leyland's wife –" Millais stopped short and gestured with his pipe stem. "Just be careful of the company you keep, James."

"Jimmy realized long ago that Manet upstages every artist in Paris, but that he could be the Manet of London." The scaffolding was up for the roof of Whistler's opulent new studio in Tite Street, and Tissot truly was shocked by the scale and expense. Jimmy claimed he would start taking students to defray the cost.

"Whistler is a very real threat, James. 'Impressionism' may be the latest fad, but it does the new generation more harm than good." Millais threw one arm over the back of the sofa and spoke with his pipe clamped between his teeth. "Young artists now think they can escape the grind by running off to Paris to learn how to paint hazes from men who don't even know how to draw. I tell them, you cannot run before you have learned to walk; you have to go through the mill like we've all done. The public is beginning to find this out now, to distinguish between genuine art and imbecile trash. We can only hope that the Royal Academy and our English art galleries and exhibitions educate even the most ignorant."

"Academic training is essential to art that endures," Tissot replied, "but I do not understand this fear of contamination from the art movement across the Channel. How can Tom Taylor support Burne-Jones but attack Manet's pictures in *The Times*?" He shook his head and pushed himself back and forth in the rolling chair. "Whistler says Tom Taylor is an interfering old fool who gives useless advice."

"Tom is a good sort – that's why I set you up with him, years ago, to help illustrate his *Ballads of Brittany*." Smoke encircled Millais' head as he spoke. "You may not know, but back when Ruskin was appointed to the Professorship of Art at Oxford, Tom also was considered. He's a few years older than Ruskin and was the art critic for *The Times* and on the staff of *Punch*. His plays are popular, but –"

"He doesn't have an original thought in his head. Everything he does is based on a French drama, or Dickens. Or Shakespeare."

"It's true," Millais admitted. "But both Tom Taylor and Ruskin fear the influence of foreign art on the English School. It's a matter of native pride, as well as simple jealousy. You see, the Royal Academy painters see British collectors buying pictures from artists like you, and that is a very real threat to their livelihoods."

Artists like me? Tissot stopped rolling his chair.

"As for Ruskin, he abhors the commercial sensationalism of the Continental art that has invaded our shores in the past several years. In his eyes, greed is immoral, and he equates the morality of the artist with the morality of the picture."

Tissot raised an eyebrow, "Ruskin, who drove a young girl to insanity?"

"He's paying for it. They say he's suffered a mental collapse. There is gossip that he murdered his cat. Evidently, Ruskin took the poor creature for Satan." Millais puffed at his pipe and laughed. "I don't believe in Satan."

"I do."

"You can't mean it!"

"*Oui*, I am cursed." Tissot could not meet Millais' eyes, could not explain more than to say, "Courbet swore, just before the Commune fell, that I would be damned to hell."

"Well, that savage is dead now, and he can do you no harm from the grave."

Tissot inhaled, straightened in his seat and tried to calm his nerves. "No matter what I paint, or how I paint it, or how popular my pictures are with the public here, my work will be criticized as immoral because I am French?"

Millais withdrew the pipe from his lips with a benevolent expression. "Why cause more controversy than we must, my dear fellow?" He smiled, "It's bad for business."

"All of this...it is so easy, for you."

"Not at all. Ruskin has turned on me once again, you see,

because he says in doing nothing but portraits, I have sold out my talent." Millais examined *Cherry Ripe* for a long moment. Then he mused, "Perhaps, after all, I have failed to fulfill the promise of my youth." He was quiet, and finally slapped his knees with both hands and burst out in his boyish grin, "*But!* Never mind that – when there are still Christmas bills to pay, and the new house as well –"

On the landing outside his studio, an uproar of indignant female voices arose.

Millais tapped out the ashes from his pipe. "The only regret I have in this life is that Her Majesty will not receive Effie."

"She is still being punished for the annulment of her marriage to Ruskin? I am sorry to hear it," Tissot murmured. He took his cue to leave, and parted from Millais with a handshake. Out on the great landing, he encountered Effie and her eldest daughter, also Effie. Tissot's eyes darted between the two attractive women, one middle-aged and the other a vivacious *débutante* in a low-cut gown and diamond earrings, who bore a remarkable likeness to her father.

Effie, the mother, was fastening a tartan sash over her daughter's shoulder with a silver clan badge. "Though I am expressly kept from the presence of the Queen, you will *remind* them that your mother is a Scotchwoman."

She looked up, infuriated and red-eyed, and Tissot asked, "Effie, are you quite alright?"

"My husband is taking my daughter instead of me as his escort to a *soirée* for Laurence Alma-Tadema," she answered. "Her Majesty the Queen will be present, as he is to be elected an Honorary Member of the Royal Scottish Academy."

Tissot was dumbfounded by yet another award made to Laurence Alma-Tadema. *The Gold Medal in Berlin last year, the recent knighthood by the King of Prussia – how it must gall him that he still is not a member of the British Royal Academy!*

"Mama, you know Papa is doing it to help me along in Society," young Effie insisted. She was a blonde beauty, and as Millais had painted several portraits of her over the years, she was a celebrity in her own right.

"*Everyone* will be there!" cried her mother. "Why must he go, when I am left behind? Ruskin is free to go where he pleases. The price is to be paid – by the woman!" At the sound of a carriage in the drive, Effie burst into tears and raced up the sweeping staircase from which she regularly greeted friends, patrons, aristocrats, diplomats, and literary figures.

James was just about to escort the daughter down the marble steps when Millais emerged from his studio. Young Effie turned to him with her confident air and said, "You must dress, Papa, and show what it is to be a great man."

"It takes *me* only a moment to change, my dear!"

He offered his arm to her, and Tissot fell in behind them.

Down amid the columns of the grand reception hall, Joe and Louise Jopling appeared, dressed for the *soirée*, and Tissot met them at the foot of the staircase and bowed. Joe accepted his outstretched hand but would not meet his eyes.

Louise greeted Tissot with an open eagerness. "Is all well with you, James?" she said. "I have seen so little of you since the Grosvenor show."

With a pang, he assured her he was fine, ascertained that her little son was flourishing, then hastily bid them all a good evening and crossed the wide mosaic floor to the doors.

The price is not always paid by women.

༄༅༅༅

Chapter XXVI

The Grosvenor Gallery
135-137 New Bond Street
Closing Reception, July 31, 1878

Affecting a careless demeanor, Tissot surreptitiously scrutinized Burne-Jones' exhibit in the West Gallery one final time before the Grosvenor Gallery exhibition closed for the season. Visitors hailed Burne-Jones' oil pictures again this year as a brilliant success, but the appeal of his despairing, frankly erotic figures in their brightly-colored medieval costumes continued to utterly confound James. And the titles! Tissot was expected to suppress the supposedly decadent influence of his native land, while Burne-Jones pretentiously gave many of his titles, like *Le Chant d'Amour – The Love Song* – in French. There was a sinister sexuality in the desolate nudity of his *Pan and Psyche*, and his pretentious Venus picture – *Laus Veneris* – was based on a poem about obsession with lust.

James suspected *he* would be run out of the country if he

had painted these pictures. A magazine critic gave his work the back-handed compliment of being "French, rather than English, alike in the ideas it suggests and the skill it shows." But another credited him, by virtue of his long residence in London, with being nearly an Englishman, remarking that both he and Alma-Tadema had greatly influenced English art.

It is a game to be played. James fidgeted with his watch chain. He understood that he was struggling to maintain his grip on the mere edge of Establishment acceptance, and that he must continue to please where he needed to please. Degas, in Paris, had written that though the fourth Paris exhibition of the Impressionists had turned a small profit, the critics were dismissing their *avant-garde* group as washed-up. James considered himself astute not to have tainted his reputation by participating in their shows.

Working harder than ever and keeping to his studio, he even painted through lunch. He stopped only when it was time for tea in the late afternoon, when Polly Hervey's nursemaid brought Kathleen's children. Sometimes Polly came with her children as well. James went out only when he needed to paint a portrait elsewhere than his studio, or to attend evening receptions where his paintings were on view. Strolling along the Grosvenor's gallery tonight, he paused to shake as many hands as possible. He knew he was losing his connections with many figures in the art world and tried to make up for it when he could. Most evenings, he stayed at home with Kate, and he had not been at the Grosvenor often this season.

James wondered how Kathleen was faring in his absence. He checked his pocket watch. The children were long gone by now, back to Polly's to be tucked in for the night. Only the butler and a maid would be on hand to see to Kate. The fear and guilt that she was in bed, again coughing blood, gripped him as it did each time he went out alone.

At the other end of the gallery, women began standing on chairs, looking toward him in a frenzy. *They cannot be so amazed by my presence!* He clasped his hands behind his back and turned to see the Prince of Wales parading Mrs. Langtry around the Grosvenor Gallery. She wore all white, with no flowers or jewels. It was true, what was said about her: profile of a Grecian goddess, body of an Amazon. She was Kate's age, in her early twenties. It was rumored that Mrs. Langtry was keen to be presented to the Queen. Tissot was startled to see how many of the gallery visitors continued looking at her, rather than the art.

Sauntering along the gallery, he observed that Mr. Langtry appeared a bit drunk, engaged in a discussion of salmon fishing with the portly Joe Jopling. James nodded to Joe, then turned his back and looked at the pictures.

The Prince of Wales, with Lillie Langtry on his arm, made his way to the buffet table, where he turned to Louise and said, "May I cut you a piece of cake, Mrs. Jopling?"

"How kind! Thank you, sir."

Tissot, from the corner of his eye, thought she looked off her head with joy when the Prince of Wales himself cut her a piece of cake and offered her the plate, then a fork. For the first time, Tissot found himself annoyed with Louise. He crossed his arms over his chest and looked away.

"You have met Mrs. Langtry?" the Prince asked Louise in his guttural voice.

"Yes, of course. At Oscar Wilde's."

In a conspiratorial tone that made them all laugh, the Prince confided to Louise, "I have told Mrs. Langtry that you ought to paint her portrait."

Lillie Langtry laughed deeply, and Louise replied, "Oh, yes, straight away!"

"What fun, to be painted by a lady!" Mrs. Langtry

simpered, clearly not intending to do any such thing. Tissot glanced at Louise, but she did not seem to feel the slight.

Millais, tall and manly, approached with young Effie on his arm. He waved genially at Tissot but headed for Mrs. Langtry. "Ah, I knew you were here from all the hullabaloo!" He took Mrs. Langtry's hand, leaned toward her ear, and whispered something that made her laugh.

"It would be an honor to sit for you, Mr. Millais. I thought you might never ask."

He winked at her. "I simply was waiting in line with the others, my dear!"

Tissot could stand no more. *I will never grovel.*

As soon as the Prince's entourage moved away, James helped himself to a glass of champagne from the buffet and strolled back into the East Gallery, where Whistler was strutting before two eager young journalists, feeding them quips. Jimmy wore a coat that nearly swept the floor and was calculated to show up in the pages of *Punch*. Meanwhile, his paintings defiantly reprised his exhibit last year. James could hardly believe that Jimmy would show *Thames – Nocturne in Blue and Silver*, a view of the Battersea skyline nearly identical to the original *Nocturne in Blue and Silver*.

Whistler bustled about, assisting the press in finding the proper line of sight to view his paintings. He struck comic poses, to assist the cartoonists for the illustrated magazines, and regaled them with Disraeli's rebuff. Whistler had happened upon the Prime Minister in St. James's Park, absorbed in thought on a bench, and tried to persuade him to sit for a portrait. "He gazed icily at me and muttered, 'Go away, go away, little man.' " Whistler paused dramatically, his eyes darting under his eyebrows as he looked at each of the reporters. "And then – what do you think? Ha! Ha! The next day, he agreed to sit for Millais!"

The public showed much less interest. Two men passed by Tissot, the first saying, "It is an insult to Burne-Jones that Whistler's art is hung in the same building!"

"Jimmy Whistler is nothing more than a Yankee buffoon," the second man replied. "He could paint well, if he would try."

"On your second point, I disagree," the other man said. "Mr. Whistler is an etcher – equal to Rembrandt himself. Unfortunately, he has not done anything worthwhile since *The Thames Set*."

James knew how well Jimmy Whistler could paint. It was frustrating and depressing to watch him self-destruct, while clinging to the illusion that he was building some sort of fantastic reputation.

On the opposite wall, Tissot demonstrated his abilities with a broad range of subjects and styles. Kathleen Newton, anonymous as she must remain, was now essential to his success. Of the nine pictures he exhibited this year, Kate modeled for the main figure in seven of them. He had painted her, luminous in the same white muslin dress she had worn the first time she had modeled for him, in a vertical, Japanese-style format, which he titled *Spring*. She had posed for him near the Regent's Park, with a direct, modern gaze in *The Warrior's Daughter*. And he had featured her in two etchings, *October* and the one that had created a public buying frenzy, *Mavourneen*. He stood back and smiled at everyone's reaction to it, courteously accepting compliments from those who knew him.

His reviews had been almost entirely positive, especially those written by Tom Taylor for *The Times*. He pronounced James Tissot a virtuoso in his handling of light. The vivid yellows and greens James was now using made his pictures stand out in the gallery. Even on closing day, they continued to attract a crowd of admirers.

He lounged around the edge of his exhibit, sipping from his champagne glass. Even the worst review he had seen of his pictures was not so bad – it merely took him to task for his devotion to painting modern women in the latest extravagant fashions as if he were illustrating dressmakers' books. He thought his pictures looked positively wholesome and thoroughly British – especially compared to Burne-Jones' women, in their nightgown-like "Aesthetic" dress. Tissot's women were at least properly corseted. He glanced toward the West Gallery, looking forward to Burne-Jones' inevitable downfall. And Lawrence Alma-Tadema's highly realistic, life-sized nude remained on exhibit at the Royal Academy, drawing a rebuke from the Bishop of Carlisle. Tissot almost wished for the power to see into the future, just to know when and where to be to witness their comeuppance. He rapped his knuckles on the chair rail behind him. *Knock on wood.*

Louise wended her way through the crush to seek James out, looking anxiously at Whistler's performance among the reporters. She quietly asked him how Jimmy was holding up under the pressure of the months before the Ruskin trial.

"His new studio in Tite Street will be completed in a few months," Tissot replied, "and he does not seem to see the avalanche of debt that will crush him."

"He is convinced he will prevail in the courtroom in November."

"Word has it that Ruskin's mental condition is too unstable for him to appear," James said, setting his empty glass aside. "If so, that is the only advantage Jimmy will enjoy. Ruskin's lawyers will tear him to pieces."

The bearded old critic Tom Taylor entered the gallery, and a broad smile spread over Louise's face as her persistent wave finally caught his eye. "Tom has bought yet another one of my paintings!"

"That is a great compliment to you," James said, suavely hiding his opinion of Tom Taylor as a mediocrity. He bowed toward Tom and told her, "As long as he keeps giving my work favorable reviews, I do not care if he buys it. His good opinion is the equal of Ruskin's." In fact, Tissot felt it was a clever thing to have prevailed over Ruskin, by earning the favor of his former competitor.

He made a sardonic face and remarked, "What I cannot comprehend is this craze for Burne-Jones."

"You don't like his pictures?" Louise smiled as if she attributed James' attitude to envy. "They are wonderful, so dreamy and of another world entirely. So modern!"

"You call *him* modern?" Tissot was offended, but smoothly replied, "They strike me as decidedly un-British." For good measure, he added, "Millais never would get away with that."

"Oh, Millais! Did you hear he has been awarded the Medal of Honor by the French nation?"

"*Non,*" Tissot said, dazed. "I had not." *Millais, the archetypal British painter!* He felt as betrayed as the day he saw the Versaillais troops marching toward his house to crush the Commune.

"He is to visit Paris for the awards ceremony in October," Louise said, pleased to be so in the know. "And Lawrence Alma-Tadema, too. He not only won a gold medal, but will be inducted into the French Legion of Honor."

The French, who bought one of my paintings for the national collection when I was only twenty-four!

But that was before the war.

❧ ❧ ❧

He sought comfort in Kathleen's arms, making love to

her twice upon waking the next morning. Though he meant to be careful with her, she was hungry for him, and gave herself with abandon.

Afterwards, Kate swung in the tassled Brazilian hammock that James had bought for her, enjoying her afterglow under the shade of the chestnut tree. He had hung the hammock at the edge of the black iron colonnade encircling his shining pond. It was a breezy summer day, and in the privacy of their garden paradise, she held her novel and let her leg drape languidly with her skirts over the edge of the gently rocking net. She wore the long-sleeved, high-collared black Worth day gown he had had custom tailored for her in Paris.

"I do love you, James," she said.

He beamed at her from his wicker armchair, sitting with his leg extended and watching her as her slender fingers brushed along the thick grass beneath the hammock. She coughed, but not as frequently as she once did. Her fits seemed to him, truly, to be less frequent. *Perhaps she has made a recovery, and the cough is the last vestige of the disease.* He wanted to believe it.

Courbet's curse weighed on him. James believed in his heart that this was how the curse had manifested itself, in Kathleen's illness. *Courbet!* Suddenly, James recalled the first painting he had ever seen of Courbet's, when he was new to Paris and eager to see the great man's solo exhibition with Jimmy Whistler and their friends. He thought of a way to exorcise Courbet's malevolent spirit.

"Stay put," he told Kate, and he went inside to gather his paint box and brushes.

"I'm not planning to move for the rest of the afternoon!" she called after him.

"A perfect model!" he shot back, over his shoulder. Soon, he emerged from the studio and tripped lightly down the stone steps with his painting materials as well as a Japanese rice paper parasol from his prop collection.

He opened the day's newspaper, folded it with a flourish, and handed it to Kate, who cried, "No, don't take my book!"

"You can read it later." He set it open and face down on the straw mat under the hammock. Then he opened the parasol with a pop and tucked its handle under the thick golden cushion behind her head.

"That's ridiculous," she giggled. "I'm afraid that's taking the pose too far, dear. Why must *I* suffer for your art?"

"It will look right, you will see. The picture needs it. It needs something else, too –" He bounded across the grass to pluck a red geranium from a planter at the edge of the graveled path. Tucking it into her bodice, he said, "To pick up the color of the berries on the branches behind you."

Kate let him fuss over her, then looked up. "This business of being a muse is hard work. When do I get to read, for goodness' sake?"

"Go ahead, I am finished!" He ran his eyes over her, *La Mystérieuse*. She made a silly face at him, and he enjoyed a hearty laugh. *If her disease progresses, there will be few days as glorious as this*. Her beauty would be ravaged with her health. He wondered how long God would allow him to have her. Kissing her red lips with passion, he said, "You look so *chic* and serene."

"Wonderful, dear. *Paint* and let me read before Violet and Cecil come for tea."

As the thrushes and blackbirds sang in his trees, James began sketching out his composition. He would paint in his finest academic style, in great detail, but with bright colors over a white canvas, in a modern take on the Pre-Raphaelites. The children's dog meandered into the section of grass he was painting, dropped his striped ball, and flopped down on its side to sleep in the shade.

James chuckled. "*Bon*, now there is black and white to break up the green. He will echo perfectly your shiny new boots and petticoat."

"Oh, my petticoat! James, must you?"

"*Oui*." He winked. "The picture needs white just there." She tossed a leaf at him. "Do not worry," he teased. "It is tasteful."

"Next you'll want to paint me in my corset and drawers like that Nana picture by your friend Manet."

"I never would!" he protested, in mock outrage. He loved to hear her laugh. "But perhaps *à la* Burne-Jones, in your nightdress! Do you think I could get away with it? I shall give it a French title and have you look sinister, with an effeminate lover in knight's armor pining away at your feet. Or perhaps, the hairy god Pan balefully worshipping you? *Non*, that has already been done..."

Kate was giggling so much that she protested for him to stop. "How am I to hold this pose?" She collected herself and sighed with enjoyment of the moment. "What will you call it?"

"Oh...I think, *The Hammock*. Let them make of it what they will. 'Do What's True, Let them Talk' – remember Manet's one-man show?"

"Don't take that risk, James. Everyone will speculate on who modeled for you."

"You are right." He examined the picture thoughtfully. "But it is a common enough thing for artists to paint women in hammocks. And in art, the dog is considered a symbol of fidelity. And here – though you will not accept one from me, I shall paint a wedding band on your finger." He gestured at the canvas. "It is a picture of a lovely young wife at her leisure in the suburbs. Much more wholesome than what we can expect from Burne-Jones next!"

Chapter XXVII

17 Grove End Road, St. John's Wood
November 25, 1878

Kate had coughed through the night and was running a low fever. Tissot had not slept until midafternoon when Violet and Cecil came for tea. He had not thought to send a message to Polly Hervey and did not wish to send the children away when the butler awakened him with a soft knock to announce their arrival. Instead, he told the old man to give them some special treat and let them have the run of the downstairs rooms.

Polly had sent her daughter, Lilian, as well, and Tissot was aware of the sounds of the three children playing hide and seek in his studio for the hour or two he lay in his great rosewood half-tester bed beside Kate. Despite all, his house was a happy home, and he looked forward to tussling with Cecil tomorrow. Violet, at eight, was becoming a little lady who often read her fairy stories aloud to Kate and kept them both good company while he painted.

Finally, he sat up and pushed the covers off himself, then ran a hand over Kate's forehead. *Better.* He gazed at her features in sleep, and thought of a verse from a Keats poem she had read him: *She will bring, in spite of frost, Beauties that the earth has lost.* On her night table lay her rosary. Tissot stared gloomily at it. Then he slipped around the bed and pressed the tangle of beads into her fist, as he had done for his suffering mother on her deathbed.

He ignored his haggard reflection in the mirrored armoire and pulled out his lounge jacket. Glancing once more at the document delivered to his house the day before yesterday, he folded it and slipped it into his jacket pocket.

Kate rolled over and opened her eyes. "James, are you going down to your studio?"

"*Oui, ma chère.*" He caressed her hair and slipped on the jacket. "I need to get back to work."

"I'm awake now." She took his hand and kissed his palm before cupping it against her check. "I want to be with you."

۶۰۶۰۶۰

The footman built a fire in the studio and helped Tissot move some furniture. Soon Kate, propped up on pillows on the wicker *chaise longue*, was devouring the details of the Whistler v. Ruskin libel trial in the *Evening Standard*. The courtroom was packed. Ruskin was not up to the strain of cross-examination, but offered statements through his attorney. *The Times* had only regaled its readers with the comedy of the lawyer at the Queen's Bench of the High Court at Westminster putting Jimmy's *Nocturne* on the courtroom easel, upside down.

James lifted his brush, observing the effect of his background – St. Paul's churchyard – and glanced over at

Kate. She was heavily shawled over her plaid wool dress. He had settled her *chaise* and side table just across from the fireplace, near the glass panels at the entrance to his conservatory. "What are they saying now?"

"Let me see...Ruskin objects to the exorbitant prices degrading paintings into 'marketable commodities.' " She pulled the paper closer to the oil lamp, scanning the long columns of print.

James snorted and rotated the piano stool under him. "Which they are, or else how is one to earn a living? Whistler asked only two hundred guineas for that painting."

"Ruskin is offended by 'the reduction of art to a commodity by purchasers who were themselves in manufacture or the finance market.' "

"*Mon Dieu!*" After a moment, Tissot chuckled and shifted his weight forward toward the lamp on his painting table. "That is the sort who will snap my new picture up – a scene of a businessman going to work in a hansom cab."

Kate leaned back into the cushions, weary physically but eager for the mental stimulation. "Ruskin's attorney says it amounts to a tradesman selling to customers who are 'gullible, artistic gentlemen from Manchester, Leeds or Sheffield.' "

"The man is an idiot. William Agnew is from Manchester – so is Louise Jopling. They will take that as the insult it is."

"Oh, James – that man, the critic for *The Times* who likes you – he has come out for Ruskin."

"Tom Taylor," Tissot said. "He edits *Punch*, you know, and has milked cartoons of Jimmy for all he's worth. He has no choice but to take Ruskin's side." He sighed. "Poor Maud! Home with Jimmy's baby while he carries on with Mrs. Leyland under everyone's nose."

"He has seen Maud at least once," Kate informed him, after a long cough, "since she is expecting his second child."

"I thought I knew the man," Tissot said angrily. "*Pauvre petite*, what is to become of her?"

They heard a nasal voice, and a door slammed in the front of the house. Whistler strutted into Tissot's studio, wielding his bamboo walking stick against his palm like a police officer with a billy club. "Leyland and Burne-Jones are stepping into it now! Leyland – that *parvenu* in his frills and buckles – called me 'an artistic Barnum' who has failed in all these years to produce any serious work." He swept off his top hat and sent his curls flying. "Our years of friendship count for nothing."

Whistler brought the winter cold in with his long coat. Tissot stood and blocked him from getting more than a few feet into the room.

Kate said, "Hello, Jimmy" and folded up the newspaper.

"Jimmy, please – Kate is resting."

"And Burne-Jones!" Jimmy sputtered, standing nearly on James' toes and flourishing his hands. "Would you believe, he is the chief witness for Ruskin's defense? He provided a statement for Ruskin's lawyer to submit to the court: 'Scarcely anybody regards Whistler as a serious person.' He said my work is merely 'the art of brag!' He is just using this to take my place under Leyland's patronage. They all hope they can drive me out of the country, or kill me! And if I didn't have the constitution of a Government mule, they would!"

He affixed his monocle and turned his chin up to Tissot, waiting for him to rally.

James hesitated, fingering the subpoena in his pocket. The memories of all their old hijinks in Paris flooded his mind. James would paint portraits of housemaids for forty *francs* apiece, and later take them dancing at the all-night student balls where Courbet would cavort in his Scottish Highlander costume. Jimmy would be there, then sleep until noon with whatever girl he brought back to his room in the rue St. Sulpice. The girl almost always would model nude for him the next day, even the one they called *La Tigresse* who ripped up all his sketches of other girls in a jealous rage. When Jimmy saw what she had done, he wept.

Whistler, continually in debt, always expecting – and getting – fresh loans from everyone he approached with his gaiety and wit. Tissot had learned early on never to lend money to the charming American. When there was money in Jimmy's pockets, he squandered it down to the last *sou*, treating his friends at the cafés. When his pockets were empty, he would pawn his coat or even his bedclothes, steal canvases and paint boxes from other students copying the pictures in the Louvre, even sleep in Tissot's bath tub if he could not pay his rent. Once, to James' astonishment, Jimmy tied a monkey to a ball of twine and let him loose in his landlady's pantry, to be pulled back clutching loaves of bread, whole rounds of cheese, and bottles of wine. It was funny until the woman appeared at her window, hollering, "You riffraff!" Jimmy was not only smaller, but stealthy – and so she saw only James, who had no need to steal from old ladies. He could never look the woman in the face again.

James ran his eyes over Kate's pale face. She shook her head with a gentle smile, inhaled and closed her eyes.

Ever since Tissot first met him, Whistler gave the impression of not working much. In truth, he never stopped working, drawing everything – his friends, the streets – but even back then, took offense so easily that he always seemed to be raging about some insult.

He looked at Jimmy's contorted features and piercing

eyes. "I have had a lot on my mind." Tissot went back to his easel and settled on the piano stool.

Whistler followed him. "Do tell."

"Jimmy, is it not enough that the great Rossetti has agreed to testify that your *Nocturne* is worth two hundred guineas?"

"It's Rossetti's *brother*, the art critic – Ruskin's *friend*," he scoffed. "He said he'd do it, but his heart isn't in it."

James had his back to Jimmy as he fidgeted with his palette and brushes. "Do not embroil me in this...this *circus*."

"Too late, too late!" Whistler rapped his little cane angrily on the floor. "You're listed as a witness for my defense!"

Tissot planted his feet on the floor, trying not to get riled. "There is no point arguing..."

"I am not *arguing* with you, I'm *telling* you." Whistler became shrill and gesticulated with his hypnotic hands. "I understand that I am not popular with the masses – like *you*, James – but this is the moment for all artists to unite in undoing Ruskin once and for all. He thinks he can treat me like a sheet of notepaper and crumple me up! And then, you are the only one who can explain that the Royal Academy has been against me from the start."

"I thought you said you had found a letter from Leighton; certainly the endorsement of the president of the Royal Academy is all the evidence you need to impress the jury."

"Not when Leighton objects to his personal letter being used as evidence. And, by way of coincidence, he has just been called away to Windsor by the Queen – to be knighted!" Jimmy banged his cane against the threshold. "You *have* to appear in that courtroom tomorrow!"

Tissot slapped his brushes down on the table at his side. "What use am I to you, if I appear in court against my will?" Every muscle in his body tense with anger, he offered, "I will write a letter to the jury, if you wish. I can confirm how long I have known you, what training you received in Paris, and name some pictures you painted that I consider to be masterpieces: *At the Piano, The White Girl...*"

"Is that the best you can do?" Jimmy's face had turned a bright red. "I will be utterly bankrupted if my friends don't come forward to defend my art. Every creditor in town is beating upon my door, from my butcher and greengrocer to my builder and Leyland!" He yanked the monocle from his eye. "Plutocrats with their millions and it is all they can do to pull a man down by his coat tails into his chair again."

"You have been careless, Jimmy." Tissot drew himself up to his full height and began edging Whistler back toward the door to the hall.

"Whereas you," Whistler lifted his chin toward Kate on her *chaise* and shot back, "have been the very model of caution?" At James' furious expression, Whistler looked shattered and appealed to his old friend. "I will have no choice but to sell my studio and everything in it. I hope someone enjoys it, as I've never yet lived there myself."

"Where would you go?" Tissot coldly asked.

"Oh, I don't know. Venice, perhaps. I will not paint for the mob of mediocrity. Joe Jopling believes he can arrange a commission for me from the Fine Arts Society." Whistler glared at him.

"You have brought this disaster on yourself!" Tissot exclaimed, with his arms folded over his chest. "Even Degas says you behave as if you had no talent."

Jimmy shook his oiled curls, and his feather of white hair wagged above them. "Degas would back me!"

"What of that? It is *my* reputation you want behind you. You expect I will sacrifice it on the altar of *your* art? When did you ever champion *my* work?"

Whistler laughed grimly and put on his tall hat. "Ruskin is portraying you as a degenerate Frenchman polluting British morality, but he is wrong." He held out his cane at Tissot. "You are nothing but a plagiarist. You always were, copying my etching techniques, copying my interest in the Thames, in Oriental art, in –"

Tissot held up his hand to halt the tirade. "We all borrow ideas from each other – Degas, Manet, Millais – and make them our own. What infuriates you is that *I* know how to make cash off ideas, and you have only your ideas."

"At least they are – *my* ideas."

"Go to the devil!"

Kate sat up and began to cough. "James, you don't mean that. You're just upset." She held her handkerchief to her mouth.

James went to her side and held her shoulders while she continued to cough. He lowered his voice as his outrage increased. "I have *worked* all these years while you pranced about London, giving outrageous quotes to journalists and posing for cartoons in *Punch*! Now, it is up to me to save you from your love affair with yourself?"

Whistler affixed his monocle in his right eye. "They say I cannot keep a friend. My dear, I cannot afford it!" He stood before the friend who had adopted his name in their youth. "I'll leave you alone, *James*...quite alone." On his way out of the studio, he pivoted to deliver one final blow, and his long coat swung in an arc around him. "If you ignore the summons, you may as well leave the country. At any rate, you're next, you know."

"They are after us all, Jimmy," Tissot replied, as evenly as he could through his clenched teeth. Kate reached up, and he clutched her hand. "But while you have made yourself a target, I have learned to keep my head down."

Chapter XXVIII

The Grosvenor Gallery
135-137 New Bond Street
May 28, 1879

Tissot ran his eyes over his third Grosvenor Gallery exhibit, eight oil paintings and four etchings forming a grid of his most strikingly original works to date. Kate modeled for all but two of them. He reached out and straightened the gilt frame around *Summer*, an elegantly simple portrait of Kathleen in her favorite, formfitting black dress. The canvas shone with the golden sun through a Japanese parasol that framed her face like a halo. James was so proud of the bold and simple composition, showing the influence of stylish Japanese woodblock prints, that he had expected critical acclaim for his modern approach to art by this single picture alone. In fact, he felt he had reached a pinnacle in style that would be both praised by the critics and sought after by collectors as much as his *Kathleen Mavourneen* two years ago.

All his compositions were bold and fresh, like *Going to Business*, showing a businessman headed for his office in the City in a hansom cab that nearly sprang out at the viewer. His favorite picture was of Kathleen swinging in the hammock in their private paradise of the back garden. He had painted two variations of it, *A Quiet Afternoon* and *Under the Chestnut Tree*. James had put his energy into each picture as never before, combining new, vivid colors with all the precisely rendered detail that he could paint with such incomparable skill.

And yet, James could hardly meet the eyes of those who passed his exhibit wall in the Grosvenor's East Gallery. He stood uncomfortably, with his gloved hands clasped behind his back, and maintained an aloof demeanor in his impeccable British suit while many visitors snickered and others cast contemptuous glances at him.

In Paris last month, Degas had doggedly organized the fourth Impressionist exhibition, this time in the avenue de l'Opéra. He showed over twenty paintings and pastels, and while numerous critics wrote sarcastic and derisive reviews of the show, more singled his work out for praise. But here in London, Tissot was enduring an unceasing storm of abuse that knocked the wind out of him.

No sooner had the exhibition opened than a review appeared in the *Spectator*, dismissing Tissot's work as nothing but "ladies in hammocks, showing a very unnecessary amount of petticoat and stocking, and remarkable for little save their indolence and insolence."

All the critics in London joined in heaping their fury and disgust on Tissot, condemning his pictures, especially *The Hammock*, as immoral and deliberately insulting.

Degas had written that he hoped to show his work in the United States, upon hearing Durand-Ruel's recent encouragement, "The American public does not laugh. It buys!" But James had even received a crushing commentary in *The New York Times*, which he happened upon at the Arts Club:

> *Mr. James Tissot, one of the eccentrics of the Grosvenor, has sent in eight pictures. They are always of a girl lying in a hammock, or in a swing or lying down, always surrounded by the green grass and green trees so you have to hunt for the figures, and you want to call him names for prostituting his talents to a silly affectation of Realism. Pre-Raphaelitism gone mad is the motive power of this wild man of the studio. Under Mr. Tissot's eccentricities lurk a laughing giant.*

It took all Tissot's courage to stand by his exhibit and watch people pass. He *was* a giant, one of the most celebrated painters of his generation, but he was hardly laughing. *It is Lawrence Alma-Tadema who is elected to the Royal Academy.* Behind his back, Tissot's hands were clenched in fists.

A Bohemian young man and a lady in a peacock blue "Aesthetic style" dress emerged from the crush in the West Gallery and sailed past Tissot on their way to the staircase. They did not look at his pictures.

"Burne-Jones is the most extraordinary artist in London or Paris!" the man said. "Such a noble imagination!"

"Yes," the lady answered, "but naturally for one with so scholarly a mind, he paints for the small inner circle of those who understand his allusions." Like others wearing the flowing new uncorseted gowns, she moved freely and with a consciousness of being at the vanguard of fashion.

"He is like the Renaissance painters of angels, of which

one is not sure of the sex. His *Annunciation* is sublime!"

"I rather fancy the nude sculpture come to life – *The Soul Attains*," the lady mused.

"What one wouldn't give to be the man on his knees before her!"

James straightened his back. He would never let them see how humiliated he felt. What was it Degas had said? *Life is too short and the strength one has only just suffices.*

Tom Taylor made his way through the mass of people, more stooped than ever, his white beard floating before him like foam on the crest of a wave. Tissot called out a greeting – once, twice – and in the moment before Tom finally acknowledged him, James realized that the critic had intended to cut him.

Tom stopped and accepted Tissot's outstretched hand, but impatiently averted his eyes from his pictures. The two men had not seen each other since before Whistler's trial, where Taylor testified that that the *Nocturne in Black and Gold* was not a good painting because he had given it a negative review in *The Times*.

James summoned some humor. "One would think Burne-Jones is the only artist in London. I hope I can count on you for a good review."

Tom Taylor burst out in indignation. "James, I have known you long before you ever thought you would come to England. I was glad to give you a leg up, illustrating my book of ballads with Millais. But what are you up to? These titles are nearly as mysterious as Whistler's –"

"My titles are not intended to express anything."

"And they don't! It's impossible to discover any meaning other than – 'an arrangement in black and green!' "

Tissot's blood boiled. "Do not associate *my* art with Jimmy Whistler's!"

Tom looked at his watch. "Look – I have to meet up with

someone." He pressed his lips together, then added, "I am disappointed in you, James." He disappeared into the swarm of gallery visitors.

Tissot drew a deep breath and squared his shoulders, determined not to let his guard down. He had to consider everyone in the crowd a potential client, a rival artist, or a critic. He pasted on a slight smile and scanned the parade of notables marching past him to view Millais' pictures in the West Gallery.

Lillie Langtry entered on the arm of the Prince of Wales. Mrs. Langtry was all mannered nods and smiles to this one and that. She pretended not to see those who were of no use to her, including the forty-three-year-old James Tissot.

The VIPs gathered before Millais' full-length likeness of Mrs. Langtry. Millais depicted her with a modest, downcast gaze, wearing the demure black mourning dress she had worn to beguile her way into London Society. He had sent to Jersey for the native flower that gave the picture its name, *A Jersey Lily*.

"Ah, the most beautiful woman on earth!" Millais cried with an avuncular air, wrapping her arm under his.

She could not have been more than twenty-five or twenty-six, but she had achieved her goal – being presented to the Queen. In the end, the Prince of Wales' attention had been attracted by another woman, their affair had ended, and her creditors were closing in. Tissot had heard gossip that Lillie was having an affair with the Prince's cousin, Prince Louis of Battenberg. Their appearance together was merely a publicity stunt, and soon they were surrounded by a crush of aristocrats including Lord and Lady Lindsay, trumpeting the success of the show.

Nothing is left for Millais but a peerage. Tissot crossed his arms over his chest and looked away.

Millais also exhibited a full-length portrait of Louise Jopling, wearing a gorgeous embroidered dress. He had painted it in five days, as a gift to his friend Joe. In it, Louise looked so striking – and faintly defiant – that the picture created a sensation with the visitors to the gallery.

Louise herself, floating on air in a dove grey gown embroidered in white, was surrounded by a circle of aristocratic, artistic, and literary admirers. She excitedly chatted about the custom-designed pair of garden studios that she and Joe had just moved to in Chelsea.

"I am able to work all alone in my glory," she exclaimed, "as Joe's studio is on the other side of the house!"

Tommy Bowles emerged from the West Gallery, and James watched the Prince of Wales turn his back on him. Tommy had drawn his malice yet again over an item in *Vanity Fair* asserting that Sir Robert Peel's personal remarks on the Queen in last month's speech before Parliament offended the Royal Family.

The Prince's Private Secretary issued a denial, and Sir Robert Peel wrote to *The Times*, insisting the Prince denied having taken offense to his remarks. Tommy followed up by publishing Peel's long, petulant letter threatening to sue him as editor of *Vanity Fair*, and challenging him to do so if he wished. When the credibility of this letter from Peel was questioned, Bowles stated flatly in the next week's issue of *Vanity Fair* that "Sir Robert Peel himself left the letter in my office." Tommy defiantly added that issues of his magazine containing Peel's ranting letter were in such demand as entertainment that they were being resold for as much as ten times their usual price. He gloated that furthermore, efforts to ban *Vanity Fair* from London's gentlemen's clubs only succeeded in doubling subscriptions.

This afternoon, still-blonde Tommy was in high spirits,

ignoring the man he privately referred to as "Prince Tum-Tum" and loudly joking with Joe Jopling about the Burne-Jones paintings in the West Gallery. "If you prefer the real women to the dream women, well you have none of the higher culture, that's all!"

He turned to see Tissot. His boyish blue eyes betrayed hurt. "Why didn't you tell me, James? I have to learn about your private life through the gossip of strangers?"

James shrugged, his back against the wall. *After three years, can one simply say, "Oh, sorry"?*

Tommy said, "A friend is a friend. At least to me. How many times have I visited your home and been barred from meeting her? How many dinner invitations from my wife did you wriggle out of?"

"I never would have expected you and Jessie to have welcomed her to Cleeve Lodge."

"James, after everything...you might at least have given me a chance." Bowles said. "*I* defended you when everyone said you were a *Communard*, damn it! Were you lying to me then, too?"

The smoking lounge was downstairs near the Grosvenor's restaurant, but Tissot pulled out his cigarette case and lit up. Tommy exchanged a glance with Joe Jopling and strode away.

Not Tommy! Tissot steadied his hand and brought the cigarette to his lips.

An old man escorting his ugly wife and daughters passed by in the stream of people.

"Oh, good Lord, not that vulgar foreign artist again," said the man, in his aristocratic accent. "Look how he's still flaunting her!"

"And her ankles..." replied his wife. "How long did he think no one would know what he's up to? What else does that girl do, but lounge around in his French garden, reading novels and newspapers?"

"This time, he's gone too far..."

The man stood before *Going to Business*. "He need not continue to advertise *his* business," he said, a glint of envy in his eyes. "We can well imagine how he spends his afternoons in St. John's Wood."

"Have you seen *Punch*?" one of the daughters laughed. "They quite skewered *The Hammock*, in a clever verse called *The Web*:

> *Will you walk into my Garden?*
> *Said the Spider to the Fly.*
> *'Tis the prettiest little garden,*
> *That ever did you spy.*
> *The grass a sly dog plays on;*
> *A hammock I have got;*
> *Neat ankles you shall gaze on –*
> *Talk – well, now, time to change the subject.*

"Exactly," said her mother. "He's gone too far."

When the younger daughter tittered at *The Hammock* again, her father said, "My dears, come see something more uplifting..." The man gently guided his wife and daughters towards the throng admiring *A Jersey Lily*.

Tissot trembled and exhaled the cigarette smoke.

I will never exhibit at the Grosvenor again. But he did not regret leaving the Royal Academy behind. The critics might revile him, but he would just circumvent them, and sell to those who had made him a success – the British public. Tissot would look for exhibition venues and dealers away from London, in the northern industrial cities. He would write to the sugar merchant who bought his etching, *October,* to ask for a recommendation to the best picture dealer in Newcastle – someone who could show all his etchings or anything else in the town.

Whistler appeared, in an overcoat longer than ever, and commented, "Millais' portrait of Louise Jopling is superb, a great work."

Tissot was taken off guard. He had not seen Jimmy since the last day of the trial, which he had attended only because of the summons, and at which he was not called as a witness. The last he had heard, through Kathleen, Whistler had left Maud Franklin, pregnant, in a London hotel room and pretended he was in Paris.

"Congratulations to you and Maud on another daughter," James said, holding out his cigarette. "And I hear Leyland and his wife have separated."

Whistler had won his suit against Ruskin, but the jury awarded him just one farthing in damages. He was bankrupted, and the bailiffs had moved into his new Tite Street studio in advance of the auction of all his household goods, even his prized collection of blue and white porcelain.

Ruskin had resigned his Oxford Professorship after the indignity of having his art criticism open to question. Burne-Jones had raised funds from the British public to pay Ruskin's court costs of three hundred and eighty-five pounds.

Jimmy Whistler looked at James, and his piercing eyes wore, not his customary sardonic expression, but a profound betrayal.

He stared vacantly at *The Hammock*, as if he were seeing past it. Then his lips curled and he began to swing his cane. "Why, James! Isn't the memory a dandy thing? I recall this *very same* composition in one of the first pictures we ever saw in Paris, at Courbet's one-man exhibition. Yes, indeed, he painted *his* mistress in a hammock. And by Jove, if *he* didn't call it *The Hammock*, too!"

Tissot's heart pounded. He had been accused of plagiarism before, but Whistler's eyes were slits of vengeance.

Quickly, he defended himself. "I am not the only artist who has ever painted a woman in a hammock."

The crush pressed in on Whistler and Tissot as Lord Lindsay's two gallery assistants made their way toward the West Gallery. They were bringing in the coveted brass railing, to protect *A Jersey Lily* from the admiring mob.

Millais slapped Joe Jopling on the back, and they put their heads together and roared with laughter.

"The future of art," Tissot murmured.

The old sly merriment returned in Whistler's blue eyes as he lifted his head high and cackled, "I'll be back in a year or two, and it will be a dandy thing to return as a martyr to the gentle circle of the *avant-garde*."

A group of women passed them, all wearing not the corsets and fripperies Tissot had so assiduously documented for a decade, but the loose Aesthetic gowns made popular by Burne-Jones. They did not spare a glance for Tissot's paintings.

"Damnation for an artist is not scorn, you know," Whistler drawled. "It's oblivion."

Tissot met his gaze for a long moment. Then he tossed his nearly-smoked cigarette to the gallery floor. He gave it a light tap with the toe of his shoe before turning his back on the horde, to make his way home to Kathleen.

It was going on tea-time, and Polly would be bringing the children over.